THE LAW OF RETURN

The LAW
of
RETURN

a novel by

ALICE BLOCH

Boston: Alyson Publications, Inc.

This is an original paperback, first published by Alyson
Publications, 40 Plympton St., Boston, Mass. 02118.

First edition, first printing: September 1983.

ISBN 0 932870 48 1

For Nancy and the moving force

I.

1

In the beginning was sound.

I was an ear in a tunnel of sound. I floated, curled and still, rocked by each deep, clear tone, resting in the rush of silence between the notes.

Music was my mother tongue, Hebrew my father. English is the language of speech. French is an elegant game, nothing more.

America is my birthplace, Israel my homeland, nowhere my home. My home is that hollow of maple, music, and flesh, remembered but lost.

She carried me under her heart and behind her cello. She did her best playing, she said, during that pregnancy. The cello balanced lightly at three points: floor, thighs, navel. The larger she grew, the richer her tone, until with a great chord she pushed me out.

After my birth, Mother kept me slung about her waist in a white linen shawl, swaying with her practice, my world circumscribed by the sweep of her bow arm. Sometimes, when a note was very deep and long, I felt even my bones vibrate.

When I outgrew the shawl and the space between Mother's belly and the cello's back, she fashioned a leash and tied one end to my overalls, the other to her heavy oak music stand.

Thus I learned to listen with my whole body, to keep still, to wait until the end of a movement. Thus I learned the meaning of confinement.

Why do I tell you these things? Perhaps I need to explain my later idiosyncrasies: my odd attraction to religious orthodoxy, and the combination of passivity and romantic impulse that was nearly my downfall. Perhaps I spent too many years in psychoanalysis, so that I now think the story of my early adulthood began in my mother's womb or lies swaddled in her lap.

Maybe I never knew what I was up to; maybe I still don't. Maybe I had to do everything I did. Maybe I want you to believe I had to do everything I did, even the mistakes, even the embarrassing, humiliating, stupid mistakes. Maybe I want to believe there are no shortcuts; maybe I want to believe I haven't wasted any of my life.

––––––––

A young woman hugs her parents goodbye at the Pittsburgh airport. "See you next month," she says. She boards an El Al airplane.

It is 1969, so the young woman still thinks of herself as a girl. She has just graduated from the University of Wisconsin, with a B.A. in French, and has been accepted for graduate school at Berkeley. She has saved enough money from summer jobs to take this summer trip to Israel.

Israel never interested her much until a year ago, when a boyfriend told her she should go to Israel, she would like it there. The same boyfriend told her she should go to Berkeley, she would like it there too. She had never gone to bed with anyone else, so he had a certain power over her at the time. He soon moved on to a new girlfriend, and she retaliated by finding someone else to go to bed with, and then someone else, so that the first affair would seem less important—but nonetheless, she is on her way to Israel for the summer.

––––––––

She is in Jerusalem, city of stone and light, narrow cobbled streets and walls within walls. A wall of sound surrounds her: *sh* and *tz* and *kh* and *im*, all around her the strange noises and familiar voices. The voices holler and grate and whisper and complain and praise and *shekket Shekket SHEKKET*! a shriek from a window over the café where she sits. She is afraid. What does *shekket* mean? go to hell goddamn brat police divorce? The waitress laughs: "She shouts for quiet. *Shekket*. Such a noisy word."

A noisy word, a noisy world. The intimate new voices mimic her ancestors, initiate her to a landscape of rough sound and sleek vowel, rough stone and smooth tile floor, clay and sandstone consonants sticking in the ear, straining her throat when she tries to imitate these sounds without meaning, guttural and sheer, nonsense syllables of rock and rough bark and golden scrolls, vowels of braided bread and consonants of goat cheese, vowels of *shabbat* and consonants of *ḥol*, a week of magic in every word, not even words yet the sounds rise and fall without separation, a song of creation and origin, the first marsh of sound before separation of light from dark, before separation of water from water, before separation of water from land, before names and meanings, before the braided candles of *havdalah*. The original language, nothing but sound, the swirling music of air.

———

That language, that city pulled on me like gravity. I needed to learn Hebrew, I needed to live in Jerusalem. The longing I felt was as simple and instinctive as my longing, a year earlier, for a lover to touch my body.

For me, at that time, there was no separating the land, the language, and the religion. I wanted all three, and to me they were one. *Sliḥa*, the solemn word of atonement, the word of Yom Kippur, the prayer for forgiveness: I learned to say this same word when I bumped into someone in the street. To use Biblical words everyday made everyday life holy, made me want to acknowledge every day's holiness through my people's ancient religious practices, in my people's ancient city, in my people's ancient tongue.

I saw no contradiction, no inconsistency then. It was simple, this religious urge of the senses, as simple as the need for body against body.

———

"You are Jewish?"

"Yes."

"You can be a citizen right now, under the Law of Return, or you can be a temporary resident for a maximum of three years, and then you must become a citizen. Which do you want?"

"Temporary resident, please."

"Last name?"

"Rogin."

"First name?"

"Ellen."

"Ellen? You don't have a Hebrew name, maybe, from when you were born?"

"Yes. Elisheva. But everyone has always called me Ellen, even my parents."

13

"Everyone *here* will call you Elisheva." The clerk looks at her an instant, his eyebrows raised—if she wishes to protest, this is the opportunity; then he writes something on her identity card. "Father's first name?"

"Arthur. Wait . . . Asher in Hebrew."

"Asher. *B'seder.*" He passes the card across the desk. "Now you must sign at the bottom."

She stares at the card. She can read nothing, recognizes only the cheap photograph of her own face at the top: hair hanging limp and straight, partially covering one eye; the other eyebrow puny, from the time she overplucked, and the hairs never grew back, so that she now looks perpetually surprised; the white sunglass ridge over the nose; the nose itself, already burned darker than the rest of the face, as if singled out by the strong sun of Israel; the cheeks rounder than she would like; the half-smile she wears when she is uncertain what is expected of her.

"I can't sign my name in Hebrew."

"So sign in the other alphabet."

"How do you spell 'Elisheva'?" She signs letter by letter, as he spells for her. The result, her own name in her own handwriting, looks like what it is: a word she is learning to spell.

"You are Jewish?"

Nowhere else in the world is it safe to answer that question. I think I knew it even then, knew I was the first Rogin to feel no fear when an immigration official asked that question.

As for the Lowenthals, my mother's family—well, the Israeli clerk asked nothing about them. Did I notice at the time? Or did I accept as normal his exclusive interest in Asher/Arthur/Dad? Perhaps I noticed but was glad he didn't ask Mother's name, Clara, because I had no Hebrew alternative to offer, the American Lowenthals having been American for so many generations. And as for the European Lowenthals, the stubborn ones who hadn't crossed a border since the Middle Ages, who tarried in Berlin until there was no leaving by choice: I must assume they had reasons more powerful than the fear of Ellis Island inspectors.

It was one of those Ellis Island fellows who bestowed the name Rogin on my grandfather. In Lithouania the name had been Roginsky. A volunteer interpreter spelled the name in American letters for the inspector, and at "n" the inspector said, "That's long enough."

14

So I probably could have taken back Roginsky while I was at it, but what was the point? "Roginsky" was the whim of some other Christian official, a few hundred years ago when all the Jews were suddenly required to take last names. One Christian official gives a name and another takes part of the name away: what does any of it have to do with me?

But Elisheva, the name I didn't even know how to spell in English or Hebrew—this name goes all the way back to the Torah; this name has been in my father's family as long as anyone can remember. I was named after my father's sister, who died in 1946; she was named after her grandmother, who died in 1910; she was named after her aunt, who died in 1845.

Nowhere else in the world has an immigration official ever restored a Jew's original name, her claim to history. Nowhere else in the world, when she has answered "yes" to the question "Are you Jewish?" does the man behind the desk reply, "In that case you must become a citizen."

Assimilation has scarred me more than I ever imagined. Parts of name lopped off like the nose job I never had. Elisheva to Ellen, Roginsky to Rogin (the next step is Rogers). Ah yes, the last name has its significance, too. "Sky" is what they removed. They took the whole goddamn sky away from us.

Those girls in the cafeteria line at school, talking about whether Jews are damned to hell. Yes, they decided. I just listened.

I wish I'd had the name Elisheva then. It would have done them good to try to pronounce it. Those girls, and Mrs. Gallagher the French teacher who couldn't even pronounce French, let alone Hebrew, and Billy Williams Jr., my first date.

"Rogin. What kind of name is that?"

"Jewish."

They always looked surprised when I said it straight out. After my grandfather died I considered going back to Roginsky in his honor. I told Mrs. Gallagher of my intention. She was my favorite teacher, accent or no, and her job was to introduce Americans to a foreign culture. I thought she might understand.

"Oh, I don't think you should change your name, Ellen," she said. "People will have trouble . . . remembering it."

Well sure, none of them are used to having to remember anything. No other language or two or three from a couple of generations ago. No other language to learn for prayers except the

15

Catholics. I recall thinking, maybe that's why the Protestants name their kids after themselves when the parents are still alive: so they won't have to memorize a new name. And Billy Williams Jr. even had the same name first and last, no strain at all.

I thought such things, but I knew better than to say them. To say them would mean I was conceited, obnoxious, improper, loud. In short, too Jewish.

And then later I was glad I hadn't said those things about poor Billy, who enlisted in the Marines and never came back from Vietnam. If only he'd waited a few years, gone to college like my brother Neil. By the time Neil was up for the lottery, I was a draft counselor and he got out on a trumped-up medical exemption. I would have been glad to help Billy too, even though I never went out with him again after that one date.

I suppose in some grotesque way, Billy lives on in my eyebrows. It was for the date with Billy that I plucked out the bushy centers, which I thought looked too Jewish, and in plucking, I permanently damaged the roots.

2

The bus winds uphill from the old Arab town to the new Jewish town, Upper Nazareth. The Arab town: stone houses built without haste, carefully-planned tile work decorating the arched windows and doors, luxuriant grapevines spreading over the roofs. The Jewish town: stucco apartment buildings, a few newly-planted sticks. The apartment buildings appear discarded, stranded on the steep hillside, perched insecurely as matchboxes. Each apartment has a view of the valley, looks down on the Arabs in a blatant expression of victory.

Elisheva stands in the aisle, just behind the driver's seat. She grasps a vertical metal pole and swings about wildly as the road curves along the edge of the hill, switchbacking, always a long drop to one side. Her suitcase is jammed between her legs. She wears her traveling clothes, the same good-girl outfit in which she said goodbye to her parents at the airport: a navy polished-cotton skirt, a white-and-navy print blouse, white-and-blue ceramic button earrings, white sandals and pocketbook.

The hot wind in the bus blows her hair into her eyes until she must release one hand from the pole, to hold the hair in a clump at the nape of her neck. She is uncomfortable, desiccated; the wind pulls moisture from her body without permitting her to sweat first. The suitcase scrapes the inner sides of her calves, which she shaved last night.

"Please?" she says to the driver. "Would you tell me when we arrive at the *ulpan*?" This is the third time she has asked him. The second time he seemed annoyed that she didn't trust him, but the bus has climbed for such a long time, surely it has already passed her destination. A Hebrew language school should not be at the very top of the hill; it should be lower, closer to the Arab town, nearer to people for whom Hebrew is not a native language. All around her, people are saying words she cannot understand: behind, the other passengers; ahead, the driver's radio. Suddenly she is certain they are talking about

17

her, making fun of her. The same language that in Jerusalem sounded like a constant prayer, here seems dull and menacing.

The driver stops the bus and casts her a weary glance. "Here," he says. "*Ulpan.*"

The building is harsh white, blinding to the eye in the midday sun. It is the newest, ugliest building on the hill. Its shape is irregular, as if styrofoam cubes were thrown into the air and then cemented together wherever they landed. The ground is utterly bare; the dust it sends up has a flat, lifeless smell. There is no sound but the feeble hiss of wind. No person is in sight, no animal, no plant. Perhaps there is a rule of silence at the *ulpan*, so that the students will learn language out of silence, as it was in the beginning. Perhaps the students are required to take afternoon naps, as it was in nursery school.

Elisheva drags her suitcase up a flight of stairs to the nearest door. No answer. She peeks into the window. No furniture, no rugs, no draperies. Plaster dust on the linoleum floor.

The Ministry of Absorption has sent her to an *ulpan* under construction. What is she supposed to do, wait for the bus to take her back? Wait to join the construction crew after their lunch break? Maybe the *ulpan* is a sort of kibbutz: first you must help build the school, then you can learn Hebrew in it. Or maybe you learn Hebrew by being forced to communicate with the construction crew until the building is finished. Then there's no need for a school, because you already know Hebrew, so the school building can be converted into still another apartment building. Maybe all the buildings she passed in the bus were once *ulpanim.*

From what seems a great distance, she hears the rotation of wheels, and a woman's voice, singing. She stumbles to the sidewalk and sees a young mother pushing a stroller down the hill—or rather, holding the stroller back from escaping down the hill. As the woman approaches, Elisheva waves frantically and calls, "*Ulpan? Ulpan?*" The woman nods, pointing uphill. The automatic, wordless gesture tells Elisheva how very often the residents of this neighborhood come upon a flustered newcomer gripping a suitcase, repeating "*ulpan*" as an infant chants, "Mama . . . mama," the first word, the first charm against loneliness.

The director of the *ulpan* is busy. Elisheva waits in a large room—a lounge, she supposes—containing some chairs, a ping-pong table, and a small television set, which a group of men are watching. The television set speaks Hebrew, with such volume and excitement as to stimulate Elisheva's curiosity. She stands behind them and sees a fuzzy black-and-white picture of two astronauts planting an American flag on the moon.

One of the men turns around and says, in English, "Congratulations, American."

She stares at him, stupid. He says something to the other men and then turns around again. "Maybe she's not American, this one?" he says in French. "But she looks American, *bien sur.*"

Finally she has caught up with him, taken in the picture on the TV, the meaning of the picture, the meaning of his congratulations, the meaning of his French words, the nature of his accent.

"Yes, I am American," she says in French. "And you, are you Greek or Turkish?"

"Turkish," he says. "Bravo."

His name is Michel in French, Moshe in Hebrew. Something else in Turkish? He is tall and thin, with a narrow beard and no moustache, intense large eyes, flirtatious and confident. He has been at the *ulpan* over a month, knows the ropes, will help her get a good room and a good teacher. His friends are Turkish and Tunisian. The Turks speak Ladino with each other, French with the Tunisians and Elisheva, and Hebrew with the *ulpan* director.

"Put this American in Sima's class," Michel orders the director—or so he tells Elisheva afterward, for she can understand nothing. "Her man just landed on the moon, and she can speak French. She must have good treatment here. Isn't there an empty room in the Tunisian girl's apartment?"

The apartment consists of three single bedrooms and a bathroom. Elisheva's two neighbors are gone, so Michel shows her to her room, which, he says, is exactly like all other newly-constructed and -furnished rooms in Israel: bright white walls, the color of which rubs off onto her navy skirt when she leans back; a studio couch on a metal frame, the mattress and bolster covered in a rough red-and-black plaid fabric; a small table with a straight metal chair. From the window, a view of the other wing of the *ulpan*, and beyond, the top of the empty housing complex she mistook for the *ulpan*.

"What is that building?" she wants to know. "Why does no one live in it?"

"Ah," says Michel. "The Bedouins."

"The Bedouins? But I saw no one. Is the building unfinished?"

The building is finished, but the Bedouins refuse to move in. The government built the ugly complex of apartments to encourage the Bedouins to live in one place, where they can be watched. The Bedouins want to continue to wander the land, as they have done for thousands of years. The government hopes the Bedouins will change their minds. The building stands empty.

"They are foolish, the Bedouins," Michel says. "They should take what is offered."

"But if they want to keep their way of life . . . "

"What way of life? They are savages. Better to become civilized."

"What civilization? A concrete building with no trees? Better to roam."

He cocks his head and grins at her. "How prim she looks, but she has a wild soul, this one. Is it not so, my little Bedouin?"

She blushes but forces herself to continue looking straight at him. "I do not know what kind of soul I have."

The answer is sincere, but she knows, hearing her own words, what she has done: without a trace of coquetry in her own manner, she has entered his flirtation. Because she answered his question seriously, rather than objecting to its familiar tone, she has consented to seduction. It still isn't too late. She could say, "I'm not your little anything," and he would leave her alone in her room. But she doesn't want to be alone, and she finds him attractive, and she likes speaking French with him, and no one has touched her since she hugged her parents good-bye, and her suitemates still have not returned; they must be in class; Michel is missing class on her account; he likes her, or at least, is intrigued by her. He thinks her wild.

Stan, her Wisconsin boyfriend, the one who sent her here, used to say, "Let's have at each other." She liked the expression, something playful about it, as if sex didn't have to be grim and terrifying, as if two people could romp and nuzzle, careless as a pair of lion cubs.

"Why are you smiling?" Michel asks, but before she can answer he is kissing her, pressing her horizontal. His beard tickles her face; the coarse upholstery of the studio couch tickles her arms and legs. The sensation is pleasant, reminds her of something familiar—what? The back seat of the first car her parents owned, the scratchy texture against her cheek when she dozed during journeys to relatives, the ridges in her face when she woke up, the lines of telephone poles and wires overhead. Michel is a skillful lover, arouses her quickly. After his orgasm, he moves away abruptly, with an angry look. He sits against the wall, stiff and silent, letting whitewash powder coat his back.

"*Qu'est-ce qu'il y a? Qu'est-ce que tu as?*" she says. "What's the matter? What's the matter with you?"

Finally he answers: "*Quel numéro suis-je?*"

"What number are you? What do you mean? Oh. I don't know."

"*Quel numéro suis-je?*" He folds his arms over his chest, stubborn, angrier. "*Quel numéro?*"

"I don't know," she repeats. "What's the difference?"

"*Quel numéro?*" he shouts.

She shrinks from him in fear. This, she thinks, could end in violence. He could start hitting me, and everyone else is in class; no one would hear. Even the Bedouins aren't there to hear.

Michel stops shouting and turns away, silent and sullen once more. She doesn't have to be afraid; he won't hurt her. Now she feels nothing but a homesickness, a sudden longing for Stan's cheerful, indifferent lust; or the quiet friendship of Daniel, her peace-movement comrade who never made a pass at her; or the rowdy companionship of Patty, her college roommate. Where are her suitemates? She wishes they would come. She wishes Michel would go.

He turns to her again. "*Quel numéro?*"

"*Sept.*" She knows even as she invents the number that this is the wrong strategy, it won't shut him up or get rid of him.

"American girls," he says with disgust. "American Jewish girls. *Sept.*"

He is engaged, he says, to a French girl. She is beautiful and innocent. She is blonde. She is Catholic. But she loves him even though he is Jewish and Turkish. Soon she will come here to marry him, even though nothing forces her to come to Israel. Soon she will come.

"*Avec elle,*" he says, "*j'étais le premier.* With her, I was the first." He repeats this sentence a couple of times, pointing at his chest for emphasis. "*J'étais le premier.*"

Finally he leaves. She lies on her back for a while, then props her head against the wall—her hair will be chalky when she gets up—and stares out the window at the flat blue sky. Why has she come here? She can't remember. Something about finding her people.

Tired though I was by then, I showered: my version of the ritual bath I should, by Orthodox law, have taken before lying with a man, not after. And hot though it was that afternoon, I found a sheet with which to cover my nakedness before going to sleep: my version of the veil, or of *tzniyut*, the modesty required of an Orthodox woman.

I slept in the dream of becoming wood. Not the live, wet center of a growing tree, but lumber: wood already sawed, bumped downstream, milled, dried, and sanded. My arms the stiff arms of a chair, or the oars of a beached rowboat.

It was the same dream that overtook me on the edge of sleep when I was a feverish child, swollen rigid with mumps. "Mama!" I called. "I'm turning into a log. Don't let them cut me up!"

But Mother was giving a music lesson—I heard the rasp of a student's bow as I came to consciousness—and Dad stood over me, the slanted ceiling spraying him with wallpaper flowers.

"No one's going to cut up my Poopsie," he said. "You're having a bad dream. Are you awake now?" He had just returned from work, was still wearing a snowy winter jacket and muffler. "Can I get you something?"

"Brownies," I said. "With chocolate frosting."

He indulged me, drove the three or four miles to Edelmans' deli and returned bearing a bag of sweets. He must have thought my craving was a sign of renewed health, and maybe it was, for that night the fever broke, after I vomited on Mother's slippers. How tenderly she held me, even though my cries of "Mama" had interrupted her sleep, even though I threw up as soon as she appeared at my bedside. "My poor little lamb," she crooned; and bleating, I clutched her shaggy bathrobe until the shivering was gone and I slept happy in our animal warmth.

Elisheva awakens to the smell of chocolate. Someone has placed a tray on the table: two open-face cheese sandwiches, a small bright-red tomato, a few extra slices of bread (*halla* left over from *shabbat*, slightly stale around the edges), and a dish of what looks like a melted Hershey bar. She dips a finger into

22

the chocolate: a good, rich flavor, like icing without the cake. She takes another fingerful, and another, and is about to lick the last bit of chocolate off her finger when there is a knock at the door.

It is Andrée, Elisheva's Tunisian roommate. A friend of Michel told her of Elisheva's arrival; she is delighted to have a French-speaking neighbor; she thought to bring a few things to eat, since Elisheva missed the evening meal; oh, you are quite welcome, it was nothing; please don't wait, go ahead and eat, you must be hungry; you will need strength for the first day of Hebrew class tomorrow; you know, they make you speak nothing but Hebrew from the beginning, it is insane; but in our rooms we can cheat a little, eh? But what are you doing with the chocolate? One spreads it on the bread, like the children after school—is it not done in America? My friend in Tunis always said it tasted better on the fingers; do you agree? Yes? I must try it that way. Have you read de Beauvoir? I am now reading *Le Deuxième Sexe*. I will lend it to you when I have finished. I would like to discuss it with someone, and these men, *bof*! Who can speak of ideas with them? Although, one must learn, no? I have always gone to schools for girls before this. But I am nearly twenty now. It is a burden to be still a virgin at my age, and I do not believe it necessary from a philosophical or moral point of view, but these men are so stupid, they simply do not appeal to me at all. Are you a virgin?

"No." Elisheva laughs. "You are the second person to ask me today." Andrée, she thinks, will be snapped up as soon as she finds a man worth talking to; she is charming and very pretty, with curly hair and smooth skin of the same sandy-brown color. "Who is the third girl in the apartment?"

"Bella, from the Soviet Union. We have no language in common. Soon Hebrew will suffice, but until now she and I have been lonely together. She is always with the other Russian immigrants."

As if on cue, Bella enters with a heavy step. She is a robust woman of thirty or so, with bright red cheeks and large features. "*Shalom*," she says, extending a hand. "Why do you leave America? America is better than Israel."

"Ah, you speak English. I don't think America is better than Israel. I am a Jew. This is my country."

"America is good for Jews. America is better than Israel."

"How do you know? Have you been to America?"

"America is good."

Although Bella's English vocabulary seems limited to statements such as these, she manages to engage Elisheva in an argument about the war in Vietnam. Bella is in favor of U.S. involvement; she repeats a simple, dogmatic version of the domino theory until Andrée has gone to bed and Elisheva has given up arguing or even listening. At this point Elisheva begins to count the days since her last period, and realizes she may have been fertile today. If she is pregnant, she will have to use the rest of her money to fly to Sweden for an abortion. Why Sweden? She heard of someone else going there for the same purpose. But who was it? And surely whoever it was went from the United States, not from Israel. Are abortions illegal in Israel? How can she find out, when she knows no Hebrew and no Israelis? Maybe Andrée knows. Andrée is better than Sweden. Sweden is better than America. America is better than Israel. No, Israel is better than America. Elisheva is better than Ellen. Clara is better than Bella. Israel is better than Clara is better than Roginsky is better than Rogin is better than Rogers is better than Moshe is better than Michel is better than French is better than English. Hebrew. Hebrew tomorrow.

————————

My name is Elisheva. I am a new immigrant. Are you a new immigrant? What is your name? I come from the United States. Where do you come from? I am a pupil at the *ulpan*. My teacher is Sima. In the *ulpan* we learn Hebrew. We will speak only Hebrew. Hebrew is our language. Hebrew is the language of Israel. Israel is our country. Now it is summer. In summer it is hot. I live in Upper Nazareth at the *ulpan*. I will study Hebrew at the *ulpan* for two months. Then I will go to a kibbutz. I will be a volunteer at the kibbutz for six weeks. Then I will go up to Jerusalem. I will live there. I will be a student at the university. I will live and work in the city of Jerusalem.

For breakfast I eat yogurt and cucumber and tomato and bread and butter and cheese. I put my food on a plate. I eat with a fork and spoon and knife. I drink coffee from a cup. I sit with all the pupils in the dining room of the *ulpan*. Some pupils are from Roumania and some are from Morocco. Some are from Australia and some are from Russia. Some are from India and some are from Brazil. We speak only Hebrew in the dining room.

Hebrew is the language of Israel. Hebrew is the language of the Jews.

The *ulpan* vocabulary included a word for "good," but none for "evil"; "love," but not "hate." There was no word for "Arab," no Zionism, no Christianity. No politics, no government, no corruption. No music, no song, no dance, no art. No protest, no disillusion, no sex, no madness, no dream, no wonder, no prayer. There were tasks and activities: buying a stamp, ordering a meal in a restaurant, applying for a job, boarding a bus, describing a symptom to a doctor.

I learned quickly, glad to recite the prescribed statements, content even to see the magical sounds of Hebrew become plain words, to see the pure truth of music disintegrate into the half-lies of taught language. I was willing to make the sacrifice, just so that I might speak, understand, read, write the language that would tell me who I was: a new immigrant who ate yogurt and tomatoes for breakfast.

Later, in Jerusalem, when Miriam and I studied the Bible together, the magic returned. *Hashmal*, the word Sima taught me for electricity, became the lightning of the ancients. *Shvita*, a labor strike, came from the same root as *shabbat*, the day of rest. *Rakevet*, a train, was the descendant of the chariots in which the Egyptians drowned, pursuing Moses and the Children of Israel.

In Upper Nazareth, in the *ulpan* full of pupils from Australia and Brazil and Morocco and Russia, I needed only the simplest, most optimistic Hebrew words and concepts, exactly the ones Sima taught. I was happy to speak of ideas only in French, with Andrée.

As she had promised, Andrée lent me *The Second Sex*, and we discussed it. I think this must have been the first feminist conversation of my life. It went on for weeks: at meals, during class breaks, in each other's rooms after dinner.

One evening Andrée and I went to the cinema together, at the Upper Nazareth shopping center. The film was the story of a young Israeli war widow, who falls in love with a friend of her late husband and is haunted by the fear that he too will be killed. The widow's obsessions filled the movie: sirens, announcements on the radio of the names of soldiers just killed, the moment when she was notified of her husband's death, over and over again, as if her husband is dying over and over again. In the bus, on the way home, Andrée held my hand. We were both silent.

That evening in the shopping center, I noticed a gynecologist's office, his doorplate considerately lettered in Hebrew, English, and Arabic. I returned there when my period didn't come. The doctor gave me a high-dosage shot of hormones every day for ten days. During the ten days I was nauseated and I gained weight in the belly. I went for walks by myself and avoided my suitemates. Mostly I walked around the abandoned Bedouin housing project, hoping no one could see me from the *ulpan* above. This, I thought, is how the Bedouins would feel if they had moved in, knowing they were here to be watched, hoping no one was watching. In fact, I would be one of the watchers, from the window of my room. I began to think I had been put in that room to watch the Bedouins. I had only just arrived, and already I was being recruited as a spy.

On the eleventh day, a Friday, my period came. I remember it was a Friday because when I saw the spot of blood I said *barukh ha-shem*, thank God, in Hebrew, and then I lit the candles for *shabbat*.

At the *ulpan* Andrée fell in love with one of Michel's Tunisian friends; I heard later that she married him. I heard it not from her but from Michel, a few months after, when I ran into him at a Jerusalem bus stop.

"How nice," I said.

"And you?" he said. "Have you found a boyfriend?"

"No," I said.

"My fiancée arrives next week," he said.

"How nice," I said. "I thought I was pregnant. But I'm not."

"Why didn't you tell me?" he said. "What would you have done?"

I told him. He called me a heartless *chienne*. Then my bus came.

But when I remember that time, it isn't Michel I think of, although he was the last man ever to get away with telling me something was wrong with me because of my being Jewish, because of my not being the blonde, Christian virgin. Nor do I think of Bella, although she and I got along better in Hebrew than in English.

When I think back now, it is Andrée I miss. Andrée, who

charmed me and lent me de Beauvoir and held my hand on the bus. Andrée, whom I avoided when I thought myself pregnant, and who later avoided me when she fell in love. Andrée, with whom I lost touch, and whose name I don't even know, because surely by now she is Aviva or Aliza or Ḥanna or Ḥava.

———

Still, I should have understood them better, Michel and Bella. Perhaps I hardly think of them today because it shames me to remember how little I understood them, how readily I allowed myself to feel superior to Bella's yearning for the country I had rejected, Michel's insistence on importing a Gentile bride. It shames me to remember how little I cared to see the difference: they both immigrated to Israel to escape persecution as Jews in their native countries; I was the only one to emigrate purely by choice.

I should have understood Bella, especially Bella, who came from Vilna, not fifty miles from my grandfather's *shtetl*. I should have known, when Bella said, "America is better than Israel," it was the same as Mottel Roginsky, still in Lithouania, saying, "The streets of New York are paved with gold."

Bella embarrassed me, Old Country Jew that she was, smelling of herring, speaking too loudly in simple sentences. I mocked her privately, just as my parents had mocked Zayde Mottel and Bubby Sadie for keeping a thick Yiddish accent and never quite learning the social rules of the America they adored.

I wonder about Sadie and Mottel. I wonder, if they had been there with me when I arrived at the *ulpan*, whether they too would have felt, watching the astronauts hoist the American flag on the moon, that they had less in common with the men than with the rocky surface of the moon itself.

———

At the end of two months the Ministry of Absorption gave me a certificate: *ulpan* completed; absorption completed. The Ministry did not mean my absorption of Hebrew, but Israel's absorption of me.

The metaphor of *klita*, absorption, is that of society as a plant, sucking up immigrants like drops of water to make it flourish. An apt image for a country perpetually in need of water, citizens, and trees. I had no objection. In America I had always hated the metaphor of assimilation, felt it as teeth grinding me up like meat, intestines digesting the parts they found useful and excreting the soul along with the gristle. I perceived no such threat to myself in Israel. I simply knew I was not yet absorbed. I was part of a community of new immigrants. I was not part of Israel.

I learned Hebrew at the *ulpan*, but I became part of Israel at the kibbutz. I became part of Israel not as a student, but as a volunteer fruit-picker for the autumn harvest. The people who stayed in my life were not those from the *ulpan* and before, but those from the kibbutz and after. Andrée disappeared but Miriam remained. Michel disappeared; Shlomo and Ilana remained. Patty disappeared, Stan disappeared. Oh, but Daniel. I forgot about Daniel. Daniel was from before, and Daniel remained. Daniel remained.

3

The first few nights, the shelling woke me with a start. After that, I slept right through, dreaming of the harmless, ornamental firework displays we used to watch from our back porch every Fourth of July. The shout of a kibbutznik, not the bombs bursting in air, roused me at 3 a.m.: "Volunteers! Out of bed! Truck at the main building, half an hour!"

The daytime shelling continued to frighten me. I never did get used to it, never learned not to jump when the noise of battle caught me about to pry a ripe pomegranate off its branch, my freshly-calloused thumb pressing the leathery skin of the fruit, my arm throbbing with new muscles. Miriam just kept picking; I could hear the snap of twigs from her side of the tree, after the rumble of explosion faded. Then I hurried to catch up, lest she and I lose our reputation as "good workers, for Americans," and find ourselves demoted to the pepper field.

The orchards were at the far end of the kibbutz, much closer than the sleeping quarters to the Jordan border. But still, it was peacetime—who was shelling, and why, I never knew—and the orchard was serene except for those short bursts of war-movie soundtrack.

I loved the work, loved the red fruit we cracked open against a tree, the juice we dribbled down the front of our gray work garments when it was time for a break. I loved bouncing to the orchard in the back of a truck in the dark, and watching the sun rise just as we arrived. I loved tucking my hair into a hat and not letting it fall to my shoulders again until the workday was over at noon. I loved the slow strengthening of my body, the coarsening of my hands as they learned to be tough and useful. I loved eating breakfast at a long table set up in the field, and after breakfast, the moment when one of the kibbutzniks would chant, *"Rabotai n'varekh*, honored companions, let us bless," and everyone would *bentsch* before returning to the trees. This,

I thought, was how our religion began: in expressing a bond with the land and the seasons, in honoring our own hard work, in knowing we and the land and the sun and the winter rains had made the food we ate.

At first I kept these thoughts to myself, fearing that Miriam would find them sentimental or blasphemous. She had come to Israel two summers earlier, immediately after the Six-Day War; her seniority intimidated me, as did her background: Zionist from a Zionist family, Orthodox from an Orthodox family.

Nonetheless, we made a good team, she and I. We picked quickly and never pleaded exhaustion, as other Americans had been known to do. We complemented each other: she tall and thin, I short and plump; she fair, I dark; she with a large vocabulary and poor accent in Hebrew, I with few words but impeccable pronunciation. Between the two of us, we managed to make ourselves understood to the most impatient kibbutznik; eventually, we managed to make ourselves understood even to each other.

––––––

Only Elisheva and Miriam are awake—and a few watchmen, of course. After the midday meal, the silence of the kibbutz is not the playful hush of an afternoon nap, but the heavy stillness of nighttime, as if the kibbutzniks have transplanted to afternoon the hours from 3 to 6 a.m.

"We can afford to sleep less than they do," Miriam says, lighting a cigarette. "Next month we'll be gone. Imagine how you'd feel if you had to get up for work in the dark, every day of your life except *shabbat* and *yom tov*. You'd start sleeping all afternoon, believe me."

Elisheva, who has been fanning herself with a gray workhat, stops to examine a new inflammation on the fleshy part of her palm. "Do you ever think you might want to?"

"Sleep all afternoon?"

"No, stay on a kibbutz. Become a member. Keep working outdoors." She extracts a splinter. "Ouch. Do you have any handcream left?"

Miriam topples a jar off the shelf over her bed. "I'm almost out. Tomorrow let's take the bus to Beit She'an. Who would have thought we'd need more than a jar of handcream each? We can visit the Roman amphitheatre, too. Okay? Good. Even if we're too hot to budge, let's go tomorrow. It won't get any cooler while we're here. We're both out of tampax. I'm almost out of cigarettes. If we were members, the kibbutz would furnish everything, and we'd never have to go shopping."

"Well?"

"Yes. I wouldn't want to stay here, but some day I'd like to start a new settlement with a group of young people. That's what I had in mind when I made *aliyah*. A *moshav* or kibbutz based on the principles of A. D. Gordon, but religious."

"Who's A. D. Gordon?"

Miriam's eyes go round. "You've never heard of A. D. Gordon? You came to Israel, and you've never even read his philosophy? Maybe you forgot his name. You know, 'People and Labor,' 'Logic for the Future,' 'Our Tasks Ahead.' Similar to Rav Kook, but more emphasis on land and labor . . . "

"Rav Kook?" Elisheva watches Miriam's face change: yes, this girl is truly ignorant; patience is in order.

Miriam dives into her suitcase and emerges holding a tattered book. "Here's Gordon: 'There is a cosmic element in nationality which is its basic ingredient. That cosmic element may best be described as the blending of the natural landscape of the Homeland with the spirit of the people inhabiting it. This is the mainspring of a people's vitality and creativity, of its spiritual and cultural values. Any conglomeration of individuals may form a society in the mechanical sense, one that moves and acts, but only the presence of the cosmic element makes for an organic national entity with creative vitality.

" 'It is life we want, no more and no less than that, our own life feeding on our own vital sources, in the fields and under the skies of our Homeland, a life based on our own physical and mental labors; we want vital energy and spiritual richness from this living source. We come to our Homeland in order to be planted in our natural soil from which we have been uprooted, to strike our roots deep into its life-giving substances, and to stretch out our branches in the sustaining and creating air and sunlight of the Homeland. We, who have been torn away from nature, who have lost the savor of natural living—if we desire life, we must establish a new relationship with nature.' He wrote that in 1920."

Elisheva's head is bobbing in vigorous agreement. "Miriam, it's wonderful. It's exactly the way I've been feeling here, but I didn't have the words. Read me more, please."

"You can borrow the book." Miriam flips to another page.

31

"Here's something from Rav Kook: 'The claim of our flesh is great. We require a healthy body. We have neglected health and physical prowess, forgetting that our flesh is as sacred as our spirit. We have turned our backs on physical life, the development of our senses, and all that is involved in the tangible reality of the flesh, because we have fallen prey to lowly fears, and have lacked faith in the holiness of the Land. As it is written in Talmud: "Faith is exemplified by the tractate *Zera'im*, Seeds—a human being proves faith in eternal life by planting." ' "

Elisheva sees on Miriam's bright face the reflection of her own flush of excitement. "I can't believe it. A rabbi wrote that? A rabbi said we should love our bodies and develop our senses?"

"Well, not just any rabbi. Rav Kook. He said a lot of things that aren't very popular with most religious Jews. Even the kibbutzniks here would be scandalized by the passage I just read you. Not to mention my neighbors in Jerusalem—they'd probably stone Rav Kook if he were alive today." Miriam looks at Elisheva and hesitates. "Your parents aren't religious at all, are they?"

"No. Not at all. My mother is musical. My father is ethical. Neither one is religious. Why do you ask?"

Miriam looks down and says nothing. Elisheva's excitement turns to anxiety. What is Miriam leading up to? She can't be friends with someone who wasn't raised religious?

"What does a cheeseburger taste like?" Miriam almost whispers the question.

"What? You've never eaten a cheeseburger? In your whole life?" Elisheva's features jump into the same expression Miriam adopted when Elisheva asked who A. D. Gordon was.

"Huh-uh. We were always kosher."

"You never sneaked?"

"Never. I grew up in New York City without ever tasting pizza. I've never eaten in a Chinese restaurant. But the only *trayfe* I'm really curious about is cheeseburgers. I like beef patties and I like cheese, so I figured I'd probably like the combination. *Nu*? So what does it taste like?"

"Cheeseburger. Shit, I don't know. It tastes like cheeseburger. Cheese and meat together."

"Thanks a lot. That's a big help."

"Listen, it's been a long time. I haven't eaten meat in over a year." Elisheva made a pact with Daniel after they co-led a Students for Peace discussion on animals; she wonders whether he is still a vegetarian, too; she wonders where he is; she wonders why she hasn't heard from her family since she left the *ulpan*; she feels a pang of homesickness. "Tell you what. Once I'm settled in Jerusalem, I'll have you over to dinner. I'll make a walnutburger with cheese. It's the closest thing there is to a cheeseburger. Deal?"

"Deal." Miriam extends her long arm to shake hands. "Mmm. That made me hungry. Isn't it time for these lazy Israelis to get up and start making supper?"

———

Dear Mother and Dad,

The Israel post office finally caught up with me. I was getting desperate for news from you—I was convinced something terrible had happened, or you were furious with me, or who knows what. Every day before lunch I went to the kibbutz mailroom, and every day I left forlorn. (Time to play "Hearts and Flowers," Mother.) At last, today there was a large packet of letters, a whole month's worth, which for some reason arrived all the same day. Thank you, thank you! And thank you for the box of vitamins and the paperback books and the beautiful red shawl from Grandmother Lowenthal (I'll write her a separate note, don't worry) and the wonderful photos of you and Neil. I'll have my friend Miriam photograph me in the orchard tomorrow so you can see my glamorous work clothes and my glorious tan. Mother, the picture of your quartet is delightful. You all look positively in love with each other. It must have been quite a concert. Dad, you look thinner than I remember. Have you lost some weight, or do I remember wrong? Oh, I miss you both!

As you'll see from the pictures I'll send you, I've managed not to lose any weight here. I've gotten more muscular, but I still have the *zaftig* Lowenthal shape. Why couldn't I be thin like the Rogins? You'd think I'd at least have sweated off a few pounds. This part of Israel is extremely hot and humid, because it's a river valley. I'm looking forward to the cooler weather of Jerusalem—but no, Mother, I won't consider leaving this kibbutz a minute before Sukkot. If I don't stay to participate in the harvest festival, for what am I working my fingers to the bone? (As Bubby Sadie would have said.) And I won't consider living in Tel-Aviv instead of Jerusalem. I don't care what Sonya says about the wonderful concerts in Tel-Aviv. Jerusalem is where I will live.

Anyway, I know your reasons for wanting me away from here and away from Jerusalem have nothing to do with Sonya. You're concerned about my safety, right? I should have known, Dad, you wouldn't be able to resist looking up my location on a map—but I wish you hadn't. You're just going to worry yourselves for nothing. I'm perfectly safe. Israel is so small, just about everywhere is near some border or other, and the Jordan border is relatively quiet. I'll be careful, I promise.

Maybe you'll understand better if I tell you how much effort it took to get me into this kibbutz. There aren't many religious kibbutzim, and they select volunteers carefully. I had to be interviewed at an office in Jerusalem. Nobody ever told me that religious girls are expected to wear long skirts and long sleeves. Well, I showed up for the interview in a skirt above my knees and a sleeveless blouse. The interviewer refused to believe I was religious. I argued with her (which wasn't easy, with the amount of Hebrew I know), and I guess we made a commotion, because a man who was walking down the hall came in to see what was going on. She recognized him right away: "Professor Cohen! Please sit down. Can you help me make this girl understand why she is unsuitable for a religious kibbutz?" She pointed to my knees, as if they told all he needed to know.

Professor Cohen asked me a few questions: Do I keep kosher? (How can a vegetarian not keep kosher?) Will I keep the sabbath? Will I go to synagogue? Will I study Torah? Then he said, "*Giveret* Goldstein, if you deny this girl a place to work, you will be responsible for turning a soul away from Israel." He started quoting Talmud, and I couldn't understand the rest, because he got pretty worked up and was talking very fast. A couple of times he knocked his own hat to the floor, from waving his arms so wildly.

Thanks to Shlomo Cohen, professor of Jewish philosophy, here I am, and here I intend to stay until Sukkot! Professor Cohen gave me his card and invited me to come for *shabbat* with him and his family when I am in Jerusalem. See how kind the Israelis are? How can you think I'm in danger?

There are no more pomegranates to pick, so Miriam and I have both been transferred to olives. I liked picking pomegranates better. Olives are no challenge at all. You just run your fingers through the leaves, and the olives drop right into your basket. There's no resistance, no dialectic. It's boring. The olive trees are lovely, with graceful silver leaves that give a lot of shade to work in—but I like pomegranates better.

If I can find a job as soon as I get to Jerusalem, I may not attend the university this fall. I can't see coming to Israel to study French, and my Hebrew isn't good enough yet for me to go into another field. Also, I want to do something practical here, make a contribution. I want to keep working with my hands, even if all I'm doing is typing in an office. (Yes, Dad, maybe you were right to make me learn to type.)

Dad, the next time you're in the library, would you look up some information for me? (The kibbutz has a small library, but no books in English.)

1. Do birds sweat?

2. Do birds of the same type have different song patterns in different parts of the world? I see some of the same birds here as in Pennsylvania: blackbirds, sparrows, swallows. Surely they must have a different dialect here? And how do they manage to live in such a climate unless they sweat?

Thanks. And Mother, please stop worrying about me, or I'll have to worry about your worrying. Okay?

> Much love,
> Elisheva

They never did let me know about the birds, although Mother sent letters fat with statistics from Dad's forays into the Middle East section of the college library: 14 "incidents" in the Jordan River valley since the Six-Day War; 5.6 incidents in Jerusalem per month; predictions by 19 out of 20 experts for another war in the near future.

Even so, I stood firm, staking my claim to adulthood on my right to live where I chose. Mother's objections became more and more trivial—fruit-picking would ruin my hands for the piano, should I ever decide to take lessons again—and eventually ceased.

Dad, although he supplied the facts for Mother's campaign, never objected directly to my geographic location. What he asked me to reconsider, as I knew he would, was my decision against the university. He was still in mourning for the years he'd wasted in Uncle Jake's grocery store before finally saving enough money to finish a doctorate in sociology. "Don't make the same mistake I made," he wrote to me. I wrote back, "Have you ever read A. D. Gordon?"

As I had vowed to my parents, I stayed at the kibbutz through the autumn holy days. And as I had promised Shlomo Cohen, I went to synagogue.

There was no shelling on Yom Kippur that year, no conflict of any kind. For the first time I had no decisions to make. I did what everyone in the kibbutz did: fasted from sundown to sundown, drank no water, wore no perfume or leather shoes, refrained from washing. I contributed to the mixture of odors I inhaled in the women's section: nightbreath of day, vaginal fluid, sweat dried on the skin. I joined the communal prayers, stood and beat my breast as a member of the congregation. I swayed on my feet and entered the collective trance of *Ne'ila*, when the ark remained open and the male descendants of the *kohanim*, the priestly clan, covered their heads with white prayer shawls and stood before the Torah scrolls, chanting, until light seemed to emanate from the scrolls, the ark, the silky cocoons of men wrapped in prayer.

If Dad could have seen me there in the back of the synagogue, growing faint and light-headed with the other women, as Bubby Sadie had done before me, he would have been even more distressed than he was about my abandoning him in academia. When Neil and I were children, Dad always insisted that we stay home from school for the holy days, but only as a gesture of loyalty to the few other Jewish students; he knew our attendance would be used as an excuse for punishing their absence. And at the last minute, he always ended up taking us to a synagogue, I suppose as another gesture of solidarity. He stood and sat at all the right points, but he refused to say the words, refused to pray to a God he didn't believe in.

I still respect Dad's integrity and follow his example. When I find myself in a synagogue, I still skim ahead in the prayerbook to see which parts of the service I can read aloud in good conscience, which parts I must not recite.

But in 1969, in a kibbutz *shul* near the Jordan River and the Jordan border, I staked my claim to adulthood on one more act of rebellion: that of rejecting the moral scrupulousness of my father Arthur Rogin, and accepting instead the ecstatic submission of my fathers Abraham, Isaac, and Jacob. On Yom Kippur 5730, I lost myself in prayer, in community, in the ancient Hebrew words that were always true, no matter what I believed.

———

When I promised my parents to be careful in Israel, I meant I wouldn't walk alone after dark in Arab neighborhoods. I meant that if I saw an abandoned suitcase in the road, I would run to a phone and call the bomb squad. I meant I wouldn't volunteer for the army, as Miriam was planning to do after finishing her degree in Computer Science.

When I made that promise, I was thinking of myself as a Jew of no gender, not as a woman. I had no thought of the danger I'd sensed for an instant with Michel: This could end in violence.

Michel, since I told him so, was the seventh man. The eighth man, may he rest in peace, assuming he did finally kill himself, was Zev. I met him at a party Miriam and I attended while I was still staying at her apartment in Jerusalem and looking for one of my own. Zev was a large and unattractive American, with a plump face and handlebar moustache. I went home with him without first consulting Miriam. Although (thanks to Rav Kook) she and I had discussed "the flesh" in abstract terms, she had never asked me Andrée and Michel's question. I didn't want to contend with her possible disapproval.

After sex, Zev stood before a small bathroom mirror all night, holding a straight razor to his throat and mumbling about his worthlessness. At dawn I finally persuaded him to put down the razor and return to bed for another go. Then I had to leave; he must let me take that razor; he must promise not to kill himself. Zev refused to give up the razor, but agreed to stay alive if I would see him again.

When I told Miriam what had happened, she expressed no disapproval, saying only, "Don't do it." I went out with Zev again anyway. Because I had said I would? I think not. Because I didn't want to be a one-night girl, as I had been for Michel. Because I thought I had saved a life. Because I needed to know what kind of soul I had, and I believed that Zev's despair, manipulative though it was, might teach me.

But the razor-blade trick was apparently the only one in his repertoire. As he saw his encore performance failing to hold my interest, he began to mumble about my worthlessness instead of his own. "Stupid bitch. You'd better not leave. You'd better see me again. If you're too stupid to see me again, there's no telling what I might do with this blade."

I stationed myself near the door and sized up my chance of escape. I was still in good physical condition, from the kibbutz. Zev was big but slow, paunchy, unmuscular. I decided to run for it.

Miriam looked at me with an odd expression when I returned. "Elisheva," she said, "I don't know you very well yet, but I thought you had more sense than this. You didn't have to go to bed with that man the first time, and you certainly didn't have to go to bed with him the second time. He is dangerous. Don't do it again."

"I won't," I said. "But I don't think he's actually dangerous. He's just depressed."

Miriam said, "You didn't give him this address, did you? No? Good."

As Miriam spoke, I felt embarrassed to have exposed to her my lack of judgment and, even more, my lack of sophistication. It was as though my nights with Zev had never happened, as though no man had ever touched me, as though my girlhood was intact, as though I would never grow up, even at a remove of 6,000 miles from my parents.

The embarrassment was the same as that of the first time I lay with Stan, when my cunt closed hard as a fist, a tight little knot that refused to admit him, although I breathed deeply and hummed "The Trout" by Schubert. Stan was in no hurry, let me go that time, just rolled off and gave instructions: "Squeeze harder, harder, use both hands, like wringing a towel, that's right, harder."

Stan, the toil, the fumbling in his dark room, the embarrassment of stubborn innocence: all that was part of my education. But now I had graduated from college, finished *ulpan*, been with more than one man, read *The Second Sex* and the writings of Gordon and Kook. I wanted my education to be over. I wanted finally to understand the strange hunger of one human being for another, the desire to burrow in one another's flesh. I wanted to know whether it was really I who performed these private acts of the senses, or someone else who temporarily crawled into my skin and took me over. I wanted to know what other women seemed to know: when to be afraid, and when to trust; when to hold back, and when to expand toward someone else without hesitation, offering the self entire.

———

As it turned out, I had nothing further to fear from Zev. Not being religious, he had no reason to show up in Miriam's neighborhood. Once or twice in the years that followed, I saw him at a bus stop or in a cinema line downtown, near Zion Square. Each for a different reason, we pretended not to know one another. *V'sof pasook*: that was the end of that.

38

Miriam's neighbors, the Hassidim and their inseparable enemies the Mitnagdim, surrounded me with harmless, exuberant disapproval. I enjoyed watching the men, dressed for a Polish winter in fur hats and long black woolen coats, gabble to each other in Yiddish as they streamed happily out of the enormous yeshiva down the street. I could not bring myself to take them seriously; and yet they seemed to take me very seriously, to consider me a grave threat.

I rather liked the sense of power they gave me, those pale bearded creatures who crossed the street to avoid walking too close to me, who interrupted the most avid discussion to turn their faces toward the wall when I passed, who without looking at me knew whether I was dressed properly, and tossed insults at my back when I wore pants or a short-sleeved blouse. They cared so very much, they feared my influence to such a disproportionate extent, that I was moved to feel something indulgent, maternal, toward them. I wrote them a letter:

Men of Ge'ula! Please do not waste your energy on me. You are making yourselves old before your time. You will give yourselves ulcers and high blood pressure. Relax a little, take it easy. I am not here to stay. Even as you read this notice, I am searching for employment and lodgings in a more suitable quarter. If you know of a job for an American immigrant who can type and speak French, or an apartment under 250 *lirot* a month, your kind assistance will rid you of my presence immediately.

Thank you and shalom,
Elisheva Rogin

I decided against posting the letter, which might have jeopardized Miriam's precarious position and cheap rent in the district. Hidden in a pocket of my suitcase, the letter did its work.

4

*S*hir ha-ma'alot: a song of ascents.
The terraced hills surrounding Jerusalem are broad stone
steps leading up to the city. Jerusalem is a crown on the
land, a tower, a breast of shining stone.

At dawn and at dusk she gleams gold and rose, at noon alabaster. Her stones are quick with light.

All Jerusalem is built of stone, the stone of the hills and the
stone of the walls. The stones are ancient first in the earth, then
ancient to human use. The stones are quarried, piled, mortared,
toppled, recovered, reused. The stones are rough, then worn
smooth, then bullet-pocked.

The stone pavements, the stone walls, the stone houses. The
air of stones, the powdery dust of stones, the sacred light of
stones, the stone towers of the Old City, the curved stone wall
entered only by gates, the gates of the city.

The stone courtyards, the courtyard of the stone house
where Elisheva will live, the gate to the courtyard, the walls of
stone, the stone staircase.

The house breathes. The stones are alive.

The apartment is available because an old man from Iraq has
died. His son, the new landlord, has no use for the old man's
personal belongings; therefore, the apartment is furnished. Elisheva will sleep in the old man's bed, on his thin mattress, under
his ragged quilt. She will bathe in his metal tub. She will water
his only plant, a woody vine with few leaves. She will eat from
his chipped plates and listen to the crabbed voice of his radio.
She will see what he saw, through the wrought-iron grillwork of
the arched windows, when she sits at his table; or on a sunny
day, when she looks down into the street from the *mirpesset*
she will share with the family in the other upstairs apartment.

Across the street, beside the *makolet* where Elisheva can buy

dairy products and bottled juices, stands a small Iraqi synagogue.
At 5:00 every morning, a friend of the dead man paces in front
of the synagogue, calling, *"Minyan! Shaharit! Minyan!"* He
walks as if already at prayer, his turban swaying from side to
side, his long yellow-white beard swinging across the front of his
striped caftan. When nine men have joined him, they enter the
synagogue and chant in a Hebrew that sounds like Arabic. Sometimes a shepherd with his flock, or a man leading a few donkeys,
passes by, and the braying of the animals drowns out the
prayers.

At 6:00 the *makolet* opens, and the bakery down the street,
and the *mikva* and public shower at the corner. Now the old
women begin to appear, carrying baskets, greeting each other
loudly—in Arabic? or in the same Hebrew their husbands use in
the synagogue? Clusters of children run by, shouting and laughing, bookbags strapped to their small backs. Young men and
women dressed for jobs emerge last and walk quickly toward
the bus stop at the end of the street. Some are smoking, some
cracking sunflower and pumpkin seeds with their teeth and spit-
ting the shells into the street; all are talking, interrupting, talking, gesturing, giving each other friendly slaps, offering seeds,
offering cigarettes, talking.

Not many cars in the neighborhood, but the street is so narrow, the residents so accustomed to walking in large groups,
that there is a perpetual traffic jam. Drivers leave their cars running in the middle of the street and jump out to say hello to a
friend, to yell at pedestrians or other drivers for blocking the
way, or to run upstairs and fetch a relative who needs a ride and
didn't respond to ten minutes of honking.

Right at this moment Ḥayim from next door is leaning on the
horn of his cab, waiting to drive his wife Yardena to a wealthier
neighborhood, where she will spend the day cleaning houses.
Perhaps Yardena does not hear him? Elisheva knocks at Yardena's open door.

"Mah atem osim? Yeladim m'shuga'im!" Yardena shrieks.
"What are you doing, you crazy children?" She turns from the
tiny wall mirror in which she has been braiding her hair at lightning speed. "Ah, Elisheva, excuse me, I thought you were my
boys. I sent them off to school not five minutes ago, but they
always find an excuse to come back for something. Would you
like a cup of coffee? Why are you up so early? Does your job
start today? Ḥayim is coming for me, he will give you a ride.

Come, sit down. Do I speak too quickly? Do you understand what I say?"

"No. Yes," Elisheva stutters. "Yardena, Ḥayim already waits for you. Do you want me to tell him you are coming?"

"*Mah pit'om*? What time is it? *Oy va voy*, this old clock." Yardena strides to the *mirpesset* and leans over the railing. "*Ḥayim! Ḥayim!* Come up for a minute, leave the car, come have some coffee. Elisheva has come to visit."

"Yardena, no. You will be late for work. Please, I just came to tell you Ḥayim was waiting."

No use. Yardena has already mixed three portions of *café botz*, "mud coffee," added three teaspoons of sugar to each cup, poured in some milk. Now she has disappeared into the kitchen, and returns with a partially-sliced honeycake.

Ḥayim bounds up the stairs. "*Brukha ha-ba'a!*" He pumps Elisheva's hand. "Welcome! It is good that you came to see us. Anything you need, just ask Ḥayim and Yardena." He turns to his wife. "We are lucky she moved in, *lo nakhon*, Yardena? What an improvement over the old man."

"Don't mention the old man to me, him or his thief of a son. Do you know how much rent Elisheva is paying him? For a room with no toilet or hot water?" The question is rhetorical; only yesterday Elisheva overheard Yardena and Ḥayim discussing her rent, expressing the hope that the new landlord would not try to raise theirs to the same level, and deciding that even a thief like him would not expect them to pay the same rent as a new immigrant from America. "More coffee? Here, have another slice of cake. You do what Ḥayim says, Elisheva *motek*. Ask us how much something is worth before you pay."

"Thank you," Elisheva says. "As a matter of fact, I am going to the Old City today. I need a rug, a tablecloth, a few other things for my apartment."

"From the Old City? Why do you want to go there? They don't have nice modern things. Everything there is dirty and old-fashioned. And they cheat you—you have to bargain hard, hard, with no mercy. Right, Ḥayim? Listen to us, we were raised among Arabs, we know not to trust them. If the landlord is stealing from you, what do you think the Arabs will do?"

"*Shtuyiot*," Ḥayim says. "Nonsense. Why are you telling her to be afraid of Arabs? This is Israel! In Syria we had to be afraid of Arabs. Here we are strong." He flexes a muscle. Elisheva is impressed.

42

Yardena winks at Elisheva. "In Israel every man is a hero. Thank God. But Ḥayim, look at her. This is Elisheva, not the whole state of Israel. Do you want to send her into the Old City alone, a young girl like this?"

Ḥayim suddenly turns paternal. "How old are you?"

"Twenty-two."

"Why aren't you married yet? You should have a husband."

Yardena nods assent. "Ḥayim is right, Elisheva. *B'ḥayai*, upon my life, you would be better off with a husband. Never mind, *en davar*, she just arrived. She will find a husband soon enough."

"But not in the Old City," Ḥayim says. "Don't go looking for a husband there."

"No, no, today I will look only for a rug and a tablecloth."

"Here is what you do." Yardena stands up and walks around the room as if examining merchandise. "Ḥayim, you be the shopkeeper. How much is this rug?—Elisheva, you be sure to speak to them in Hebrew. If you use English, they will ask a higher price.—*Nu nu*, how much for the rug?"

Ḥayim smiles broadly. "Ah, *giveret*, you have chosen my best rug. My daughter wove it with her own hands. A beautiful rug. For you, one hundred *lirot*."

"One hundred? You're telling me a joke. Down the street I can get the same rug for fifty. Fifty *lirot*, no more."

"*Mah att omeret*? The thread and dye alone cost sixty. But you are so nice, I will sell it to you for ninety."

"Too much." Yardena walks to the door. "*Shalom adonee.*"

"*Rega, rega!*" Ḥayim calls after her. "Eighty-five." She keeps walking. "Eighty."

Yardena returns. "Seventy-five, not a *grush* more."

"*Giveret*, please. I will lose money. . . . *B'seder*, okay, seventy-five. For good luck. My first sale of the day. Seventy-five."

Yardena struts over to Elisheva. "You see, *motek*? You have to bargain hard, like me."

"Bravo! You two should be actors, *b'emmet*, honestly. What a performance!"

"Actors!" Ḥayim laughs heartily. "*Betaḥ*, we have acting jobs today. I have to play a driver, and Yardena has to play a maid. Come on, Elisheva, we'll give you a ride to Jaffa Gate."

————

The wall and the gates are what held her off until now. If the Old City wanted to make itself known to her, it would not have set itself apart and girded itself with the thick wall of a fortress.

43

If the Old City wanted her to enter easily and without hesitation, it would not require that she pass through a gate. Like an established family, the Old City demands a letter of introduction, a purpose for her visit. The Old City tolerates no idle curiosity; only a sufficiently strong need or desire can earn her the right to enter one of its gates.

Elisheva stands where Yardena and Ḥayim deposited her. She watches large numbers of people pass through Jaffa Gate: German-speaking tourists, Israeli soldiers strapped with *uzi* machine guns which pat the young men on the back when they walk, Israeli civilians, Arab women in embroidered black dresses who balance bronze trays on their heads, Arab boys pushing carts of fresh bread and calling, "*Bageleh bageleh, bageleh ḥamm bageleh ḥamm.*" Elisheva buys a loop of warm sesame bread from one of these vendors.

"*Zattar?*" he asks.

"*Zattar?*" she repeats. "What is *zattar?*"

He hands her a pinch of newspaper, which contains a fragrant brown powder.

"*Zattar,*" he says. He shows her how to dip the bread into the spice as she eats. The combination is delicious, pungent, an utterly new flavor.

As if the *zattar* were a drug to give courage, Elisheva marches forward, through the gate and into the world of the Old City. And as if the *zattar* were a stimulant, she feels a rush of sensory pleasure: how splendid everything looks, how good it smells! She enjoys the press of people around her, even the boys who jostle her on purpose, the men shouldering heavy boxes who shout, "Allo, allo," when they want to pass. The sudden scent of dry mint leaves pricks her nostrils and then vanishes. She walks past mosques, churches, desecrated synagogues under reconstruction; all are worthy, all are of equal beauty in her eyes. She must explore everywhere, taste and see everything. Wares are so abundant, they spill out of the shops: pottery clutters the narrow walkway and trips her feet; garments hung overhead brush her face; trinkets suspended like wind chimes tinkle in her ears. Shop after shop, arch-covered alleys intersecting at strange angles, soft light filtering down from domed skylights where the arches meet, plants crawling through cracks in the walls, in the arches, in the glass of the skylights.

A voice beckons from inside a shop: "I *have* what you *need.*"

She needs everything: fabric rich with embroidery; tooled

leather ottomans to stuff with newspaper; harsh camel-rugs of woven hemp dyed red, purple, orange, pink; a bright blue enamel pot for Turkish coffee; halva so sweet it closes the throat. She bargains fiercely, pretending she is Yardena, knowing Yardena will grill her this evening about each purchase.

The tape-recorded cry of a *mu'ezzin* leads her to an open space guarded by soldiers, one of whom examines her parcels and asks her to open her pocketbook for inspection. He waves her into the arena, which is as large and barren as an American parking lot. The bright sunlight blinds her for an instant, and then she knows where she is, recognizes the place from photographs in books: the *kotel*, the western wall of the Temple; and above it, the huge golden Dome of the Rock.

Elisheva waits her turn to approach the Wall from the women's side, which is much more crowded than the men's. Are more women praying? At first it appears so, but no; the men's side is simply twice as large. A ragged *mehitza* curtain separates the two portions, as blatant and unabashed a display of unfairness as Grandmother Lowenthal giving her puny son-in-law Arthur the largest helping at a holiday meal; or Yardena this morning, cutting her husband a slice of cake twice as thick as her own, although he will sit in a cab all day while she climbs, kneels, scrubs, polishes.

The other women don't seem to mind. They bend in prayer, they weep, they kiss the stones of the Wall, they press their wet cheeks against its surface. Many centuries ago, these massive foundation stones were set in place without mortar, rock cut to fit rock; in the two years since the Six-Day War, the narrow crevices between stones have been all but plugged with crumpled, rolled-up scraps of paper; each woman adds her wish to the collective written offering.

Higher, beyond the reach of hands, small shrubs and grasses grow in the crevices, and some doves have managed to build nests; their cooing blends with the voices of women weeping and praying.

When Elisheva's turn arrives, she stands before the Wall, her parcels at her feet. She touches the Wall with a hand, and rests her forehead against its cool, weathered skin of stone. She is unable to weep for the past, unable to pray for the future; she feels only the sensations of the present.

I got the job through one of Miriam's friends at the same university I had decided not to attend. I was to be the Israeli version of a Kelly girl, going from department to department, wherever an English-language typist was needed. A few departments (Archaeology, Sociology, English) had electric typewriters; most had machines resembling my old gray Remington Rand portable with dark green keys.

My first weeks on the job coincided with the *hamsin*, the hot, dry desert wind that blows into Israel before and after the winter rainy season like a pair of billowing parentheses. The sensation of typing, clumsy, in an uncomfortably hot room, made me homesick for Pennsylvania, for Mother and Dad, who had given me the Remington Rand when I turned thirteen; especially for Dad, who had insisted on my learning to type. Mother was gone that summer, teaching at a music festival; Dad stayed at home to work on his master's thesis; Neil went to day camp; a program was needed for me. Dad came up with one: typing class in the morning ("you never know when it might come in handy"), and bicycling across town in the afternoon for at least an hour of swimming in the Jewish Community Center pool ("you have to start getting regular exercise"). All I wanted was to read novels and daydream, as I had done the previous summer, curled up in the faded green armchair Grandmother Lowenthal had given us when she redecorated her house. I especially liked that chair in the summer, because its satin brocade upholstery felt so good against my legs as I sat there in shorts, reading all day and watching robins flap water under their wings in the concrete birdbath Dad had installed when we first moved in; watching Mother's peonies open bright and round, and then the roses and the glads.

Dad said he knew what was best for me and some day I would thank him. So I spent the summer typing business letters and speed drills. The classroom was hot and full of sound as intricate and vivid as music. A kitchen timer perched on the teacher's desk, and when it rang, everyone had to stop and compute speed. Crazy double-time records of classical music spurred us to type faster and faster; the one I remember best was a frantic version of Schumann's "Träumerei." And the frenetically stimulating noise of a typing pool, many typewriters clattering in a single room, a huge rhythm section, noisy and comical and distracting, fracturing time, and the clock over the teacher's head, and the timer ringing on her desk, time's up time's up time's up.

Typing pools and swimming pools, the noisy world of morning and the muffled waterworld of afternoon. At first I cursed Dad and his plans for me with every pump of my legs on the bicycle, with every lap I swam. But then I began to enjoy swimming underwater to retrieve red and blue rubber rings at the bottom, moving slowly down through water in a way that had nothing to do with gravity, pushing the water away from me, pushing down, down, then letting the water buoy me up, rising through the blue slow ripples, graceful for the first time in my life, my body not separate parts flailing about, but one body moving easily through the water; and the hushed forms of other people in the pool, just essences of color at a great distance; and light streaming down from the glass roof into the water, down through the water in green and yellow curves. I liked combing my wet hair into a ponytail, using the wide mirror to look at the bodies of the women in the locker room. The women dressed and undressed slowly, chatting with each other. They had none of the self-consciousness of gym class, none of the haste with which girls of my age hid from one another. They showed me every kind of body a Jewish woman could have; they taught me to see my own body as it was then, just budding, and as it would flower and fade in some greenhouse like the Center pool.

That summer I got my period. I asked Dad to drive me to a drugstore but wouldn't tell him why; surely he guessed. It must have been after typing class, because I was wearing school clothes: a pink-and-white striped seersucker dress, with white flats and peds on my feet. I remember walking toward the car, a straw purse dangling from my elbow, the same arm holding the Gray's Drugs paper bag against one breast, the other arm hanging free, brushing the seersucker. I remember the shock of heat at the exit of the air-conditioned store, so that I began to sweat immediately, and I could smell my sweat and the new odor of hot menstrual blood. Then I saw Dad staring at me from the car, watching me cross the parking lot. His gaze was unfamiliar, intense, as though for the first time he was focusing his attention on me as a person separate from him, a person with her own life independent of his will. I knew that his concentration on absorbing this image of me had something to do with my new status as a menstruating woman, but there was in his stare no lust or pity or envy or condescension, no reaction in any way demeaning or aggrandizing. His response to me in that moment permanently changed my own perception of myself. I had no choice in the face of that stern acceptance but to turn it inward, to give up something of childhood forever.

———

During the autumn *hamsin* I noticed the bereaved woman across the street. Oh, I had seen her before, a middle-aged woman sitting for hours on her *mirpesset*, staring down. Sometimes she sat alone, sometimes her husband joined her for a while. But during good weather everyone in the neighborhood sat outdoors as much as possible, so it was not until the *hamsin* that I noticed something was not right with her.

In a *hamsin*, clothes dry on the line in ten minutes. If you leave them out for twelve or thirteen, they turn rigid and pale as angry demons or neglected children. Yardena had warned me when she saw me hanging laundry: "Be careful, Elisheva *motek*. It's the wind of Satan. It tries to ruin everything." So as I rushed around my apartment, tidying up and beginning preparations for *shabbat* dinner, I looked outside frequently.

At the end of eight minutes came a dust storm. Suddenly the air was thick with sand, as if all the rocks of the city had been battered by the wind until they broke down into powder, all of Jerusalem disintegrated and swept up into the fierce desert wind. I ran out to save my clothes from the dust. Although I quickly tied a towel about my face, my eyes burned and grit scraped my gums. I felt afraid.

Once inside again, I looked out the window. The sky was yellow-pink, the sun hazy and vague as a moon in fog. Directly across from my window, on the *mirpesset* over Avraham's tiny grocery store, the woman still sat. She held one end of her shawl over her face, like the veil of Islam. I could have sworn she was staring at me, as I was staring at her, through the heavy swirl of dust.

Then the storm ended, the wind faded for a moment, and the woman slowly lowered her shawl back into place on her shoulder. I thought back through the few weeks since I had moved in. Never had I seen the woman talk with anyone, not even her husband when he sat with her. Never had I seen her in the cluster of women at Avraham's *makolet*. Never had I seen her walk out into the street.

As abruptly as wind had become sandstorm, frightening and destructive, the woman's vigil took on a sinister, threatening aspect. Like a malevolent spirit she sat there, brooding, cursing the neighborhood, cursing me. She was evil. She wished me ill. Perhaps it was too late, and the damage was already done; some disaster awaited me, as it had awaited the old man who died in this house.

When Yardena came over to borrow some sugar and make sure I had taken proper care of my laundry, I flung my arms around her neck, clutching her long, thick braid as in sickness I had clutched my mother's bathrobe.

"*Mah yesh, motek?*" Yardena said, half-laughing with surprise. "What's the matter, sweetheart? Did the dust frighten you? Don't you have dust storms in America?"

"The woman," I said, pointing to the window. "Who is she? Why does she sit there, even with the dust blowing? What is she doing?"

"Ah, that one." Yardena shook her head and sighed. "*Miskena.* Poor thing. She lost her son in the last war. She is not the same since then. *Kakha zeh b'aretz*: that's the way it is in this land."

Yardena said no more, and I knew she was worrying about Nadav and Yonah, her own small boys. I felt awkward, cowardly, tactless, selfish, a brat whining over my fantasy fears when the people around me had bigger things to dread than a dust storm or a sad neighbor. I hastened to pour Yardena her cup of sugar and let her return to her family.

It was a dismal *erev shabbat*. Miriam came to dinner, but I was poor company for her, and she found the promised cheesewalnutburgers a disappointment. "It's the *hamsin*," she said. "Everyone is miserable and crabby until it ends."

"Miserable" was as good a word as any for my gloomy restlessness. I had looked forward to making dinner for Miriam and spending the evening with her, but now that she was there, I felt dissatisfied, as if she and I were together by default, because we each lacked a boyfriend, or a husband and children, with whom to spend *shabbat*. We had no one to love, no one to worry about, not even anyone to mourn.

"Old maids," I said. "That's what we are. Nothing but old maids."

Then I spent the rest of the evening apologizing and explaining: I didn't mean it, I was just in a bad mood, I was upset about the woman across the street, I'd been saying the wrong thing all day, maybe it was getting to me that Israeli girls of my age all seemed to be married.

Miriam insisted she wasn't hurt and she understood perfectly; but I didn't quite believe her. To make up for my ill temper, I walked her back to her apartment. The night air was cool and calm; the strong winds had returned to their home in the desert for *shabbat*. The Hassidim were still at the yeshiva, singing and dancing with their *rebbe*. Miriam and I sang along as we walked:

> *Evven ma'asu ha-bonim*
> *haita l'rosh-pina.*
> The stone the builders rejected
> has become the keystone, the chief cornerstone.

Jerusalem was reconstituted, the dust assembled into stones, every stone restored to its rightful place. The walls that had crumbled stood firm once more; each gate had its arch, each arch its keystone, the one stone holding the rest as a hand holds a bow, in a taut curve of stone lovely and strong as the arch of bone in a foot, the arch of a spine, the arched backbone of a city.

5

It must have been after my first winter in Israel, because I was already seeing Dr. Feinstein. Between Purim and Pesach, because I had been transferred from Jewish History to Anthropology. No, maybe it was after Pesach. But in the spring, it was definitely in the spring.

I'm beginning to sound like my parents:

"I was pregnant with Neil, so it had to be 1949."

"No, Clara, you were pregnant with Ellen. It was 1946."

"But Arthur, your Aunt Etta wasn't there, so she must have passed away already. It was 1949."

"Aunt Etta was visiting Aunt Guttel in Brooklyn."

"But Ellen was there. Remember, darling? No? Well, you were only two years old, how could you remember? Arthur dear, you simply must believe me. It was 1949. I had just auditioned for the Pittsburgh Symphony Orchestra, remember?"

"No, the Pittsburgh hired you in 1950. It was 1946, right after you started playing with the Erie Philharmonic."

"The Pittsburgh hired me in 1951 to fill in for the summer, but my first audition was in 1949, when I was pregnant with Neil."

So. It was 1970, in the spring. I was not pregnant. I hadn't been with a man since Carl, the ninth man, whose streak of violence scared me enough to send me into psychoanalysis. I was typing for the Anthropology department, where I first heard the Yemenite melodies that have haunted me for ten years, humming in my ears and breathing into my bones like the sounds of an ancient flute, enchanting, beckoning.

No one has called her Ellen in nearly a year, so it takes her a moment to respond, to recognize the voice as she whirls around, just an instant before she sees the face. It is Daniel. God, he looks good to her. His sweet, gentle smile sets him apart from the aggressive mass of soldiers, reserve soldiers, and future soldiers stampeding across Zion Square, just as it set him apart from the belligerent young men who hollered into bullhorns at Wisconsin anti-war rallies. She sees in him now what she saw before: a man of peace, a man with no tendency toward violence or domination, a man she can trust never to turn on her with growling and snapping, never to become her enemy; a kind man, brother to her best self.

"Daniel!" She runs to hug him, but there is a shyness in his demeanor, a reserve she senses and remembers, which stops her short, as the wall held her off from the Old City until it was ready to open a gate to her, until she was brave enough to enter. She stands before him, almost tottering on her feet from the arrested momentum toward touch. How tall he is, how much more slender he has become; how forlorn this observation makes her feel, as if he has abandoned her in the plumpness they used to share, as if he suddenly shot up into tall, lean manhood, as her brother Neil did in adolescence, leaving her behind. She takes a half-step back, in order to see Daniel's face without having to tilt her head. "Daniel. How are you? What are you doing here? I thought you were in rabbinical school."

"I am. This is my semester in the Holy Land. What are *you* doing here? What a surprise! I felt bad for not writing to you at Berkeley, and here you are. You wouldn't have gotten the letter I never wrote. That's not fair, Ellen, making a friend feel guilty for no reason."

"I'm sorry. I guess I didn't expect we'd still be friends after graduation. Shit. I don't mean that the way it sounds. It's just, at Wisconsin we were always *working*—attending meetings, leafleting . . . Even right now, it seems funny to be talking to you without stuffing envelopes at the same time. It's good to see you, Daniel. I guess I never thought I'd see you again, so what was the point of writing? I'm living here, and it's so far away from where I thought you were. Cincinnati, right?"

"You're living here, permanently?"

"I think so. Almost a year now."

"Don't you love it?" His warm smile again, and the large dark eyes like those of Yardena's sons. "I have to return to the U.S. in a couple of months, but I'm thinking of coming back here to live some day."

"You're kidding. I never would have pictured . . . because of the Army and the wars . . . "

He nods, serious. "I wouldn't have pictured you here, for the same reason. But once you're here, there's something very special about the place, isn't there? It takes you in and wants you to stay."

A crowded bus pulls up to the curb, and a large number of people rush to board, grabbing at the still-unopened doors and pushing each other aside. Someone shoves Elisheva into the elbow of a large woman carrying two shopping bags at her breast like twin babies.

"Stupid tourist!" the woman yells. "Either push like everyone else or get out of the way."

"*B'vakesha, giveret.*" Elisheva wedges herself, like Daniel, against a shoestore display window. "Please go ahead. There is no need to shout. Have a little patience. *Savlanut.*"

"Patience is all I have," the woman shouts. "Do I have a seat on the bus? No. I have patience. I was wrong about you. I thought you were a tourist. If you're telling me, '*Savlanut, savlanut*,' you've already been in this country too long. You can keep your *savlanut*, you and your handsome husband. You have time to be patient. Me, I'm getting old. I have no strength, I have no time. Why aren't there more buses in this country? More buses and less patience, that's what I need."

"Here, *giveret*." Daniel steps in. "Let me hold your packages until the next bus arrives."

"Ah, here it comes already, and almost empty. *Ezeh mazal*! What luck! Thank you. Such a nice young man." She casts an eloquent glance at Elisheva—hold onto him, you lucky girl—and jostles her way back into the throng of passengers.

"She's right," Elisheva says. "It was nice of you to offer to help her."

"I'm just a sucker for anyone who tells me I'm handsome." Daniel blushes. "She's about my mother's age. So maybe someone in New Jersey will be nice to my mother now."

"Come for *shabbat*," Elisheva says, remembering the woman's glance. "I'm having some friends over. Can you come?"

"No, I'm already invited somewhere. Maybe another time? Can you stop for a cup of coffee now?"

Elisheva looks at her watch. "No, I don't have time. '*Eyn lee koah, eyn lee savlanut*. I have no strength, I have no patience.'"

"Good imitation. Your Hebrew is better than mine."

"Well, I've been here longer. Listen, I really do have to go. I have an appointment. I've started seeing a psychiatrist—well, I'll

53

tell you about it some other time." She rummages in her bag and finds a slip of paper, which she tears in half so that she and Daniel can exchange addresses.

He stares at what she has written. "Elisheva?"

"Yes. Everyone here calls me Elisheva."

The first time I saw Dr. Feinstein, he asked what problem had led me to seek his help. "I can't seem to get along with men," I said. "My relationships with men are short and not very sweet. I always seem to be pushing men away, wanting to get rid of them. I seem to lack the necessary patience or motivation to work things out. I am irritable, easily annoyed. It feels like a bad habit: a habit of irritability."

Irritability, indeed. Just look at my choice of lovers in Israel: Michel/Moshe, who did not want to be Jewish; Zev, suicidal; Carl, one-armed; then Milton, one-eyed. This list was the most humiliating evidence of all that something was not straightforward in my relations with men; so humiliating, that I was in psychoanalysis a year before recounting it to Dr. Feinstein.

He lit up like a birthday cake and wrote down practically every word of that session. I can still hear his German accent: "You want to hurt men. You do not want the guilt of hurting men. So you choose men already hurt." He added something about the wish to castrate, but that never rang true to me, there was no thrill in the fantasy. I'd rather have done something to make sure none of them could punch me in the face. Not that any of them ever tried. What gave me the idea that any of them might? Or nearly any: not my father and not Stan and not Daniel.

And Carl in fact did pin me down with his one strong arm. When I struggled free, he pushed me against the wall and held me there by the neck, saying, "I could strangle you, you know."

I looked him in the eye and said, "Yes, you could, but you won't."

The bluff worked: he loosened his grip just slightly for an instant, probably thinking, "Is that true? Won't I?" I escaped in that instant and ran to the door, opened it and yelled, "Get out!" in English and then in Hebrew, "*Aḥutza! Lekh ha-bayita!*" loud enough so he would know I'd awakened Yardena and Ḥayim for sure, and using the masculine form of the Hebrew verb so Yardena would know it was a man I was kicking out.

Carl stood there staring at me, dazed. He seemed very large and his arm was very large. Then he turned into a kid disheveled from a baseball game down the street, how about some milk and cookies, Mom? Boyish, he said, "Can I spend the night? The buses have stopped running."

I actually hesitated for an instant no longer than the loosening of his forearm on my neck, but he was slower; it wasn't a long enough instant to do him any good. I grabbed my purse, found the paper money, extended a wad in his direction—"Here. Take a cab."—still holding the door open with a hip.

"I don't need your fucking money," he muttered, pushing past me and down the stairs.

He was gone, but furious. I knew that if he ever came back to kill me, it would be because of my offer of cabfare, nothing else, just this affront to his manly pride.

"This time it's gone too far," I thought as I locked the door. The next day I called Dr. Feinstein.

The odd thing is, I still don't quite believe that Carl tried to strangle me. The memory is not entirely real; it is like those once-removed memories of someone telling me what happened, what I did and why. It is not the direct memory of experience. Something in me has never wanted to know that it happened.

For instance: I kept my door locked at night for only a week or so after Carl stomped out, even though I must have realized an anger like his could have increased with time, could have smoldered rather than extinguishing.

And a year later, when I told Dr. Feinstein, when I described Carl's lunge at me and his huge arm at my throat, I asked, "What could I have done to make him so angry?"

Even now, I think, "No. It never happened. A person like me doesn't get into a situation like that."

Carl was American. He had served in Vietnam at the same time as Billy Williams Jr. I've thought a lot about Carl and Billy. They seem to represent my two views of men: the dangerous, unpredictable makers of war and violence; and the helpless victims of a war machine. Which is true? Perhaps someone like Carl killed Billy, but then Billy could just as easily have killed Carl. I would never have killed either of them.

Dr. Feinstein said I wanted men to be hurt. Some men are hurt. Okay. But when Carl wanted me to be hurt, he didn't go into psychoanalysis. He came to my apartment and tried to strangle me.

He did try to strangle me, didn't he?

Another day, Dr. Feinstein asks, "Well, what *did* you do to make Carl so angry?"

Elisheva thinks for a moment. "I wouldn't let him fuck me and read the newspaper at the same time."

"Excuse me? I do not understand."

Elisheva repeats, this time in Hebrew: "I wouldn't let him fuck me and read the *Jerusalem Post* at the same time."

"Why would he want to do that?" Dr. Feinstein lights his pipe. "He was so busy, he had no other opportunity to read the paper?"

"He just wanted to prove he could do it."

"Oh. Why wouldn't you let him?"

"Because I didn't want to be his proving ground. What, you think I should have let him?"

Dr. Feinstein puts down the pipe and uses both hands to center his *yarmulke* on his bald head. "You know the tradition, that while enjoying sex with his wife, a man is supposed to recite a prayer in his mind? This way he will not be tempted to evil thoughts, and Lilit and the other demons will be unable to seduce him. Perhaps the newspaper is like prayer for Carl."

"But he's not even Jewish!" Elisheva tries to stay calm. "Look, I don't care how he prays, he had no right to attack me. What's the matter with you, did you forget what we were talking about? We were talking about a man who nearly killed me. How dare you! How dare you excuse his attack on me because I might have interrupted his goddamn form of prayer? How dare you, you pious jerk!" What delicious freedom it gives her to know that Dr. Feinstein does not understand words like "jerk" in English. She can say whatever she damn pleases; the more insulting and colloquial her vocabulary, the less likely he is to recognize its full significance.

Quietly, Dr. Feinstein says, "You were the one who seemed to think you had provoked this attack." He looks back through his notes and reads aloud: " 'What could I have done to make him so angry?' "

"Oh." Elisheva sinks back into her chair. "Well, I guess I don't really believe that. Do you?"

Dr. Feinstein carefully replaces the page of notes. "That you did something to make him angry? Maybe. That he had a right to attack you? No."

"But I don't even think he had a right to be angry." She leans forward again. "Why should I let him fuck me and read the paper at the same time?"

"I did not say you should have consented. I only said that your refusal made him angry."

"Oh. Okay."

Dr. Feinstein puffs on his pipe for a moment. "But why did you choose a man like this?"

"There is another kind?"

"Isn't there?"

Elisheva sighs. "Yes, there is another kind. My father is another kind. Daniel is another kind. Stan was another kind."

"This Stan, what did you like about him?"

She rattles it off as if she has rehearsed: "He made me laugh. He demanded nothing. He was decent. He didn't care. He had no wish to hurt me. He weighed less than I did. He was tone-deaf. He was good to his mother. He liked being Jewish. He understood me. He accepted himself. He didn't frighten me. He wasn't afraid of me. He liked appetites. He got turned on when I sang to him in French. He knew how to love, although he didn't love me. He wouldn't buy anything in the supermarket without reading the label first. He liked the way I poached eggs. He told me I was tough-minded. He sent me here."

And Daniel. In spite of our auspicious meeting at Zion Square, we managed to get together only once before he left Jerusalem. I suppose we were avoiding each other.

One evening I took the bus to his address and stood outside, counting windows, figuring out which apartment must be his. The lights were on; he was probably at home. But I couldn't make myself walk to the door, perhaps because of the same barrier I had sensed when I almost hugged him.

"He probably has a girlfriend," I told myself. "The one who already invited him to *shabbat*. She's up there with him. I don't want to barge in."

So I just stood on the sidewalk until the next bus came. I rode to Milton's house. Milton was a member of the *hevra*, the group of friends with whom Miriam and I spent nearly every *shabbat*. He had been pursuing me for some time. That night I bedded with him.

A few weeks later, after work, Yardena came over with a note for me. "A very good-looking young American left it," she said, winking. "He even has two arms, two legs, two eyes, and two ears. I said to Ḥayim, '*Mah pit'om?* Elisheva is finally interested in someone normal?' "

The note read, "Can I still take you up on the invitation? I leave in two weeks."

So I made dinner for Daniel that Friday night. We were uncomfortable together, didn't know what to talk about at first.

"I see you're still a vegetarian," he said. "I'm not anymore. It's hard when you don't live alone and your roommates eat meat. And we're all so eager now to prove that Reform Jews can keep kosher, and who can tell that you keep kosher if you're vegetarian?"

He waited for me to laugh, and thus pardon him for abandoning me in this way too. I kept an angry silence. It was all his fault. It was his fault that I was fatter than I wanted to be; he had treacherously slimmed down by eating lean meat, while I was still padding my hips with starchy vegetables, breads, cakes. It was his fault that I was lonely, his fault that I had started sleeping with Milton.

Finally I said, "I don't consider myself a Reform Jew. I'll take the excesses of the Orthodox any day over the watered-down version of Judaism I grew up with."

We had found our subject: religion and philosophy. Daniel argued in the lovely, earnest manner I remembered from meetings of Students for Peace. I was out for blood, and used sarcasm and veiled insult. I won the debate; I felt rotten about it.

After Daniel left Israel, I missed him intensely for quite a while, even though I'd hardly seen him. I missed the knowledge that he was in Jerusalem, in that lighted room, giving me some kind of hope. I began to see Milton more often.

———

There was no music then, no music for a long time, maybe a year. Or rather, I remember no music. Of course there was music, as there always is. I passed under windows where someone was playing the piano or practicing the violin. I walked down the street and heard the rhythmic click of my own heels, the brushing together of my thighs. These things must have happened, but I cannot remember noticing. My keenest sense, the one in which I had luxuriated since before my birth, became dull and useless to me. Life was not without pleasure; but sound, which had been my chiefest pleasure, was gone.

I remember the absence of music, but I do not remember

exactly when it occurred. It began at some time after I heard the Yemenite songs, but when? And was music really gone from me, or was it working silently within me, slowly changing something?

When I complained to Dr. Feinstein, he said, "Why don't you go to a concert?"

No. I didn't want to go to a concert. "I could go to a concert in the U.S.," I said. "Why should I go to a concert here?"

"But you do many things here that you could do in the U.S. You eat meals, you ride on buses, you type in an office."

"That's different," I said. "Concerts belong to my mother. Music belongs to my mother. How will I ever grow up, if I stay in my mother's world?"

"Is that why you came to Israel? To get away from your mother?"

"That's part of it. But I could have gone many places to get away from my mother. I came to Israel to be a Jew. You know that."

"And a Jew is not permitted to enjoy music?"

"Of course a Jew is permitted to enjoy music. *I* am not permitted to enjoy music."

"This is a punishment you are imposing on yourself?"

I suppose it was. Or a discipline of sorts, a way of resisting what I found most seductive. Or a way of intensifying frustration until I could resist no longer. When I could resist no longer, I returned to music. My ears opened to sound, and music vibrated through my body once more.

6

Each winter Miriam and I crocheted an afghan: the first
winter, for her bed; the second, for mine. She had begun
the first afghan alone and worked on it whenever we sat
together, talking, drinking cup after cup of coffee. The stone
walls and tile floors, which had made both our apartments so
comfortable in hot weather, retained the damp chill of winter;
and the loosely-fitting windows, which had provided such delightful breezes, now permitted cold winds to blow through the
houses. Our tiny kerosene heaters warmed us up to the knee if
we placed our feet directly on the grate. Even wearing our coats
indoors, we shivered a great deal, until Miriam's afghan grew
large enough to cover her lap and thighs. Then I shivered alone.
She soon took pity and taught me to crochet; we spent enough
time together that winter to finish her afghan with the last rains.
The afghan was yellow, orange, and brown—Miriam's favorite
colors—and it was a lovely piece of work, although my stitches
were considerably tighter than hers.

More and more as we crocheted, Miriam and I found ourselves discussing religious questions, often inspired by the weekly Torah portion read aloud in the synagogue on *shabbat*: Why
a red heifer, why a golden calf? What does the second commandment really mean? How could Moses have written the Torah,
when his own death is described in the last chapter of Deuteronomy? On *Simḥat Torah*, after the last portion of the Torah has
been read, and before the first words of Genesis are chanted,
why does the congregation recite, "*Ḥazak ḥazak v'nithazek,*
strong strong and we will strengthen ourselves"?

After the first winter Miriam and I formalized these discussions into three sessions every week to study the Torah portion
for the coming *shabbat*. First we sat and crocheted for an hour
or so of conversation, and then we let the unfinished afghan sit
in our lap like a sleeping animal while we read the Torah portion aloud in Hebrew, consulted dictionaries and scholarly

works, offered our own interpretations, argued when we disagreed with one another.

Although the second afghan got less of our attention than the first, practice had improved our speed and skill. The second afghan, for which I chose yarn of purple, blue, and magenta, was an even greater success than the first, more beautiful and harmonious, more consistent. It reminded me of that moment I used to hear, in Mother's practice with her friend Sonya, when they had played a sonata together so many times, had so thoroughly absorbed each other's rhythm and phrasing, that they no longer sounded like two musicians playing two separate instruments.

The yellow, orange, and brown afghan still warms Miriam, or one of her children. This thought makes me happy: that something of our friendship is useful to her today. I also like the thought that the purple, blue, and magenta afghan has stayed in Israel all these years, even though I left. It now belongs to Yardena's son Nadav, who will be married as soon as he finishes Army service. No one in his family will ever be able to say, "Here is the part that Miriam made, and this part is Elisheva's."

————

"I was walking down a deserted road. Suddenly I came upon a stone wall. This wall marked the border, and I had to take my place behind it and fight to protect it. The enemy began to advance. I could see them through a hole in the wall at eye level. The hole was intended for a rifle, but I had no rifle, no weapons at all. I looked around for something I could use for the battle. My crochet basket sat in the corner behind me. It was full of balls of yarn, red, purple, blue. I knew that my weapons were hidden in the balls of yarn. I pulled one ball open, and in the center was a seltzer bomb."

Dr. Feinstein chuckles. "So begins the Seltzer War, your true initiation as an Israeli."

"I felt good when I woke up. Happy and safe."

"As well you might." The doctor chooses a pipe from the stand on his desk. "The dream is a good sign, Elisheva. It shows that you are making progress. No longer will you reject your femininity. Now you will find the—how do you say—ammunition? Yes, you will find the ammunition you need in your womanliness."

Never has he seemed so pleased with her. She should be

pleased, too, but she isn't. Why should she need ammunition? Doesn't he remember she was an anti-war activist in the States? Maybe he takes war imagery for granted; maybe his other patients are constantly dreaming of battle. Not Elisheva. This is the first dream in which she has ever envisioned taking up arms. She did feel happy and safe when she awakened, but now she feels confused and tense. Is she losing all her old ideals? And why doesn't she tell Dr. Feinstein what she is thinking?

She doesn't want to destroy his satisfaction with her feminine dream. She stares past him, out the window, to the slashes of sunlight diving to the ground between the branches of the Jerusalem pine. It's a staunch tree, twisted almost beyond dignity, clinging to its bit of soil. Dr. Feinstein's father planted the pine in 1929 to commemorate the family's arrival from Germany, and just the sight of it has often calmed Elisheva during a painful session. Perhaps that's why Dr. Feinstein chose this room for his office?

Beyond the pine, beyond the low stone fence built by the same patriarch, *Giveret* Feinstein is walking the dachshund, Felafel. At least, Elisheva assumes Felafel to be at the end of the leash; she can see only down to *Giveret* Feinstein's waist. A handsome woman, Elisheva thinks for the hundredth time. Also for the hundredth time, she wonders how such an attractive, strong-looking lady could have married a tubby, bald psychiatrist. But this is common in Israel. Also in the U.S.?

The silence is too long. Dr. Feinstein will think she is resisting therapy.

"What a beautiful day!"

"Yes, I'm sure it is a beautiful day for you," says the doctor. "How could a day not be beautiful after such a dream?"

"That's not what I mean," Elisheva protests. "You shrinks are all alike. You sit in here listening to people's problems, and you forget there is a world outside. Turn around and look out the window! It is a beautiful day, objectively. Anyone with any sense would see that, whether she'd just had a good dream or not."

Dr. Feinstein turns to look out the window, and he waves to his wife, who waves back but doesn't smile. Good. He writes something on his pad.

What is he writing this time? "Over-reacted in defensive fashion"? "Negative attitude"? No, that's what teachers write on report cards. An analyst would call it "negative transference."

And this analyst wouldn't even call it that in English. How do you say "negative transference" in Hebrew?

Elisheva has tried several times to read Dr. Feinstein's notes about her, by leaning over his desk as she talks, but she still doesn't know Hebrew well enough to read it upside-down. She once heard him speaking German to his wife, so she asked why he keeps notes in Hebrew. "In order to use them for presentations at professional conferences," he said proudly. Well, anyone who can do therapy in four languages has a right to be proud.

Dr. Feinstein is still writing. She peeks over his pipe stand and makes out a sentence, half in Hebrew and half in English: "Look up 'shrink.' " For the first time in the hour, Elisheva feels pleased with herself. Only once before did she ever succeed in deciphering Dr. Feinstein's notes. That time, too, the note was half in English. It said, "Look up 'blow job.' "

———

Really it was nothing like that. I was walking down a deserted road, but more than the road was deserted. For miles, all was desert. The wind kicked up dust, it swirled around me, I hid my face in a scarf. I looked for shelter, but I saw no hut, no wadi, no tree, not even a rock large enough to sit on or crouch behind. Only the sand and the dust and the small stones that would soon be dust but that still bit the skin as dust could not. And the light all around, the desert sunlight that could find you and scorch you through the thick of a sandstorm. And strangely, I could see through the cloud of dust that surrounded me. I saw each particle of dust, its shape and being, and beyond the dust I saw the horizon and the pure light of distance. Then suddenly the dust was gone from around me. I had walked into a clearing in the storm, and while I could see the dust spinning in the air on all sides, I was myself free of the dust. And I took off my shoes, for I knew I was standing on holy ground.

The enemies, the crochet basket, the seltzer bombs came later, perhaps even on a different night. The seltzer bombs were all right for a laugh, a show of imagination. But the dream of dust and light, that dream was to other dreams as the sabbath is to the other days of the week.

———

Friday's buses are full of women. Women make *shabbat*, do the shopping, cooking, and cleaning, all the preparations that transform each house into a place of serenity. The busdriver knows it. He sings along with *Kol Yisrael*, "Voice of Israel," the national radio network: *"Kaḥ l'kha isha uv'neh la bayit.* Take yourself a wife and build her a house."

The busdriver is married. Everyone in Israel is married. The busdriver is the only man on the bus. All the other men are building houses for their wives, so that the wives can make *shabbat* in the houses.

Shabbat is the wife of the Jewish people. In synagogue at sundown, everyone stands to greet her: *"Bo-i kala, bo-i kala.* Come, O bride; come, O bride." The Jewish man welcomes *shabbat* as a bridegroom welcomes his bride. Milton has told Elisheva this.

How does the Jewish woman welcome *shabbat*? Milton smiled. *Shabbat* is her reward. First her husband sings to her from Proverbs at the table she has set: "A woman of valor, who can find? Her price is higher than that of rubies." Then, after she has cleared the table and put the children to bed, she lies with her husband. It is a *mitzvah* for the Jewish man to lie with his wife on Friday night. This is her reward. If she is lucky, she will conceive; a child conceived on *shabbat* is specially blessed. The husband must give his wife pleasure, not just take pleasure for himself. If he fails to give her pleasure and she conceives, she will bear him a girl child; if he is a good husband and gives his wife pleasure, she will bear him a boy child. This is his reward. The busdriver is smiling because he knows it. Milton smiled because he knew it. Elisheva did not know it, but now she does.

And how does the Jewish woman who has no husband welcome *shabbat*? Milton did not know.

Elisheva knocks a hand against the side of her head, to induce a change of subject in this conversation with herself. She should have talked more freely with Dr. Feinstein. The dream of war is still bumping around inside her, not understood, not resolved. All this bitterness about men and women is fallout from the seltzer bombs.

When did the bus get so crowded? Elisheva relinquishes her seat to an old Arab woman loaded down with parcels. Standing now, she bends to peer out the window. The bus has left Dr. Feinstein's elegant neighborhood and entered the dirtier streets of the downtown area. Hurried shoppers mill around. Soon Elisheva will be one of them.

She is making *shabbat* for eight people tonight. She isn't in the mood, would prefer one of those solitary sabbaths she used to have when she first moved into her apartment. An evening of reading by the kerosene lamp, after a leisurely walk to the Western Wall at sundown, the smell of roasting and baking in the air, the special stillness of Jerusalem at peace, the private leafy courtyards, the stone houses rosy and porous as fresh loaves of bread; then the narrow arched alleys of the Old City, and finally the Wall, the place of the Temple, the Holy of Holies.

Elisheva feels tears in her eyes and doesn't know whether to attribute them to the Wall, the dream of war, or the memory of a lonelier time. It's all very well to wish for a quiet *shabbat* when she has spent every weekend for months with the group, but to know that she would be alone, to have no choice? No, that was not pleasant.

The old woman to whom Elisheva just gave her seat opens a box and holds out a wafer cookie. Elisheva accepts it, and the two women chew and smile at each other. Elisheva promises herself to take an Arabic class in the fall.

The name of the bus company is *Egged*. It's a good name for Friday's bus, which is a bit like an egg, or rather an ovary: a container bulging with lives. Elisheva looks back through the bus. That woman with the angular jaw. The timid blonde in thick glasses, nervously fingering her face over and over again, as though her hands could re-form every feature and line, if only she could decide how she wants them. And way in the back, sitting next to an open window, a lively dark-haired girl smiling as she talks, tossing her head, her hair divided by the wind so that an ear shows.

The bus lurches; the Arab woman spills a large number of cookies on the floor. Elisheva kneels to pick them up, but the floor is filthy, the cookies ruined. The woman says something and makes a sign with her hands, but Elisheva can understand neither the words nor the gesture. The cookies line up on the floor like a little army.

Elisheva looks closely at the woman. "Are we enemies?" she thinks. "Who says we are enemies?"

She pauses to pull her shawl closer around her shoulders, to readjust her vision to the shade of the canvas canopies. At her right, a mound of eggplants like plump purple bellies. Before her, stacks of long green and yellow squashes, bright tomatoes, hills of food as far as she can see in this shadow world. But vision is secondary here; only the primary colors stand out in the half-light. The more primitive senses are assaulted by the strong odors, the clamor of voices; vegetables are chosen by their feel, their texture, not their color.

She takes a deep breath and plunges into the sea of shoppers, all pushing along in one direction between the two rows of stalls, making return all but impossible. Alleys cut away at right angles, but today there is no time to wander; Elisheva will stay on the main path, stopping at a favorite stand here and there until she has everything she needs.

Underfoot are smashed tomatoes, flattened pieces of sheep dung. Between the vegetable stands, barrels of pickles and sacks of spices fill the nostrils with discrete scents, the brown smells of cumin, dill, garlic, saffron, cardamom, cinnamon, Turkish coffee. Above the general din, the loudest merchants lower their prices by the minute as *shabbat* approaches and they foresee their fine produce going to waste.

"Beautiful tomatoes, four *lirot* a kilo!"

"Wonderful, wonderful eggplants, only a *lira*!"

"One-of-a-kind tomatoes, three-and-a-half *lirot* a kilo!"

The uproar feels pleasurable, necessary: *shabbat* would not be *shabbat* without this overstimulation of the senses as overture. It is as though the quiet of that one day requires a nearly intolerable climax of motion and noise first, so that the contrast makes the special day a gift, a blessing, not just an obligation or an inconvenience.

Most women do their shopping Friday morning; the afternoon crowd contains the hard-core bargain hunters, and they fight to reach the best zucchini, they shove their evidence in the merchant's face: "Look at the bruise on this tomato! How can you charge me the full price, Yitzḥak, you thief? Have a heart, friend!"

Yitzḥak turns as red as the tomato. "I'm already giving you the cheapest price in the market, Esther! You don't believe it? Go give your business to Moshe over there, you'll see what is a real thief! Upon my life, Esther, you're giving me high blood pressure. See this vein standing out on my neck? I'll have a stroke before the sun even goes down. Give me one last *shabbat* with my family! Here, I'll throw in another tomato with the kilo."

Elisheva's two string bags bulge with food: *ḥallot* and poppyseed strudel from the bakery, oranges, bananas, grapefruits, paper bags of lentils and almonds and raisins, small eggplants to stuff with tomatoes and cheese, shiny green and red peppers, squashes, carrots, turnips. The food she is carrying seems like parts of women's bodies, assembled in some strange order and stuffed into the netting of the shopping bags. Orange breasts and purple thighs protrude exuberantly in all directions, as if about to burst from the flimsy bags that hold them together.

If these fruits of the earth and the tree were really parts of women's bodies, they would come from the bodies of the women surrounding Elisheva, the amply fleshed shoppers in flowered housedresses, their dark wavy hair tied up in white kerchiefs, small gold earrings flashing against their brown necks. These magnificent Sephardic women, most of them twenty or thirty years older than Elisheva, elbow their way through the crowd with great purpose. Elisheva positions herself behind one woman, and watches the throng part ahead of her as this older immigrant—from Syria? Iraq? Kurdistan?—moves confidently, steadily forward.

A few years ago, before Elisheva came to Israel, a bomb exploded in this market on a Friday afternoon. Fruits and vegetables spattered the walls in all directions, stained the clothes of the shoppers. How many were killed—three? four? If a bomb exploded right now, she would grab the woman walking ahead of her, and duck together for safety.

Elisheva sees some beautiful artichokes and moves toward them. Every year the kibbutzim introduce one new vegetable or fruit for Rosh Hashana; the year of the big immigration from Morocco, the new vegetable was the artichoke. By now, artichokes are plentiful, cheap, delicious. Still, they're not so popular as most of the other vegetables; probably they take too long to eat for the impatient Israelis. Elisheva chooses several artichokes and pays the merchant, who wishes her a sabbath of peace.

She picks up some almost-overripe cooking tomatoes at a bargain price—at this stand she does her own share of elbowing and shouting—and finds herself ejected from the end of the market, blinking in the strong light of afternoon.

———

Daniel's letter was waiting in my mailbox when I got home

that day. It was maybe the third or fourth letter he'd written me; the first was a thank-you note for *shabbat* dinner. In the time since then—almost a year—we'd maintained a polite, leisurely correspondence.

When I recognized Daniel's precise handwriting on the envelope, I made a mental note to open the letter before sundown. There was no time for reading letters on a Friday afternoon, and besides, Miriam was already at my apartment to help with the cooking. Impersonal though Daniel's letters always were, I preferred to read them in solitude.

Once the letter was open, I knew I could read it late that night, after my guests had gone, without violating the laws of *shabbat* by tearing the envelope. That was the way I thought then, quite automatically. It seems strange now; but not as strange as it might. Letters had to be ripped open before sundown on Friday. I had to make a trip to the outhouse before sundown, to tear strips of toilet paper and leave them in a stack. I had to heat enough water for coffee and tea, and keep a small flame under the pot all night Friday and all day Saturday. I had to decide whether I wanted electric light for Friday evening; if so, I had to sleep under its beam all night.

I wish I could forget some of the rules now. I learned them so late, and they are no use to me anymore. Why can't I dismiss them? Why can't I take for granted the simple act of writing on Saturday morning, or driving to a restaurant on Friday night? Isn't it enough to carry around the memories of childhood, the laws of the soul, formed so early, without rational control? I have forgotten nearly everything I learned at school; why can't I forget the laws I chose to learn, follow, and reject as an adult? That time in Israel, that apprenticeship to Orthodoxy, was a kind of second infancy, an influence so powerful and deep that I will never completely lose it.

———

Elisheva thinks: "Who are these people to me? They are my friends, but who are they to me?"

The group calls itself a *ḥevra*. The Hebrew word implies an almost mystical association, people as necessary to one another as the arms and legs of a body. Israelis use the word too loosely, Elisheva and Miriam agree. But who in this room is *ḥaver* to Elisheva? Perhaps only Miriam.

Milton begins to sing Elisheva's favorite *shabbat* song: *libee*

68

uv'saree y'ranenu l'el hai. "My heart and my flesh will sing the praise of the living god." Everyone joins in for the chorus, and Milton hams up his solos with Hassidic hand-waving, finger-snapping and foot-thumping. Sharon and David use their spoons to tap on the table; with every verse the rhythm becomes more intricate, until Elisheva cannot resist, and picks up her spoon to join the percussion section. Henry, Josh, and Tova invent a three-part harmony, and Miriam chants her own monotone version as usual.

All of this has happened before; all of it will happen again. Milton always begins the singing, and Sharon and David always tap in unison as they smile at each other, and Henry always finds the first chord, and Miriam is always oblivious to the melody, and Elisheva always resists at first before giving herself up to the music, even when the song is her favorite. The group always meets for *shabbat*, and aside from *shabbat*, the only group members Elisheva ever sees are Miriam and Milton. Miriam, because she and Elisheva are *haverot*, true friends; Milton, because it would be indiscreet of him to spend the night with Elisheva on *shabbat*—everyone in the group would know about their half-hearted affair—so he sometimes stops by during the week.

Perhaps the group is a family more than a *hevra*. Tonight, for instance, Elisheva is the mother, Milton is the father, and Miriam is the oldest daughter who helps with the cooking and cleaning. Elisheva sighs. She has traveled thousands of miles, at least in part to separate from her family and find some larger or deeper identity, and now she has fallen into a pseudo-family here: a group united by blood tie, ritual, and habit.

It is time for *birkat ha-mazon*, the blessing after the meal. Elisheva removes all knives from the table, so that the blessing can be sung in an atmosphere of peace. On the way back from the kitchen she stops at the threshold. The *shabbat* candles and the kerosene lamp have given this ordinary room a glow, almost an aura of holiness. Elisheva sees the crumbs of bread on the white tablecloth, the faces of her friends, the curved iron grillwork outside the French windows, the shiny yellow rainhat resting on the bureau by the door. The room is alive with so many textures that Elisheva trembles with delight. She wants to touch everything in this room, to know how everything feels right now, to keep the memory of this moment in her fingers.

"*Nu nu?*" says Milton. "The hostess is in her own world. Come sit down. Time to *bentsch*."

Elisheva sits and opens her *siddur*, aware of the thin pages in her hand, the smooth skirt on her legs, the hair that tickles her neck and cheeks, the hot kerosene lamp behind her, the heat from the lamp and from the envelope beside it radiating into her shoulders. She feels Daniel's presence in that envelope, and remembers the last time she experienced this rare acuity of sensation. It was here, in this room, in his company, at the end of their evening of debate. The subject was Buber: Is Buber's philosophy a Jewish philosophy, or does it show too much Christian influence? Daniel spoke ardently, with great sincerity, in defense of Buber, and Elisheva became more and more sarcastic and irreverent, until there was no reconciling their positions. They sat in silence for a moment, and Elisheva knew she had hurt Daniel and he would soon get up to leave, and suddenly she became aware of his body beside hers and she wanted him as she had never wanted any other man. This desire was something new, not exactly sexual, more tactile and diffuse. She felt the air around her and the outline of her body, and the air was thick and charged with an almost tangible substance, and every molecule of this substance touched every other molecule and touched her skin. She laid her hand on Daniel's cheek; he looked confused and startled. Then he kissed the palm of her hand, and left. This was the only time they ever touched.

Now that she knows the unread letter from Daniel to be responsible for her extraordinary sensitivity tonight, she is reluctant to read the letter and find this magic dispelled by what will surely be one of Daniel's formal and uninspiring messages. She decides to pretend she has not opened the envelope at all. She will read the letter after *shabbat*.

The group begins to sing *shir ha-ma'alot*, one of the songs of ascent: "In the return of god, when god caused the return, we were like those who dream."

———

Half in this world, half in the next: in such a state she awakens. She has been dreaming about the old man whose place she took in this house. Not a nice man, according to Yardena: the landlord, always yelling at anyone he caught wasting water by doing laundry too often or scrubbing the steps for *shabbat*. He shook his cane at the children and frightened them.

Still, Elisheva imagines him a learned man in his white beard, turban, and striped robe. This is how he appears in her dreams,

70

to give her advice in beautiful Hebrew phrases. She tries to remember his words in the dream from which she just awakened. Something about sacrifice. "The sacrifices of today will be the pleasures of tomorrow."

What the hell is that supposed to mean? What sacrifices? What pleasures? When will it be tomorrow? And will the sacrifices themselves be the pleasures, or will the sacrifices make the pleasures possible?

"Too bad, old man," she mumbles. "You're losing your touch. Your advice is beginning to sound like bad fortune cookies. Did you ever hear of a fortune cookie? Probably not."

She will write down the dream as soon as *shabbat* is over; perhaps Dr. Feinstein can help her make something of it. He'll like this dream. It's just the kind of advice he would give, too: postpone gratification, do what must be done first. Oh, maybe he wouldn't say that. Maybe it's just her own advice to herself.

———

The dream, as I remember it now: My hands and my feet are tied together, and I hang like the bundle of a hobo's possessions from a stick slung over the shoulders of two men, who are carrying me—where? to market? to the house of the priests? I am bound together, roped and tethered, bound for the city. Other men pass, carrying similar bundles; they wave to one another. They all know each other, but I know none of them. I know only myself, my own flesh that aches and cries out to me for food, for comfort. For I want, I want, and I am found wanting. I am flesh, they are sticks. They intend to sacrifice me to their god, who is also my god, or so they tell me. I give them my body for this act, which they say is necessary, which their god has commanded. They say they own me, and I must agree to do what they want. For now, I agree; but some day my flesh will be my own, I will own my flesh, and I will glory in the flesh that today is used for their purposes. My flesh will make me brave; through the flesh will I be made whole; through the flesh will I be sanctified; through the sanity of my flesh, the flesh of my courage, will I be made free. And they will say, Amen.

———

When the Torah is brought out from behind the curtain, the women reach toward it and then kiss the tips of their fingers. Elisheva watches and is moved, but she does not do what the

71

other women do. Like them, she is in the balcony looking down on the important proceedings in the men's section, but unlike them she is not willing to pretend to make contact with a scroll thirty feet away. It's not fair that she is forbidden to touch the Torah just because she is a woman. No matter how many ways Milton explains this rule to her, it will never seem fair. They have had this argument dozens of times.

"If you touched the Torah when you had your period, then no man would be allowed to touch it after you."

"What if I swore not to touch the Torah during my period? What if I agreed to go to the *mikva* after my period, before touching the Torah?"

"That wouldn't be good enough, because a woman's oath is not binding. The men would never be sure you weren't lying. And you couldn't read aloud from the Torah in the presence of men, because the voice of a woman is a sexual temptation."

"Well, that stinks. Is there anything to prevent a group of women from holding a separate service?"

"No, there's nothing to prevent it. It just hasn't been done since the Middle Ages. So, if you want to be old-fashioned . . . "

At this point Milton grabs her, and she pulls away.

"Aren't you forbidden to touch me unless I've been purified by the *mikva*? If I'm not allowed to touch your Torah, you're not allowed to touch me."

Every time Elisheva tells Miriam about these fights, they swear to each other that they will continue to study the Torah on their own and that some day they will find a group of women to pray with. And Miriam and Elisheva consider their vows binding, even if the men don't.

The reader is just beginning to chant today's Torah portion, from the middle of Exodus, God's instructions to Moses for worship at the altar: the oil lamp, and the priests' clothing, and the offerings of bread, wine, rams, bulls, lambs. Elisheva and Miriam didn't have much to say about this portion when they studied it. They sped through the lists of animals to be slaughtered, the requirements for sprinkling blood and entrails on the altar.

Elisheva said, "This part of the Bible is disgusting."

Miriam agreed. "But don't forget," she said. "When we pray for the rebuilding of the Temple, we are praying for animal sacrifices."

"Then I'm glad there's no Temple," Elisheva said. "Just don't tell the *ḥevra* I said so."

72

A phrase in the reading now catches her attention: "And the ram shall be for Aaron and his sons by law forever from the children of Israel. . . ." Why didn't she and Miriam notice this? Of course, Aaron and the other priests would have lived off the meat of the sacrifices! How convenient for Aaron, that his brother Moses wrote up the laws, and the laws say everybody has to bring food to Aaron. Elisheva glimpses here a self-serving system of priests who made the laws and whom the laws benefited. She is furious for an instant, then uncomfortable. No, it can't be so crass; her understanding must not be deep enough yet.

The Torah reading ends. The men and some of the women continue their prayers. Elisheva looks down at the crocheted *kippot* on the men's heads, bobbing like beach balls as the men sway and duck in prayer. They suddenly look ridiculous; she suppresses a giggle. She hears two women behind her talking quietly, about their children and about the food they will serve when they get home from synagogue. Elisheva flips pages until she finds the right spot to begin her prayers. She is not concentrating very well today. Would she rather be down there with the men? No.

Much later, I found a book about Jewish women in the Middle Ages. There were women scholars, women scribes, women who led prayer for all-women congregations. This was the "old-fashioned" time Milton derided, the time before Jewish women learned to live through their husbands.

One of the medieval women said: "Do you see this cloth covering the ark? I wove it, with my sisters and daughters. This fine work is ours, a worthy apron for a worthy scroll. This embroidery, the crown and the lion's head, ours too. The well embroidered in the center is my own creation, for my name is Rebecca, and Rebecca our mother found the well and uncovered the large stone from upon it, and brought forth fresh water. For it is written: 'She is a well of living water.' And: 'She is a tree of life; all her ways are ways of pleasure, and all her paths are peace.' "

Another woman wrote: "This scroll is my work, and this book. I learned the craft of the scribe from my mother Raisel, may she be remembered for a blessing. This book I set in type with my own hands, from first to last. If it contains any error I beg the reader to forgive me, for I was nursing my son as I worked."

A third said: "Women! We must pray to our mothers Sarah,

73

Rebecca, Rachel, and Leah, to increase our knowledge of herbs and healing, that we may end this plague. Women! Now you must weep."

And the women wept.

––––––

Elisheva stands alone in the kitchen, washing dishes on the eve of the first day of the week, under the glare of the first light bulb. Her refrigerator bulges with leftovers.

Shabbat always begins too soon and ends too soon for Elisheva. She has just a few more things to do when it is time to stop and light the candles on Friday night, and she is just beginning to feel at peace when it is time to light the *havdalah* candle and return to the week's worries. At least Miriam and Henry can look forward to the pleasure of their first cigarette. Elisheva considers taking up smoking and decides that's the stupidest idea she's had in many days.

The teakettle whistles for the first time; now she will have enough hot water for the dishes. The old wringer-style washing machine groans as it heats more water, for the bath Elisheva really wanted Friday afternoon but had no time for. She finishes the dishes and waters the plant in the doorway. It's a good thing the old man isn't alive to see how much water she is using.

Then she notices: the old man's plant is producing buds. Yardena has told her that this plant blossoms only once in seven years, and Elisheva will be lucky enough to see the flowering this spring. She tries to guess the color of the flowers; the buds are solid green; it is much too early. She could ask Yardena, but that would spoil the surprise.

She finds herself humming a leftover *shabbat* song, *Yismaḥ Moshe*: "Moses was happy with the gift of Torah." How hungry she has been for a surprise, even a small one! The purpose of *shabbat* is to refresh the soul, and sometimes it does. But this *shabbat* she felt bored with the rituals, unable to concentrate; the moment of true refreshment came last night with that sudden flooding of her senses. And the *havdalah* spice box, the fragrance she and her friends inhaled less than an hour ago, didn't really sweeten the departure of the sabbath for her; it is the tiny buds, the unexpected promise of color and fragrance in the future, that have eased her into the new week.

Strange: when she first arrived in Israel she was eager for ritual and community; she took in the ancient Hebrew words and

74

they filled an empty space in her; she relished the seasonal holidays and took comfort in the regular, common calendar. She loved filling her house with friends and prayers, and she was happy to be living in the place where it all started, among the stones of her origin.

And now, after such a short time, she is already dissatisfied. She wants something fresh and new. She wants a private revelation, something all her own, not the same words that have been repeated for thousands of years. She wants to forget that her feet still cling to soil and rock. She wants to feel the buds of promise emerge from her fingertips.

She pulls the old metal tub out from under her bed and drags it into the kitchen, where she fills it with hot water from the washing machine outlet hose. Before undressing, she turns off the kitchen light, so that she can see out but no one can see in. She watches the steam rise from the tub, kneels to test the temperature with one elbow, and adds some cold water from the tap. Just right. She shivers as she takes off her clothes in the drafty kitchen, then slowly she lets herself down into the warm tub.

Across the street, over the small grocery store, the bereaved woman, bundled in a sweater and a shawl, sits on her balcony, staring down. A lamp from inside the woman's apartment throws some light on her face; she looks sad and tired, as always. Elisheva normally avoids staring at her—not out of fear anymore, but because the woman's prolonged mourning is so intense and private. Tonight, however, Elisheva's nakedness, her engagement in the private act of sponging her own body, somehow give her the right to observe her neighbor's sorrow.

"Is there a way I can help you?" she asks the woman in silence. "Is it possible to cheer you up? Has your husband given up trying? Does he lie with you on Friday night? Does he sing to you from the book of Proverbs, calling you a woman of valor? or has he given that up, too? Can I organize a serenade for you? We will sing under your balcony, Miriam and Yardena and I. We will charm you out of your depression. Even the tuneless voice of Miriam will sound sweet to your ears. We will sing the lovely Yemenite melody, the one so complex and serpentine that I can never remember the whole of it. Throwing you handfuls of blossoms from the old man's plant, we will sing. Our song will rise to you, and you will believe it:

> Who can find a woman of valor?
> She is worth more than rubies.
> She is like the merchant ships;
> she brings food from afar.
> She rises while it is still night.
> She considers a field, and buys it;
> with the fruit of her hands she plants a vineyard.
> She girds her loins with power,
> and makes strong her pelvis.
> Strength and dignity are her clothing;
> and she laughs at the time to come.
> She takes care of her household,
> and eats not of the bread of idleness.
> Give her of the fruit of her hands;
> and let her works praise her in the gates.

As though she can hear Elisheva's thoughts, the bereaved woman stands. She goes to the rail of the *mirpesset*, and very deliberately she spits into the street below.

7

Dear Elisheva,
   I've never written a letter like this before. I hope I can do it well.

There is much about me that you don't know. It feels important to me to be honest with you now, so that we can be closer to each other. I have cherished our friendship, and I have been afraid until now to tell you the truth about myself because I didn't want to lose your good opinion of me. So before you read further, please know that you are very dear to me. I hope that even if you are shocked at first, you will be able to find your way to understand and accept me, and we can have a harmony between us that is based on truth instead of lies.

First of all, I am a convert to Judaism. I tell people that I am from an Italian Sephardic family, but actually my parents are Italian Catholics. Their last name is Lucarelli. When I converted, I took the last name Yamenu, which as you know means "our days" in Hebrew. I chose this name because it comes from my favorite prayer, the one for returning the Torah to the ark: "*Hadesh yamenu kakedem.* Renew our days as in the beginning."

I converted and changed my name just before I met you, so you were one of the people I lied to about my background. Some day I'll explain to you how I decided to become a Jew. It's a long story, and right now I only want you to understand why I felt I had to lie. By the time I converted, I knew I wanted to go to rabbinical school. I thought people would look with suspicion on a future rabbi who wasn't brought up Jewish. The Talmud says a convert is a real Jew, but we both know that people who were born Jewish often feel superior to converts.

The second thing I've lied about is rabbinical school. I dropped out last fall. My letters telling you about my courses and plans were full of lies. Even my return address was a lie: I've been living in New York, and the school has forwarded your letters to me from Cincinnati.

Why did I lie to you about rabbinical school? It has to do with the third lie, the hardest one to tell you about.

When we first met in college, maybe it seemed strange to you that I never asked you out on a date. We liked each other right away and had a lot of the same interests, so why didn't I ask you out? I used to say to myself, "What's the matter with you? She's nice, intelligent, attractive. Why don't you ask her out?" But even while I was asking myself, I really knew the answer. You see, I've never dated a girl in my life. From the time I was a child, I knew I was more attracted to boys than to girls. When I met you I had had casual affairs with men, but no serious relationships. Then last fall I got involved in the gay liberation movement, and I met Bill. He and I started living together. That's when I dropped out of rabbinical school.

Bill and I love each other very much, even though we fight a lot and things may not work out between us. We've broken up a couple of times but then we always get back together again. But even when things are good between Bill and me, I'm still not really happy, because deep down, I want to lead a good Jewish life, be a member of the Jewish community and have a wife and children. Sometimes I think that what I want more than anything is to get married and settle in Israel, maybe start a kibbutz of like-minded serious people with ideals. I hope you and I can talk more about these plans some day.

Since I quit rabbinical school, I've had a job as a library file clerk. (Bill calls me a "homophile clerk," ha ha.) I'll probably go back to school, but I don't know in what field.

Whatever my future is, I hope you'll be in it. I think you're a very special person, Ellen, and somehow I feel I can trust you with the truth about myself. I feel relieved just having written to you and knowing I don't have to lie to you anymore, but I'm very anxious to get your response and know that we can still be friends and you don't think I'm a terrible person. So please write soon! And please, please don't tell anyone else what I've told you. You're the only one I've told any of this to, and I couldn't stand the idea that anyone else would know. I'm trusting you to keep this confidence.

Shalom,
Daniel

Shit. Goddamn. Fuck. Shit.

How long has she been doing this, pacing and muttering? Her robe has come untied; anyone could see in. She hastily closes the curtains and continues to pace, trying to halt the flow of expletives and compose her thoughts. But it is no good. She struggles to recall her state of mind before she read Daniel's letter. She can remember nothing. Before that letter, her life was neat and orderly—wasn't it?—but what on earth did it contain? And "after" swirls ahead of her until she is dizzy and has to sit down.

"Stop being melodramatic," she tells herself. "It's only a letter, and it's about Daniel, not me. It's his life. I can still go on with mine. But what is mine? If only I could remember."

She stands, bracing herself against the table, and turns the dial of the old man's radio. The wail of an Arabic love song fills the apartment: *"Ya-a-a-ḥa-bee-bee, ya-a-a-ḥa-bee-bee. . . ."* Beloved, beloved. Most popular songs in Arabic seem to consist of that one word repeated over and over. Why this uniformity? What secret code is hidden in that word?

She writes *"yaḥabeebee"* on Daniel's envelope, first in Hebrew letters, then in English transliteration. She counts the letters, rearranges them, figures their numerological value. The exercise clarifies nothing.

How dare he! She gives the floor a good stomp, turns off the radio in mid-syllable, and paces more vigorously than before. How dare he lead her on for three years. How dare he make a fool of her. How dare he let her hold him up as the exemplar of purity, the one man whose goodness she could trust, when all the while he was lying to her and lying with men. How dare he take away her hope that maybe some day he and she would be lovers, or maybe even get married, and then everything would be wonderful.

What a fool she is. How could she not have guessed. How could she not have known better. How could she have allowed herself to adore him. How could she have given him the power to insult her in this way. How could she have been so gullible. How could she not have picked up all the cues—

She stops short. All what cues? If she knows there were cues, then she must have known what the cues were telling her. Did she already know? No. Yes. No.

She ties her robe tighter and returns to pacing. The letter. The letter. Okay. The truth. She was shocked to learn that Daniel is a convert, but not that he is a homosexual. His telling her surprised her more than the fact itself. So, she must have wanted him to keep lying to her? She must have known already, or at least suspected? But how could she have known? Because he never made a pass at her? No, surely she isn't as vain as that. She always assumed he wasn't attracted to her; or he didn't want to spoil their friendship; or she just wasn't his type.

How right she was! She isn't his type. His type is boys, not girls; boys, not girls. She repeats the words with each step, like a marching song: boys, not girls; boys, not girls. Then the words change: faggot queer, left right; faggot queer, left right; faggot queer—

She stops again, horrified. What is happening to her? And where did she learn the word "faggot"? She can't remember ever hearing anyone say it, but there it is in her head. So she must have heard it; or maybe she read it in a book.

She will have to answer the letter immediately. But what will she say? That none of it matters to her? No, that would be a lie. That he has spoiled her fantasy of falling in love with him? No, that would be humiliating. That she is angry with him? No, that would be heartless, when he is in such distress. That she understands? No, she doesn't understand. She can't answer him until she understands—what? She doesn't even know what it is that she must understand before she can write to him. How will she ever be ready?

She wishes she could talk with Miriam. But Daniel has asked her not to tell anyone. That means she can tell no one but Dr. Feinstein. Her next appointment is two days hence. How can Daniel expect her to wait so long? How dare he lie to her and then tie her hands like this? Well, he asked her not to tell anyone, but she never agreed. What right does he have to ask anything of her at all? She sighs. Maybe Miriam isn't the person to talk with, anyway. Miriam is so naïve, so inexperienced. How can she help Elisheva with this? How can anyone? Even Dr. Feinstein seems to live a pretty sheltered life. Maybe there's something Elisheva can read? So she'll understand better?

"Damn you, Daniel," she groans. "I don't want to understand. I don't want to know. Why did you have to tell me? Of all the people in the world, why did you have to tell me?"

———

While typing rejection notices for the Admissions Department, Elisheva begins to cry. At first the crying is only a mild tearfulness, the kind of sadness she might expect from having to dash the hopes of so many people in a single day. When her shoulders start to heave and choking noises escape from her, she runs to the ladies' room to hide and try to stop herself.

She can't stop. She sobs for a long time, great guttural sounds that come from a place deeper in her chest than she's ever felt. She cannot recognize anything of her familiar voice in this keening; a jackal has taken possession of her and is forcing its howls up from her belly; her throat bruises itself in the effort to hold back these frightful noises, but she is powerless to contain them. Her personality is weakening, dissolving in yelps of pain. Soon nothing will be left of the Elisheva she knows. She will collapse on the floor like an exhausted animal, and she will bite anyone who approaches.

Through the veil of her own sobs, she hears some people speaking Hebrew just outside the door. Oh God. She can be heard outside this room. She has never cried in public before. Her dignity is lost forever. Everyone in the department—the other secretaries, maybe even the administrators, God knows who else—is out there witnessing her breakdown.

With an enormous shudder she enforces silence upon herself. Immediately the door opens, and Rina, the head secretary, enters and sits beside Elisheva on the plastic divan. "Elisheva, what's the matter? *Mah yesh*? Are you sick? Was that a friend of yours who was killed in the border shelling last night?"

This is the first Elisheva has heard of a border shelling. Thank God, she is well, her parents are well, her friends are all alive. Her problems are very small. It is not her son who was killed in the war, not her friend who was killed in the shelling.

"I'm okay," she says. "I had a fight with my boyfriend."

"Oh, that." Rina makes a gesture that dismisses the nonexistent boyfriend from the human race. "Don't worry, *motek*, he'll be back if he has any sense. And if not, you're better off without him. *Nakhon*? Right?" She goes to a stall and returns with a wad of toilet paper.

Elisheva blows her nose. "*Nakhon.*"

"Why don't you take the rest of the day off? Go home early. No, don't go home, that will only depress you. Go to a sad movie. There's a good one at the Paladin. Cry to your heart's content. You'll feel better tomorrow. *B'seder*? Okay? Good. You're welcome, it's nothing, *motek*. Just go. Go already."

The movie Rina recommended is the same one Elisheva saw

with Andrée, nearly two years ago. How can she bear to sit alone through a movie about the aftermath of war, about the same war that took the bereaved woman's son? How can she see this movie without Andrée's warm hand to clasp, without Miriam's comforting presence beside her? No, it is impossible. She will go straight home. She will sit on her balcony, the mirror image of the bereaved woman. She will think the woman's bitter thoughts.

What kind of country is this, what kind of world? Nothing is fair. Too many young women are widowed, too many mothers plunged into grief. Too many wars, too much hate. Too many Jews were displaced, displacing too many Arabs. Too many, like Bella the Russian, have been forced to come here; too many have been forced to leave. Too much anger, too much grief. Too many Sephardim, like Yardena, do menial work for the Ashkenazim. Too many Arabs do menial work for the Jews. Too many Jews, like Andrée, like Yardena and Hayim, like the bereaved woman, were forced to leave Arab countries. Even the birds do not know whether to sing in Hebrew or in Arabic, and so have settled on the sounds the two languages have in common, the sounds from the back of the throat, the sounds that express pain and hunger, the sounds that cause pain in giving voice to pain. The sounds are the ululation of a wedding and the wail of a funeral and the choke of grief and the hoarse voice of love and the shrieking of the siren that calls for silence on the day of remembering the war dead and the bellow of the horn ripped from the head of a ram for the call to prayer. Even the birds know this dialect. Even the birds.

———

Miriam is already at Elisheva's apartment, several hours early for their study session. She sits at the table with the newspaper spread before her, smoking a cigarette with one hand and with the other, twiddling the strand of hair that would be a *payes* if she were a Hassidic man. Elisheva stands in the doorway and watches her friend, who does not yet know Elisheva is there. Miriam twirls and twirls that piece of hair around her finger, twirls it and twirls it. Because of this habit of Miriam's—twiddling her hair as she daydreams and a cup of coffee goes cold and a cigarette burns itself out in the ashtray—she has one permanent Shirley Temple curl at each ear, while the rest of her hair is perfectly straight.

Elisheva looks around to make sure she hid Daniel's letter before work. When her glance falls once more on Miriam, she sees that Miriam is weeping.

"Miriam, what's wrong? What is it?" Elisheva rushes to the table and examines her friend's face. She has never seen Miriam cry before, and her own eyes fill with tears. She holds them back: Miriam has never seen her cry either, and Elisheva is afraid she will lose control as she did at work.

"Miriam, please tell me. What happened?"

Miriam seems unable to speak. She shakes her head slowly, miserably; her tears fall on the newspaper; she points to a picture on the front page. Elisheva sees the face of a chubby young man with a moustache, and his name: Shmuel Mordekhai Abramovitz. The name means nothing to her. She reads the headline and the first paragraph of the story: this was the person killed in the shelling at the Lebanese border, the one Rina thought Elisheva was crying over in the ladies' room.

"Who is he? Do you know him?"

Miriam nods, still without speaking, and cries harder. She draws her sweater around her, like a lonely old woman. Elisheva has never seen such vulnerability in Miriam. She knows some new gesture of consolation is called for, but she hesitates awkwardly. She and Miriam are each other's closest friends; yet they lack the easy physical affection Elisheva shares with Yardena, for instance. By unspoken agreement, they hug and kiss on the cheek only when one of them gives the other a present.

Elisheva pulls her chair closer and puts her arms around Miriam, who collapses into the embrace. This is so easy, Elisheva thinks. It is so easy to touch and help each other. Why have we denied ourselves this comfort?

Her eyes fill again, and this time she lets the tears come. The jackal does not return; this crying is quieter, softer, not a threat but a peaceful merging with the still unknown sorrow of her friend, which somehow shelters her own confused pain.

Miriam pulls back and wipes her eyes on her sleeve. "I'm sorry. I don't know why I fell apart like that. I didn't even know him very well."

"Who was he? How did you know him at all?"

"He was Sam." Miriam begins to cry again. She picks up her coffee cup and runs into the kitchen. Elisheva hears her in there, clattering around and crying. She considers following Miriam, to prolong their moment of intimacy, but then decides no, Miriam wants to be alone.

Elisheva never met Sam, who was Miriam's one fling, possibly the only man she will have gone to bed with when she marries. He was obnoxious but taller than Miriam. "One out of two ain't bad," Miriam said with a laugh. "I don't even like him. I just want to know what sex is. It's kind of like the cheeseburgers. I don't want to keep wondering."

They giggled and made fun of Sam together, and Miriam soon stopped seeing him, but Elisheva felt uncomfortable about the whole thing. She worried she had influenced Miriam too much, and maybe neglected her for a while after starting the affair with Milton, thus leaving Miriam easy prey to tall and obnoxious men.

Miriam returns with two cups of coffee, lights a cigarette, and begins to twiddle her hair again. "It's just that he's the first person I've known who died in an incident. Also . . . I know it's stupid, but I keep thinking I should have had his baby. I could have kept something alive, and now there's nothing. Not that he was such a great guy, but it doesn't seem right for there to be nothing at all. . . . I just feel very empty." She looks away and drinks some of her coffee. "Could we do our studying now? I think it would make me feel better."

"Are you sure you're ready? Are you positive you don't want to talk some more?"

Miriam tries to nod and shake her head at the same time, and they both laugh feebly. They put away the newspaper and bring out their holy books.

In preparation for Purim, they study *Megilat Esther*, reading aloud the text and commentaries, discussing each point that interests them. They agree that although it is Esther who saves the Jews, Vashti is a more admirable woman, for refusing to display her beauty before her husband's drunken friends. On this point Elisheva and Miriam wax so enthusiastic that Elisheva forgets the pan of leftovers warming on the stove and Miriam forgets the cigarette burning in the ashtray, and suddenly there is pungent smoke, a combination of burnt vegetables and burnt filter.

They open the windows to let in the moist, cold air from outside, and they continue their study. A magic wind enters the room and transports them like two figures in a Chagall painting, and for a short time they forget that they are cold and the kerosene is almost gone and there may soon be another war and Sam is dead and Daniel is gay. They float into a world of royal turbans and seven-day banquets with vessels of gold, a world in which everything has its place and there is one bad man and everyone knows who he is, and when he is gone there can be rejoicing in the land.

"And why is this so upsetting to you, about your friend Daniel?" Dr. Feinstein does not appear shocked, and this amazes Elisheva.

"Well, of course I'm upset! Wouldn't you be upset, if a good friend of yours told you he was homosexual?" Dr. Feinstein says nothing. She feels she must convince him that she has good reason to be upset. This is not at all what she expected. "Listen, he's the only man I really feel attracted to, okay?"

"Isn't that interesting, that the only man you find attractive happens to be homosexual."

"What's that supposed to mean? I didn't know. Honest, I didn't know at all." Elisheva hears her voice turning shrill. She stops and takes a breath. "I'm upset about Daniel because I'm worried maybe I'm the same way." Absolute silence. She can't look up. She can hardly believe she just said that. She wants to take it back. There is no way to take it back.

"Go on. Don't be afraid." His voice is surprisingly gentle.

"The night I read Daniel's letter," she says very quietly, still without looking up, "I dreamed I was kissing your wife, with great excitement. Other women were in the room: Yardena, Miriam, Rina, Andrée, Bella, my mother, some women I've only passed in the street. Everyone seemed happy, like at a bar mitzvah or a wedding. The one man there was Daniel. He was over in the corner, nodding his head and smiling at me, as though he was proud. . . . Oh God, I'm so scared! I'm not homosexual, am I, Dr. Feinstein? I don't want to be homosexual."

She finally looks up. Dr. Feinstein has a kind, calm expression, like an indulgent father.

"What would it mean, if you were homosexual?"

"I would be an outcast. Everyone would think I was a horrible person. I couldn't have any kind of life here. I mean, it's hard enough being single in this country, let alone . . . "

"So it's just this country that's the problem?"

"No, no, even in the U.S., what kind of life could I have? I can't even imagine it. I've never known any homosexuals. I don't know anything about what they're like, but I'm sure they're not at all like me. I wouldn't have anything in common with them. I mean, I've read a little bit and heard a little bit, and it all sounds so awful, these lonely outcast people who live in some kind of sordid half-world. It's always dark and they're always drinking in seedy bars. I don't even like to drink, so what kind of life could I have?"

Dr. Feinstein is writing furiously on his notepad. When he finishes, he puts down his pen.

"Elisheva," he says, slowly and deliberately, "I have something very important to say to you, and I want you to listen carefully. I know you are frightened by Daniel's letter and your dream, but I am very glad this has happened. This will speed up your analysis tremendously. I have been waiting for lesbian imagery to appear in your fantasy life. It was inevitable in your case. Everything pointed in this direction. Now that it has finally surfaced, we can work past this stage to a real maturity." He pauses. "I promise you, Elisheva, if you will only stay with this analysis to the end, you will be ready to marry and have a family. You will not be an outcast. You will be a happily married Israeli woman." He beams at her, not unlike Daniel in the dream.

"One more thing," he says. "Your attraction to my wife, do not worry about it. This is the most optimistic sign of all. You are finally forming an attachment to me. This is the first step that will prepare you for marital love. It was too threatening for you to have a sexual dream about me, so instead you dreamed about my wife. She is a substitute for me. Surely you can see that. All right? Time is up."

———

Milton has invited Elisheva to a Purim party. She gets ready slowly, assembling a costume that will transform her into Vashti, the rebellious queen. A long black Gaza dress, with panels of red and purple embroidery. A heavy bronze necklace with amber beads, and matching earrings that graze her shoulders. Dark eye makeup. Her hair piled high. A filmy scarf for a veil.

She goes next door for Yardena's approval. Yardena is propped up in bed, sewing costumes for her sons to wear to school the next day. Her cheeks are flushed. When Elisheva touches her forehead, it is very hot.

"Yardena, get yourself to a doctor! You're sick."

"You think I don't know I'm sick?" Yardena sounds weary. "You think I haven't already been to a doctor? All week, every morning I go to the clinic before work. Every day it's a different doctor. They take my temperature, they tell me, 'Go home to bed and bring another bottle of urine tomorrow.' It gets no better and no worse, so how can I stay at home? If I knew it would be gone soon, then I could take a day off. But this way, it could go on forever. I have to work."

"Why didn't you tell me you're sick, Yardena? I'll make food for you. I can help you out."

"*Yahabeebee*, all I need is more food! I can hardly eat as it is. My mother makes me so much food, I'm stuffing the boys until they won't be able to fit into these Purim clothes!" She inspects Elisheva's costume. "You're an Arab lady?"

"I'm Vashti. She was a Persian lady, *lo nakhon*?" Elisheva goes to the mirror. "I look more like a hippie from Brooklyn."

"What's a hippie? Where's Brooklyn?" Yardena sinks back into her cushions. "*En davar*, never mind, you go and have a good time. You'll have enough work to do when you're married. Enjoy yourself while you're still single."

In spite of Yardena's intermittent protests, Elisheva washes the dishes in the sink and straightens up the apartment, then makes a cup of tea for Yardena before returning to her own place to add some more makeup and an ankle bracelet.

Milton arrives, dressed as Queen Esther. He looks pretty, but he doesn't seem at all pleased when Elisheva says so. At the party his good humor returns, and he quickly takes advantage of the requirement to get drunk on Purim. Then he flirts and dances with all the women, ignoring Elisheva except to look in her direction and wink a few times as he straightens his wig with one hand and feels up his dancing partner with the other.

Elisheva has never seen this side of him, but a couple of hours is quite enough. She finds the hostess' bedroom and empties her purse of Milton's wallet, keys, and breath spray. Then she walks home as fast as she can, locks the door, pours herself a glass of wine, and takes out some writing paper.

Dear Daniel,

My response to your letter was so strong and so confused that I was reluctant to write back until I understood my own feelings better. By now I see it will be some time before I understand completely, and I don't want you to be worried by a silence on my part, so I will have to write in stages, as I know more and more.

What I know now is, first of all, I absolutely want to remain your friend. In fact, I feel much closer to you than ever. Your letter threw me into such a turmoil because I care about you a great deal and because I feel a certain identification with you.

That's about as much as I can say right now. I will write again soon.

Love,
Elisheva

She is awakened by a loud knocking on the window. It is Yardena's boys, Nadav and Yonah, both wearing long red robes and gold cardboard crowns, with very elegant black moustaches and beards painted on their faces.

"Who's this? Two King Ahashueruses? *Ezeh yofi*! What beautiful costumes! But which of you is the real king?"

"Not him," says Nadav with a sneer. "He's just a stupid kid. I'm the *gever*, the real man."

"Says who!" Yonah hollers. "If you're such a *gever*, how come you wet the bed last night?"

"You wet it the night before, tattle-tale!"

The two boys begin to tussle, hitting each other with their Purim noisemakers.

"Stop fighting, you're going to smear your beards." She pries the children apart. "Here, I've got something for you."

When she returns from the kitchen with two bundles of cookies, Yardena is kneeling before Yonah to arrange his crown. She still looks sick.

"Do you want me to come with you to the clinic?" Elisheva hands a sack to each of Yardena's sons.

"No, no, you have better things to do. Yitzhak down the street is giving me a ride in his truck. Come, boys, off to school, Elisheva has to get ready for work."

Elisheva escorts them to the staircase, and she stands for a moment at the top of the steps to look around. A chilly fog is still hovering over Jerusalem; the street dissolves into mist in less than a block. Directly below her, small kings and queens parade to school for the day's festivities; an old Arab herds his sheep and donkeys among the children; Avraham the grocer arranges loaves of bread on a tray; and Milton appears in the courtyard, waving sheepishly and carrying a parcel.

The parcel contains poppyseed strudel, which he knows is her favorite. He must be ashamed of himself. Good. He should be. He cuts two slices of strudel, gives her one, and clears his throat.

"Elisheva, I know I behaved terribly last night, and I wouldn't

88

blame you if you never wanted to see me again . . . "

"How'd you guess?"

He winces. "Okay, go ahead. I deserve it."

"You want to be punished? You want absolution? Go see a priest. Just leave me alone, okay?"

He stares at his strudel in silence. She suddenly feels tired and not very angry.

"Listen," she says more gently. "We shouldn't be seeing each other anyway. There's just not enough happening between us. It's nobody's fault. Now, please go home."

"Okay."

Doesn't he care at all? She was expecting him to put up at least a little fight. Then she sinks into fatigue again; better for this undernourished affair to die as easily as possible.

"I won't be at your house for *shabbat*," she says.

"Okay."

"Now go. I have to get ready for work."

After he is gone, she sits for a while, holding her belly and rocking. No tears come. She gets up and dresses for the day. She will walk to work. The holiday atmosphere will cheer her up.

The fog is still dense, and all the royal children have vanished into schoolhouses. The only hint of Purim is the occasional din, when Elisheva passes a synagogue, of the hoots and buzzes that drown out the name of Haman the villain and the names of his ten sons during the reading of *Megilat Esther*.

With one finger, Elisheva lightly scrapes a stone wall as she walks. The stones are rough, hard, distinct. Yet only a few meters ahead, the wall is hazy and the stones are pale heavy pillows.

A man is lying on the sidewalk, exerting a superhuman effort to push a slab of rock off his chest. His head is slightly raised and taut with strain. As Elisheva rushes forward to help him, his head transforms into a stone, harsh and heavy as his concrete body.

A building has been demolished; a new one is going up. Nothing more.

She taps the stone head, almost expecting some liquid to gush forth: honey, oil, even water. A cloud of dust rises and merges with the fog. Elisheva steps out into the street to skirt the rest of the rubble.

She needs to get away for a few days. Now that she has decided not to go to Milton's for *shabbat*, she can do whatever she pleases. She has a couple of sick days coming, and Rina will understand if she takes them now. She can leave Friday and stay till Monday—where? She has already seen the green North; this time she will go south, to the desert. Something new. She will get away from her family of friends, maybe travel as far as Elat, where she can be alone, relax, read in the sun, swim in the Red Sea.

She walks on, avoiding the business district and taking an unfamiliar route, through steep, narrow streets named after prophets. When she reaches a deserted square, she sits for a moment on a bench. By now the fog has cleared, and small white clouds float past television antennas over the Old City. Farther in the distance, more glittering white igloo-houses perch on a hill; more antennas.

The square where she sits is scraggly, wide, sandy. Shreds of barbed wire hang from trees, and jagged pieces of metal rust on the ground. This place was once a no-man's land between the Arab and Jewish sectors. It is only a matter of time before new buildings are constructed here, too, but as of now, the square is still empty. It is one of the few spots remaining in Jerusalem that look as though battles have been fought here. This square is an identifiable war zone. She looks around and tries to absorb the image of these surroundings as a reminder of danger, as she has absorbed the small square photograph of Sam in the newspaper, the rectangular balcony where the bereaved woman sits, the long marketplace where bombs can explode at any time, the dark box of a movie theater where Elisheva and Andrée learned the widow's obsession with loss.

She lifts her eyes to the Old City and tries to imagine the Temple rising above the wall, the City full of Jews carrying first fruits to the Temple. She shakes her head: the scene she has summoned is much too corny, a Cecil B. DeMille creation, corrupted by her modern experience. But maybe the thing itself was corrupt: a clan of wealthy priests ruling the nation.

Maybe she has to go back farther still, to the time before religion, the time even before people. Jerusalem was once considered the navel of the world, the original place where the earth was connected with the heavens before the cord was cut. In a time before war and peace, this was the place of the first crater, the volcanic mixing-bowl that spewed river rock and molten stone, a huge roar of primal material flowing over the entire globe in rivulets of lava until it hardened into cities.

Miriam ices the last corner of the cake. "I can't study to-night," she says grimly. "I'm going to take this to Sam's mother. I'm sorry, I should have called you at work. I overslept today, and then I never caught up."

"It's all right. Are you okay?"

"Yeah, I guess so." Miriam sits down and lights a cigarette. She doesn't look okay; she looks . . . like a mourner. Her hair is greasy, and she is still wearing the nightgown she slept in. "I really don't want to face that woman. Sam took me to meet her once, and I think she knew we were going to bed together. She was polite and everything, but I know she must hate me."

"Why would she hate you? Even if she did guess about you and Sam, that wouldn't make her hate you."

Miriam seems startled. "It wouldn't? No, I guess it wouldn't. I must be going nuts. You know why I thought she would hate me? Because I had the nerve to go to bed with Sam without get-ting pregnant. I feel so guilty and awful, not being pregnant. Do you think I'm crazy? Do you understand?" She clutches Eli-sheva's hand and exhales into her face the stale breath of anx-iety. "Please tell me I'm not crazy. I just feel so guilty. I couldn't stand to be crazy too."

"No, you're not crazy. You're not crazy at all. I understand how you feel. I might feel the same way in your position." Eli-sheva speaks very slowly and loudly, as though she is trying to wake Miriam up, or as though Miriam's face is a telephone re-ceiver and this is a long-distance call with a bad connection. "Listen, I don't think you ever felt right about going to bed with Sam in the first place. Maybe you want to be pregnant partly to punish yourself."

Miriam begins to cry. Her grip on Elisheva's hand loosens. "I feel like such a bad person. I'm not a bad person, am I?"

"Of course you're not, of course you're not," Elisheva mur-murs. She shouldn't be touching Miriam. Miriam wouldn't want her to, if she knew about Daniel and about Elisheva's dream of kissing Mrs. Feinstein. Elisheva pulls back. "How about if I come with you to see Sam's mother? We'll walk over to the Turkish bath first and take a shower. Then we'll come back for the cake. Okay?"

Miriam nods gratefully, wiping her eyes with the back of her hand. "Would you? Oh, good. I'll go find my hair dryer."

Tonight there is no time for a swim in the pool, so Elisheva and Miriam go directly to the steam room. Eight or nine women are already there; they seem to have been there for hours, and most of them seem to know each other. They sit and lie in pairs on the marble benches, slapping one another with lufas and braiding each other's hair. Their skin is brown even where the sun does not hit it; their breasts are large and pendulous; black hair curls in tendrils around their flushed, wet faces. When one of them is too hot, she gets up and splashes cold water on her body, from one of several faucets set in marble basins around the room. Occasionally two friends splash each other playfully, giggling and hooting like children engaged in a mild water fight.

How do these women know each other, Elisheva wonders as she and Miriam find a corner for themselves. Are they friends outside this building, perhaps neighbors, seeing each other every day, lending and borrowing sugar and extra chairs? Or are they menstrual sisters, women who didn't know each other until they were married and began coming to the Turkish bath for their monthly immersion in the *mikva*? Elisheva likes this idea, that these women have come together simply because their periods occur at the same time, that they meet each month to splash and play and they have never even seen each other fully clothed. She decides to return for the next full moon, to see whether the same women are here again.

Why doesn't she just ask them? She feels shy, perhaps because she and they are naked. If she happened to be waiting for a bus or shopping for fruit in the company of these same women, maybe then she could ask them, but here she is shy. She looks down at her own body, which usually seems quite plump; but here, her breasts appear pitifully small, almost as though they have been squashed flat, and her belly and thighs are puny and inadequate. Her skin is too pale, and her hair, though as dark as anyone's, is thin and straight. She should have kept her gold earrings on, instead of leaving them in the locker. The earrings would have given her more dimension, more texture, more color.

She resists the temptation to return to the locker for the earrings, instead rising to throw some cold water on herself. The woman at the next basin smiles and says, in a Hebrew that sounds much like Arabic, *"Ḥavera shelakh g'vo'a me'od*, your friend is very tall," as though Elisheva deserves some of the credit for Miriam's height.

"Yes, and I am very short," Elisheva replies.

"*Lo*, not too short," says the other woman. "*B'seder gamur.* Just right."

"Thank you. You are just right too."

"No, I am too fat. But, my husband likes me that way."

The woman's friend nudges her in the side. "Stop bragging about your husband and come get dressed, Shoshanna." She winks at Elisheva. "Both of our husbands are eager to see us tonight."

Laughing, the two women leave the room. Elisheva feels reassured about her body. She is just right. So much kindness. So much kindness.

She glances in the direction of her tall friend. If she has felt out of place here, how must Miriam feel, with her long, slender arms and legs, fair hair, white skin? But Miriam seems to be giving no attention to her physical being. She sits stark upright, while everyone else lounges; and she stares straight ahead and twiddles her earlock. Her cheeks are rosy as pomegranates, from the steam.

Several of the women discuss Miriam's appearance in a stage whisper. A few words stand out: "tall," "beautiful," "like a ballerina." Elisheva thinks, how strange, these women want to look like Miriam as much as I suddenly want to look like them. Miriam is the ideal they can never attain, the Western model whose image fascinates them in fashion magazines. Why do we all wish to be what we are not?

"There is something else I have to talk with you about," Miriam says in a dull voice, still gazing straight before her. "Last night very late, Milton came over. He tried to get me to go to bed with him. I didn't do it, but I was tempted, I felt so lonely and awful about Sam. I think if he had been just a little more persistent, I might have done it, that's how low my resistance was. When he left I felt terrible, like I wasn't any kind of real friend to you. I'm sorry, Elisheva."

"Jesus Christ," Elisheva snaps. "You waited this long to tell me, couldn't you have waited a little longer? I was enjoying being here, I was enjoying that it was all women. I was having a good time. Why'd you have to bring Milton into it, here of all places?"

"I'm sorry." Miriam looks confused. "I thought I should tell you right away. I felt bad for waiting this long. I thought you'd be angry with me . . . "

"Why should I be angry with *you*?" Elisheva is surprised by the vehemence in her own voice. "Did you go to Milton's house? Did you try to get him to go to bed with you? Of course it was hard for you to say no, but you did, didn't you? Why would I be angry with *you*? He's the creep, not you. Get yourself together, Miriam! Not everything that happens is your fault. You had nothing to do with that shell exploding in Sam's face, and you didn't make Milton come over and proposition you." Suddenly she is laughing; she just realized why Milton was so very contrite this morning, and why he let her go without a fight. "Men are so ridiculous," she says, laughing, knowing she shouldn't be laughing right after she mentioned Sam's death, but laughing anyway.

Miriam starts to laugh, too. "They are."

After a minute, Elisheva says, "Miriam, you are my best friend. You are very important to me. I don't give a shit about Milton, and he doesn't give a shit about me. We agreed this morning not to see each other anymore. Are you interested in him?"

"I don't know. How can I know right now? I'm upset. I don't know."

"Well, if you decide you are interested in him when you feel better, it's all right with me. Just wait a little while, okay? The way I feel today, I don't think I could stand being in the same room with him, and that would make things awkward between you and me if you got involved with him right away. Okay?"

"Sure. Okay. I'll wait. I mean, I'll wait before I even decide whether I'm interested. Are you all right? Are you sure you're not mad at me? Do you want to go shower now? Oh, I feel so much better, I don't even mind going to see Mrs. Abramovitz. I'll go by myself. It'll be fine. I'll bring you back a piece of the cake if it's any good. Oh, I feel so much better."

8

For about an hour Elisheva has been sitting on the Jerusalem-Elat bus, listening. She has already heard many things: the names of the two small boys, Boaz and Yonatan, who sit with their Kurdish grandmother in front of her; the price the grandmother hopes to get in Beer Sheva for her chickens, now cackling in a cage on the floor; and the favorite English-language song of Dina, a four-year-old girl who sits next to Elisheva and is not related to Boaz or Yonatan or their grandmother.

Dina's favorite song is "The Itsy-Bitsy Spider," performed with hand gestures. She learned it a year ago from an American student of her father, and she loves the song so much that the first thing she said to Elisheva was, "Are you American?" The second thing she said was, "Sing 'Itsy-Bitsy.'"

Elisheva has also heard that Dina has three brothers: Ḥanania, Yossi, and Ephraim. Her parents are Shlomo and Ilana. Ilana, sitting across the aisle, doesn't want Dina to bother strangers on buses, and thinks that Elisheva should not have brought a sleeping bag, for there are beds with linens at the Elat hostel and a young woman alone should not camp on the beach, especially on *shabbat*.

The Kurdish grandmother takes a parcel of food from the large cloth bag at her feet. Elisheva watches the checkered kerchief wrapped around her head dip and return, dip and return, as she eats, then feeds her grandsons, then eats some more, then feeds them some more. One of the boys pulls her long braids, and she gives a shriek. Dina looks upset, so Elisheva sings "Itsy-Bitsy" another time to make her laugh.

"*Ima*, why are they all wearing the same clothes?" Dina asks Ilana. It is true: the grandmother's dress, the grandchildren's shirts, and the cloth bag on the floor are all made from the same dark, flowered cotton.

"Sha," whispers Ilana with a frown. "It's not nice to talk about people. They can't help it, *motek*. They make their own

95

clothes. See how lucky we are, *hamuda*, that we can buy our clothes?" She leans across the aisle and kisses Dina's elbow.

Now Dina frowns. "I want a dress just like yours," she says. "Make me a dress just like yours."

"So that's it! You want a dress like *ima*'s. Of course, *betah*, sweetheart, we'll get a dress just the same for you and me, maybe for Pesach."

"For Pesach, for Pesach," Dina sings.

Hanania, who is even younger than Dina and has been sitting in Ilana's lap, starts to cry. "Me too, me too! Make me a dress like yours, *ima*!"

"Hanania, what's the matter with you, you're not normal?" Ilana says rather sternly. "Boys don't wear dresses. I'll get you a shirt just like *abba*'s for Pesach, *b'seder*, *motek*?"

"*B'seder*," Hanania whimpers. He throws his arms around his mother and buries his face in her neck.

The Kurdish grandmother pulls a plastic sack out of her cloth bag and vomits into it. Then she eats some more bread and gives more bread to her grandchildren. Elisheva opens the window.

"I'm hungry," cries Hanania. "I want to eat."

"When we get to Beer Sheva, *motek*. We'll buy you something in Beer Sheva."

Shlomo gets up, lays *tefillin*, and begins to say his morning prayers in the aisle, a few rows ahead. He has a fairly heavy German accent and belongs to what Miriam and Elisheva call the Big Sway School; he rocks his body so energetically while mumbling his prayers that his hat falls off a couple of times. He picks it up and returns it to his head without dusting it off and without missing a mumble. There is something familiar about his rasping voice, and even more, about the way he picks up his hat.

"My husband," says Ilana, shaking her head. "He is so absentminded, if he didn't have me to check up on him he'd probably leave the house with his shirt inside-out. You know,—"

"Excuse me, but is your last name Cohen? Is your husband a professor of philosophy?"

"Yes, *nakhon*." Ilana beams proudly. "You have taken a course from him?"

"No, but he helped me once—"

"Shlomo, Shlomo! This girl knows you."

"Oh, don't interrupt his prayers, please."

Too late. Shlomo, with a disgruntled expression, is peering

into her face, the black *tefillin* box on his forehead almost touching her. He smells of tobacco.

"*Ach!*" He leaps into the air. "Of course, this is the girl who wanted to go to a religious kibbutz. Are you still on the kibbutz? Do you like it? It is good that you stayed in Israel. Are you a citizen now? Are you married yet? Why didn't you ever come to us for *shabbat*? Did you lose my card?"

"Shlomo, please. Leave the poor girl alone for a minute. Go, go finish your prayers. You can talk with her later. We will be on this bus for a long time still."

Like an obedient puppy, he returns to his spot in the aisle and resumes swaying.

Ilana sighs. "You must forgive him. A brilliant intellect, but in some ways he is like a child. He always asks strangers too many questions . . . but you are not a stranger now, since you met my husband quite a while ago. So you must defend yourself. Don't let him overwhelm you. Okay? *B'seder?*"

"*B'seder.* Thank you." Ilana, Elisheva thinks, is also a bit overwhelming in her own way, and also likable.

The Kurdish *savta* and her two grandsons have fallen asleep in a great heap of flowered cotton; one of the boys still clutches a piece of bread. The wind entering the bus is hot and dry, with a harsh dusty smell. Elisheva looks out: the forested hills to the west and south of Jerusalem are gone, and the soil here is brown and chalky, the land nearly flat, zigzagged with the jagged gullies of flash floods, punctuated by clumps of dry brush and occasional Bedouin tents.

"You skirt is very interesting," says Ilana. "How much did you pay for it?"

Elisheva returns her attention to life inside the bus. She thinks for a moment. "Six *lirot.*"

"A good price! You will be an excellent Israeli. Most Americans don't know how to bargain. They pay whatever is asked."

"I am no exception. I'm still not so good at haggling. I bought the skirt in the United States, at . . . *ekh omrim*? . . . a 'thrift shop.' " Ilana doesn't understand the English words, so Elisheva tries again. "Someone else owned the skirt before. Then she didn't want it anymore, and she sold it to a shop, and I bought it."

"*Zeh lo higeni,*" says Ilana with disapproval. "That's not hygienic. Is your family poor?"

"No. I just liked the skirt." Elisheva shrugs. She still likes the skirt, which is loose, long, handpainted in swirls of white, charcoal, coral, gold. She usually wears this skirt, without underwear, for camping trips in hot weather; in it, she can squat and pee on the ground in perfect modesty, or even pull the elastic waistband up to her neck and change into her bathing suit on a public beach. How wrong her mother was to urge her to leave "that *schmatta*" at home! She'll have to remember to tell her mother this summer that Ilana praised the skirt and praised her bargaining skills.

Elisheva is pleased with herself. She will be an excellent Israeli. Ilana the sabra says so. Elisheva is glad she ran into the Cohens today. They take her back to the time when she first came to Israel, the time when she met Shlomo in the Office of Religious Kibbutzim: her eagerness to learn the magic language of Hebrew, to be absorbed into Israeli culture, to become part of a religious community.

"You speak well," Ilana says. "*Kamma zman att b'aretz*? How long have you been in 'the land'?"

"Two years."

"How old are you?"

"Twenty-four." Elisheva steels herself for the next inevitable question.

"Why aren't you married?"

"*Anee yoda'at*? I should know?"

"Who knows if not you?" Ilana laughs and adjusts her *mitpahat rosh*, the hair-concealing kerchief that is the badge of an Orthodox wife. "Here, we're almost at the Beer Sheva bus station. Look, children, see the buildings? Time for lunch."

She jiggles little Hanania, who has fallen asleep, and pats the rear end of Dina, who is draped over the armrest between her and Elisheva. The children lift their heads groggily, and as soon as Dina knows where she is, she mumbles, "Itsy-Bitsy, Itsy-Bitsy."

"No, *hamuda*, no time for songs now, leave the *giveret* alone." Ilana strokes Dina's head. "Here, *motek*, let *ima* comb your hair. *Ezeh hamuda*! *Ezeh yalda matuka*! What a darling! What a sweet girl! Where's *abba*? *Oy va voy*, talking philosophy, always talking philosophy."

"*Oy va voy*," Hanania croons, "*oy va voy*."

Shlomo is standing in the aisle near the back of the bus, waving his hands and hollering at a seated Hassid. Shlomo apparently talks philosophy as energetically as he prays; without Ilana's interpretation, Elisheva would have thought he was telling the

98

Hassid to go to hell. But no, Ilana is right: the Hassid yells back, and Shlomo jerks his watch off his wrist to make a point, dangling it in front of the Hassid's face as he vociferates, and then the two men laugh and shake hands.

The bus passes some brand-new housing developments and lurches into the station.

"Twenty minutes," shouts the busdriver. "*Yallah!* Get going!"

The passengers race for the exits, pushing and elbowing exactly as they did in Jerusalem to enter the bus. Elisheva has learned to push when necessary, and it is always necessary to push in order to get onto a bus. Getting off the bus in a station, however, is another matter; she would rather have eighteen minutes instead of twenty for lunch than push her way through this crowd.

After the bus is empty, she uses her sleeping bag to reserve her seat, and climbs down to the pavement. The station smells like Friday: extra exhaust fumes, extra food, extra sweat. She walks to a vendor's cart and gulps down a glass of fresh grapefruit juice, then one of orange juice. She finds a young Arab woman sitting in a corner, surrounded by paper bags, and buys from her a sack each of pumpkin seeds and sweet golden raisins, for the trip to Elat.

Once the bus is moving again, almost all the passengers fall asleep. Ilana leaves a sleeping Ḥanania in the arms of a sleeping Shlomo, scoots across the aisle, lifts Dina into the seat she just vacated, and sits down beside Elisheva.

"Don't worry," she says confidentially, patting Elisheva's arm. "I wasn't married at your age either. You will find the right man. I was 28 when I met Shlomo. He is a good husband, thank God, and he gave me these two darling children."

"But Dina said you have four children."

"Yes." Ilana frowns. "Yes and no. Yossi is Shlomo's son. Shlomo's first wife died. Oh, you will like Yossi! He is a fine boy, a soldier six months now. We are going to Elat because of him. He is stationed in the Sinai, and he will meet us for his *shabbat* leave."

"And Ephraim, he is also from Shlomo's first marriage?"

Ilana looks startled. "How do you know his name? Oh, yes, Dina told you. Isn't she a friendly child?" She gazes fondly at her daughter. "And so intelligent. Ephraim is another story. He was not meant for this country. He was always sensitive, nervous." Her eyes are wet.

"He passed away?" Elisheva says quietly.

"Not exactly." Ilana takes a clean white handkerchief from her purse and dabs at her eyes. "He is in an institution for special children. He was always too sensitive, but when there was the fighting—you know, the Six-Day War—he went over the edge. All the noise, the confusion, the shooting, the wounded people everywhere! He couldn't stand it. He has never been right since then." She shakes her head. "*Kakha zeh b'aretz, ha-ḥaim kashim.*" This is Yardena's expression, the expression of everyone here when discussing casualties: "That's the way it is in 'the land.' Life is hard."

Ilana wipes her eyes again. "*Masbik.* At least, thank God, I have my sweet healthy children, and a good husband. And I know it's all part of God's will, it's all for a reason. Don't you believe this too?"

"I don't know," Elisheva says. "I don't think that way. I don't really believe in things like God's will and God's plan, but I wouldn't say I exactly believe these things don't exist."

"So, you're not religious?" Ilana looks disappointed.

"Yes, I'm religious," Elisheva protests. "I keep kosher, I keep *shabbat*, I study Torah, I try to be good to people. I just don't know what I think about God."

"Oh, that's all right! Shlomo will talk to you, he understands these matters better than I do. Shlomo says it's more important to act right than to believe right."

"I think so too," says Elisheva, "but I don't think there's only one way to believe right."

"Shlomo will talk to you," says Ilana with a firm nod. "You know, I was not religious until I married him. My parents are socialists, kibbutzniks. So, at first I didn't believe, I just kept a kosher home for my husband, but you will see, after a while you believe." She pats Elisheva's arm again. "You and I, we are very much alike. I can tell."

"*Ken*? Yes?" Elisheva scrutinizes Ilana's tight features, her perfectly neat pink dress and matching kerchief. She doesn't feel as though she and Ilana are much alike, but maybe they are. Maybe she will be a lot more like Ilana in ten years.

"*Att betula?*" Ilana says, raising her eyebrows. "Are you a virgin?"

"No." Elisheva blushes. No one has asked her this question since *ulpan.*

100

Ilana appears delighted. "See, I told you! We are just alike. I was not a virgin when I married Shlomo, either! Do you have a boyfriend now?"

"No."

"Don't worry, you will find a boyfriend, you will find a husband. . . . Ah, it's so hot! The heat makes me sleepy. I will sleep now." Ilana trades places with a limp Dina again, and falls asleep on Shlomo's shoulder.

It is very hot indeed, but Elisheva feels quite alert. She has always feared the desert, and for the most part she has avoided it, spending her vacations instead in the green hills of the Galilee or at the Mediterranean coast. She knows of people who got lost or stranded in the desert, and who survived through ingenuity, by sucking the moisture out of crayons or burning a tire to make black smoke signals. Her own ingenuity has never been tested, but she senses that it may be inadequate, that she might crumple under pressure, that she might be one of those who have no matches to make the tire burn, no plastic sheet in which to catch dew at night; that she might be the one who dies of exposure and whose body is eaten by the five survivors, who then have enough strength to reach civilization.

She shudders. What is the matter with her? A moment ago she was talking with Ilana, feeling just fine, answering question after question, hearing the history of the family sleeping to her left. They are the survivors, she thinks. They know how to go on. They had to sacrifice Ephraim, the one who was too sensitive, who couldn't bear up to the difficulty of life in "the land." Now they can go on, the strong ones.

Elisheva has never lived through a war, but in her imagination, wars take place in deserts: fierce battles under the blazing sun, with all but the strongest and bravest perishing, to be buried under the shifting sand.

My God, she thinks, I sound like a Nazi, with all this crap about the bravest and strongest. This has nothing to do with real survival or real deserts or real wars. This battle is taking place only in my head.

She forces herself to look out the window again, at the real desert. It is not the desert of her imagination, flat sands stretching forever. There are hills, gorges, wadis. The hills are built up, layer on layer of rock, with strata of gray, brown, orange, yellow. Some of the mountains are perfectly flat on top, as though the tablets of the Law once descended and imprinted themselves on the landscape, squashing each hilltop flat as a commandment.

Of course, of course. This is the *midbar*, the wilderness where the children of Israel wandered, where *dor ha-midbar*, the generation of the desert, died without ever seeing the Holy Land. They traveled through these same rocky hills, they felt the rain that created these gorges, they sat under the thorny acacias of these same wadis.

"Beep. Beep. Beep." She jumps, along with all the other startled passengers. The bus driver has turned on *Kol Yisrael*, "the voice of Israel," for the hourly news broadcast. Everyone listens in silence until the newscaster signs off by wishing them all *shalom rav*, great peace.

"*Barukh ha-shem*," Ilana murmurs. "No casualties today. Yossi is all right."

"*Ḥaverim*," says the bus driver over the P.A. system. "We are reaching Mitzpeh Ramon. Prepare to drink like camels."

The juice bar where Elisheva drinks like a camel is located on the rim of a gigantic crater. The long, flat basin below is a jigsaw puzzle of red clay and black basalt; down the center runs a thin line of bushes, where the water flows for a few hours each year. The walls of the crater rise in multicolored layers, as far as she can see in every direction.

"Look." Shlomo holds Dina up to the window and points to the opposite edge of the crater. "We are up higher, over there is down lower. *Att yoda'at lama*? Do you know why?" Dina shakes her head. Shlomo puts her down, and speaks very slowly and dramatically. "Many, many years ago, even before *abba* and *ima* were born, the land broke open right here." He makes a violent gesture, like Moses shattering the tablets. Dina's eyes widen. "That place over there and this place here were very close together, as close as this." He holds his hands together. "Then, *oopa*! The land broke open, and this part rose up, and that part sank down."

"*Ima*!" Dina screams, running to her mother and clutching Ilana's legs. "I want to go home! I don't want the land to break!"

"*Mah pit'om*? *Mah yesh*, *motek*? What's this all of a sudden? What's the matter, sweetheart?" Ilana kneels to smooth Dina's hair. "Don't be frightened, darling. *Abba* was just making up a story. The land won't break, *ima* promises you."

"*Abba* was not making up a story," Shlomo says peevishly.

"That was a geology lesson. This is science, not grandmother stories. She is old enough to learn science! In the times of the Talmud she would already be engaged for marriage."

His hat has fallen on the floor again. When he stoops to retrieve it, he straightens up suddenly, his face very red. *"Ezeh ganav!* The Hassid stole my watch! Ilana, my watch is missing! *Ach, kulam ganavim!* They're all thieves, the Hassidim."

"Excuse me," Elisheva says. "Didn't you put the watch in your pocket?"

"Ach, you are a genius!" He hugs her spontaneously. "Such a good girl, so practical, just like Ilana. Here, I will buy you another glass of juice. Ilana, she found my watch, this Elisheva. You are right, she is *b'seder gamur."* He turns back to Elisheva. "My wife and I, we have decided we like you," he says in the tone of an official proclamation.

"Thank you," says Elisheva, somewhat stunned by this outburst. No wonder Shlomo frightens Dina! And no wonder Ilana warned Elisheva about him. But he is charming in an odd way; she understands why Ilana would have chosen to marry this erratic, homely professor instead of one of the stolid, boring, handsome kibbutzniks she grew up with.

"Yallah!" cries the busdriver. "Next stop Elat."

The road crosses through the crater, and then the terrain flattens into a monotonous plateau covered with chalk. Elisheva soon dozes off. When she awakens, Shlomo is seated beside her, smoking a cigarette and writing on a clipboard, and Ilana and the two children are sleeping across the aisle. The plateau is gone; all around are hills and rock formations in increasingly vivid shades of pink, red, purple.

"Ezeh yofi!" Elisheva exclaims. "What beauty! It's just like Dante."

"You are a student?" Shlomo asks.

"No, I was, but I quit and got a job."

"Good!" He caps his pen. "That's what I should have done. I should have gotten a *useful* job, as a porter or a stonecutter. Why are you laughing?"

"Please don't be offended," she says. "I just pictured you trying to cut stones, with your hat falling off all the time."

Shlomo cackles wildly. "You are right. I have no talent for anything but philosophy. Good! You have a sense of humor. Do you want to join us for *shabbat*?"

"It is kind of you to ask. No, thank you, I need some time

103

alone. I have spent every *shabbat* for months with a group of friends."

"Very good," he says. "You are honest. You say what you think. You are just like us. You will get along well in Israel."

Good Lord, Elisheva thinks, he and Ilana have been rehearsing from the same script. Does this happen to all married people?

He adopts his formal tone again. "My wife tells me that you suffer from a confusion of the spirit. She wants me to help you." He takes a wrinkled handkerchief from the same pocket that earlier hid his watch, and he wipes a great deal of perspiration from his face. He seems so nervous, so ill-at-ease with his new responsibility for Elisheva's spiritual welfare, that she wants to make him feel better.

"Please do not worry," she says. "I already have a psychiatrist. And all I said to Ilana was that I'm not sure I believe in God."

"*Ach*, my wife," he says, looking considerably relieved. "She is a wonderful woman, but she cannot tell a story correctly. I am a German Jew, a *yekke*. I have a logical mind, and I never misquote anyone!" He pounds a fist on the armrest. "I am a professor, not a psychiatrist. So, I will now lecture, and you will listen. For fifteen years I have been teaching at the university. I have seen many students come and go. Also, I have observed the behavior of my own family and of other people. Do not tell my wife I said this, but listen and remember: A lack of faith is the sign of intelligence. Many of these Orthodox Jews, they are simple people; they want someone to tell them what to do and what to think. My brothers are like that. All they need in life is to preserve tradition. Every year during the Days of Awe, I watch them. They fast and pray, and then they go about their business once more. They are happy, good-natured, uncomplicated. My father was not like that, and neither am I, and neither are you. We are intellectuals!" He jumps up and down in his seat. "We think, we reason, we wonder. Of course we are not sure about anything! We see the different sides of the issues. So, every year before Rosh Hashana, I begin to suffer. I question my beliefs, I question my worthiness, I question everything." He mops his forehead vigorously. "People like us have a more difficult life than the others, but it is a better life!" He nods firmly at Elisheva and waits for her response.

"I am not sure I'm such a great intellectual," she says. "There are many things that make me suffer and cause me confusion, but until now belief in God has not been one of them. May I be honest, since you have praised my honesty? You say I am like you, and Ilana says I am like her. This makes me think I have not made myself understood to either of you. The truth is, the idea of God does not interest me. When I read or hear discussions about God, they seem too impersonal, too . . . *ekh omrim?* . . . 'abstract.' These discussions are far away from any concerns I have ever had. I think the minds of the people who make these discussions must be very different from my mind. Then I worry: maybe I am strange or stupid or too . . . *ekh omrim?* . . . 'subjective.' So, I am not bothered personally by lack of interest in God; I am only bothered socially, in comparing myself with others."

"Yes, I can understand this," Shlomo says, "although it is an unusual attitude, not one I have seen expounded in a philosophy journal. . . . But tell me, then, what things do cause you confusion?"

"*Ha-min*," Elisheva says, using the one Hebrew word for sexuality, sexual activity, and gender.

"*Ha-min?*" Shlomo laughs his wacky laugh. "*Betah*, of course, everyone is confused by *ha-min*, but this is not philosophy!"

"I think it is," she insists. "What makes men the way they are, and what makes women the way we are? This is a difficult and complicated issue, *lo nakhon?*"

"*Ken, nakhon*. There you are right. After many years of marriage and philosophy, I still could not begin to answer your question. Perhaps your psychiatrist is better skilled in this area."

"Perhaps. Don't you want to know what else causes me confusion? There is war, violence, cruelty, destiny, survival . . ."

"Halt! No more! This is already enough to think about for a lifetime. Have mercy on a poor philosopher!" Shlomo places his hand over his heart, as though he is about to collapse. Then he sits up straight and raises an index finger in a Socratic gesture. "No, I will be a masochist. I will ask you one more question. If you don't believe in God, what *do* you believe in?"

"Nature," Elisheva responds without pausing to think. "The seasons. The earth. The wisdom of the body. Land and water. History. Compassion." She stops, amazed to hear herself telling this strange man the truth. In English she would not have been so blunt and direct; she would have slithered away from Shlomo's probing questions. But she lacks vocabulary in Hebrew, and she lacks experience with politeness in this country; she has no choice but to blurt out the bare, direct truth.

"*Ach!*" Shlomo claps a hand onto his forehead, once more knocking off his hat. "A pantheist! All this talk, and she is nothing but a pantheist!" He looks utterly dismayed.

"*Rega, rega,*" Elisheva says. "Just a minute. Was Rav Kook a pantheist? I don't think my beliefs are so different from his. 'Our flesh is as sacred as our spirit.' Didn't he say that? Didn't he urge all Jews to have faith in Nature?"

"Yes, of course. But Rav Kook did not mean what you mean." Shlomo's manner is suddenly more respectful and patient; thank God Miriam gave her that book of essays to read at the kibbutz; thank God Shlomo helped her get to the kibbutz, so she could meet Miriam there; why is she thanking God when she just said she doesn't believe in God?

Shlomo offers Elisheva a cigarette. When she refuses, he lights one for himself. "You don't smoke? Good. Also good that you have read some of Rav Kook's writings. This is a start. But the sentence you quote must be taken in context. In the same book, Rav Kook says, 'Jewish secular nationalism is a form of self-delusion: the spirit of Israel is so closely linked to the spirit of God that a Jewish nationalist, no matter how secularist his intention may be, must, despite himself, affirm the divine. An individual can sever the tie that binds him to life eternal, but the House of Israel as a whole cannot. All of its most cherished national possessions—its land, language, history, and customs—are vessels of the spirit of the Lord.' "

"But you told me that a lack of faith is a sign of intelligence."

"*Ach!*" Shlomo pounds the armrest once more. "You even quote *me* out of context! This will not do. I was speaking of the questioning mind and the suffering that grows from an inability to accept simple answers. I was not speaking of a simple-minded rejection of God, or even worse, your American beatnik pantheism. Even to the questioning mind, faith in God must be the goal, and obedience to God's commandments is the highest good. You may reject God if you wish,"—his volume grows in a steady crescendo—"but do not use the words of Rav Kook and Professor Cohen to justify yourself! This is like the Christians who take what they like from Buber and forget that he was a Jew. Do not forget that Kook was a holy man who was waiting for the Messiah and preparing himself for the office of priest in a rebuilt Temple! Do not forget that pantheism is rejection of the one true God!"

Ilana, roused by her husband's shouting, leans across the aisle and grasps his arm. "Shlomo, *mah yesh l'kha?*" she scolds. "What's the matter with you? On a hot bus you must holler philosophy at this girl? Give her a rest."

"*B'seder, b'seder.*" Shlomo sounds grumpy. "First you tell me to talk to her, then you tell me to leave her alone." He jumps across the aisle and hugs his wife, whispering something to her, and they both laugh. Dina wakes up and laughs too.

Shlomo turns to Elisheva. "When we get back to Jerusalem, I will send you some things to read about pantheism. You are an intelligent girl; you will soon see that pantheism is no philosophy to have. Now I must make *minha.*"

He stands abruptly and begins to sway and chant in the aisle. Ilana, radiating indulgence for her eccentric husband, leans back in her seat again and closes her eyes.

––––––

In her room in a youth hostel circled by date palms, at the edge of the desert and the lip of the sea, on the afternoon of *Shabbat Parah*, the Sabbath of the Cow, Elisheva reads about Lilit. According to rabbinic tradition, Lilit was Adam's unruly first wife. She had wings and long, loose hair. When she refused to lie beneath her husband, he tried to force her. Instantly, she rose into the air and flew to Elat, where she swam in the Red Sea and copulated with other demiurges. Three angels were dispatched to persuade her to return to Adam.

"How can I be a wife again," she answered them, "now that I have been to the Red Sea?"

Elisheva likes Lilit, although the rabbis have interpreted her willfulness as evil, and many folk practices have evolved over the years to resist her influence. Thousands of lying-in beds and babies' cradles have been decorated with charms against Lilit, who supposedly delights in killing infants. Thousands of parents have slapped a child who smiled in its sleep, because this is a sign that Lilit is playing with the child, and she must be frightened off. Thousands of men have awakened to find their semen on the sheets, and they have trembled to know that Lilit seduced them and straddled them invisibly, while they slept. For this reason a man is to avoid sleeping alone in a house. Even Milton, who considers himself enlightened, keeps a charm against Lilit on the wall over his bed.

Elisheva finds this fear of a disobedient woman excessive, confusing, upsetting. What is so terrible about simple disobedience, and what is so wonderful about simple obedience? It makes no sense to her, but what does she know? She is nothing but a pantheist.

Maybe Shlomo is right: pantheism is no philosophy to have. Certainly it is no philosophy for an observant Jew to have. She tries to remember the exact list of beliefs she summoned for Shlomo yesterday. Do all of them fit under pantheism? No, a belief in history and a belief in compassion don't really seem pantheistic.

She feels angry with Shlomo. Why did he encourage her to speak, to put her most fundamental beliefs into words for the first time in her life, only so that he could dismiss her thoughts immediately with an inaccurate name? He gave her something and then took it away before she could even begin to enjoy it.

Whatever the real name for her philosophy, though, it is not an adequate system. It doesn't help her to answer any of her questions about obedience, about Lilit, about this morning's Torah portion, about the horror that filled her body at the sight of family after family strolling in the boulevard, all dressed up, husband wife children, husband wife children, an endless string of families that could trip her or strangle her, and the hot sun beating down on her unprotected head until she could die of thirst there on the main street of Elat, surrounded by families. It was for escape from this unbearably oppressive sensation that she returned to the hostel, drank some juice, and began to read about Lilit.

She gets up from the straight-backed metal chair and starts to pace her small room. She feels restless, trapped, hemmed in. The hem of her skirt is unraveling, and she will have to wait until nightfall to mend it. She watches the loose thread drag on the floor with her pacing. What an annoyance, not to be permitted even to snip off the string until after *shabbat*.

"Do it now," says a mischievous voice in her head. "Who will ever know?"

Who indeed? She has removed the skirt and is foraging in her bag for scissors and a needle when she stops short, horrified by her eagerness to desecrate *shabbat* after a two-year perfect record. What the hell is the matter with her? She sinks back onto the bed. During the week she's never in a hurry to do mending. Why now can't she wait a few hours?

"Have it your way," says the mischievous voice. "Who cares if your skirt falls apart? A neat hem only ties you in. Let it all out, let it fly!"

It is the voice of Lilit. Elisheva pictures Lilit flying out of the book, up into the air, out the window, over the Red Sea. Her hair trails behind her, and in her left hand she holds the thread of Elisheva's skirt. The skirt unweaves; a long, long multicolored thread winds out over the sea, floating loose until it tangles upon itself and makes a design as intricate as pubic hair.

Elisheva twiddles the rough curlicues of her own crotch. She fondles the hairs gently, not to excite but to smooth. This is the way she has comforted herself, soothed herself to sleep, since she was a small child. She has never masturbated to orgasm. Dr. Feinstein doesn't seem to believe this, but it is true. "I need to know that I am safe with my own hands," she explains to him.

But today the spirit of Lilit is with her, and she is not safe with her own hands. As she plays with the hairs, the sensitive folds of skin underneath begin to jump and throb, and a warm liquid rises in her. Alarmed, she withdraws her hand and quiets her breathing. "Out, Lilit." Lying on her back, perfectly still, she mutters the ancient formula. *"Hutz Lilit. Hutz Lilit."*

The formula does not chase Lilit away; instead, the playful goddess responds to the sound of her name by coming closer. She stands at the foot of Elisheva's bed and laughs. She is young and naked, and her long hair blows all around her face. *"Hutz Lilit. Hutz Lilit."* Now Lilit changes into Giveret Feinstein, with her stocky body, short gray hair, bulldog face. The face softens and draws near, until Elisheva can see the tenderness concealed by Mrs. Feinstein's tough demeanor. "Choose me," Mrs. Feinstein whispers, "choose me."

Hutz Lilit. Choose me. Hutz Lilit. Choose me. Hutz choose Lilit me. Choose Lilit me hutz. Hutz me Lilit choose. Choose choose choose choose

———

The voice of Lilit enters Elisheva's dream. Sweet and full, the voice sings a Yemenite folk melody, the one Elisheva heard on a record and has tried to remember ever since. The words are from the Song of Songs:

Libavtini ahoti kala
Libavtini b'ahad me'eynayikh
B'ahad anak mitzavronayikh.

You have ravished my heart,
my sister my bride.
You have ravished my heart with one of your eyes,
with one bead of your necklace.

Mah-yafoo dodayikh aḥoti kala
Mah-tovoo dodayikh miyayin
V'reyaḥ shmanayikh mikol bsamim.

How beautiful is your love,
my sister my bride.
How much better than wine is your love,
and the smell of your oils than all the spices.

Nofet titopnah siftotayikh kala
Dvash v'ḥalav taḥat l'shonayikh
v'reyaḥ salmotayikh k'reyaḥ l'vanon.

Your lips drop honey, my bride,
honey and milk are under your tongue,
and the smell of your garments
is like the smell of Lebanon.

Gan na'ool aḥoti kala,
gal na'ool ma'ayan ḥatoom.

A walled garden is my sister my bride,
a closed spring, a sealed fountain.

Shlaḥayikh pardess rimonim pree m'gadim,
k'farim im nradim.
Nerd v-karkom kaneh v'kinamon
im kol etzeh l'vonah,
mor v'ahalot im kol rasheh bsamim.

Your shoots are a pomegranate orchard with precious fruits,
henna with spikenard plants.
Spikenard and saffron, calamus and cinnamon,
with all trees of incense,
myrrh and aloes, with all the chief spices.

Ma'ayan ganim b'er mayim ḥayim
v'nozlim min l'vanon.

You are a fountain of gardens,
a well of living waters,
and streams flowing from Lebanon.

Under the voice is a drumbeat, a complex, syncopated rhythm, enchanting the feet, which move to dance even in sleep. The melody is ornamented with trills and leaps of the voice, decorated too by the Middle Eastern vowels of the lyric, the Sephardic pronunciation which emphasizes the sounds of emotion: *ayin* and *ḥet*. *Ayin* is a sob of a vowel, the vowel of the soul; *ḥet* is the wind of Creation, a focusing of the breath through a narrow throat, strong and tight, the breath of the spirit.

This is the voice of Lilit, the first woman. This is the song with which the world was born. In the beginning was this melody.

Lilit sings it through from start to finish. Lilit teaches the song to Elisheva, plants it in Elisheva's mind so firmly that it can never be forgotten. Like the sound of her mother's cello, Elisheva will carry this song and its rhythm through her entire life.

————

When Elisheva awakens, it is dark outside. She fumbles about for the *havdalah* set: the spice box, the braided candle, the wine goblet. She quickly recites the blessings that separate *shabbat* from the six days of the week, then turns on the overhead light. She hums the melody Lilit taught her. Yes, she remembers it, all of it. Something like this once happened to someone she knows. Who? Oh yes, her brother Neil: when he began to play with Crazy Fingers, his band, somebody famous—Stéphane Grapelli, was it?—came to him in a dream and taught him a difficult fiddle part. Elisheva found that remarkable when Neil described it. Why doesn't the same thing seem remarkable when it happens to her? These visitations must run in the family, or maybe Neil gave her the idea, so he gets the credit.

She finds a needle, mends her skirt, snaps the thread over one finger, and puts the skirt back on. Then she sits at the small table in the corner and begins to doodle on a letter tablet. She makes a staff and quickly transcribes the Yemenite melody. Then she takes a new sheet of paper and draws the face of Lilit, that of Giveret Feinstein, that of Grandmother Lowenthal. "Shame on you," she writes, and she repeats the three words over and over, maybe a hundred times, like an elementary school punishment. Shame on you, shame on you, shame on you.

A knock at the door makes her jump. Lilit? No, a young man in uniform. He is so beautiful—tanned, well-formed, golden-haired—that she gulps. He stands awkwardly, holding an overnight case and looking at her.

"I am Yosef Cohen," he says in very slow English. "My father told me about you, and I thought maybe you would like to go for a swim."

Who is Yosef Cohen? Who is his father, to have told him about Elisheva? She knows no one in Elat. Then she connects. "Ah . . . Yossi!" She switches to Hebrew. "How nice to meet you. Please come in."

As soon as he sees that she knows who he is and that she can speak Hebrew, he relaxes. "That's my father," he says, sitting down at the table. "He tells me everything about you, even that you are a pantheist. He tells me you are intelligent and pretty, but he doesn't tell me you can speak Hebrew."

Elisheva laughs. "Soon everyone in Israel will know I am a pantheist, and I'm not even sure it's true."

"*Lo ḥashuv*," he says, "not important. At least it is true that you are pretty, and my father is always right about intelligence."

She blushes. He is unusually smooth-talking for an Orthodox boy, and especially for the son of Shlomo. His mother must have been quite something.

"Would you like a glass of juice, a piece of cake? I don't have much else here, but . . . "

"No, no, thank you. Ilana has filled my stomach until I can hardly move. I have only a few hours before I must get my ride back. Do you want to go to the beach? The water should be nice and warm tonight."

"*Tov, b'seder.*" Elisheva nods. "Please go into the hall while I put on my bathing suit."

"No, come just like this, this is fine. I don't even have a bathing suit with me. We will be okay; it is dark out, we won't be able to see each other."

His tone is so matter-of-fact that she is hardly shocked. She takes a towel and follows him down the corridor. The air outside is balmy, soft. Her limbs loosen; how tense they have been, ever since this morning's Torah reading. How tense she has been, except in the dream of song.

"Yossi," she says, "something has been troubling me about today's Torah portion. Perhaps you can help me to understand better?"

"*B'vakesha.*" He makes a gallant half-bow. "Please go on."

"It's the part about the golden calf, when Moses and Joshua return from the mountain, after Moses has received the first tablets of stone. They hear the singing of the people around the calf, and at first Joshua thinks it is the noise of war. Then he says no, it is not the sound of victory or of defeat, it is singing and dancing. And this is why Moses gets so angry that he breaks the tablets, *lo nakhon*?"

"Betaḥ," says Yossi. "Of course this makes him angry, it is idolatry."

"Yes, yes," Elisheva says impatiently. "I know it is idolatry. That is not my question. What bothers me is that Joshua and Moses consider war better than singing and dancing. What kind of ethic is this, what kind of religion, if it is okay for Moses to order the massacre of three thousand men as punishment for singing and dancing?"

"This is a good religion," Yossi says. "War is not praised in our religion, but war is considered preferable to idolatry."

"But that doesn't seem right," Elisheva persists. "I would rather see people dancing around a calf than going to war."

Yossi thinks for a moment. "This is probably because you are a woman and an American . . . and a pantheist, too. The lesson of the Bible is clear: loyalty to the one God is more important even than life itself."

"Good Lord, you sound just like your father. Did he coach you?"

"Of course not. Maybe sometimes he and I happen to agree. In that case you can know he is right. *Yaḥabeebee!* You are too serious! Look, we are on the beach."

Elisheva looks around and relaxes again. They have almost reached the edge of the water, and contrary to what Yossi has said, she can see very well by the light of the moon. The waves are silver, slow and gentle, and the sand is cool on her feet.

"Ezeh yofi," she exclaims. "Let's go swimming right now."

"That's better," Yossi says, laughing. "I see that you are a girl who enjoys life."

"And you are a boy who is a terrible flirt. You look this way, and I'll look that way, and we'll undress. I bet I can be in the water before you!"

She tears off her clothes and runs into the water. She can hear Yossi splashing nearby.

"Tie!" he yells. "Very good, American girl. See, wasn't I right? The water is beautiful. Here, come closer. Have you ever been to a *mikva?*"

"Mah pit'om? I have never been married."

"Az mah? Married or not, you are now in a *mikva.* The sea is a *mikva,* you know. Look, try, immerse yourself once."

She ducks under the water and comes out sputtering.

"Now say the *brakha* and immerse yourself again."

She praises God who has commanded immersion, and then she dips under the water again.

"*Lo kasher*," says Yossi. "Not kosher. Your hair was floating on top. You have to be completely under water. Every bit of you must be touched by living water. Here, watch me." He holds his arms out in front of him, his fingers spread. His lips are apart, his eyes slightly open. "See, now the water can touch me everywhere. Come, we'll do it together."

She stretches her arms and fingers, spreads her toes, parts her lips. She and Yossi plunge deep into the water and emerge purified. Then they swim farther out to sea; not so far as to take them into Jordanian waters, but far enough. They float on their backs and try to find patterns in the blanket of stars overhead, and they tread water and argue about the precise phase of the moon, which is no longer full.

"I know I am right," she says, "because my menstrual period always comes with the new moon."

"And I know I am right," he says, "because my name is Yosef, and Yosef the son of Jacob dreamed that the sun and the moon and the eleven stars bowed down to him."

"Big deal," she says in English, for lack of an equivalent expression in Hebrew. "The experience of my body is better evidence than the dreams of your namesake."

"Says who? Where is it written?"

"It isn't written. It's just true. *Oy va voy*. I don't want to talk with you anymore. We don't agree about anything."

"So don't talk. There I agree."

He disappears under the water, and in a few seconds he is tickling her feet, then sliding up her legs, around her hips, her waist, shoulder blades, breasts, and back down to the soft inner thigh. How can he be touching so many places at once, is that his tongue his lips his hand his toes, how can he be touching her everywhere as the living water touches her and so smoothly, how can he and how can her skin be so sensitive to his touch his kisses how can her body enjoy him so much how can she?

She is washed in pleasure, gasping at the moon, which whirls in the sky like an ivory pinwheel. He comes up for air, and they smile, they slide around each other, they open and swim into one another as sweetly as if there were no friction or violence in the world, as if all resistance of matter vanished, as if their bodies were liquefied, as if the order of creation were reversed, and the fluid sky and the liquid sea were reunited as one element, indistinguishable from the stream of their bodies.

They swim back to shore slowly. She is full of wonder. She has never been touched the way he touched her. This is the way she imagines a woman would touch her, a woman or Daniel.

They sit on the sand, draped in towels. "When I was a little boy," Yossi says, "my father told me that men and women are different from animals because we make love face-to-face. Do you think it's true?"

"I don't know. Maybe. No, I don't think so. You made love to me many ways, not just face-to-face. That's what was so special."

He looks puzzled. Then he shakes his head. "No, no, that's not what I mean. *Betah*, I did all that." He waves his hands in the air. "Women like that, but that isn't the real lovemaking. The last part was the making love, don't you even know that? You're a sophisticated American girl, don't you even know what making love is?"

"And you sound like a stupid yeshiva boy." How disappointing. He thinks the same way as Milton, as all of them. She liked him better in the water. "Where'd you learn to touch a woman so well, a yeshiva boy like you? You know, no man has ever touched me with such grace and gentleness . . . "

"Grace! Gentleness! What are you saying? A man is not graceful. A *gever* is not gentle. I am a soldier of Israel! I am not soft when I make love to a woman. My penis was hard, surely you could feel that? What's the matter with you? Crazy American!" He pulls his uniform furiously over his body.

"Yossi, wait! I wasn't insulting you. Maybe I didn't use the right words in Hebrew. You don't understand. I *liked* the way you made love to me."

"I understand enough. I have to get back to my unit. I will call you in Jerusalem."

"No you won't," she says.

He doesn't call, but Ilana does, to invite Elisheva to the Passover seder. She accepts, even though she knows Yossi will be there and they will be uncomfortable together. She is still trying to make sense of what happened. She can't understand why anyone would want not to be gentle.

"It's Israeli society," says Dr. Feinstein.

"Fuck Israeli society," says Elisheva.

"That's not so gentle."

"Fuck you."

"Good!" says Dr. Feinstein, writing it all down.

———

115

The red heifer, the golden calf. The message: burn the cow, do not worship her.

What good is any of this?

All of it, the version of men.

Cows are neither red nor gold. They are black, white, brown, mottled as the herd of Jacob and Rachel. They are large and beautiful.

The cow the cow and the golden calf.

The blood and the milk. Our fluids, which are holy, set apart, separated. *Kadosh*.

Our power to nourish from our bodies, to make life from liquid, to make milk from blood. Our breasts of nourishment and pleasure. Even if one is lost, there is always the other.

In celebration we hold out our breasts: life is here, and nourishment. Drink.

In mourning we beat our breasts: life has failed, our spirit has been defeated.

The horns of the wild cow the ewe Leah and Rachel the horns of the altar Sarah the horns of the moon Rivka the hive of the bee Devorah the bitter sea Miriam the eyes of the judge Dina the weak eyes of Leah the wild squall of the infant where his mother Hagar placed him in the fragrant desert of the beloved Yokheved my pleasure Naomi the daughter of vows Batsheva the vow of god Elisheva god's contentment the contentment of the beasts the breasts shadayim shadim the demons the spirits of wind and storm lilitu Lilit Lilit.

The cow the cow Parah the fruitful the breasts the hooves the arms the flying hair Tziporah the holy milk the holy blood the holy sweat the honey of the hive Devorah.

Eretz zvat ḥalav u-dvash: the land pours milk and honey this food of our bodies our breasts our wings and spirits Lilit.

As it is written:

> The wildcats will meet the jackals
> and the wild goats will call to their neighbors,
> for Lilit will repose there
> and find herself a place of rest.

> None of the nobles of the land will be called to power
> and all its princes will be nothing.

> The wilderness and the arid land will exult,
> and the desert will rejoice, and blossom like a rose.
> For in the wilderness waters will break forth
> and streams in the desert.

9

S pring came to Jerusalem while Elisheva was in the desert. A pair of doves have made their nest in the fluted rain-spout over her door, and the seven-year plant is about to bloom. The green skin on each bud is now pale and taut; through the thin membrane Elisheva can see a coral color.

Each day her belly seems rounder, and her body wants to move more slowly. Perhaps she is pregnant. She stands on a chair to see her torso in the mirror. Yes, she looks pregnant. She is not upset. This time, she thinks, I would have the baby. It would be okay; I could manage. I would not fly to Sweden. I would stay in Israel and have the baby, fathered by a soldier of Israel. Miriam would feel better then. My parents would have a fit, but they would come around. I would take up music again, and the baby would dance in my womb.

She hums all day, to entertain the embryo. She hums at the typewriter and at the stove, the melody she learned from Lilit, and all the other songs she has learned in Israel: the *shabbat* songs and the popular songs from the radio and the love songs in Arabic and the prayer chants from the synagogue across the street. When she walks outside, she hums the music she learned from her mother: the cello suites of Bach, the string sextets of Brahms, the concertos and symphonies and sonatas, every theme and every variation.

Music is what she has always loved, what she has forsaken in order to grow up, to separate from her mother, to leave the circle defined by the short radius of a leash, the circle the center of which was always music, the heavy wooden music stand and the music of the mother cello.

She has had to step outside the circle of music, but if she bears a child, then she can give music to the child. Not for herself but for the child. That would be okay. She could manage. The child would thrive, and she would thrive with it.

What if she is not pregnant? If she is not pregnant, she will find someone to marry. A good, kind man, who would not ask too much of her, would give her a child, would treat the child well. Someone trustworthy. Someone who would never beat her or her child. Who? Daniel? But Daniel lied to her. Maybe he isn't trustworthy anymore. And he is gay. Why should she marry someone gay? He has hinted that he wants to marry her, that he wants to get married and have children and settle in Israel. Isn't that what she wants too? If he wants to marry her, that means he doesn't want to be gay anymore. And if she wants to marry him, then she doesn't have to worry anymore about her dreams of Lilit and Giveret Feinstein. Especially if she has a child. If she has a child, then she will be a normal woman. She won't have to worry anymore. She will be okay. The sooner the better. If she isn't pregnant, she will get married and have a baby, the sooner the better.

————

Ellen darling,

I wish you could see the springtime here. We had a harsh winter, but now it's all worthwhile. No more antifreeze, no more shoveling the driveway. The brooks are running, the ground is soft and wet, and the hills are green with feathery new grasses and leaves. Our fruit trees are blossoming—they smell so sweet! Come home this summer, please, dear. There will be plums and pears and cherries and berries galore, and of course those silly crab apples you and Neil used to throw at each other. Remember how shocked you were that time you tried to play baseball with them, and the fruit splatted all over your dress? And then you were afraid I'd be mad, so you ran the wash yourself before I got home from rehearsal, and you added too much Tide, and the washer overflowed and flooded the kitchen, and then I really *was* mad!

I don't know why I'm going on like this—probably boring you to tears. They say nostalgia is a sign of old age. (No wisecracks, please. I'm even more sensitive on this subject than I used to be.) I only wanted to tell you how glorious this weather is, and how it lifts my spirits in times of stress. All winter I curse your father for having dragged me to this drafty farmhouse, but then in the spring I think he was brilliant to see the possibilities of this place. Honestly, each morning some new flower is blooming, and all the new life somehow gives me hope.

Dear, it's very hard for me to imagine that you really are so far away, and that you do intend to stay there. I know Israel is our people's homeland, but it doesn't seem fair for a homeland to be so far away from home! Do come for a visit this summer, please.

Your father's asthma is always bad this time of year, as you know, from all the pollen in the air, and this year it seems worse than usual. He has to sleep sitting up, and even at that he's often up half the night wheezing and gasping. It doesn't frighten me as it used to, but it is terribly difficult to see him so uncomfortable and to be able to do so little to help him. He's wonderful—you know that as well as I—never complains, and he's so appreciative of every little attention.

Ellen sweetheart, I hope I haven't alarmed you about your father. It's a chronic condition, you know, and he has very few really serious attacks—I suppose we should be grateful for that.

Neil is fine—you do remember that he graduates in June, don't you? He's still in that silly rock band, and I'm still hoping he'll go back to serious music some day and stop wasting his talent. Maggie seems to be a good influence on him. Once he's gotten the results of his law school applications, maybe he and Maggie will decide it's time to get married and start a family. I just can't wait to be a grandma! And it would give your father quite a boost.

How is your job? your social life?

Do let us know when to expect a visit from you, so we can get Neil and Maggie to come—and so I can start counting the days.

All my love,
Mother

Before Elisheva has finished reading her mother's letter, she knows she will do as Clara asks and go home for a visit this summer. She has not seen her parents for two years. That's long enough. She is ready. And she can use the opportunity to see Daniel, too.

There is something worrisome about the letter, something that leads her to read it through again. Her father. Is his asthma as bad as her mother implies, or is Clara exaggerating because she misses Elisheva so much? Probably the latter, Elisheva decides. Not that Clara would do such a thing on purpose, but she might unconsciously use a few key phrases to arouse Elisheva's concern and get her back to Pennsylvania quickly.

Yes, definitely the latter. Otherwise Neil would have written after his last visit home, would have shared his concern about their father.

Elisheva is pleased to note her own equanimity. A few years ago, such a manipulation by her mother would have made her quite angry. Isn't this proof that she has achieved the separation she wanted, that she has finally grown up, that she is now ready to have a child of her own? And Clara is eager to be a grandma. If Elisheva is pregnant, she can remind her mother of that line.

Humming to her belly, Elisheva goes out to the *mirpesset* to take her wash down from the clothesline. Absently, she smiles and waves to the bereaved woman across the street. The woman doesn't even blink. Would she be happy if Elisheva had a baby? Of course she would. A new life in the world, on the street, in Israel. How could she not be happy?

Below the bereaved woman's balcony, Avraham the grocer waves and calls, "Elisheva! Elisheva!" He must have thought Elisheva was waving to him. Or perhaps there is a phone call for her. She goes to see what he wants.

"Elisheva, your neighbor is in trouble. Her husband asked me to tell you when you got home from work."

"Her?" Elisheva points up.

"Her? No, no, *miskena*, poor thing, she has no more or less trouble today than yesterday. Your neighbor Yardena. She is in the hospital. Ḥayim took her this morning. She is very sick, a high fever."

"Which hospital?"

"*Mah pit'om*, which hospital? Which hospital do you think? The free one, on Yaffo Street. Where do you think she would be, at Hadassah? People in this neighborhood have no money for Hadassah Hospital. When anyone from this neighborhood is in the hospital, you know which one. The free one. The one for poor people. The one for Sephardim. That's where you'll find Yardena."

For several days, while Yardena is being treated for contagious diseases, she can have no visitors except her husband and her mother. Ḥayim gives Elisheva a report each day: still a high fever, delirium. Yardena calls out for her sons: "Don't kill them, please don't kill them! I'll do anything you want, just don't kill my boys."

As if in response to Yardena's fears, Ḥayim cares for the boys

120

with unsuspected gentleness. Sometimes Elisheva sits with them for the evening while Ḥayim is at the hospital. "Be careful," he says as he leaves. "Don't let any harm come to them." Yardena will be pleased, Elisheva thinks, to hear what a good father her husband is. Yardena will be pleased.

Finally Yardena is transferred to a wing where Elisheva can visit her. On the way to the hospital, Elisheva stops at a bakery for a bag of sesame seed cookies, Yardena's favorite kind, as sweet and brown and healthy as she wants Yardena to become again.

The hospital is so crowded, Elisheva has trouble finding her, and the nurses are no help. "Look," they say, "just look. How should I know which is which?"

Everywhere, women in wards, on beds in the corridors, every-where, women moaning and turning their bodies, women in identical hospital gowns, everywhere, sick women.

She spots Yardena on one of the extra beds in the hallway. So pale and weak she is, so very pale is it really—

"Yardena? Is it you? Yardena?"

She stirs, yes, it's Yardena, the same beautiful face, but thin-ner, whiter, and the white hospital gown, the sleeves flutter like wingtips fanning Elisheva's face as she leans to kiss Yardena's hot forehead.

"Elisheva," Yardena says, and her desperate eyes, get me out of here, please, make me well and get me out of here. *Brukha ha-ba'a*. A blessing on your arrival. You see what the govern-ment has done to me?"

"The government? *Mah pit'om*, how the government? Yar-dena, what has caused this fever? Yardena, are you going to be all right? Yardena?"

"*Anee yoda'at*? If I get well in this place it's no thanks to anyone but me and *ha-kadosh barukh hoo*, the Holy One bless-ed be He. *Ken, ken*, I'll be fine. You know me, Elisheva. I'm a fighter, a *davkanikit*. I won't give up. What's in the bag? *Yaḥa-beebee*! *Sum-sum* cookies! *Yofi*! Now I will get well, one hun-dred percent. If you saw the food here, it would make you sick even if you were well when you came."

"Yardena, I'll bring meals to you. Ḥayim will tell me what you like. I'll make your favorite foods."

"Thank you, but my mother is already bringing me food, every day a nice surprise. I swear, I would be better off in her hands. She would care for me better than these strangers."

121

"Yardena, don't wear yourself out. Don't talk too much if it tires you."

"No, it does me good. I am lonely here. Everyone is sick, nobody talks except to complain. How are my boys? Are my boys all right? How are my boys?"

"They're fine. Ḥayim is talking excellent care of them. Really, you would be surprised how much he knows how to do."

"Ḥayim, bless him, he is a good husband. He must know why I am here, but he asks nothing and says nothing about it."

"About what? Why are you here?"

"Come closer, Elisheva. I will tell you but no one must hear."

Elisheva leans closer. Yardena whispers, "I went to the Bureau of Housing. I asked for aid to get a larger apartment. It isn't healthy to live the way we do, all in one room. The boys are too big now. All this I tell the man. He says, 'Have a third child and we will get you a bigger apartment.' I say, 'First I want the apartment, then I promise to have another child.' He says, 'No, the child first.' I say, 'You want me to have a third child, and then maybe you say no again, and I'm still in one room but with three children. No! How can I manage? Give me a bigger apartment first.' So, he says no, I say no, finally I say, '*Tov, b'seder*. I will get pregnant, I will bring you the proof from the doctor, but you must give me the apartment then or I will find an abortion, which is illegal and will be on your soul.' I don't tell him I am already pregnant. So, I went to the clinic and got a letter for proof. Then the man at the Housing Office says, 'This is too soon. I don't believe you are pregnant. You don't look pregnant. Come back at eight months.' I say, 'You think I'm crazy? At eight months I can't get an abortion!' So, it breaks my heart but I go to my mother and she gives me the address of somebody, and I get rid of the baby. This is when I start to feel sick, with this infection. The doctors say if I recover, I may not be able to have another child. Whether this is a blessing or a curse, I don't know. I wish only to get out of this place and go back to my family. Elisheva, am I feverish still?"

"Yes. You must rest."

"Elisheva, talk to the doctor. He tells me nothing. Everyone here, we're just ignorant *Sephardiot* to him. You are educated and American, he will talk to you. Find out why I must stay here. Ask him if I can go home."

"Of course, Yardena. I'll talk to him. Is there anything else I can do for you?"

"No, just talk to him. Dr. Shapira is his name."

"Yardena, why are all the Sephardic women put together? I thought medicine was socialized here."

"Ha! I should live so long. *Betah*, we get free care, in a place like this, in the hallways and the wards. The *Ashkenaziot* pay some extra money and go to Hadassah or other fancy places, the modern hospitals. *Kakha zeh b'olam*. That's the way it is."

Dr. Shapira says, "Why do you take an interest in this patient? She is no different from the rest. You are a social worker, or what?" He looks Elisheva up and down.

"I am her neighbor and friend. I see that she is not getting proper attention here—no one is. How can they, when it's so crowded? Is there some reason she must stay, or can she go home? Her mother and her husband and I will take good care of her."

"*Ken, betah*, the same good care that brought her here in the first place. No, no, absolutely not. She must stay in the hospital at least another week. She needs to rest and eat well, and she must get her medication on schedule. I know these women, I see how they live. Almost no meat in their diet, pregnant all the time, illiterate. How can I trust her to take a prescription she can't even read?"

"Yardena can read. Her husband taught her. And she gets plenty of protein. I myself eat no meat, and I am quite healthy." The doctor frowns, and Elisheva quickly adds, "But if Yardena needs extra meat in her diet, I will see that she gets it, and so will her family. Please, doctor, just give me instructions. I promise to carry them out exactly."

"What authority do you have over her? You aren't even a relative. I would not consider releasing such an ignorant woman without the permission of her husband."

"*Yofi*! Wonderful! Her husband will authorize her release immediately. I'll go get him now."

"Just a minute. Not so fast. I didn't say I would release her on her husband's say-so, only that I would not release her without. I am the doctor here. I make the decisions."

Elisheva takes a deep breath. This is not the time to lose her temper. Yardena is counting on her. "Doctor, please," she says. "I know you have Yardena's best interests in mind. But look how overworked you are. How much attention can you possibly give each patient? Not nearly enough, I am sure. This must be a great frustration for you. I see that you are a dedicated physician, and I am glad you are being so cautious. But please believe me, I will make absolutely sure that Yardena gets the proper care at home."

"Okay, *b'seder*." The doctor shrugs. "Take her home tomorrow. Only first I must have her husband's permission. I will write down everything to do. You are sure she will be able to rest at home, with her children there?"

"I am sure. Her mother will take the children for a while if necessary. Yardena will rest, if I have to tie her down."

The doctor laughs. "You are American, yes? A student?"

"No, a typist."

"Why aren't you married yet? Find yourself a husband and get out of this neighborhood. It is a dirty place, not suitable for an American girl."

"If this neighborhood is dirty, it's only because the garbage is collected less often than in the wealthy areas. Is this the fault of my neighbors? They are cleaner than I am—I bet one of them cleans *your* house—and they work very hard and pay taxes they can't afford, and they send their sons off to be killed just like the European Jews. You should have more respect for your patients, doctor."

"*B'seder, b'seder*! I am a busy man. I don't need your sermons, miss rabbi. Come back tomorrow with the woman's husband. I will leave instructions for you."

Elisheva walks home firmly, quickly. There is much to do. Ḥayim must be contacted at work, and Yardena's mother. The apartment must be readied. Elisheva will spend the evening cooking, so that there will be lots of good food in Yardena's refrigerator.

She enters the courtyard. Her door is ajar. A face at the window: the bereaved woman. Elisheva runs up the steps, half-expecting another vision or hallucination, or whatever it was that made Lilit appear to her in Elat. But no, there she is, the bereaved woman, sitting at Elisheva's table, looking down at her hands.

"*Giveret*? *Shalom, giveret*, can I do something for you? Would you like a cup of tea or coffee? My name is Elisheva."

Still staring down, the woman says, "My name is Zahava. Have you gone to see Yardena?"

"Yes, just now. She is very sick, but the doctor will permit her to come home tomorrow if Ḥayim agrees."

"Good," says Zahava. "I want to help take care of her. She did many things to help me in the time of my trouble. Now I want to help her. I am good with the sick. I know what to do." She looks up for an instant, her expression almost fearful, as though she anticipates an argument.

"*Yofi*! Yardena will be very glad. Thank you. Would you like something to drink?"

"No. Thank you. I must return home. I will make some food. I will come back tomorrow. Thank you." She speaks slowly, with long pauses between each phrase and the next, like someone who is relearning social habits after a stroke or a spell of amnesia. "It is time for me to do something again. I want to be useful again. You understand?"

"Yes, I understand."

Zahava stands up slowly, bracing her weight against the table. "You should not stay here."

"*Sliḥa*? Excuse me?"

"You will not have a good life here. You should go back to America. I know what I am saying. Go back to America. You will have a better life there."

Elisheva is shocked. No one in Israel has ever suggested anything but that she should stay forever. "Why do you say that?"

"Because I know. This is not the place for you. You will not have a good life here."

"Why?"

"I know it. That is all." Zahava leaves, slowly, heavily, her black dress swaying with each step. At the door she stops but does not turn around. "*Shalom*. I will come back tomorrow."

When she no longer hears Zahava on the staircase, Elisheva looks out the window. Up and down the street, pedestrians are stopping in their tracks, conversations are silenced, as everyone watches Zahava cross the street and climb the stairs of her own house.

"*Kol ha-kavod*!" calls Avraham the grocer. "More power to you! *Shalom*, good evening, Zahava."

Zahava does not answer, but Elisheva thinks she sees a flicker of a smile as the woman pulls herself up the steps.

At that same moment, a dove coos over the door; and Elisheva feels the lining of her womb begin to tear free and slide out of her body. Standing up, she knows now that she is not pregnant, she recognizes this rich loosening of the abdomen, the gush between the legs.

No child. Not for Yardena, not for Miriam, not for Zahava,

not for her. It is not to be. No baby. No music and no baby. Not until she is married. She will have to get married. She will have to do what everyone keeps telling her to do, and get married. She will not bear the child of a soldier of Israel.

On the way to the kitchen for a tampon, she sees the first blossom on the old man's plant. The flower is not large and orange as she had anticipated. It is quite small, with many tiny petals in concentric circles: a circle of gold, a circle of rose, another circle of yellow, another of pink. Tomorrow she will take it next door to show Yardena and Zahava.

At last, she thinks, at last someone has told me the truth.

Then she remembers the hint of a smile on Zahava's face. It is the sly smile of Lilit.

———

A soldier of Israel! This should be a contradiction in terms, would be, in the world she wants. But it isn't, not at all, it isn't even one of those new Hebrew phrases invented for modern circumstance. *Hayal yisrael*: an honorable term from the Bible. War and military strength are a glory in the Bible, God is a man of war, a soldier is a servant of God. This is the heritage of her people.

Her people?

This is what has happened to her, this is what she has done. She makes herself say it all to herself in sentences, not just in thought-flashes: This is what has happened to me. This is what I have done. This is what I have become. I, a lover of peace, a fighter against war, have chosen to make my home in a country perpetually at war, firmly warlike, a country of soldiers.

It is the land of her ancestors, but so is Lithouania, so is Germany, so is Pennsylvania. It is the land of her earliest ancestors, but so what. Her earliest ancestors lived more like the Bedouins than like the Israelis of today. The Israelis of today want more than anything to live like Americans.

She remembers a phrase from the anti-war demonstrations: "Bring the war back home." But the war never came back home. American houses have never been bombed, not in any of America's wars. Americans go elsewhere to kill and be killed, nice work if you can do it, don't soil the nest.

If she is to live in a world at war, she wants to be at the center, in a contested city built on contested land. She wants the conflict to be on a scale she can understand: her own home at stake, not a bomb half a world away. She wants to join those in danger. Those in danger are her people.

But who is more in danger, Yossi the soldier of Israel or Ephraim his half-brother who was shell-shocked without even being drafted? Yossi, or Yardena who lies in her fever, dreaming that her sons are under attack? Yossi, or Miriam who will grieve for a long time over the loss of a man she didn't even love, the loss of a baby she was never meant to have? Yossi, or Zahava who already lost her son and a good part of her vital spirit, on that balcony of depression, and even the balcony may be lost in the next war, may blow up and dump Zahava into the vegetable bin below, or throw her into the street.

Who is more in danger, he who may die in war but who may live to make the next war, or she who may die in war but who never has made any war, never will make any war, not even in this country where women are dressed in soldiers' uniforms to do office work for soldiers. She may die in a war she didn't create, or she may die by the hand of a lover she would never kill, or she may give birth to a soldier who will die or kill or both, or to a lover who kills, or to a killer who comes out of her holding a rifle ready to strangle or shoot or pillage or rape, a man of war like God who is also called the father of peace in the *kaddish*. When the man of war has killed someone you love, you have to thank the father of peace who is the man of war in disguise. *B'rikh hoo.* As in the news, the modern form of *kaddish*: give the names of the dead, then wish everyone great peace *shalom rav*. Modern peace smooth and clean the great cleanup after the war at home. Modern peace the smooth greeting in the street *shalom* a beautiful word and comforting but it cleans up all the dead bodies, washes them too quickly and sits them at table as though they're only napping full of good food.

No more cleanup! Maybe that's the solution, a general strike, all the house cleaners starting with Yardena, all the office workers in soldiers' uniforms, all the mothers wiping the blood from their babies to send them off to battle. No more. Let those who want war make war. Let those who want peace withdraw, have nothing to do with war, supply nothing to war, not even our love, nothing. We will keep ourselves for each other. We will make peace with as much vigor as those making war, not a namby-pamby peace of boredom and floating harps, but a real solid earthy peace, an honest peace deserving of the word *shalom* which we will speak with reverence, not politeness.

As it is written:

We will withdraw war from the earth,
we will set love upon the land.
We will pour forth peace in the midst of the earth,
we will increase love in the midst of the fields.
It is impossible to stand against us, the mothers of all
    tribes.
It is impossible to stand against our will.
We will withdraw war from the earth,
we will set love upon the land.

"Now eat a spoonful for Nadav." Elisheva teases Yardena by using the game she learned from Bubby Sadie, who always knew how to get reluctant grandchildren to finish their oatmeal. "And this one is for Yonah." She feeds Yardena another spoon of *sahlav*, a thick concoction of sweetened milk and tapioca, spiced with cinnamon and nutmeg. "And this one is for Ḥayim. And for Avraham across the street. And for Zahava. And for the old man."

"*Masbik, masbik*, Elisheva." Yardena feebly pushes the spoon away. "Enough. I am full. Thank you." She draws Elisheva's afghan more tightly around her. "Is it cold in here?"

"No. You must be feverish again. Let me get Zahava. She will make you the poultices to lower your temperature."

"Call her from the *mirpesset*. Pretend you are Israeli." Yardena grins. "Remember how I taught you to bargain like an Israeli? Now you must yell like an Israeli."

Elisheva presses Yardena's hand. "How could I forget? Yardena, you are beautiful in purple. You must be descended from queens."

"*Mah pit'om*? What's this? You think flattery will cure me? Go call Zahava."

Elisheva goes to the *mirpesset*, cups her hands around her mouth, and shouts, "Zahava! Zahava!"

Zahava appears on her balcony. "*Mah yesh*? What's the matter? Does Yardena need me? I'll be right over. I'm just making stuffed onions. You know how to make stuffed onions?"

Elisheva and Zahava carry on a fairly lengthy conversation, in which they are joined by Avraham and several of his customers. Yardena is beaming when Elisheva returns to her bedside.

"Okay?" Elisheva asks. "Did I perform like an Israeli?"

128

"Like a sabra," Yardena says. "I couldn't have done better myself. See how much good you did me? I feel warmer even without Zahava's poultices."

"Yardena? Can I ask you something?"

"Anything, *motek*."

"At the hospital you said Ḥayim had not asked about the cause of your sickness. What would happen if you told him you had an abortion?"

"Elisheva, don't tell him! Promise me you won't tell him." Yardena sits up straight in bed.

"I won't. I promise. I'm sorry. Please lie down and rest. I'm sorry. I shouldn't have asked anything that would upset you."

Yardena lies back. "It's okay. He knows anyway, I'm sure he knows, but it is important that no one tells him. It would kill him to hear this, and who knows what he would do to me. No, no, he must not be told. He needs to feel like a *gever*, a real man who can support a large family. 'What do you think, Yardena,' he would say, 'you think I'm such a failure that we can afford only two children?' That's what he would say. And he would beat me. No, no, he must not be told."

"He beats you?"

"What are you saying? You live next door to me, don't you think you'd know if he beat me? No, he doesn't beat me, not anymore. He is a good husband. Only in the beginning he beat me, when we were young. Now he doesn't. He loved me so much in the beginning! It isn't good for a man to love you too much, Elisheva. It isn't good. Some of the love spills over. There is too much feeling. He can't contain it. This is what happens. Too much *koaḥ*, too much power in the love of a man."

"The sick one is teaching you about love?" Zahava appears in the doorway. "What do you know about love, you young girls? I could teach you both about love." She begins to sing in Arabic and to dance a slow, graceful dance, her arms extended like the branches of a tree. At the end of the dance she seems embarrassed and rushes to the kitchen to make Yardena's poultices.

Elisheva follows her. "How do you know so much, Zahava? Where did you learn about herbs and poultices? Where did you learn the dance you just did?"

"My mother, of course." Zahava looks surprised by Elisheva's question. "I learned everything from my mother. The songs, the recipes, how to heal—she was a midwife—she knew everything."

"Did she write it down for you?"

129

"Write it down? She couldn't write. And I can't read."

As Yardena recuperates, so Zahava opens herself. After four years of silence, she now wants to talk. After four years of depression, she now wants to express all that she feels. The daytime hours of companionship are not enough. Late at night, from across the deserted street, Elisheva hears her moan:

"Ah! for the lover of my youth, the one who brought me almond cakes and honeyed fruits, ah! He, he was the one I loved, my small boy of a lover, ah, how I yearned for him. Under the olive tree, ah, the old root rough on my skin, my back curved in pleasure like a supple branch. Gone, gone. In autumn I remember. Ah. He was . . .

"Those days are gone. I hobble now, and I huddle in my bed away from my husband's crackling hide. Ah, for the sweet smooth flesh, the skin like a baby's, like my son's, my little boy, my Yoram, gone. Gone. Ah.

"I promised him too much. 'Yoram,' I said, 'the world is yours. The world is yours, my sweet, my tender one, my boy.' The world. A Syrian grenade was his. I spit on this world. From my *mirpesset* I spit, ptui, you can all go to *azazel*, ptui, I want my boy, my sweet one, ptui, a grenade I would spit on this world.

"In autumn I remember. In winter I spit. In spring I ferment. In summer I dry up a little more every year.

"Ah. Never. Never."

In giving voice to her despair, Zahava recovers from it. Each day she is livelier, as each day Yardena is stronger. Miriam and Elisheva begin to teach her to read and write; she teaches them her dances and songs and recipes. She teaches them what she learned from her mother.

Miriam is not pleased with Elisheva's plan to visit the United States in the summer. "Why do you have to go?" she says.

"To see my parents."

"Make them come here."

"To see Daniel."

"Aha! What did I tell you? A true romance."

"Don't be silly. We're friends, that's all."

"Then why are you blushing?"

"Well, he just wrote to me that he's broken up with the . . .

person he was going with. And he's been saying things about wanting to start a family and live in Israel. And he says he really wants to see me."

"Elisheva! That's practically a proposal." Miriam jumps up and down in her chair. "Will you say yes? How exciting! You'll only say yes if he truly intends to live in Israel, won't you?"

"I don't know what I'll say. I just need to see him. I'll know when I see him."

"That means you're going to say yes. How long will you stay there?"

"Just a few weeks. First I'll see Daniel in New York, then I'll spend a couple of weeks with my parents. Don't frown, Miriam. I'll only be gone a few weeks. I'll quit work at the end of June—the summer's always slow at the university anyway. I'll take a week in the Galilee, same as last year. Then I'll come back to Jerusalem, and in August I'll go to the U.S. I'll be back by the end of the summer. Now what do you want to study tonight?"

"I have just the thing." Miriam opens her Bible with a flourish. "Psalm 137. Repeat after me:"

Im eshkaḥekh yerushalayim
tishkaḥ y'mini.
Tidbak l'shoni l'ḥiki
im lo ezkrekhi
im lo a'aleh et-yerushalayim
al rosh simḥati.

If I forget you, Jerusalem,
let my right hand forget all it knows.
Let my tongue cleave to the roof of my mouth,
if I fail to remember you,
if I fail to set Jerusalem
above my greatest joy.

Elisheva repeats after Miriam. At first she is joking, parodying this ceremony of swearing on a Bible. But by the time she finishes, she means every word.

"I'll be back." She promises her friend, and she promises her city. "I'll be back."

———

Dear Daniel,
Thanks for your letters. Once again I've fallen behind in our

131

correspondence. I hope you haven't been insulted or worried by my silence.

My wonderful neighbor Yardena has been very ill. (Remember her? You left a note for me with her last year, and she invited you in for Turkish coffee.) Anyway, she's almost good as new now, thank God. While she was sick, I was one of three women who took turns caring for her. The other two were her mother and another neighbor, Zahava, who was prodded out of a long period of mourning for her son by the desire to nurse Yardena back to health.

The whole experience has been remarkable. It's hard to describe, but I feel I'm learning a tremendous amount from these women who are scorned and disdained by Ashkenazi society. Also, I am discovering that something very special can happen to the atmosphere of a room where women are together. I have felt it at the *mikva* where I sometimes go to take a shower, and at the Turkish bath, and in the women's section of the synagogue, and in kitchens, and in my apartment when Miriam and I study Torah together, and lately in Yardena's sickroom.

It is an atmosphere that I crave, and yet I fear it too. I fear that it will separate me from the world. There is something ironic in this fear, because really it is "the world," governed as it is by men, that thrusts us out; the separation is not entirely our choice. We make the best of it, and then the pleasant surprise is to find out how much we can give each other, even how much fun we can have together.

I feel strange to be writing this to a man, vaguely disloyal, as though I am divulging a secret. But I know you are trustworthy.

Daniel, it does worry me some that I am so comfortable among women. It seems like a temptation, the more seductive because it is gentle and undemanding. I've always felt a little different from other people anyway, as though I'm on the outside of things, and I worry that I could gradually turn into a real freak, or a recluse, and then it would be too late.

I guess what I'm trying to say is that I understand your desire to get married and "settle down," as they say, and that I feel the same way a lot of the time—that is, I feel the tug in both directions.

Did you have a good Pesach? I went to the Cohens' for seder; they're a zany, sweet family I met on the bus to Elat. I was a little anxious about the seder, because of an emotional complication between me and a young man in the family, but he's a soldier and didn't get a Pesach leave. So everything went fine—for me, that is; I'm sure Yossi wasn't too pleased about spending Pesach in the Sinai. Although in a way that's the most appropriate place, isn't it?

Well, I'm just chattering on and on. Enough!

I'm sorry to hear about your breaking up with Bill. I know it's painful for you both. But as you say, maybe it's for the best.

I look forward to seeing you in the summer. We have a lot to talk about.

Love,
Elisheva

10

Elisheva travels north, north to the Galilee, to the Kinneret, the lute-shaped lake. The bus takes her through hills furrowed as though some floury baker's fingers had passed through the mud, shaping dust-coated ridges and sprinkling weeds with white powder. Then the rocks, balls of red clay, baked solid. Steeper mountains, black volcanic rock, cactus and carob trees, and below, that sudden green valley and the surface of lake like a bright blue penny, a Dutch porcelain saucer. Red-tipped terebinth branches spray sunlight into her face, and the bus descends through terrain green and greener, the gray stone ground cured by vegetation, lifted beyond itself by green shoots feeding and pushing out, lush and vital.

Land so green it doesn't seem a part of Israel; but neither is it the Pennsylvania farmland become suburb where Elisheva grew up. No winters here, no snow, none of those tall hardwood trees. Here, low shrubs, and a harshness even in the green. It's almost too bright, garish, as if it's trying to prove something: Fertile! Fertile!

An awkward brag: See? You thought this country was nothing but desert, didn't you? Surprise!

Maybe it wasn't always this way. Maybe the problem is the kibbutzim, the orderly fields and new buildings, the predictable pattern of fish ponds, orchards, vegetables, animal sheds, houses. Yes, it's not the land that's out to prove something; it's the people, with this display of fecundity.

But the food is needed. What else could have been done? When you find the good soil, you have to farm it. What else could have been done?

For a moment she thinks, This was a mistake, I shouldn't have come back this year, the desert has ruined me for good; now I will always crave stark rock and salt. But the closer she gets to the lake, the more natural and gentle the green becomes, as though the foliage can tell the difference between irrigation and rainfall.

From Tiberias she takes another bus ten miles around the lake, to her favorite hostel, old white plaster buildings right on the lake, with peacocks roosting on the roof, shade trees all around, flowers in the doorways this time of year: geraniums, hibiscus, plumbago, bougainvillea, Judas tree with its lavender clusters almost lilacs. Her favorite room, white and clean, quiet. Her favorite place to swim, a beach sheltered by eucalyptus and cottonwood, with ducks waddling out into the water. Cool damp rocks to sit on, dabble the feet, behind her a grove of banana trees, the fruit almost ripe. At the next inlet, a flock of goats and sheep slurping from the lake and nibbling the grasses. She sits until it is dark out.

The next morning she is drinking orange juice in her room when she hears a man and a woman speaking English outside the window.

"No good," says the man. "I will have to leave this place immediately. There is nothing I can eat here."

"Really?" says the woman. "I thought the breakfast was fine."

"Look out!" says the man in a loud voice. "They may have poisoned you."

"Oh?" The woman sounds as though she would like to escape instantly but doesn't want to offend the man too much.

Just what I would do, Elisheva thinks. She likes the woman's voice; it is warm and expressive, East Coast Jewish. New York or Philadelphia.

"Look in the Bible," the man continues. "I am careful to eat only those foods mentioned in the Bible. Very important. I recommend you do the same."

"No kidding? What foods did I eat that aren't mentioned in the Bible?"

"Oh, most of them. That is why I must leave. The most dangerous food on your plate was the tomato."

"But I've eaten tomatoes all my life."

"Humph! You are still young. It will catch up with you."

"I see."

"Do you know Hebrew?"

"No."

"Learn your Hebrew, young lady. Look in the Bible. The

135

word for tomato is *agvania*, specifically designated in the Bible as a poison. No more tomatoes, that's my advice. Now, I must go right away. Would you care to join me?"

"No, thanks. I'm staying until tomorrow."

"Very well. But no tomatoes!"

"Right. Well, it was nice meeting you."

Elisheva wants to glimpse these two strangers before they both disappear. She moves to the window, peers out, and sees the man receding, older than she expected, bald on top, with a long fringe of white hair and a straggly white beard. A pack on his back and hiking boots. A healthy gait: maybe he's right, she should give up tomatoes.

But where's the woman? Elisheva steps out and almost bumps into her on the walk.

"Oh, I'm sorry," she says. "I just overheard that crazy man talking to you, and I had to see what he looked like."

"Yeah." The woman smiles, a nice friendly smile. "He's quite a character, isn't he? Well, at least he wasn't trying to pick me up. That's more than I can say for most of the men around here."

"Then you're traveling alone? Me too. My name's Elisheva."

"Deborah. Hi." A firm handshake. Elisheva likes her. Something straightforward about her manner. A strength in the shoulders. A bit taller than Elisheva, but not much, and about the same age. Very attractive, Elisheva decides, especially that beautiful hair: long, curly, auburn, held back over each ear with an old-fashioned comb, the kind Bubby Sadie used to wear. And slender tanned arms, bracelets at both wrists, the silver bands intricately carved. Without thinking, Elisheva reaches toward one bracelet and runs her fingers over the textured metal, as if the design were braille and held some message for her hand. Deborah looks startled, then relaxes.

"Oh, I'm sorry," Elisheva says again. "I was just admiring your bracelets. They're really beautiful and unusual. Damn. I don't know what's the matter with me today. I'm not usually so . . . forward. First eavesdropping on your conversation, and now inspecting your jewelry. I'm sorry."

"Hey, it's all right. I'm glad you like the bracelets. I made them a couple of years ago. Here, look." She slips off the bracelet Elisheva touched. "This was the last one I did. It's still not very good, but I switched to painting right after that. Maybe some day I'll work in silver again, who knows? But look, I want to show you the images I carved. All of them are symbols of female power. I found them in a book called *The Great Mother*. Here's a cow, and a lioness, a crescent moon, a pomegranate, and—well, this one's not very clear, but it's supposed to be a woman with her arms raised, like this, in a sacred dance."

"Please, may I look at it some more?"

Deborah lets her arms fall from that graceful gesture; she suddenly seems embarrassed. She shrugs and drops the bracelet into Elisheva's hand. Elisheva turns the bracelet around and around, each image three times, four times—what is the magic number? —and then she feels embarrassed too. She gives the bracelet back to Deborah without looking at her. "Thanks." She wants to get away, she is afraid, she has made both of them uncomfortable, she has been nosy and tactless, she should rescue them from this awkward moment. "Well, listen, you must have things to do. It's bad enough that you were pestered by that man . . . "

"No, I'm enjoying talking with you. I was just feeling very selfish, going on like that about a stupid bracelet."

"It's not stupid at all. The bracelet is beautiful. And here we go again." They both laugh.

Deborah says, "Look, I have the use of my aunt's car until tomorrow—she lives in Haifa—and I thought I'd like to drive all the way around the lake today. Want to come?"

They stop in town for picnic supplies. "No tomatoes," Deborah warns, so they settle on goat-milk cheese, pears and plums, and down the street, hot flat bread from an Iraqi bakery. The fragrant, fresh bread is irresistible; they finish it before they even get back to Deborah's aunt's battered old Volkswagen. So, they turn around, go right back to the bakery and buy more bread for later.

Elisheva taps the dashboard. "Reparations?"

"Huh?"

"Reparations. From Germany. After the war."

"Yes, that's right. Hey, you know a lot about this country. And your Hebrew sounds pretty good—at least, the shopkeeper understood you the first time you said whatever you said. You've been here awhile, haven't you?"

"Two years. Now, if you were Israeli, the next questions would be: 'How old are you?' and 'Why aren't you married yet?' "

"Tell me about it!" Deborah nods energetically. "I've only been visiting for a month, and I don't know how many times I've heard that routine."

"Have you ever seen such a gorgeous lake? God, I love this place. I've never been all the way around, though. I've heard the best beaches are on the other side."

"Yeah, and the worst roads. But old Batya thinks she's a jeep, so we ought to be okay."

"I think I like your aunt. She calls her car Batya?"

"No, the name was my idea."

"Well, then, I think I like you." Another awkward silence. Goddamn, Elisheva, you've done it again. Just shut up. Watch the trees, and the bright light reflecting off that calm lake. Watch the trees, bay and cyprus, olive, sycamore, oak, Syrian maple, Oriental plane, date palm, eucalyptus and poplar, and there—"The rockroses are blooming. And that's a Judas tree, the one with the purplish flowers."

"Ooh! I'm going to stop for a minute, okay?"

"Sure."

Deborah reaches into her woven bag and takes out a pad and pen, goes to sit under a eucalyptus, and in a little while returns.

"May I see your sketch?"

"No, it's not very good."

"That's what you said about the bracelet, too. Come on, let me see it."

"No, this time I mean it. The sketch is no good. Okay?"

"Okay. I'm sorry. I shouldn't have pushed."

"No, it's all right. Let's talk about something else. Or let's not. Look, I'm sorry. It's not your fault. I just don't know what I'm doing, that's all. I'm supposed to go back to the U.S. at the end of the summer to finish art school—I only have one term left—but the more I paint what interests me, the less my teachers like what I do. I don't know what the problem is. I came here for the summer to get away and figure things out, but it doesn't seem to be helping. I just don't have enough confidence in my work. So I thought, what the hell, maybe I'll stay here—I like Israel in a funny kind of way, and the landscape is a painter's dream—but this is no place for a feminist."

"Huh. I think that's what a neighbor of mine was trying to tell me a while back. Do you think it's true?"

"Absolutely. Women aren't valued here at all, from what I see, and there doesn't seem to be any alternative to family life—not even on the kibbutz. Don't you agree?"

"Yes, but . . . I like it here."

"I'm not saying you shouldn't stay, Elisheva. I'm just saying it's not the place for me. I must be boring you to death. I can't believe I'm running off at the mouth like this, and I just met you this morning . . . "

"I'm not bored at all. Honestly I'm not."

Deborah suddenly pulls the car over and jumps out with her sketchpad again. Elisheva looks around: no houses anywhere, just vegetation and water, and where Deborah sketches, a lagoon, tall rushes, a herd of water buffalo. They are magnificent, huge and lethargic, and the camera is back at the hostel. Shit. As if on command, one of the animals begins to shit.

Elisheva is still chuckling when Deborah returns.

"What's so funny?"

"Not you. The water buffalo. I like them. I feel elated. What's that pile of straw up ahead?"

The pile of straw is a bridge over the Jordan River. Elisheva gets out of the car and jumps up and down on the rickety structure a couple of times to test it. Then she moves out of the way and watches Batya and Deborah leap to the other side.

"Bravo! Bravo!"

"Just don't ask for an encore. Please."

It's a dirt road from the river on, but Deborah handles it fine.

"Deborah, I bet you're good at athletics, right?"

"Yes, as a matter of fact, I am. Why?"

"You drive like an athlete. Oh, let's stop here for a swim. I don't think we'll find a nicer beach anywhere."

The beach is small and private, and the water is so clear that Elisheva can see every pebble and rock at the bottom, as many colors as the fish swimming over them. She leaves her clothes in a pile on the beach and goes in for a swim while Deborah sits and sketches.

"The water's perfect," Elisheva calls. "Refreshing but not cold."

She swims out farther. Just by opening her eyes under the water, she can see everything, maybe the whole lake full of fish and water and shiny pebbles. When she comes up for air, Deborah has entered the water too. Elisheva watches her clean, sure backstroke, her smooth skin at the surface of the water, her long golden body, the wavy hair floating out like seaweed. Elisheva wants to touch her, wants to lose self-consciousness and fear as she did when she reached for the silver bracelet, wants to touch Deborah and learn the message of her body, but doesn't dare, doesn't dare, swims far away and doesn't return until Deborah is out on the beach, dressed again.

"I thought you said you weren't an athlete," Deborah says. "You're quite a swimmer."

"All stamina, no form." Elisheva quickly pulls on her clothes. "That's always been my problem."

They eat lunch and then lie back in the sunlight.

"What do you like about Israel?" Elisheva says.

"Oh, I don't know. The way the white paint from the walls comes off on your clothes if you lean back for a second."

"How about the mayonnaise in toothpaste tubes?"

"Yeah, that's pretty good too."

"You know, I admire the way you just pull out that pad and sketch, wherever you are and whoever's around. I've never known that kind of discipline."

"It's not exactly discipline. It's enjoyment, too. What kind of work do you do?"

"Oh, I have a job as a typist. Pretty boring."

"Something else in mind?"

"I don't know. I was supposed to go to graduate school in French, but that doesn't interest me anymore. If I went back to school now, it would be to study Sephardic music, Yemenite especially." In a rush of words, Elisheva tells Deborah about the melody she heard in the Anthropology Department, the one Lilit taught her in a dream.

"Do it," Deborah says. "Look how excited you are. Go back to school in that field—what's it called?"

"Ethnomusicology. The study of folk music." Elisheva shakes her head. "No. I can't. My mother's a musician. I swore I wouldn't go into music. I need something of my own."

"But studying folk music isn't the same as being a musician."

"So much the worse. She already considers it a tragedy that my brother's in a rock band. I kept clear of her expectations by staying out of music altogether, but if I do anything that involves melody and harmony and tempo—forget it. Folk music isn't 'serious' music to her. She'd consider it as big a betrayal as Neil's wasting his perfectly good violin instruction by becoming a rock fiddler. Huh-uh. I can just hear her: 'Ellen darling, was it for this I was named after Clara Schumann? Was it for this I persuaded the assistant concertmaster of the Pittsburgh Symphony Orchestra to teach violin to you and your brother? You and Neil both had so much talent. What went wrong?' Huh-uh. Not music. Not for me."

Deborah is laughing. "Okay, okay. I get the picture. I guess I'm lucky. No one in my family is artistic. They all think I'm crazy, but at least they don't say I'm wasting my talent. My mother expects me to marry in the next few years, but I guess she'll have to get over it."

"Don't you want to get married some day?"

"Definitely not. Look what happened to your mother—she gave up an exciting career to raise a family. I don't want that to happen to me. I'm not nuts about kids, anyway."

"I am. When we were in the water, I was thinking about a little girl I met on a bus in the Negev. Dina. Her parents invited me for Pesach, and when everyone was getting ready for the seder, Dina came into the living room, naked, and started marching around, chanting, 'Guf ḥamud. Guf ḥamud.' That means 'adorable body' in Hebrew. I expected her parents to be mortified—they're Orthodox—but Ilana just laughed. I thought it was wonderful. Don't you?"

"Yes, terrific."

"Miriam doesn't agree—she's my best friend in Jerusalem. She thought it wasn't nice to teach a child conceit."

"That's not conceit, it's—well, I don't have to convince you, do I?"

They lie in silence for a while. The sun is warm, pleasurable. Elisheva feels so relaxed with this new friend, more relaxed than she's ever felt with Daniel, freer to say whatever comes into her mind. Maybe Deborah has the right idea. Maybe it isn't necessary to get married. Maybe Elisheva could live her whole life like this, relaxed and free, swimming and sunning with someone as beautiful as Deborah.

Deborah sits up and runs a hand through her abundant hair, then begins to braid it over one shoulder. "I imagine it would be very hard to resist the social pressures here," she says. "If you do stay in Israel, you probably will be happier if you get married and have a family like everybody else."

"Yeah." Why does Elisheva feel so disappointed? Deborah is right. It's a simple matter. How could Elisheva have thought otherwise, even for an instant? Of course she has to get married. Deborah doesn't have to get married, but Elisheva does. Even Deborah sees it. Elisheva has to get married. "I have a candidate in mind."

"You do?" Deborah sounds a little upset—or is it that Elisheva wants her to be upset?

"Yes. I have a good friend in the U.S.—his name is Daniel—

and we've been carrying on a very intense correspondence this year. Well, I'm going there for a visit, and if it works out I'll marry him and bring him back here."

"I see." Deborah is using the same guarded tone she used this morning with the crazy man. "You sound pretty sure."

"Oh, I'm not sure at all. But maybe it's a good plan."

"Do you love him?"

"I don't know. Yes, in a way. Yes, I guess I do."

"And he?"

"I don't know. But he wants to marry me, that much I know. He hasn't said it yet, but I know he does."

"Well, then, you're all set, aren't you? We'd better be heading back."

Deborah sounds very brusque and businesslike all of a sudden. Elisheva wants to pull her close and say, "No, please, don't let me do it. Let's go off together and swim, always. Please, don't let me do it." But she can't say anything, and Deborah hates her now, and she hates herself too. But what can she do? She wants a normal life, doesn't she? What else can she do?

She sits in the car with her eyes closed, and hears Yardena's voice in her head: *"En brera. Kakha zeh b'olam.* There is no choice. That's the way it is. *En brera. Kakha zeh."*

In the morning Deborah is not in the dining hall. Elisheva goes for a walk, to the banana-tree grove, and when she returns, Batya is missing from the driveway. Elisheva wants to cry. In her room, on the table, she finds a large envelope, with a note in it.

> Dear Elisheva,
>   Thank you for one of the best days ever. If I decide to stay, I'll look you up in Jerusalem. If not, I hope we meet again somewhere.
>
>   In sisterhood,
>   Deborah

Inside the envelope are two things: the silver bracelet, and a drawing of those silly old water buffalo.

Dear Deborah,
    I think I'm going crazy there's so much I didn't get to tell you and now it's too late I'll never get to tell you any of it I'll

never see you again I know it why should I care but I do I can't help

See what's happening to me I'm a typist that's what they pay me for and what use am I if I can't even punctuate? Good a question mark maybe there's hope after all.

I know you've gone back to the U.S. because it's been a while and you never looked me up I'm here in Jerusalem but where are you? You could be anywhere I don't think I ever told you my last name so even if you are here how could you look me up? I know you never gave me your last name or address why the hell didn't we think ahead a little I can't even send you this letter not that I'd want to probably anyway I don't want you to know how crazy and confused I am after all we hardly know each other we only spent one day together so why should I care but I do. I know you do too or at least you did or why would you have left me your best bracelet I love it Deborah I wear it all the time and everyone admires it I wish I could tell you what they say. And the water buffalo drawing I love it too and I can't even thank you it's on my wall and I swear it will always be on my wall wherever I live.

Deborah I keep dreaming about swimming with you in clear clear water just like that day only this time we graze each other's bodies in the water it's so nice I never want it to stop. We swim together and then apart but we always come back together in the shimmering ripples we float on our backs then on our bellies and we watch the blue sky and the pebbles at the bottom so many colors such pleasure and great peace shalom rav like a return to music. Green mountains all around the lake and I know on the other side of the mountains are the cities of men full of noise strife violence enmity. I don't ever want to have to go back there I just want to stay in the water with you always. You know that whole day it never occurred to me but only a few years ago we couldn't have gone to that side of the lake we couldn't have crossed the Jordan or seen the water buffalo or swum at that perfect beach. Even in Tiberias even at the hostel there would have been guns aimed right at us and maybe we would have exploded. Even now there are mines up in the hills and if we made the wrong move that day we could have been blown up. It's scary you know to think we're both alive just by luck or at least I'm alive and I must think you are too somewhere I couldn't stand to think you wouldn't be.

The next thing in the dream is a circle of women dancing

around a fire wild flames and freedom of motion we lift our arms in an arc of light that same image of female power you called it in the silver bracelet. Deborah I never told you I worked on a kibbutz when I first came to Israel right after the ulpan and my work was to pick pomegranates another image from the bracelet. It was wonderful work beautiful and satisfying with a good tired feeling at the end of the day. It was the best work I've ever done and when you asked what kind of work I do I probably should have told you I'm a pomegranate picker temporarily unemployed. In Hebrew the word for pomegranate is rimon the same word means grenade and this kibbutz was near the border so we'd be picking fruit as if on a peaceful island and then we'd hear shelling somewhere not far away. The first time it happened every day someone would say They're shooting and everyone looked at someone else for an instant before going back to work. Have you ever eaten a pomegranate they are delicious and the red juice drips while you eat all those tiny dark red seed cells of the six-chambered fruit there's nothing like it we used to take a break in the field and just open a pomegranate and eat it right there because who cared if you stained your uniform it was old and ratty anyway. Now don't laugh but here's my secret even today I can't eat a pomegranate with any kind of politeness. I just strip and sit naked in the bathtub and let it drip all over me and then I take a bath after I'm done.

Deborah in a week I'm going to the U.S. I wish I knew whether you're there and where so I could see you again but maybe it's better this way did you know did you do this on purpose? I wish I knew I wish I could ask you.

You see what I mean I'm pretty nutty these days acute anxiety is what Dr. Feinstein calls it he's my shrink I don't think I told you about him and now I never will Deborah I can't stand it. Panic he says and that's the way it feels too Deborah I'm so scared what the hell am I going to do I wish I could talk with you I think you would understand. Deborah I can't stand this feeling so empty and full at the same time so scared and lacking. Dr. Feinstein promises I will get my defenses back but I don't know whether I even want them now once I get them back again maybe it will be too late but for what I don't know. More and more I think marrying Daniel is the right thing to do maybe I'm crazy but I think he and I could get along and I do find him attractive I yearn for something he has or is this doesn't make

144

any sense does it. What I mean is marrying Daniel would be a mitzvah it would help him and me both to live a better life to be normal people not perverts. When I was with you Deborah I didn't feel perverted I just felt drawn to you but I know that kind of attraction has no right to exist it would be bad for both of us everyone would think we were perverts it could ruin our lives and we're not bad people so maybe it's better this way that I should marry Daniel. Did you know all this Deborah I wish I could know what you think.

I think I should marry him that's what I think and it makes me feel calmer just to write it down so it must be true. Deborah I think I should marry him because that attraction does have a right to exist and it would help instead of hurt and then nobody would have to be a pervert.

Deborah I feel very sleepy now I'm going to bed and then I will leave for the U.S. and I feel calmer now but I wish I could talk with you again there's so much we didn't have time to

II.

1

*L**a'alot*: to go up, to rise; to immigrate to Israel. *Laredet:* to go down, to sink; to leave Israel.

But I rose to New York on the airport escalator, which ascended very slowly toward the customs inspection that would readmit me to the land of my birth, the land my grandparents struggled to reach, the land in which my parents struggled to move up.

Above the escalator, behind a glass partition, Daniel was waving to me in time with the muzak version of "Don't Fence Me In." I waved back, and then we both stood quite still and looked at one another for a long moment, until the escalator had passed under the partition, under the floor on which Daniel stood.

For me, it was almost as if I had never seen him before, because never before had I seen him as a gay man, and never before had I seen him as a potential fiancé. These two new images came to me simultaneously, so that they blended into one rather than contradicting each other: "This is the gay man I am going to marry."

I looked for clues in his appearance to confirm the double-exposure image in my mind. All the clues were there, the ones I had noticed before and the ones I hadn't. His large, dark, sad eyes: I now saw them as the eyes of one of those beautiful Arab boys who drive men wild; and I knew in the same moment that these were the eyes of the man I wanted to marry, because they showed me that he was alone and ashamed as I was alone and ashamed. I saw his smile, warm and shy as my own, and it was the smile of a gay man and of a husband.

In our mutual gaze, we agreed to become a pair, to try to join the secret society of married couples from which we had both been excluded. Neither of us knew the rules of entry, the initiation rite or hazing we would have to undergo; but this was part of the initiation, that we had to guess what the ritual was, before we could perform it.

"All right," we said to each other in that gaze. "We will do it.

We will join up. We will fake if necessary, to penetrate the circle and learn the secret from inside. We will bite into the sweetness of knowledge, even if we must steal it first. We will live no more as outsiders."

———

The air is sticky and dirty, with the special mosquito-ridden humidity of New Jersey in August. Elisheva and Daniel sit on the front porch of his parents' house, drinking iced tea and mopping their sweaty faces with small napkins engraved in gold letters: "Happy Anniversary Tony and Angela."

They talk first of small everyday plans, as though, like Tony and Angela, they have already been married for thirty years. Tomorrow morning they will drive to the farmers' market and buy food for the two large meals of *shabbat*: Sephardic baked fish for Friday night, and lasagne after synagogue on Saturday.

"We'll drive to synagogue," Daniel says. "It's five miles away."

"There isn't one closer?"

"Well, yes, but the people in that congregation would know my parents are Catholic. I'd be in a funny position. I'd rather not, when you just arrived. Maybe next week we can go to the temple in this neighborhood . . . "

"No, by then I'm supposed to be visiting my parents in Pennsylvania. Never mind. If you prefer, we'll drive to *shul*. Why are you living with your parents? Didn't you have an apartment in New York?"

"Yes, but I can't afford it alone. This is just temporary—I moved in here a couple of weeks ago, when Bill left."

Daniel's eyes fill with tears, and he turns away. Embarrassed, she turns away too. The air between them grows thicker and heavier.

"Do you miss him?"

"Yes. A lot. But it's my fault he left me. As much as I loved him, I never made a real commitment. He wanted me to stop tricking, but I couldn't, or I didn't want to. I don't know which. Then I started talking about wanting a family, and he saw one of my letters to you. I guess that was the last straw . . . I don't blame him, but I do miss him."

Elisheva knows she should be pleased that Daniel's correspondence with her was such an important matter, but she feels nothing but fatigue and an unfamiliar sort of nervousness. She can't seem to take in the significance of Daniel's words. Instead, she hears them as a kind of music: his lilting, almost singsong speech; the blur of consonants; especially, the glottal *l*, which makes his English sound almost Arabic: "left" sounds more like "gleft," and "love" is nearly "glove."

"What does 'tricking' mean?" She feels like Dr. Feinstein, hopelessly uncolloquial, as though English were no longer her own language.

Daniel laughs, as Elisheva would have laughed at Dr. Feinstein. "It means picking up a stranger. Look, on Sunday I have to go into the city, to get a few last things out of the apartment before the lease expires. If you want to come with me, I'll show you around the neighborhood. You can see where the men go to cruise—that means looking for tricks." He pauses; then in a rush of words, he says, "I'd like you to come, I'd like to show you. I want you to know everything about me."

"Thank you."

"Please tell me more about you. I've been doing all the talking. How have you been?"

"Okay. I thought I was pregnant for a while, but I wasn't. My neighbor Yardena is fine now. Miriam and I have been studying *Ḥumash* almost every day. We agreed to continue by mail while I'm in the U.S. I went on my yearly trip to the Kinneret, and I met a woman there who attracted me. But nothing came of it."

Somewhere in the middle of the list, Daniel stopped paying attention. He is tapping his fingers together and looking at the floor. Well, no wonder. Pregnancy scares must be as foreign to him as tricking and cruising are to her.

"My parents," Daniel says, "don't know about Bill and me. What I mean is, they don't know about *me*. I don't think they could take it—they both have heart conditions, and my dad was hurt enough when I stopped using his last name . . . Mom and Dad have been pestering me to give them grandchildren before they die." Daniel blushes and looks away. "They love kids."

Elisheva blushes too. Was this his proposal to her? She suddenly feels as inexperienced with men as Daniel is with women. She doesn't know what the rules are with him, how to interpret anything he says.

"They like Bill," Daniel goes on. "They invited him to all the family get-togethers: Christmas and New Year's Day and Easter. When he and I split up, I told my family that he was moving to another city. He went along with the story, to make things easier for me. I wanted you to know . . . "

"So I can make things easier for you, too." Damn. That sounded sharper than she meant it to.

"Yes, I suppose so," Daniel says quietly. "Well, now that you're in the U.S., do you want me to call you Ellen or Elisheva?"

"Elisheva. Please."

She is proud of him: he pronounced it better than anyone but her neighbors in Jerusalem. He has a talent for languages, just like her. He is just like her, but different, larger, heavier, darker, his fleshy odor of muskrose, his flesh, his voice, thick and rich, like Turkish coffee flavored with *hel*. Cappuccino and cannoli, thick and creamy, heavy petals of vowel, muskmelon, is that a cologne or his own sweat, colorful and warm, spicy, turbans and embroidered cloth. He makes her homesick for Jerusalem, so soon, she just left, how can she be already but she is, and a longing for his flesh, his weight against her, his smell on her skin, Near Eastern, she is sleepy, dazed, she wants him, she wants to make love and sleep, she wants Deborah no Daniel, the shoulder in the sun, how good it smells, and the neck, warm brown skin, warm brown sun, please where am I, I want to sleep.

After Elisheva has taken a nap and a shower, after she has eaten dinner with Daniel's parents, she and Daniel go for a walk. They do not touch; they hardly speak. There is almost no traffic now, and the hot, moist air smells fresh and sweet. Every house is brick below and wood above, with a front porch and rows of carefully tended rose bushes lining the path to the sidewalk. The houses are about as old as Elisheva and Daniel; the couples sitting on the porches are about the same age as Daniel's parents. The neighborhood is quiet, sedate. A few of the front-porch couples greet Daniel as he passes; the others simply stop conversing for a moment, to see who it is.

At dinner Elisheva felt clever, alert, entertaining. She told amusing stories and answered questions about her life in Israel. Daniel was proud of her; his parents, impressed. Alone with Daniel now, she has nothing to say, nothing to ask. The silence between them is not the usual one of tension and discomfort; it is the silence of preoccupation, daydream, individual thought.

Elisheva Yamenu. That is the name she will have if she marries Daniel. It sounds funny. It sounds like a restaurant where you have to sit on the floor. A tongue-twister that eight-year-olds try to say fast and faster. A secret language. A place you climb all morning to reach. One very long name instead of two fairly long names. A prayer. A joke. A folksong.

She likes it. After she and Daniel are married, she will go visit Mrs. Gallagher, her first French teacher, the one who thought she shouldn't call herself Ellen Roginsky . . .

"Elisheva? Here. We're home. Unless you want to go around the block another time?"

"Oh, are we back already? No, fine. I'm ready."

Angela and Tony have already gone to bed, no doubt in order to give Daniel and Elisheva some privacy. The inside of the house is hot and stale. Elisheva has forgotten to expect this; in Jerusalem the summer nights are always cooled by a mountain breeze, so that she needs a blanket for her bed even after the hottest days. Here, the houses stay hot all summer long.

"I want to play a record for you," Daniel says.

"*Yofi*. Great." Elisheva follows him upstairs to his room. With great reverence he places a record on the small phonograph and gives her the jacket to read. "Won't this wake up your parents?" She sits on the bed and examines the record cover, which shows the face of a young, plain-looking man.

"No, I listen to music every night before I go to sleep. This is my favorite record."

The singer has an unusual voice—first smooth and gentle, then suddenly jarring, almost a howl—but the songs are routine ballads, about sitting in the sun and needing someone. Now he seems to be singing to a woman, now to a man.

Daniel sits beside her. "This was our song—Bill's and mine," he says softly. "One time we had a fight, and I walked out. When I came back he'd written down all the lyrics to this song, and left them on the kitchen table for me."

"Uh huh." Elisheva examines the lyrics closely, but they still seem utterly undistinctive, impossible to differentiate from those of a thousand other popular songs. She listens to the sad words, the whirr of the fan, Tony's loud snoring in the next room. At last the song ends, but the record has been set to start again automatically.

She clears her throat. "Do you mind turning off the record? It's very pretty, but I'd like to be able to talk with you."

"Oh. Sure." Daniel looks puzzled. "Would it be okay if I just turned it down? We can talk with the music playing."

"Maybe you can. I can't. I don't know how to use music as a background. When music is playing, I listen to it." She feels annoyed: why can't he just do what she asks? She agreed to drive to synagogue with him. The least he can do is to give in on something, too.

There it is again: the "habit of irritability" she presented to Dr. Feinstein, nearly two years ago. Hasn't she changed at all? Maybe it is unreasonable of her to ask Daniel to turn off the music. Maybe he needs the music in order to talk. Maybe he is worried his mother will hear their conversation without the shield of music. But he has already switched it off. Now she must think of something to talk about.

She clears her throat again. "You promised to tell me about your conversion. Is this a good time?"

"Oh. Yes, as good as any. It's hard to explain. Nobody ever understands—my parents didn't, Bill didn't—but I'll give it another try. Okay. It happened in college, a couple of years before I met you. I was taking a European History class. I already knew about the Holocaust, but I never saw before that the Holocaust fit into a pattern. The more reading I did for that class, the more I saw that Jews have been victims all through history. I've always felt like a victim, too, or at least an outcast—I guess because of being gay, but more than that—I just felt that I was a victim in the same way that Jews have been victims. I started feeling that I was meant to be a Jew. I was born into a Catholic family, but I was really a Jew. See, you're frowning. You don't understand, either."

"No, no, it's just—well, it seems so negative. I mean, Judaism has many positive things to offer. I find it upsetting that you saw Jews as victims and nothing else."

"That was the first step. Now that I'm a Jew, I see a lot more. But that was the first step. It's the truth. What can I say?"

Oh God, those suffering eyes. She has hurt him again. She is always hurting him. Why?

"I'm sorry. I didn't intend . . . I'll try to understand, I promise I will."

"I know you will." His sweet voice, sincere, blameless. "Elisheva—" He places his hand on hers. She looks down at the two hands, the large one on the small one, large above small. What a strange pattern the fingers make. Some lesson here: large above small, and the fingers.

Elisheva! Pay attention. This is an important moment. Don't just stare at the hands, try to feel his hand on yours, good, warm and steady, this will be your husband, *ba'ali, ba'al ha-*

bayit, the master of the house. Master? Calm down, Elisheva, this is Daniel, look at him, he's as frightened as you are, he's not anybody's master. He's just Daniel, your friend Daniel.

She places her other hand on top of his. A Daniel hand sandwich.

"—all of this has a lot to do with why I invited you here." He is speaking very quickly now, slurring his words together. "What I mean is, I think we should consider getting married. We get along well, we have a lot in common, I think we could be happy together, it would be good for both of us . . . "

"I agree. Okay. Let's get married."

"What? You agree? Really? But I had five other arguments ready in case you said no. Really? You agree?"

"Yes, you silly person. I'm going to marry you."

She picks up his hand and claps it between her two. They both laugh. She keeps patting his hand until they are giddy, and the patting evolves into a slap-happy version of patty-cake. She teaches him the chant she used with her girlfriends on the playground: "Eenie meenie pepsodini ah bah bubalini, achi pachi Liberace I pick you up, have a peach, have a plum, have a stick of chewing gum, if you want another one, this is what you say . . . "

When they tire of the game, they fall back on the bed and begin to kiss each other, very slow, long kisses. "There is no hurry," their tongues tell each other. "We will have our whole lives together."

These tender kisses arouse Elisheva tremendously; Daniel too seems excited. They lie there, kissing and kissing for hours, like two high school kids in a car. Even with the fan on, the room is very hot and still, making their bodies sticky, then drenched. They roll from side to side, kissing, covered with sweat, soaked, until Elisheva feels as though she is a boat rolling through the water, gliding back across the ocean to the places her grandparents left by steerage.

She goes to unbuckle Daniel's belt; he pulls back in shock. "I don't think we should," he stammers. "I mean, if we're going to get married, we should do it right. Besides, my mother's sleeping right across the hall."

Elisheva blinks. "You mean you don't want to make love until we're married? You're crazy!"

He sits up with a stubborn expression. "I think we should wait. I want to know we've done this right."

155

"You really mean it! But you've never made love to a woman. How do you know you'll even want to, once we're married?"

"Don't worry. I'll want to. Don't worry."

As soon as she has left for her bed in the guest room, Daniel puts on the record again. She hears it play three times through before she falls asleep.

———

Each morning when she peers into the bathroom mirror, the rosiness of her cheeks surprises Elisheva. The tough black fibers on Daniel's face have given her a permanent blush, a bloom of naïveté, which she can tolerate for the first few days of her engagement, but no more than that. Maybe she should persuade him to let his beard grow, so that it will become softer. Maybe she should persuade him to marry her immediately, instead of waiting a sensible year.

At night, after his parents have gone to bed, Daniel puts a schmaltzy record on the phonograph, and he and Elisheva kiss and rub their faces and necks together. She remembers Yossi saying that human beings are different from animals because we make love face-to-face, but she and Daniel have taken this idea to an extreme: they act as though faces are all they have, as though their bodies don't exist.

Or rather, Daniel acts as though Elisheva's body doesn't exist. How she yearns for him, how she longs to feel his hands on her belly and thighs! She can't take much more of this. Soon she will get him drunk and seduce him. Soon she will find her own apartment, and his mother won't be sleeping right across the hall.

Good Lord, she deserves to look like a teenager. Where is her maturity, her patience? This obsessive desire is unworthy of her pact with Daniel. They have agreed to live this year for the future, not the present. At the end of the year they can have Israel, marriage, sex. In the meantime, they will stay in the U.S., work hard, save their money, go to bed alone, get up early and study and work.

Study. She hasn't studied Torah since she arrived three days ago. She is letting Miriam down, and Daniel as well, and the children they will have. What kind of mother will she be if she doesn't know Torah? if all she can think about is sex?

She marches downstairs and installs herself at the card table on the front porch, to study *Ḥumash* and make notes for Miriam. "In *B'Midbar* 11," she writes, "when the Children of Israel complain that there is nothing to eat but manna, and they are punished by being forced to eat flesh for an entire month: is not the lesson here that we should appreciate what we have, rather than wanting something else?"

Elisheva hears Angela's high heels clicking up the sidewalk, on her way back from Mass. Her pink hat disappears around the corner of the house; she must have seen Elisheva studying on the porch and decided to enter by the kitchen door, so as not to disturb. She and Tony are both being extremely considerate. Elisheva reminds herself to buy them something for the house this afternoon, when Daniel takes her into New York.

Daniel's voice emanates from the kitchen, then Angela's, then Daniel's again. When did Daniel get up, and why hasn't he come to say good morning? He doesn't give Elisheva enough attention, doesn't seek her out, waits for her to come to him, wouldn't even kiss her at night if she didn't move toward him first.

And what has happened to her resolve to live for the future, to work hard and keep her goals in mind? If she can't even concentrate on the Torah, what good is she to anyone? She returns to her books, and is just finishing today's study when Daniel appears with a cup of coffee for her, as if to reward her self-control.

"What are you writing?"

"Notes on *Ḥumash*, to send to Miriam. What's the matter, you don't like *Ḥumash*?"

"No, it's not that, it's . . . Oh, never mind, we'll talk about it some other time."

Angela is standing in the doorway, wearing a flowered housedress she must have just changed into. She forgot to remove the pink hat, though; it is still perched on her gray curls. "How about some French toast for the lovebirds?"

"Don't say no, Elisheva." Daniel winks at his mother. "Mom's French toast is the best in the world."

"I don't like to brag, but it's true." Angela sits on a little stool by the door. "What are you kids going to do in the city?"

"A whirlwind tour of Manhattan." Daniel waves his arms around. "We'll pick up a few last things at the apartment, and then we're taking Mr. Wilbur to dinner and a Carmen Miranda movie."

157

Elisheva says, "Who's Carmen Miranda?"

Daniel and his mother exchange a look and a chuckle.

"Go ahead," says Angela. "Do your imitation. Wait till you see this, Ellie. You may want to think twice about marrying my son. He can be pretty crazy sometimes."

Daniel, with a sly grin, is already dancing. At the end of the porch he bumps his hips to both sides and bobs his head: "Boom chicka boom, boom chicka boom."

"You should see her," Angela sputters. "She sings and dances just like that. And she's wearing—puh, puh—a hat made of— puh—a hat made of FRUIT!"

Angela raises her hands to show the shape of Carmen Miranda's fruit hat, and encounters the obstacle of her own church hat. This sets her off even more, and she laughs until she has to reach into the bosom of her housedress for a handkerchief. She dabs at her eyes with one hand and removes the hat with the other; the sight of her prim little pillbox makes her laugh even harder.

By this time Elisheva has joined in, and she too laughs until she is weeping. The two women pass the handkerchief back and forth.

The more Angela and Elisheva laugh, the more pleased Daniel seems with himself, and the more sensuously he dances. He watches them out of the corner of his eye as he sambas, and his body sways in long waves from his legs, up his back, to his neck, as though his bones have dissolved and he is one sinuous muscle.

Elisheva suddenly stops laughing and catches her breath. With a new generosity, Daniel is sharing his body with her in this dance, and she can hardly restrain an impulse to touch him as he moves before her, elegant and fluid.

His dance is a wonderful surprise, an engagement present. A new side of him, a lithe certainty she has never seen before. He is wrapped in his own body as he bends and sways, and yet he is performing for her. It is as though his body is telling her: "This is my true nature, my undisguised beauty. This is what you will have some day. Aren't you glad that you will know me? Oh, I see that you want me, and I enjoy your desire, but most of all I take pleasure in myself."

Yes, this is the difference: other men dance as though they are reaching for something outside themselves or stomping something under their feet, but Daniel dances from within his own body, to a rhythm that seems to emerge from his breath and blood, so that all his cells rise and fall in a cadence as much his own as the lilt of his voice.

He ends the dance with an awkward little bow, in which he almost stumbles, in which he re-enters his stiff everyday body, the body of camouflage, the clumsy body with which he shakes hands in the synagogue and shelves books in the library. Angela applauds heartily, and Elisheva, startled by the sound, claps her hands too. But the applause feels wrong to her, as though she and Angela are commending Daniel for going back into hiding, for slumping his shoulders and knocking his feet together as he bows once more. No, no, this is all wrong, she thinks, still applauding. We should have clapped while he was dancing; we should have clapped a Latin rhythm and cried out like jungle birds. We should have entered the pleasure of his tropical body as it uncoiled into luxury, we should have urged him to blossom more and more. We should not praise him for squeezing his ample urges back into the frame of this crowded house. She thinks all this, still hitting one of her hands against the other until they both hurt.

By the time the applause is over, Daniel is once more an ungainly young boy trying to appear a man. Only one hint remains of his natural, exotic beauty: those dark, moist eyes, which stare at her now with a kind of voluptuous sadness, an almost impersonal longing, as though he is pleading with her: "Can't we do better than this? Please help me to do better than this."

———

Elisheva and Daniel remove a number of items from Daniel and Bill's apartment: a set of blue-and-yellow handpainted dishes from Spain; a very dark, carved wood night table ("distressed wood," Daniel says); a small packet of razors; a mirror, also framed in distressed wood; and a red, white, and black poster advertising the first commemorative Christopher Street March, which took place one year and two months ago.

Elisheva stares at the poster for a long time. It shows two women flanked by two men, arms extended around each other's shoulders, running energetically and happily toward the camera. The two women in the center of the poster look especially happy. Elisheva wonders whether they are lovers. She has never seen a picture of lesbians before, and these grinning young women whose hair flaps around their faces are not what she expected, although now that she thinks about it, she doesn't know what she expected instead. Both women have dark hair, fairly long, and the one wearing glasses resembles Elisheva. For an instant she thinks that woman is winking, but no, it's only a reflection in the woman's glasses. Elisheva takes the poster from the wall and rolls it up quickly.

Then she sits on the wooden living-room floor, tapping an absent-minded rhythm with the rolled-up poster and listening to Daniel clean the kitchen for the last time. Now he's sweeping the linoleum, now he's sponging the formica, splash in the sink, tap of poster cylinder on the floor.

Usually she finds empty apartments depressing, as though their past occupants have taken away all their vitality, and they are desolate, devoid of personality, waiting in loneliness and sorrow for new people to bring them new life. But in this apartment she still feels the presence of a couple, two men who made a home together here. The warmth and fragrance of their bodies still permeate the apartment, so that she feels cozy and sheltered even in this room without furniture. The plaster walls are blank, but their texture seems to have retained fragments of the shadows of the men who loved each other here, and quarreled, and ate dinner together on those bright Spanish plates.

It makes her sad to think that all of this is over, this love that she senses to have been deeper and more whole than anything she has yet experienced. And it makes her angry with Daniel to know that he was the one who ruined it, he was the one who turned away from this rich home, who now is wiping every trace of his presence and Bill's from the surfaces of the kitchen. Elisheva is glad he can't do anything to clean the plaster walls of the living room, even though someone else will soon paint them over for the next tenants. At least it won't be Daniel who is responsible.

She is silent in the car. Daniel probably thinks she is jealous as she sits there, frowning, still clutching the poster. She doesn't let go of it until they arrive at Mr. Wilbur's building.

Mr. Wilbur is Daniel's supervisor at the library. He too is gay, and he too recently lost his lover, who died of a liver disease. They lived together in this elegant old building for thirty years. Today is Mr. Wilbur's birthday; Daniel is the only one who cares enough to celebrate it with him. Elisheva warms to her fiancé again. He really is a good man, a kind person.

Daniel has warned her that Mr. Wilbur tends to drink too much, and he does seem a bit tipsy as he crosses the lobby to meet them. The doorman raises his eyebrows in Elisheva's direction. Is he expressing disapproval at Mr. Wilbur's alcoholism, or surprise at Daniel's being accompanied by a woman?

"So this is the lucky girl." Mr. Wilbur leans over to shake her hand. Are all homosexual men tall? She tries to remember the heights of the two men in the poster, but she seems hardly to have registered their presence at all, so preoccupied was she with the two lesbians. One of the men was blond and had a beard. No, the doorman is blond and has a beard. She is confusing the doorman with the poster men, and she doesn't even know the doorman to be gay.

"Congratulations." She jerks back to Mr. Wilbur's pink face, his gray head. Another surprise: not all homosexuals are young. Why did she think all homosexuals would be young? What's supposed to happen to them when they get older? If they're all like Daniel, they get married and aren't homosexual anymore. But won't Daniel still be homosexual after he marries her? What will they do about that? She must remember to discuss this important subject with him during their engagement. First, she must remember to converse with Mr. Wilbur.

"Thank you." This is conversing? Try harder. "Happy birthday."

"Now why'd you have to tell her, Danny boy?" Mr. Wilbur pats Daniel's cheek affectionately. "You know this is the year I lose all my sex appeal." Why does Mr. Wilbur care about appealing to *her?* Mr. Wilbur is homosexual. But so is Daniel. Maybe Mr. Wilbur wants to marry her, too. Maybe she should marry both of them. What the hell is the matter with her today?

The theater is full of men. Men in couples, in trios, in large groups. Mostly Anglo-Saxon young men. A few older ones with pink faces, like Mr. Wilbur. Very few women. Elisheva counts five: four, like her, young women with male escorts, and one older woman who appears to be with her son. Maybe he too imitates Carmen Miranda for her amusement.

Elisheva doesn't find the movie very interesting; she got much more enjoyment from watching Daniel dance this morning. Besides, she has the confusing and unpleasant sensation of being out of sync with the rest of the audience. The men all laugh at odd little things that she doesn't find funny at all—Carmen Miranda's accent, for instance, and the opulent settings for the

161

dance numbers. Then, when Carmen Miranda has a few rather clever lines, in which she makes mincemeat of a stupid suitor, Elisheva is the only one who laughs.

At this point she hooks her hand over Daniel's arm and leans toward him to whisper something, but he is staring straight ahead, with an uncomfortable expression. Then she notices a hand caressing his right thigh. Mr. Wilbur's hand.

She instantly feels guilty and embarrassed, as though she has invaded Daniel's privacy and Mr. Wilbur's. She tries to stop looking, but she seems paralyzed in this position, her gaze permanently fixed on a patch of trouser leg, and on the hand that moves slowly over it, stroking gently and rhythmically up and down the thigh, toward the inside of the leg, and back to the outside again, over the knee, and back up to the hip.

As she watches, the feeling of guilt slowly leaves, and instead she becomes indignant. How dare they carry on like that in her presence? It is an insult. She and Daniel haven't even announced their engagement yet, and already he is betraying her. And Mr. Wilbur, the hypocritical old lecher! One minute he is congratulating her, and the next he is groping her fiancé. And right in front of her! How dare they?

Suddenly the hand withdraws, and Mr. Wilbur, Daniel, and all the other men begin to applaud and cheer. Elisheva turns groggily back to the screen: the famous fruit dance is under way. Half-dazed, she watches Carmen Miranda do a parody of Daniel's sensuous dance—but that can't be, he was parodying her—and then the chorus marches around, carrying gigantic strawberries, peaches, bananas. Two lines of men, all holding bananas as large as they are, hoist the fruit toward each other in a strange salute, while Carmen dances down the middle. As though at a signal, all the men in the audience jump to their feet, whistling and screaming.

Elisheva has never felt so lonely.

———

"Why'd you let him do that?" Elisheva tries to control her voice. She and Daniel are in a café, there are other people around, she does not want to shout or cry.

"Why'd I let who do what?"

"Why'd you let Mr. Wilbur feel you up?"

A woman at the next table turns to see who is speaking. Elisheva blushes and then gives the woman a hostile stare, until the woman turns away in embarrassment. Good, Elisheva thinks, I won; maybe I'll get along okay in New York, after all.

"Oh, you saw." Now Daniel looks embarrassed. Good again. "I didn't want him to, but what was I supposed to do? He *is* my boss, you know. The poor guy was drunk, and he's very lonely. It seemed harmless to give him a little bit of pleasure. I would have stopped him if he'd gone any farther."

"Oh, no, why stop him at all? I think this is a wonderful precedent. Why don't we invite him along on our honeymoon? He can feel you up, and I'll invite someone else to feel me up. It's obvious that *you* don't want to."

"Wait, that's not true. I'm more attracted to you than I've ever been to a woman . . . "

"That's not saying much, is it?" She realizes they are both whispering; this is the way they will fight some day when there's a baby asleep in the next room.

"Ellie, please, don't be sarcastic with me." His eyes go soft and vulnerable again. Is he really hurt, or is he just after her sympathy? She can't tell; if it is a manipulation, it's working. "I want to marry you, but you have to understand that this is a difficult adjustment for me." He looks down and fiddles with his napkin.

"I understand that." She puts her hand over his. He glances around nervously, as though afraid someone will see them. "I know you're gay, Daniel. I know I have to be patient with you. But just because you're gay, do you have to let some dirty old man feel you up in a movie house? If someone put his hand on my leg and I didn't want him to, I'd move his hand away. Why didn't you?"

Daniel looks confused, uncomprehending, as if she just addressed him in Urdu or Hungarian. He shakes his head, over and over. Finally, he says, "I couldn't."

The next thing he says is, "The pastries here are terrific. Want to split one?"

———

"See," Daniel says, "that's how you can tell when a guy is cruising."

A man is walking a terrier on a leash. He stops to look into a shop window. Another man is looking back over his shoulder, into the same window. Their glances connect on the glass. The man who looked back now walks more slowly, until the man

163

with the terrier catches up to him, and they walk on together.

The light changes. Daniel turns right, waiting first for a large number of male pedestrians to cross.

"What cute little asses they all have," Elisheva says. "What happens to the fat ones, and the ugly ones?"

"They don't cruise the streets. They go to the trucks, where it's dark. Or they pay someone."

"Even the apartment buildings are pretty. And the pastry we ate was pretty. Everything is pretty here."

"Sure. It's the West Village. Do you want to see the prettiest thing in the West Village?"

Daniel circles the block and finds a parking space. Elisheva puts on her shawl, for the night air has turned fresh and cool. She and Daniel stroll along, her arm about his waist, his hand on her shoulder.

She has visited New York before, but never this part of New York. She likes it, even though she doesn't think it fair that ugly men are banished from these streets. She feels safe here: there are so many people walking around, and none of them are dangerous. They are simply out for a good time with each other. The brick buildings are stately and well-maintained; the trees are healthy; the old streetlights give off a special radiance.

"Here," Daniel says. "The library."

The West Village library is a small red brick castle, with turrets and stained-glass windows and brass bannisters. It's not imposing or scary, like the 42nd Street library with the white stone lions guarding all knowledge inside. This library looks cozy, happy, friendly. It looks like a home. Elisheva will come back here. She will get a card and use this library all year, until she and Daniel return to Israel together. She will come to this library, and she will feel welcome and happy and not afraid. This is where she will live.

"I knew you'd like it," Daniel says. "My bookworm girlfriend."

He kisses the top of her head, and she is happy. She snuggles her head into his chest for an instant. Then they become part of the parade of young men again, until they reach Daniel's car. As they start the drive back uptown, to the George Washington Bridge, to New Jersey, he points once more to the stream of men on the sidewalk.

"These men," he says, "are my people. They're my people as much as the Jews, or the Italians. When I come here, I'm at home. I can't help but feel that I'm deserting them now. I wish I didn't have to desert them."

"So do I. No, I mean it. I wish we could get married without either of us having to give up any part of ourselves."

"We can't," he says.

"I know we can't. But I wish we could."

"I love you," he says for the first time.

Dear Miriam, my havera,

Here are my notes on B'Midbar 13. I got such a pang of homesickness when I read about Moses' scouts returning from Canaan, carrying grapes and pomegranates and figs. Eat an extra pomegranate for me!

I miss you a lot. I wish we could be in the same part of the world this year. Has the hamsin started yet? I'd take a hamsin any day over a muggy New Jersey hot spell.

I am very happy that Daniel and I are going to be married, but I still feel disoriented and out-of-place here in the States. Maybe it will get better when I find a job and an apartment. Tomorrow I have three job interviews: one for legal typing, one for teaching Hebrew School, and one for leading a temple youth group. Please don't laugh. Remember, this is the U.S., where my skimpy knowledge of Hebrew and Judaism is more than most Jews have. So all of a sudden, I've been promoted from ignoramus to mavin.

The day after my interviews, I take a bus to Pennsylvania to visit my parents. Daniel will drive out next weekend to meet them. Then in a couple of weeks, more job- and apartment-hunting.

Would you please send some of my clothes? Just the ones I wear all the time. Everything else is yours. Except for a few items I especially want Yardena to have: my comforter (you already have a nice one, and she really needs it for the boys), and those kitchen towels she admired, and the blue enamel coffee pot. And I'd like to give Zahava the old man's flowering plant.

Good grief, this sounds like my Last Will and Testament! Don't worry, I plan to stay alive.

I'm writing to you from the West Village library. Have you ever been here? It's lovely, comfy, very old. Well, not old by Jerusalem standards. I guess my sense of time has already been re-Americanized.

Daniel is at a dance class right now. He's coming to pick me up afterwards. Here he is—he just entered and hasn't recognized me yet. I love him, Miriam. Do you understand?

Hugs and kisses,
Elisheva

Daniel looks at her pile of Bible commentary books, some in English, some in Hebrew. "Ellie," he says, "I have a big favor to ask."

He looks so sweet and serious, his black hair still damp and curly from exercise, his huge eyes damp too. How could she refuse him anything? She wants to hug him and say, "Of course, dear one, of course," smoothing his hair, stroking his face; but they are in the library.

"You," she whispers, "are irresistible. What's the favor?"

"Well, maybe I don't have the right to ask this, but I'd like you to stop studying Torah until this year is over and I'll have time to study too. Then I can catch up to you, and I'll feel better. As it is, you're just getting farther and farther ahead of me—your Hebrew is already a lot better than mine—and I find it humiliating. The other men at the synagogue all know so much more than their wives. How will they ever accept me if you've already got a head start? I feel inadequate enough as a Jewish husband, and as long as you keep learning more, it'll just get worse . . . Hey, I'm sorry. Please don't cry." He pats her shoulder awkwardly.

She is shaking her head, over and over, and tears fall onto her books, making darker spots on the dark covers. She can't seem to say anything. Finally she says, "Let's get out of here."

They go down the street and begin to walk. Even though there are more people on the sidewalk than in the library, she feels more private down here, freer to cry as she and Daniel walk in silence.

After she has cried enough, she begins to speak, still walking and still looking straight ahead. "I refuse. Of course I refuse. How could you not have known I would refuse? Don't you know anything about me at all? What made you think I would agree to hold myself down, so you would look bigger by comparison? What gave you the right to make such a request?"

"I'm going to be your husband," he says quietly.

"Is that the kind of husband you're going to be? Is that the kind of goddamn husband you're going to be?" She wheels around to face him. He looks frightened. "You listen to me, Daniel Yamenu, or whatever the hell your name is this week. You just listen. I'm not in a goddamn race with you. I study because it's important to me and I love it. You want to learn Torah? I'll teach you what I know, but I won't stop my own studies. And if that means I'm 'ahead of you' when we get married, too bad. . . . What the hell are you looking so pleased about? Were you testing me? See this fist? You'd better say no."

"No. I just all of a sudden feel proud of you. I picked myself a tough cookie. Look, I'm sorry. Maybe you're right, I shouldn't have asked. It's just . . . I've been to rabbinical school and everything, and I want people to think I was born Jewish, so it's embarrassing . . . Never mind. I'm not going to put my foot in my mouth again. Come on." He takes her hand and pulls her down the sidewalk. "Let's go for a hot fudge sundae."

"Don't you want dinner first?"

"No, come on! Everyone has dinner first. Let's be different. Anyway, a hot fudge sundae always makes peace. Trust me."

"It's not enough that I'm marrying you? I have to trust you, too?" She claps her hand against her forehead, like Shlomo. "*Ach*, this boyfriend, he asks so much!"

That night Elisheva dreams she is going blind. All she can see is a thin line of light. Nothing else.

It is *shabbat*, but what is the use of going to synagogue when she can't see? She will have to rely on Daniel. He can rig up a *shul* in the basement of his parents' house. He can read the service aloud to her. He can pray with her. She will thank God that she still has her hearing. In the afternoon she and Daniel will discuss the Sayings of the Fathers. She will have to rely on him. He will read the Sayings of the Fathers aloud to her, and he will read aloud to her his own interpretations.

Her blindness may be temporary. She thinks it is temporary. When her blindness ends, then she will be strong and whole. She will see and hear everything. How long will it take? She does not know. But when her blindness ends, she will see everything, and everything she sees will be changed by her vision. Nothing will be the same as it was. She will be strong and whole, and nothing will be as it was.

Daniel sees her off at the Port Authority terminal, dark parking lot of smelly buses underground, early in the morning. But it's always dark down here; early morning doesn't make it any darker. Still, it looks darker.

He seems reluctant to let her go. What does he fear? What does he think will happen in her absence? She is not afraid—well, she's a little bit afraid to go back to her parents. She's afraid that they will swallow her up or nullify her, that she will lose something she has worked hard to gain—what?

But she is not afraid to leave Daniel. If anything, she is pleased to get away from him for a while, to have some time alone on the bus and then in her family before and after his visit. Why isn't he pleased too? Doesn't he know how to be alone for a few days? Hasn't he ever been alone?

They stand in line with the other passengers, moving slowly. Daniel says, "I don't want you to leave. I'm going to miss you terribly." He sounds very much upset. How can he be? This is nothing.

She says, "Don't be sad, Daniel. We'll see each other in a few days. And then I'll be back before you know it."

He shakes his head. "Ellie . . . I don't trust myself when you're gone. I need to have you with me all the time, or I can't be trusted."

"Stop that right now!" It's the sharp schoolmarm voice, the same one she used when he asked her to stop studying Torah. Daniel jumps back, as if expecting her to slap him.

Wait, wait, this is all wrong. Has it been only a week since he met her at the airport? Surely this has happened thousands of times already. She has been angry or annoyed with him forever. Over and over again, like the sappy music he plays at night, the same scene repeated: he says or does something she doesn't like; she gets angry; he gives her that hand-shy spaniel routine; they make up.

Nothing ever changes. What is the purpose? It gets nowhere, it's boring, she is frustrated, she wants something new to happen, she wants something, she never gets what she wants, neither does he, why? Why can't they give each other something, why can't they help each other, please?

Okay, try to be patient. Explain to him. Say something calm and quiet. Breathe first, oh God these fumes, so don't breathe, just say something.

"Daniel, please. I want you to understand. A few days away from each other is nothing. It's nothing. You can do whatever you want when I'm gone. Just pay attention to yourself. That's all I ask. Pay attention to what you're doing and what you're feeling, because we're practicing for marriage, and that's not nothing. Do you understand? I don't care what you do. I honestly don't. I just need to know that you want *me*, and I need your respect. Your love and your respect, that's what I need. Nothing else."

He clasps her to his chest; his whole body is trembling. She holds him tight until the trembling stops.

Then it's her turn to board the bus. She runs up the narrow steps. After she is seated, she looks out the window and sees him standing there, waving, as forlorn and anxious as he was at the airport when she arrived from Israel. She opens the window, and he approaches and takes the hand she extends to him.

She says, "I love you, Daniel. Please don't be sad."

He nods, but his expression does not change. He backs off and waves to her some more, and she, to make the moment lighter, fishes in her purse for a kleenex and waves it as if it were a fine embroidered linen handkerchief, white on white, and she, the romantic heroine. When the bus pulls away, he just stands there, wistful as an abandoned child.

She feels annoyed again, and oddly insulted, that he values her so much more in her arrivals and departures than in her presence. Nostalgia and guilt, she thinks. Those are his finest emotions, nostalgia and guilt. His finest emotions are worthless to both of them.

2

Nobody sits next to her. No conversation, only the bus moving her through Pennsylvania, sneaking her back, back to the land of her birth. The Pennsylvania Turnpike, sounds like Benjamin Franklin and the Founding Fathers, sounds like the Thirteen Colonies collecting pennies at the gates to the West. The route her grandparents and great-grandparents took through these hills, snaking west on the narrow road, will there be any other Jews? Will anyone else be called Hymie Sadie Mottel Guttel Roginsky Schwartz Lowenthal Friedkin?

To them it was strange new territory; to Elisheva it is familiar, like an enormous backyard she used to play in. But the direction was reversed for her: not west toward the Ohio border, toward Great Lake country, toward steel mills and cornfields; but east, once every year, to the big city. An annual pilgrimage to "culture," Clara called it: concerts, plays, museums. And a quick visit to the burroughs, to see the relatives who were left behind on the trek west, the great-aunts and -uncles shriveling in Brooklyn apartments, the cousins cultivating hydrangeas in Queens. Strudel and iced tea, then back to Manhattan for a performance. "A bite to eat," Clara used to say, "and then we'll take in a matinee." The kids—Ellen and Neil—made it a family joke, a way to tease Clara: "We'll take in lunch and bite a matinee." Arthur usually stayed at home, working, coughing, joining them in the City just for the weekend.

Elisheva knows this route so well that she remembers the names of all the long tunnels that cut like mineshafts under the highest iron mountains; she remembers every gray stone Howard Johnson building, the fat flavor of the Ho-Jo French Fries, the pink scent of the ladies' rooms. Surely they must have driven home every year in the same direction the bus now takes, but she remembers only the trips out to New York, not the returns. So she goes through the list of tunnels in her mind, west-to-east, and then reverses the order: Blue Mountain, Kittatinny, Tuscarora, Allegheny. . . .

Here they are, those feathery green hills, the landscape she has known longer than any other. If the earth is a body, then the Negev is its skeleton, bony rock stripped of the skin of soil, the hair of grasses and trees. And this gentle Pennsylvania landscape contains the limbs, the soft downy arms and legs, the moderate mounds of hill and dimples of valley, the placid rivers, the generous tufts of trees, leafy and serene in their green comfort. It is a temperate land, well-nourished and content.

Elisheva shivers as the bus plunges into the hollow core of Blue Mountain. No blue here, no green, no soft soil: darkness and the dark pronged ribs of steel holding up the weight of that mountain, which curves over her now, its hard innards exposed. Granite and ironstone, a rocky surface, unpolished, stone, stone, a dull gray gleam and a harsh metal smell. She is under the earth. Under the earth. And just then, a tiny point of light, like the beam from a miner's forehead, very far away but the bright circle expanding already to welcome her back. Like Hayim and Yardena's bright voices shouting, *"Brukha ha-ba'a.* Blessed is she who arrives."

"When we get back to the house, I must play the Rachmaninoff sonata for you. Or maybe I'll call Sonya and ask her over this evening to accompany me. Oh, that would be lovely. Would you like that, dear? Yes, that's what we'll do, and I'll make the berries up into a pie, instead of just serving them with cream after dinner. Here, darling, you hold the basket. What a beautiful bracelet! Did you buy it in the Old City? Ouch! Oh my, be careful, Ellen. I really don't think it was a good idea for you to come out here barefoot. These brambles are quite prickly. Your father will complain, of course, but it will be three against one, if Sonya can make it. Anyway, a little concert will do him good. And Sonya is just dying to see you—oh, but she wanted to meet Dan too. Well, never mind, we can have her and Igor over again during the weekend."

"I bet she calls Daniel my 'young man,' right?" Elisheva examines one berry. It is like a cluster of tiny beads, each containing a seed and deep red juice, so dark it's almost black, but nearly translucent too, how can that be? A mystery and a miracle. Shlomo was right, she is a pantheist. She holds the berry up, watches the sunlight filter through it as through a perfect brooch, better than rubies, darker and juicier, the one Grandmother Lowenthal promised to give her when she marries. In her mouth, the berry is warm and succulent; it dissolves without any chewing and leaves a few seeds behind on her tongue, as though they would take root there.

"Why, yes, that's just what she calls him: 'Ellen's young man.' How did you know? Oh, these berries are heavenly, aren't they, darling? It saddens me to see the bushes reverting, ever since old Mr. Bailey died. They're so leggy now, and they don't bear nearly as much fruit."

"Mm, but delicious. Exactly the flavor I remember. I like the bushes this way, wild and trailing."

"Watch your skirt, darling, you'll tear it on one of these canes. See how they run all over the ground? The pattern is rather nice, I must say. But the fabric is wearing thin. You know what your Bubby Sadie would say . . . "

" 'What's this? Wearing such a *schmatta*? Is this a dress for a young lady? Feh! Cut it in pieces, *bubbele*, make from it a pot-holder.' "

"Oh my, I see I've used that one already. Here, bring the basket. My hands are absolutely full. Oh, look, I'm purple to the wrist. Really, that bracelet is simply gorgeous, Ellen. You have developed such good taste. You know, Grandmother Lowenthal will want you to choose silver and china patterns, and you'll have to register in the Pittsburgh department stores. Don't bother objecting, I agree with you, it's a pile of nonsense, but you know how she is. . . ."

By the end of her stay Elisheva will have had more than enough of Clara's chatter, but she just arrived yesterday, and it is a pleasure to be walking with her mother through this green and purple field, it is a pleasure to hear that quick, light voice, which Elisheva never remembers quite accurately, because her mind confuses it with the resonance of Clara's cello.

"Mother, your voice is just like a violin. The E string and the A string."

"Not exactly a compliment, coming from you." Clara stops for a moment and pops a berry into her round little mouth.

"Oh, I like the sound of the violin well enough, just so I'm not the one playing it. Remember how awful I was?"

"Not so bad, as I recall. You and Neil were about evenly matched for talent. But you never took to the instrument the way he did."

"Never took to it? I *hated* it. And if I didn't sound so awful, how come you and Dad wore earplugs when I practiced? That was very demoralizing, you know."

Clara holds up her berry-stained hands. "Guilty, guilty. I know the whole Freudian shpiel, and it's all true. I ruined your life. I pressured you too much. I didn't praise your efforts enough. Well, what did I know about rearing children? You were my dress rehearsal, darling. I learned by making mistakes on you. That's the penalty you paid for being the first child. But you've turned out fine in spite of me."

"You didn't ruin my whole life, Mother. Only my musical life. Why didn't you just let me take piano lessons in the first place? Why did it have to be a string instrument? And then when you finally relented, you made me study with Sonya. God, was she a terrible teacher."

"Well, who else could I have sent you to? Sonya would have been furious. She never would have forgiven me."

"Do you know what she did once? I don't think I ever told you about this. She gave me some horrible mushy piece to memorize—that one by Gustave Lange." Elisheva hums a few bars. "She said I had to learn to stop playing like a little machine—"

"And quite right she was. You must admit, dear, you never played with enough feeling. Although I would have chosen something by Liszt, perhaps, or Chopin . . . "

"Wait, wait. There's more. I memorized the piece, and then when I played it for Sonya, she rapped my hands with a pencil and shouted, 'No, no! All wrong!' Then she gave me a dreamy look and said, 'Ellen! Have you ever been in luff?' Just like that. I said, 'Sonya, I'm only thirteen years old.' She said, 'Ellen, you must fall in luff. Before your next piano lesson, you must fall in luff.' She was serious, too."

"She actually did that? You poor baby!" Clara makes as if to tear some hair out of her loose gray bun. "Oh, look, sweetheart, there are some wonderful berries over here. Now let me think, why did we insist on violin instead of piano? Oh, yes. Well, I suppose it's all right to tell you, now that you're spoken for. Promise you won't be angry? You were always such a solitary child. Really, you're fine now, though I never did like it that you were living all alone in that apartment in Jerusalem. Well, be that as it may, you just weren't very sociable as a child. And then there were hardly any other Jewish children in your school. So we thought, why should she learn a lonely instrument like the piano? Better to encourage her to take up an orchestra instrument. We thought maybe you'd want to join Junior Symphony in Pittsburgh, and you would meet some Jewish children . . . "

"In other words, you wanted me to meet a nice Jewish boy. A second violinist with acne and a hernia."

"Well, I didn't exactly have the acne and hernia in mind. But that's all in the past, and now you've found your nice Jewish boy. . . .You know, I was surprised that you decided to come home alone. I would have thought you'd wait to accompany Daniel the first time."

"What for? I haven't seen you and Dad in two years. I wanted some time alone with you. Anyway, Daniel will be here for the weekend."

Clara's face acquires a familiar expression. What is it? Cagey. Shrewd. She says, "Aren't you a little worried, leaving him alone in the big city?"

"Worried about what? He can take care of himself."

"Oh, that's not what I mean, darling. You don't really know each other very well yet. Maybe he'll find another girl while you're gone, and change his mind."

"No," Elisheva says. "I'm not worried about that."

Clara looks pleased. "Well, you certainly have gained some confidence, haven't you? You once told me you were very pessimistic about ever finding the right man and ever keeping him if you did find him."

"I said that? When?"

"No matter. I'm glad you don't feel that way now. It must be the psychoanalysis."

"It has nothing to do with the psychoanalysis. I just know Daniel won't find another girl and change his mind."

"Oh, then he's the loyal type."

The basket is full, but Clara and Elisheva continue to walk anyway. Occasionally one of them picks a berry and eats it on the spot.

"Do you love him, Ellen?"

"Of course I love him. What is this, the Inquisition? Why would I marry someone I don't love?"

"I'm sorry if I'm being a pest. I just worry; you know it's one of my favorite occupations. After you called to tell us about your engagement, I was delighted, of course, but then I began to worry. I hope you're not just trying to please us, dear. Are you certain this is what you want? You're still a very young woman, Ellen. Remember, I didn't marry your father until I was 31. There's no reason for you to be in a rush."

"I'm not in a rush, Mother. Mother, can't you just be happy for me? I'm happy, Mother. Please, just be happy for me."

Clara looks at her with some intensity. "I am, darling. I'm very happy for you." She embraces Elisheva quickly and then rubs at her eyes. "Well, we'd better be getting back to the house. How much do you want to bet your father's listening to Mozart? I still haven't been able to convert him to the Romantics. 'Too high in cholesterol for me'—that's his latest line. You know your father, a real classicist. I say, the classical period is fine if you play clarinet or harpsichord, but what on earth is a cellist supposed to do with Mozart or Haydn? What's the use of playing cello if you have to make all those diddle-diddles? The cello is meant to sing, not prance." Clara demonstrates with sweeping motions of her strong right arm. "The broad, slow stroke of the bow across the strings: that's what the cello was made for. Now *Brahms*." She smiles in contentment. "Brahms is the perfect composer for a cellist. He knew what I need. That man knew just what I need."

————

When Elisheva and Clara return from berry-picking, Arthur is lying on the couch, with the newspaper spread on his chest. He is watching a baseball game on television. The sound is turned off, and in its place he is listening to a record: Act Three of *The Marriage of Figaro*. It is his favorite act of his favorite opera. Clara makes a face and goes to the kitchen with the basket of berries.

Arthur sits up and motions for Elisheva to join him. Then he begins to conduct the music, and after a while he seems to be conducting the ball game too. The players run and catch in sprightly 4/4 time; even the coaches scratch their heads on the downbeat. Elisheva laughs with delight. Her father puts a finger to his lips, and she quiets herself, but then she sees, no, he is not gesturing for her to be silent; he is signaling to the orchestra and singers, *piano*, *pianissimo*. And they obey.

Now Figaro the valet is about to be reunited with the noble parents from whom he was kidnapped as a baby. "Here is your mother," someone sings in Italian, "and here is your father."

175

Mia madre? Mio padre? Suo padre? Sua madre! Suo padre!

Why this fascination with mistaken identity and impossible reconciliation? Arthur loves these crazy plots in which everyone is disguised and then discovered. Why? The reassurance that everything will come out all right in the end? Or the possibility that he too might have a set of noble parents somewhere, waiting to adopt him back again?

Daniel is the same: he must think his parents aren't the right ones, or why would he have changed his last name and why would he be concealing their existence from the entire Jewish community of New Jersey? Maybe all men feel that way, maybe all of them are dissatisfied with the circumstances of their birth. Or maybe birth itself isn't quite real to them, so it seems a game, and they can change the rules at any time.

Her father the sociologist would have a fit if he could see her using a sample of two to generalize about all men. "Scientific method, Poopsie. Always use scientific method."

Scientific method. Start from what you know. Elisheva knows that this is her family, here in this house. She isn't always satisfied with this father, this mother, but she knows them to be hers. They're not the evil king and queen; they're not going to lock her up in the attic or cut off her hair. They mean her no harm. They're her parents: good people who love her. She has never questioned this connection or wanted to change it.

Yet now she is about to change her last name, too. She is going to trade it in for the name Daniel invented for himself. Could her father be insulted that she wants to give up his name?

She looks at the pale, thin man conducting Elisabeth Schwarzkopf's mournful aria. No, of course he's not insulted; it would never occur to him that she might do otherwise. And it is her mother who has resisted Elisheva's decision to use the Hebrew name she was given at birth, rather than the American name Clara has always called her. Why the resistance? Because Clara still wants to control her daughter, by keeping the power of naming? Because Clara does not wish to be reminded of Elisheva's decision to live in Israel? Because Clara is still the daughter of Grandmother Lowenthal, who disdains the use of Jewish names, who disapproved of Clara's decision to marry Arthur, because he seemed too Jewish?

What a fool, Elisheva thinks. Mother couldn't have found a better mate for herself. Of course, Grandmother Lowenthal's criteria were somewhat different. She was dismayed by this frail, skinny young man with thick glasses and asthma, who worked in the steel mill by day and went to school by night. She was dismayed too by the heavy Litvak accents of his parents, their herring and onions on rye bread, their thick borscht, their overcrowded dwelling.

Clara always teased her mother—"I suppose *you* came over on the Mayflower?"—but the disapproval must have hurt. Did Clara ever wish Arthur had a different family, a loftier background? Elisheva doesn't think so, although Clara was never entirely comfortable with Arthur's relatives, seemed to shrink slightly in their presence, maybe even disdained them secretly herself, just a little bit.

Still, Clara learned a lot from the Rogins; she quotes some morsel of Bubby Sadie's wisdom at least once a day. And while Elisheva was growing up, Clara always used the Rogins as an example of a "real family," devoted to each other, completely loyal. They were her model for family life, for the kind of family she wanted to create in this house.

Elisheva runs her fingers along the designs Deborah carved in the silver bracelet. By now she does not need to look. Her fingers tell her: this is the cow, and here is the pomegranate, and here the crescent moon. She remembers Deborah's voice, commenting on Clara's life: "Your mother gave up an exciting career to raise a family." Is it true? Could Clara have become a concert soloist, one of the ten or eleven in the world? Elisheva knows this is what her mother wanted, but so few arrive at that goal, even of those with talent and determination. When did Clara realize she was not to be one of the ten? When did she realize she would have a respectable but not illustrious career, playing in orchestras and giving lessons? Was it during the months of pregnancy, when the fullness of her tone astonished her, when she played more beautifully than she had ever played before? Did she know that the same baby who floated inside her, swelling her belly, swelling the sound of her cello, would soon call, "Mama," and interrupt her practice? Did she know what it might cost her to start a family? Did she think it was worth the cost? Does she now?

Arthur begins to wheeze rather heavily. Elisheva runs to get his inhaler, and as he sucks adrenalin into his lungs, a batter strikes out and a festive chorus ends the opera: "*Cantiamo, lodiamo, sì saggio signor.* Let us sing and praise our wise master."

By the time the record clicks off, Arthur is breathing normally. Maybe her mother wasn't exaggerating; maybe he is sicker than he was. "Dad? Is your asthma getting worse?"

He shakes his head vehemently. "Absolutely not. No better, no worse. Has your mother been alarming you? Is that why you were outside so long?"

"No, we were talking about Sonya and my piano lessons. Honest. But are you sure your asthma isn't worse?"

"Positive. August is always a bad month, because of the ragweed. And May is a bad month, from the pollen. Every year your mother insists it's worse than the year before. But it isn't. I wouldn't lie to you, Poopsie." He ruffles her hair. "So. My Poopsie is going to be a married lady."

"Dad? Do you think Mother would have become a famous cellist, if she hadn't had kids? Do you think we held her back?"

"We'll never know, will we." He lowers his already quiet voice. "She doesn't like to talk about it. You know your mother: no regrets, everything's fine, she has just the life she always wanted. 'Arthur, darling,' she says, 'when have you ever known me to give up anything for you or the children?' She reminds me of the summer when she went off to a music festival, and all the times I had to cook dinner and take care of you and Neil because she was giving lessons or playing in a concert somewhere. She makes me sound like a saint. Do you remember when I was still working at Uncle Jake's store, before I went back to school? None of our friends could understand how we managed—not just financially—how we got along with each other, when your mother had more of a profession than I did." He shrugs. "I don't know, Poopsie. Maybe we were ahead of our time. But I still think she compromised some, didn't travel as much as she should have to advance her career. That sort of thing. Who knows what might have been? I think it would be different today. If we were just getting married today, the way you are. Things are different for your generation. Girls of your age aren't expected to make the same sacrifices. Once you choose the right career for yourself, it won't matter that you're married. Even if you already have children, nobody will expect you to hold back from achieving as much as you can. Things are different now."

"Do you really think so? I'm not so sure." How different can things be, if Daniel is already pressuring her to hold back until he can catch up and then surpass? Her father's ideas about men and women are more progressive than her fiancé's. A distressing

178

thought. But when Arthur gives her a quizzical look, she says no more.

My dear Elisheva,

I and my wife offer many blessings and good luck to you and your bridegroom in the time of your betrothal. When you will return to Israel, we will be honored in receiving you and your Daniel as guests in our home. Maybe you want to make your wedding here? Ilana is ready to perform all anticipations.

Our health is good, thanks be. Only one difficulty, Dina cannot suffer our singing of "Itsy Bitsy Spider." I return here your letter with all corrections of Hebrew language. I will be happy if you can polish my English also. (You know this joke? "Polish my English? But my English is already Polish enough!") You see that even this "yekke" has a little sense of humour. I save other jokes for telling to you in person and in Hebrew.

Now I am afflicted from embarrassment. I read English excellent, but I do not have occasion to write in this language unhappily. I will anyway send this letter to you, with urgency for you to teach the teacher. Then soon I will know English writing so well to convince you against pantheism in two languages.

All the Cohen family send wishes of respect and happiness to your esteemed father and mother.

> In friendship and blessings,
> Shlomo Cohen.

"How formal he sounds!" Clara raises her eyebrows.

"I hope you'll meet him, Mother. You'd really get a kick out of him. He's even crazier than your musician friends."

"Impossible. Crazier than Sonya? Crazier than Igor?"

"Well, maybe not. Crazy in a different way. Anyhow, Sonya and Igor—all your friends—still think I'm a kid. Shlomo treats me pretty much as an equal, even though he's old enough to be my father."

Clara takes a sip from her glass. "Older men who treat young girls as equals usually have designs on them."

"Mother!" The word comes out in an adolescent whine. Goddamn, Elisheva thinks, there it is. Every time I come home, I turn into a teenager again. This isn't the way I want to be. This isn't . . . "Mother, that's really creepy of you, to make assumptions like that about my friends. And I'm not a 'young girl,' and

I'm not friends only with Shlomo. I'm friends with the whole family. I like Ilana a lot, too."

"But she's not the one who wrote to you, is she?"

"Mother, stop it! Shlomo and Ilana are my *friends*. They're like a second family to me." Oh, shit, now I'm out to hurt her. If I need a family so much, why don't I just stay here? Elisheva pours herself some more wine.

Ever since college this has been something of a ritual for Elisheva and Clara: once during each of Elisheva's visits home, they stay up late, drinking wine and talking. Because both of them drink infrequently, it doesn't take them long to reach the desired state of easy speech and loose limbs.

"*Mah nishtana ha-laila ha-zeh?*" Elisheva says. "Why is this night different from all other nights? On all other nights we giggle when we drink, but on this night we bicker."

Clara sighs. "I'm sorry, love. I'm just not myself tonight." She gets up and closes the door that separates the kitchen, where they have been sitting, from the rest of the house.

"Uh-oh," Elisheva says. "Bad news time."

Clara pours some salted nuts from a can into a seashell, and brings it to the table. "No bad news. Your father is doing exceptionally well for hayfever season. No, everything's fine. But tonight I want to tell you a secret about my past."

"Oh, goody! Let's tell each other secrets. You tell me one, and then I'll tell you one, and we'll keep going until we can't think of any more secrets that we're ready to tell each other."

"Please, darling, let me get started, or I won't even be able to tell you this one."

"Okay, I'm sorry. Go ahead. I just wanted to . . . Go ahead."

"Even your father doesn't know this. All these years I've been living a lie." Clara laughs and takes another sip.

Oh my God, Elisheva thinks, she's a lesbian. That's why she married so late. Or she's been cheating on Dad. Oh my God. Don't look scared, don't look . . .

"Don't look so frightened, Ellen. It's not all that horrible. I've just never told anyone about it."

"Jesus, Mother, what is it?"

"I was married once before."

"You were? To whom? Why didn't you ever tell us? What happened to him?"

Clara holds up her hand like a traffic cop. "All in good time, darling." She dips the same hand into the seashell and takes some nuts, which she eats one at a time. She chews very slowly, looking simultaneously weary and pleased with herself.

In the same slowed-down manner she once used for bedtime stories, Clara says, "When I was even younger than you are now, I fell in love with one of my professors at the conservatory. He was a handsome man, gray and distinguished, really quite dashing." She smooths back some of the hair that has escaped from her bun. Then she looks straight at Elisheva. "He too treated me as an equal, and I was most flattered."

"Mother, cut it out!" Teenager time again. "Are you just making this up, to warn me about Shlomo?"

"Don't be a ninny," Clara says sharply. "Don't you understand? It's just the opposite. The only reason I became so concerned about your friendship with Shlomo was that it reminded me of the first stage of my romance with Reginald."

"You're kidding! You actually married someone named Reginald? Then he wasn't Jewish. You fink! You always put so much pressure on us to date Jews."

"Shush. I didn't want you to make the same mistake I made."

"You mean it didn't work out because he wasn't Jewish?"

"No, no. It didn't work out because . . . he wouldn't consummate the marriage."

"How long were you married?"

"Six months."

"And you never made love?"

"Never. I finally got an annulment. To this day I wonder what the problem was. I don't know. Maybe he was frightened for some reason, maybe he didn't find me attractive."

Elisheva mumbles, "We may have a lot in common after all. . . .Shit, I must be drunk already."

"Now, now, no excuses. It's your turn for a secret. Let's have it."

"Look, I don't want to talk about this. I mean, Daniel's coming tomorrow, and I want you to like him. I don't feel right about badmouthing him now."

"No excuses. I'll like him fine. Even if I don't, I'll pretend I do. Oh dear, I guess I'm drunk too. Well, then, you're safe: you can tell me anything you like, and I won't remember a word of it tomorrow."

"Ha! I've never known you to forget anything, Mother. Okay, okay. It's nothing terrible, really. It's just that Daniel wants to wait until we're married to go to bed together."

"Why, Ellen, I think that's lovely! What's the problem? He must be an old-fashioned boy, and he truly respects and loves you."

"Or he's frightened, or he's not attracted to me, or whatever else was going on with Reginald."

"Oh, I think that's most unlikely, dear. After all, times have changed."

"That's just it. I've had sexual relations with men before. Why do I have to wait a year to go to bed with the man I'm going to marry? And he's never been with a woman before. Maybe he won't like it."

"Now why wouldn't he like it?"

Elisheva takes a deep breath. She tries to think clearly. How did this happen, that she allowed the conversation to take such a direction? Here she is, one step from revealing Daniel's homosexuality to her mother. Dr. Feinstein would have a field day with this. She can hear his voice: "Perhaps you wanted your mother to forbid this marriage? Or maybe you were testing her, to see how much she can accept?" No, no, no, not a good idea. Do something, Elisheva. Mother is waiting. Mother is not a stupid woman. Say something first, or she'll guess without your even telling her.

"Mother . . . Why didn't you ever tell Dad about your first marriage?" Good. Clara looks relieved. She wants not to be told. Good.

"Oh, I don't know, sweetheart. It wasn't even a real marriage, so why muddle things? I was already 30 when I met your father, and I didn't want him to think I was a reject."

"Mother!" Elisheva leans over and kisses Clara on the cheek. "No one could ever think you were a reject."

"Thank you, darling. Well, now, I haven't felt like a reject in many years, but I did then. And I was so young—I really had very little confidence in myself in those days."

"So young? But you were 'already 30,' remember? Caught you, Mother. I've got all the time in the world at 25, but you were an old reject at 30. So, by my fuzzy calculations, I don't have all the time in the world. I have less than five years, right?"

"Nonsense. The world has changed. Twenty-five is younger now than it was then."

"Tell that to the Israelis! They all see me as a hopeless old maid. 'You're not married yet? Why not?' Even Ilana did that routine when I first met her . . . Mother, if the same letter had come from Ilana instead of Shlomo, you wouldn't have even thought of any sexual intrigue, would you? I mean, the idea wouldn't have ever crossed your mind, right?"

"Yes, probably right. Why?"

"I just wondered."

"What an odd question." Clara goes to the door and opens it for a moment, listening, attentive as an animal, to be sure Arthur is not stirring. Then she closes the door again and returns to her chair. "Ellen, are there any other secrets you want to tell me?"

Elisheva takes another deep breath. "No, Mother, I don't think so."

"Are you sure?"

"Yes, Mother, I'm sure."

———

"Ellen, a car just pulled up. It must be Daniel. Yes, there he is, he's getting out. Ellen, he's wearing a suit and tie! In August! Ellen, hurry up, come and see. Arthur, Daniel's here. He's wearing a suit! Can you believe it? Ellen, there you are, good, you should be here to introduce us. Well, now I know he loves you. I've never seen a young man so eager to make a good impression. Look at him, darling!"

Elisheva joins her mother at the kitchen window, peeking between the yellow curtains. A young man, Daniel, her fiancé, is carefully straightening his tie. Why is she staring at him like a nosy neighbor? Why is she joining her mother, against him? Just by standing there with her mother, she is being disloyal. She is ridiculing him by remaining silent. Leave this kitchen, Elisheva. Go to the driveway. Go, run to him, embrace him in full view of Mother and Dad. It's okay, you're engaged.

But she can't seem to do it. She stands there, silent and paralyzed, awkward and sweaty and ugly. She is 14 years old. This young man is her first date. Her mother will not like him. Her father will wait up and greet her at the door before she can even get the key out of her purse, before the young man can lean toward her.

She is wearing an emerald-green brocade semiformal gown, and a pink-and-red corsage the young man brought her. The corsage does not match her dress but does match the pink-and-red hives she got all over her arms and face from sunbathing too long so that she would have a lovely tan.

It's a good thing the young man doesn't have time to lean toward her, because then he would smell the calamine lotion her mother smeared on her face and then covered with a pale powder so thickly that when Ellen left for the date, her face was even whiter than it had been before sunbathing. By now, though, most of the powder has brushed off, and she can feel the calamine crack when she smiles or talks.

If she is red and pink, the young man is yellow and orange: one of those farm kids with freckles on top of his freckles, and cowlicked hair the color and texture of straw. Her own hair is limp, though she sprayed it stiff while her mother was dabbing the calamine. All evening she has been sleepy, from the antihistamine pills she took to make the hives go away. She can't wait to go to bed. She can't wait.

She can't wait any longer. Daniel is walking up to the house. Her mother has left the window and is calling her to the living room. But she still can't make herself budge. She is planted in this spot, as firmly as if she were growing roots back into the kitchen floor, down to the cellar, and on down into the soil of this corner of Pennsylvania where she grew up, where she knows she will never live again. But still she stands there, like a small tree that was permitted to stay in its place while a house was built around it, a stubborn tree that has grown up through a hole in the roof, while its trunk thickened and thickened, and finally it threatens to tear apart the structure that has sheltered it, and it must be chopped at the ankles.

She wants to shout, "Mama! Please, Mama, don't let him take me away. Please, Mama, I just want to stay here with you. Don't make me go."

But she left her mother's house long ago—it has nothing to do with him—and she knows this impulse of return to be the last temptation of childhood. The temptation to return to the mother. Regression, in Dr. Feinstein's terminology.

She is no longer a child; this is not her first date; soon she will be a married woman. "When you grow up and get married . . ." That's what her parents always said, and she said it too: "When I grow up and get married." Soon she will be married. She is no longer a child, and soon she will be an adult. Soon she will know the secret.

She goes to the door and lets him in.

———

184

Several hours before Daniel's arrival, Clara put an extra leaf in the dining-room table and set six places. Although she and Elisheva removed two settings as soon as Neil called to cancel, it seemed pointless to go to the trouble of making the table smaller. The resulting arrangement reminds Elisheva of movies about English nobility: very few people seated at a very long table, with as much distance as possible between them. She hopes Daniel knows this is not her family's typical way of eating together; she hopes he is not utterly overwhelmed by her mother.

"I do hope Maggie's all right. Those summer flus can be simply miserable. More brisket, Dan? Are you sure you don't want any, Ellen? I know, I know, you've been a vegetarian three years, but I keep hoping. I just don't see how you can consider a meal complete without the meat course, dear. Don't you agree, Dan? Oh, don't answer, I don't want to put you in the middle of these mother-daughter disputes already. I should wait at least until tomorrow. Well, no matter, you'll meet Neil and Maggie soon enough. Perhaps it's better this way—not Maggie's illness, of course, but now we can spend an intimate weekend together, and then you can see Neil and Maggie in quieter circumstances. But I do love to get my whole brood together. Is your mother like that too, Dan?"

Daniel has just taken a bite of brisket, and he is in such a hurry to answer Clara's question satisfactorily that he starts to choke and has to leave the room for a moment. Clara follows him with a glass of water. Elisheva and Arthur raise their eyebrows at each other.

Daniel and Clara return and sit down. Daniel looks very serious and nervous. "I'm an only child," he says, and quickly adds, "but I hope Ellie and I will have a large family. I like large families."

"How remarkable! Oh, not that you like large families, but that you're an only child. How did your mother manage?"

"Clara! Will you please let Daniel eat his dinner in peace? I hope to enjoy his company as my son-in-law for many years to come, but he won't last long if you keep asking him questions just when he's taken a mouthful of food."

"That's all right, Dr. Rogin. But I don't think I understand Mrs. Rogin's question."

"Please, Dan, call us Arthur and Clara."

Elisheva reaches across the table to put her hand on Daniel's. He jumps. He was so intent on her parents that he forgot she

185

was sitting there. She says, "I've already told them that your parents are Catholic. It doesn't matter to them at all."

"Oh." Daniel relaxes immediately. Then he remembers Clara's question. He blushes. "I don't know what my mother did. I never asked her."

"Really," Arthur says, "these matters are none of our business. I'm surprised at you, Clara."

"You're right, of course, dear. I didn't mean to pry, Dan. I hope you understand. Oh, well, that's just the way I am. Curious Clara, they used to call me. At least you know I'm being myself. You just tell me if I ask you anything else that seems too personal. Promise? Good, then I won't have to worry. How about some dessert?"

After dinner Elisheva reads Shlomo's letter aloud to Daniel and Arthur.

Arthur says, "Are you really a pantheist?"

Daniel says, "Do you want to get married in Israel?"

Elisheva says, "I don't know. I don't know. I haven't thought at all about wedding plans. I don't much care where we get married. I just want a small ceremony, maybe with a *huppa* right here in the back yard."

"Oh, yes, let's have the wedding here!" Clara practically jumps out of her chair. "It's so beautiful here in June, and we can hold the ceremony under the fruit trees. Let's see, Sonya can play some music—maybe we can even have a nice quintet. We'll play whatever you like . . . "

Unable to contain herself any longer, she runs to the next room, and soon she is playing the Mendelssohn wedding procession on her cello. Everyone listens in silence, but then she begins to practice chords and arpeggios. Daniel looks somewhat confused.

"Don't mind Mother," Elisheva explains. "This is perfectly normal behavior for her."

"Absolutely," Arthur agrees. "Playing her cello is the only thing she loves more than talking."

Daniel still seems concerned. He clears his throat a couple of times. Finally he says, "Ellie and I haven't discussed it yet, Dr.— I mean, Arthur—but I kind of have my heart set on a New York wedding. I thought we could be married in the Sephardic synagogue, and I had something larger and more festive in mind than what you're talking about, Ellie."

186

"You're kidding," Elisheva says. "You mean you've been thinking about it that much? I couldn't care less about a big wedding."

"Why not? It's a big event in our lives, isn't it?"

Arthur says, "If you're worried about the expense, Poopsie, I don't want that to be a consideration. You kids should do this however you want."

"No," Elisheva says, "I wasn't even thinking of the cost, but that clinches it. I don't want to spend a whole lot of money on a ceremony. What's the difference? We'll be married our whole lives anyway; that's the important thing." She turns to Daniel for support, but he has such a disappointed expression that she relents. "Well, we'll have to talk about it some more."

Daniel leans forward. "Arthur," he says, "I want you to know that you can count on me to take good care of Elisheva. I mean, my parents aren't very well off, but I've always worked hard, and I've saved some money, and now I'm planning to go back to school and make a successful career for myself. And I'll try hard to be a good husband to her."

Arthur says, "I know you will, son."

Elisheva is flabbergasted. What is this, the eighteenth century? Her fiancé is asking her father for her hand in marriage. And her father goes right along with the scenario. Is this the same father who sounded so progressive, who said things would be different for women of her generation? And now here he is, talking with Daniel about her as though she were absent, as though she can't take care of herself, as though she will never earn a cent in her life.

Daniel will get his big wedding, and Clara will get her quintet, and Arthur will get a son-in-law to pat on the back, and Elisheva will get . . . what? A husband. A family of her own. A life as an adult. But how can she be an adult when everything is being decided for her? Well, let them talk, what the hell. They can't do any of it without her.

She stands up. "I will leave you gentlemen here to decide my future," she says. "I am going to bed."

She sits in the bed of her childhood, making a list of things to do here after Daniel leaves:

1) Visit Grandmother Lowenthal in Pittsburgh.
2) Send get-well note to Maggie.
3) Decide on policy for wedding plans.
   (when, where, how)

By a great effort of will, she stops herself from writing "why" after "how." Then she sits motionless until Daniel knocks on her door.

He comes in, sits on the bed, and takes her hand in the same manner he would use, say, if she were in the hospital to be treated for some serious disease. "I'm sorry, Ellie. I shouldn't have started talking about wedding plans in front of your dad without you and me discussing it first. If it's really important to you, we can get married here."

Elisheva shakes her head. "That's not the point. It's not important to me. None of the formalities matter to me at all. To hear you talk, the wedding counts more than the marriage." She starts to cry. "It's as if you want the wedding to prove something, I don't want to have to prove anything, Daniel. I want us to be happy together. I feel so far away from you. Daniel, hold me, please."

He holds her, though a bit gingerly. It is some help, just that he is there and stays with her while she cries. It is almost enough.

He says, "Do you want to get married right away?" His voice cracks in the middle of the sentence.

She is moved by Daniel's willingness to be flexible, to honor her needs even if this means getting married before he is quite ready. She places her hands on his cheeks. "No. Thank you but no. Getting married sooner isn't the point."

"I like your parents." Daniel is stolid in his suit and tie. A stolid son-in-law, a stolid husband. A stolid husband who lets men feel him up in movie houses?

"Good . . . Daniel, would you stay here with me tonight? We don't have to do anything. I just want you here with me. Please."

He hesitates, then says, "No, Ellie, I don't think it's a good idea. I'm sorry, but I don't think it's a good idea."

"Okay. Never mind. I shouldn't have asked."

He strokes her hair for a moment, then holds her face and kisses her. She wraps her arms around him, and they kiss each other's face and neck greedily, as they did when they first decided to marry.

Then it happens again: he begins to withdraw from her, and she reaches out farther and farther as he pulls back. Abruptly, he gets up and leaves her there, her body still sticking out all over. Her breasts feel long, pointy, distended; ungainly, they poke out in front of her. Her arms and legs are long and grasping, with nothing but a down comforter to hold. Her hips and thighs are soft and large, like a puddle of butter gradually spreading.

This is the trouble. She is supposed to be neater, more compact. She is supposed to take up less space.

She looks around the room. A small, neat room. She should become smaller, until she is just the right size for this room again. But the room does not feel like hers anymore. Her room is in Jerusalem, in the recent past; or in New York, in the imminent future. The slanted ceiling of this room is making her dizzy, is pushing down on her head.

When she returns to New York, she will find herself a room of the right size. Immediately. She will get away from Daniel's family and her own family, and she will find a room for herself, not someone's baby room, not a leftover room. Then, later, she and Daniel will find a larger room, for the two of them. A marriage room with a marriage bed.

She takes up the tablet and draws a line under her list. Beneath the line, she writes:

When I reach out to him, Daniel feels I am pushing. He wants me to be smaller than I am. He wants my desires to be smaller than they are.

I am always pushing toward him, pushing while he shrinks back. He cares for me, so why does he pull away? It makes no sense. It isn't fair.

He promises it will be different after we're married, but why will it be different? What will make it different?

Then she remembers that tonight is *shabbat*. She has been writing on *shabbat*.

———

All night she dreams, the same dream over and over. She is in the bathroom, naked, about to get into the tub. Through the window, she sees a very beautiful woman—Deborah?—climbing a vine on the side of the house. The vine is a bougainvillea, lush and healthy. Although it is a single plant, it has many kinds of blossoms: large golden ones like ripe apricots, and rich purple ones, and scarlet, and bright pink. Elisheva stares in wonder, flattening herself against a wall so that the woman will not see her. The room is perfectly dark, but the plant outside seems to

189

be glowing. Does the radiance emanate from the plant itself, or is it a reflection of moonlight? She cannot tell, but the colors are vivid, vivid.

Then she is climbing onto a tall metal bunk bed. She reaches from the bed to the top of a bookcase, to take a book to read, a large leather volume of Biblical scholarship. But the bookcase is too far away; the bed teeters; she falls off the edge. As she falls, she is both frightened and excited, for she knows the dream will now begin again, and she will once more see the woman and the plant.

"Daniel? Are you awake?"

"Mmm."

"It's *shabbat*. We forgot all about it. Want to make a service together, someplace outdoors?"

"No, do it without me. I'm too sleepy. See you later."

"Some rabbi you would have been. It's a good thing you quit."

No answer. She goes to the far end of the yard, under an apple tree, opens her *siddur*, and begins the sabbath prayers. It's hard to concentrate when there's no one to pray with. She misses Miriam. Miriam, and the apple tree . . . what? Oh, yes. Miriam's lovely irreverent version of the Ten Commandments. Miriam singing monotone, "Don't sit under the apple tree with any other god but me."

Don't sit under the apple tree and don't climb the bougainvillea, the old man's vine. Deborah is there, don't climb to Deborah. Don't reach for the books of scholarship; they recede farther each day, and you will surely fall. God requires fidelity, not scholarship, and marriage too requires concentration. Forsake all others and cleave unto Daniel—but that's not even Jewish, is it?

Prayer requires concentration and intention, *kavannah*, to hear each word in the mind, to say each blessing with awareness of its significance. How long since she has done this? She will try, she will try, but something in her loves distraction, enjoys the wandering of attention. Not the planned distraction, not the background music Daniel uses to change a mood or temper a conversation, with no intent to listen. Not this, but the spontaneous interruption of serious listening: the delightful moment when the soloist begins to hum along with his own performance, unaware, his off-key voice nearly drowning the sound of the piano. Unaware not because of lack of focus, but because he has ceased thinking of effect, has lost all self-consciousness, has allowed the music to move freely through his body, so that naturally it must emerge as song. Or the noisy men in an Orthodox synagogue, each one immersed in his own prayers, the clamor of their sincerity rising to the women's gallery with all the exuberant disorganization of an orchestra warming up.

So this is the problem. She still imagines herself in the women's gallery, not a participant but an onlooker. For the noise of prayer distracts not the men who create the noise, but the women who make up the audience.

She will try. She moves slowly and deliberately through the prayers, pronouncing every word aloud, swaying and chanting as she has seen the men do. It doesn't work. The necessary *kavannah*, the required attention, is missing. The words lack significance. When did the words lose significance? Since Deborah? No, earlier, but especially since Deborah.

Elisheva turns the silver bracelet on her wrist, examines the hieroglyphs of womanhood. Their texture under her hand makes her whole body tingle, and when she holds the bracelet up, sunlight glints off the engraved figures. Oh, Deborah, such a distraction you are, such a difficult gift you have given me. Did you know? Sometimes so heavy, like a shackle; sometimes swift and beautiful like you. Deborah, you're so hard to find. Deborah, I am giving you up. Forgive me, Deborah.

———

"Poopsie, is that you?"

Elisheva turns around in mid-step and enters her father's study. "Yes, Dad. I was just going to make myself a glass of iced tea. Want one?"

"Come sit with me for a minute first. Your mother's giving a lesson. I want to talk alone with you a little bit."

"Okay. Sure." She sits stiffly in the chair that would be the patient's seat if her father were a psychiatrist.

Arthur removes his reading glasses and looks straight at her. "Are you angry with me? You've hardly said a word to me since Daniel left."

"No, I'm not angry. Well, maybe a little bit. Yes. I'm angry about the way you acted with Daniel the first night he was here. Maybe you were only trying to be nice to him, but I felt like you and he were starting some sort of fraternity. All that stuff about a big wedding, and how well he would take care of me, and you just listened. I might as well not have been there. Before Daniel arrived, you talked such a good game: times have changed, I don't have to be trapped, I don't have to be just a wife. What I heard you and Daniel saying was that I have to be just a wife."

"Oh, honey, I'm sorry. I suppose I was trying to be nice to him. Let me think. That's not all. There's an old-fashioned side to me, and the situation brought it out. I've never had my daughter get married before. I guess I feel someone should protect you in the world, and your husband should do it when you're too old for your dad to do it anymore. I'm sorry. I didn't mean to insult you. What can I say? I'm still a product of my generation. In a way, what I did is proof that it's too late for people of my age—but you and Daniel can make things different if you want to."

"Yeah. But look how Daniel was acting. He was worse than you. You went along with him, but he was the one who said all the things I'm objecting to. And he's in my generation, not yours. What's his excuse?"

"A good question." Her father's expression, his position in the chair, suddenly change: he is poised for attack. There is something he disapproves of, strongly. She hasn't seen this expression in many years. It frightens her. She watches him lean forward, his eyes intense, focused on a principle, then refocused on her, seeing her fear, relenting, softening. Almost in unison, they sigh. Almost in unison, his long breath of effort, recomposing him into a stance of patience and forbearance; and her long breath of relief, recomposing her into a stance of adulthood.

"What, Dad?" Now that he will not lunge, she can ask. "What are you holding back from saying?"

Arthur sighs again. "Well, you asked what Daniel's excuse is. To tell you the truth, you and Daniel are both a mystery to me. I don't understand what you're doing, why you're so enchanted with Orthodoxy. You both seem as if you're trying to turn back the clock and live the way my parents did. I just don't understand it. You especially. I saw you Saturday morning, out in the back yard, bowing and swaying in prayer, and—well, you could have been my mother."

"Bubby Sadie was a good woman. I could do worse."

"You could do a lot worse, honey. You know that isn't the point. I just don't understand what appeals to you . . . You know what I mean. Religion. Your mother and I raised you in the liberal tradition. If anything, we expected you to move a few steps to the left of us, as we did with our parents. When you got involved in the peace movement, I understood why. But when you started going to *shul*, keeping *shabbos* . . . ”

She tries to think how to explain herself, how to do in English what she did so quickly in Hebrew for Shlomo Cohen: define her beliefs. "Dad, it has nothing to do with God. It has to do with being a Jew, being part of the community of Jews everywhere, saying the oldest words of our first language. It's the language that drew me in, the sound of the language . . . Dad, I think you and Mother did a great job of raising kids. All you left out was our history, our identity as Jews. That's what your parents had, what Israel has. That's where I've needed to return. Can you understand?"

"Not really . . . Well, almost. I guess I'll have to modify my belief in Progress." He laughs at himself. "Things aren't as simple as they seem."

They sit in silence for a moment.

"Poopsie, can we come back to Daniel? There's still something I want to say. Okay?"

"Yeah. Okay." She hears an edge of nervousness in her own voice. But surely the hardest part of this conversation must be over?

"First of all, I want you to remember that whatever you do, your mother and I will stand behind you. We know you're an adult now, and we trust you to do what's right for you. Okay?"

"Please, Dad, don't keep me in suspense. What's on your mind?"

"Well, honey, I'm a little bit concerned about your engagement to Daniel."

"Great. Join the crowd. I sure did misjudge you and Mother. I thought you'd be thrilled, or at least pleased."

"It's not that I'm not pleased. Hear me out, honey, okay? Sometimes I get hunches about people. Something worried me about Daniel. Oh, he seems like a fine young man, very nice and sincere, quite intelligent. It's not his personal qualities I doubt. It's his love for you. Maybe it was the way he kept stressing money, emphasizing that he would make a good living, he would support you well, all that. I know he was probably just trying to please me, and maybe it doesn't mean anything, but . . . I guess I'm an old romantic at heart."

"That's not what Mother says. She calls you a real classicist."

"Oh, sure, in music and intellectual matters. But when it comes to marriage, I'm convinced financial security isn't what holds two people together. Money isn't very important, just so you have enough to live on. But I love you so much, honey, I don't want to see you marry anyone who doesn't appreciate you. I want you to marry somebody who is so crazy about you that he doesn't think at first about money or wedding ceremonies or anything but making you happy. I want you to marry someone who loves you passionately. Please, honey, before you marry Daniel, be sure he loves you passionately."

Elisheva gulps. "Thank you, Dad. You really care, don't you? Thank you." She squeezes his hand.

"Yes, I do. Poopsie, don't make the same mistake I made . . . Oh, I don't mean marrying your mother. That's the best thing I ever did. I've never regretted it for a moment. I mean waiting so long to find the right kind of life for myself. I could kick myself when I think of all the years I wasted, working in the mills, ruining my health, and then working in Uncle Jake's store across the street from the mills, ruining my health some more. Oh, I know I'm lucky. Some people never get out of the rut. They stay in a job they hate all their lives. And at least we had this house, so you kids could grow up in a healthy environment, and then with your mother's help I did manage to finish graduate school. But it's just . . . time is so precious, honey. I lost so much time along the way, and no one lives forever. Now don't look scared, Poopsie. I wasn't lying to you. I'm still going strong. I just want you to know it's important to use your life in the way you were meant to use it, whatever that is. Value your life, Elisheva. . . . Damn, I'm getting corny today. Well, once in a while I'm entitled. Right? Now give me a kiss, Poopsie, and I'm going to take a shower, and then if you want, we'll take a walk together."

Elisheva kisses him. "Thank you, Dad. Thank you." She can't think of anything else to say, so she leaves the room quickly.

In a few minutes she hears him singing in the shower, in an almost-strong baritone. *"Non più andrai . . . "* Figaro again. The shower stops and Arthur, wrapped in a large red towel, rushes out into the hall. He extends one of his thin arms for her inspection.

"Look, honey! I gave myself goosebumps. My own singing gave me goosebumps. Do you know how many years it's been since my own singing gave me goosebumps?"

3

In a museum in Israel, I saw a granite sculpture of a young man carrying a calf on his shoulders. I can still visualize the young man's body, the musculature of his stomach, thighs, forearms. The navel like a decorative button or decal stuck in place, as though the sculptor wanted to forget the meaning of the navel, as though he did not want to think this beautiful young man had been born of woman. All the muscles of the young man's arms and belly, all his strength, focus on the animal's feet, which he holds bound over his heart.

The calf does not know she is headed for slaughter. She trusts the young man, knows him, has been carried in this way before. She relaxes, settles comfortably about his neck.

I stared at the sculpture for a long time. I wanted to ask the young man, "How can you do this? You raised the animal, gave her a name, led her to trust you. How can you now hand her over to the butcher or the priest? Her blood will be dashed upon the steps you climb. How can you walk there?"

Later, I remembered that statue, and I remembered the words of my father. I understood then what he meant. "If you marry Daniel and he does not love you passionately," he was saying, "it will be as though I raised you for the butcher."

It was during our visit to Pennsylvania that Daniel began to sleep too much. First I couldn't get him up to *daven* with me on *shabbat* morning, then I couldn't get him up for brunch, then he needed an afternoon nap and fell asleep over dinner. At the time I thought he was just being ornery, avoiding my parents; now I know he was depressed.

"Poor boy," my mother said. "He must be working too hard."

He was working too hard, all right. Trying to become hetero-

195

sexual, trying to impress, trying to please, trying to ignore his most urgent longings. It was enough to tire anyone.

The more he slept, the more tired he seemed. The more he slept, the more wakeful I became, and the more I resented his sleep. I would lie awake in my new apartment, listening to traffic and voices in the street, worrying. I worried about the mattress upon which I lay: I had found it on the sidewalk and dragged it up with the help of the super, and although I sprayed and aired it well, I still suspected bedbugs or fleas. I worried about the ugly stripes of blue and purple tape on the wall: who had decorated the apartment so horribly, and why, and how could I remove the tape without ruining the wall, and how could I remove the feeling of an ugly presence in the room with me? I worried about Daniel: why was he avoiding me by sleeping so much, and why was he so grumpy when I asked him about it, and what had happened to the sweetness I loved in him, and when would he shape up and let us be happy together? I had moved into his neighborhood, the West Village, to live among his people, the gay men, and yet he was less and less accessible to me.

And I worried about myself. What had happened to me, that I had so little sense of who I was anymore? I wasn't a wife and wasn't a new immigrant and wasn't a New Yorker. I had three jobs and no career. I was engaged to marry a man who didn't love me passionately. I had cut loose from Mother, had snipped the leash that tied me to the sound of her cello. I had left Israel and lost the religion I justified to my father. I had written on *shabbat* and quit studying Torah and couldn't concentrate on the prayers that made me look like my grandmother.

Late at night when I couldn't sleep, I wrote letters to Miriam. I made Miriam my conscience.

"Miriam," I wrote, "something has changed. None of the rituals have meaning for me anymore. It's as though religious observance were once a large circle, and I stood in the center with Jews everywhere. And then the circle shrank, and I found myself crouching at the edge, with the circumference pushing in on me, until I want to break out altogether.

"If I had been raised Orthodox, I would know what to do now: go on keeping the umpteen little laws, in the hope that sooner or later the meaning would return. This is what Shlomo does, and what I imagine you do. But I wasn't raised Orthodox. I learned the rules only recently, and they don't make logical sense; you have to really believe in them, or you have to have practiced them all your life, until you almost can't imagine any other way to live.

"Jewish identity continues to be as important to me as ever. But I seem to be abandoning the rituals and laws. Can you understand? Can you accept?"

"Miriam," I wrote, "something has changed. Daniel does not want to be around me. He avoids me, avoids touching me. He responds to me with mild distaste. Nothing extreme, but still it is a form of disgust, and I feel it whenever I am with him.

"How can I marry someone who does not want to be around me, who does not want to touch me? And who am I now, if I do not marry him? I dropped something to run to him, and now I can't seem to pick it up again, or even remember exactly what it was.

"Can you understand? Can you remember for me?"

I mailed the first letter, but not the second. I did not want Miriam's reply to the second letter. I did not want her voice added to the dismal chorus: the admonitions of my mother and father, and the whispers of the men cruising outside my window. "Don't do it," they all said. "Don't marry him. Don't do it don't marry him don't do it don't do it don't do it."

———

Elisheva stands on the ladder she borrowed from the super and paints the ceiling of her new apartment. Although she is being as careful as she can, tiny drops of off-white paint spatter onto her face and hair, onto the old AM radio Daniel gave her, onto patches of wood floor. Before starting to paint, she covered the floor with yesterday's *New York Times*; but she has already been working for several hours, and every time she moves the ladder, the sheets of newspaper slide together in a pathetic effort to reconstitute their original order.

It's hopeless, she thinks. The pages that belong together will never find each other; even if they did, most of the words are covered over with paint and dirt. The newspaper will never be the same; the world it describes will never be the same; this wood floor will never be the same; I will never be the same.

A voice on the radio croons, "You've got a friend," and tears spring to Elisheva's eyes. Oh, come on, now. Get on with the work. It's already two in the morning, the paint will harden in the can, no time for self-pity, get to work, turn off the radio if necessary. That's right, spread the paint, spread the paint, leave the radio on, move the brush in time with the music, one two three four, just like Dad conducting a record, just like Mother sweeping her bow across the strings, that's right, paint, paint, move the ladder and paint, one two three four, four are the mothers, Sarah Rebecca Leah and Rachel, three are the fathers, Abraham Isaac and Jacob, two are the tablets of the Law, one is our God our God our God who is in the sky and in the land. *Eḥad Elohenu Elohenu Elohenu she-b'shamayim u-v'aretz.*

No, no, that's a Pesach song. It's not Pesach, it's almost Rosh Hashana and where the hell is Daniel? He was supposed to come help at three in the afternoon, he still wasn't here at eight, so she left a note on her door and took the subway uptown to his new old duplex apartment in Washington Heights, how strange, he is in the Jewish neighborhood and she is in the gay neighborhood, he didn't want to get a place near her, he doesn't want to be near her, no that's not what he said, he said he didn't want to be in the Village, too much temptation, too many but he wasn't in his apartment, so she left a note on his door and came back and started painting by herself.

Fuck him, ha, that's probably what he's doing, getting fucked, well, fuck him. He was supposed to come at three, he didn't come, he didn't even call, where the hell is he? She already put off painting the apartment how many days, must be at least ten, ten are the words of the commandments, nine are the months of pregnancy, eight are the days to circumcision, seven are the days for *shabbat.* Ten days ago he couldn't come to help, then it was weekend and he couldn't help on the weekend, then there were classes and jobs and where the hell is he? At least he used to call, or come late and apologize, it wasn't a good time to help her install a new lock, it wasn't a good time to paint, he forgot his work clothes in New Jersey or he had to get up early tomorrow, let's just go out for a hot fudge sundae.

How many hot fudge sundaes have they consumed together? Twelve are the tribes of Israel, eleven are the stars of Joseph, ten are the words of the commandments, nine are the months of pregnancy. Daniel can fuck anytime he wants and never get pregnant, how many months until we will we won't?

The ten words of commandment: don't don't don't don't don't don't don't don't and don't. Ten words in one don't is our God our God our God who is in the sky and in the land but not in the West Village in the elevator and mattress and wall of tape. Don't tape the wall should have been the eleventh commandment, thou shalt not tape the wall because the tape never comes off and then you've got a friend a fiancé who doesn't show is better than no fiancé at all but not by far. Who needs him find somebody else no they're all the same but some want to fuck and some want to get fucked and I picked the wrong kind or the right kind depending on your point of view what is my point of view? Doesn't matter, doesn't matter, picked this one make it work with this one make it work. Work, work, how when he doesn't come at three or eight or eleven? Doesn't matter you've got a friend but where is he?

In the morning he sleeps, later and later, doesn't get to morning classes, doesn't wake up until I knock on his door when will he get a phone installed when will we talk by wire by cord by hook or by crook? When will the painting be over? When can I turn off the radio and go to sleep? By hook or by crook I'll do it by myself I'll show him fuck him. A burglar or worse could have broken in and what did he care fuck him.

So she changed the lock yesterday by herself, did a good job too but went out into the hall to try it and forgot the key. Had to call the cops, two of them came and kicked her door in. She could have kicked in her own door but her boots were locked in the apartment with the key. At least she had a dime in the pocket of her second-hand jeans, dime came with the jeans, lucky for her she'd just bought them that day. At least the neighbors came out on the landing to see what was happening when the cops kicked her door in, and again when the locksmith was fixing the door today. Doesn't necessarily mean they would do anything to help if she were in trouble, but at least they stepped out to see. One woman said, "You okay?" Yes, I'm okay, false alarm, but now if I really do need their help they'll think I just locked myself out again. I blew it I need his help where the hell is he?

The tape wouldn't come off the wall without making holes in the plaster, and by the time she started painting, it was too late to find a hardware store open and buy solvent for the tape, so she left it there and painted right over it. Ugly wall ugly apartment, ugly and smelly, a few roaches under the sink too, and the tape is covered with paint but the ridges still show on that ugly wall.

There, she's done and the drops of paint in her hair have turned hard, little off-white chips that fall around her when she climbs down from the ladder, and where the hell is he?

All night she breathes paint fumes and dreams about paint. Daniel is driving her somewhere. The white line down the middle of the road thickens and thickens until the whole road is white, a white painted strip stretching ahead of them. Finally they arrive at a campground. Daniel disappears. She peeks into every tent, but he is nowhere. Then he walks toward her, accompanied by another man. Both Daniel and his friend are wearing makeup: two coats of lipstick, red first and then blue covering the red. She stares at them in fascination. What do they know that she doesn't know?

―――――

"Okay. You want to know where I was last night? Here's where I was. You see those big long trucks? Over there, by the warehouse, near the dock. See? That's where I go at night. You said you don't care what I do. This is what I do. I climb into the back of one of those trucks, and it's full of men. We fuck each other in the same place we shit from, you know what that means? You know what that feels like, wiping some guy's shit off your cock? That's what we do. We do everything we can to each other, over and over, all night long we squirm around in there, and the truck gets all wet and smelly inside, and it's very degrading, and that's just the way we like it.

"We like it that way, do you understand? I like it. I've always liked it, and I'll always like it, are you listening? That's sex for me, and you and I can never have it the way I like it. You want to know what I like? I like diving in there, into that pile of male bodies and male smells. First I suck some guy's cock, and maybe some guy starts sucking my cock at the same time, and maybe some guy is screwing me too. I like it, do you understand? I like the feeling of a cock pushing into my asshole. I like the feeling of a cock filling up my whole mouth until I'm about to gag. I like the taste of sperm, and I like the taste of a man's asshole, and I like the taste of a cock that's been dipped in sperm and spit and shit. Sometimes when some guy is fucking me in the ass, I get so excited I come, without my cock even being touched. Sometimes I get so excited I faint for a minute, and when I come to, some guy is sucking my cock and some other guy's cock is up my ass, and I like it. Do you understand? That's what I like. I come here because I like it. I can't give it

200

up. I won't give it up. I like it too much ever to give it up. I wouldn't give it up for Bill, and I sure as hell won't give it up for you. Do you understand, Elisheva? I want you to understand. This is sex for me. This is sex. This and nothing else.

"If you marry me, I will leave you alone in bed at night, and I'll come here, and then I'll come back smelling like sweat and sperm, with some guy's shit on my cock. Are you going to put up with that? Are you going to want to make love after that? Are you? Can you still say you don't care what I do, just so I respect and love you? Can you still say that? Say something, dammit. Say something!"

She opens her mouth, but no sound comes out. She has lost her voice. She sits in his car with her mouth gaping open, round as a silent howl. She cannot move, she cannot speak, she can do nothing. She is paralyzed, powerless, fixed in place with her mouth open, weak and silent. She wants to close her mouth, if only to be less unattractive to him, but all the muscles of her body have gone slack.

He sits beside her, heavy and hard, his face closed up and turned away. He has taken her strength. His body has stolen the firmness that her muscles require to protect her, to cover her over, to pull her together and move her away. He is a boarded-up house. He has boarded himself up with her strength. Give it back, Daniel, give it back.

When he turns to look at her, she sees no strength in his face; she sees only fear. He has taken her strength, and still he is afraid of her. Give it to me, Daniel, give it back, but he hides from her like a frightened animal crawling under the porch after stealing a dinner. He has taken her strength into the darkness, and she is alone in the blinding light that surrounds her, shines into her face, so that all can see her but she can see no one. He has swallowed her voice, and she cannot hear even an echo. She looks at him, and his face disappears, taking hers with it; she cannot see even a reflection of herself. She sees nothing. She is surrounded with light, and he has stolen her shadow. She is flat and white against a bright white wall, surrounded by flat white light. He has stolen her voice, her face, her shadow. She is mute, flat and silent, and although there is light all around her, she can see nothing.

Never has Daniel been so attentive. He calls several times a day, and when she refuses to speak to him, he begins to leave notes in her mailbox. He says things like "I'll always love you," and "It's not you I'm rejecting, it's marriage and heterosexuality," and "We can still be friends." She doesn't believe a word of it. The more messages he sends her, the angrier she feels. What good are his attentions to her now? For weeks he ignored her—worse, for years he deceived her. His kind, gentle demeanor was only a front. All this time, even while he was planning to marry her, he has been crawling around in dirty, smelly trucks, indulging in grubby, anonymous sex. It makes her sick to think about. Her Daniel, doing disgusting things with disgusting strangers. Not even bringing them home with him, but fucking in alleys behind warehouses. Never even seeing their faces, never talking with them, knowing them only by the sound of their zippers, the taste of their semen.

Her Daniel. She offered him her whole life, and he rejected her. He prefers a mass of writhing penises to her whole life. He is superficial and disgusting. He is a liar and a cheat. The suit he wore to Pennsylvania was a lie, his constant sleep was a lie, his promises to her were nothing but a lie. His avoidance of her body was a lie, led her to feel ugly and unappealing, led her to think there was something wrong with her, when in reality there is something wrong with him.

He is sick and disgusting. He says he will always love her, but what does he know about love? He doesn't even make love like a human being, face-to-face.

For years she was quick to anger with him, picked fights for no apparent reason, gave him a hard time. She always seemed to be hurting him who never hurt her, punishing him for the bad behavior of others, taking advantage of his good nature, failing to treat him as well as he deserved. Now she knows why. All those years, she was waiting for the moment when he would hurt her worse than she has ever hurt him. All those years, she was building up to this large, righteous anger, which knows its cause and its target.

She will never forgive him. She swears she will never forgive him.

———

At the end of two weeks, Daniel appears at her door. He looks tired and upset. She lets him in, gives him a cup of coffee.

She says, "How could you just change your mind like that? One minute you want to marry me, the next minute you don't. It's not fair." She is crying.

He puts a hand on her shoulder. She twitches him away.

He says, "Would it be more fair of me to marry you when I don't want to?"

"That's not the point."

"Do you still want to marry me?"

"No. I don't."

"Then let me be your friend. Please. I know you're hurting, and I want to help you. Please let me help you."

"Don't you understand at all?" She tries to control her voice, but it comes out in a horrible shriek. "Don't you understand? You were my last hope. You were my last goddamn hope."

"Elisheva—"

"What the hell am I supposed to do with my life now? Huh? What am I going to do with my goddamn life?"

"I don't know, but—"

"And you have the *hutzpah* to offer to help me? Get the hell out of here."

————

Elisheva looks at her Jewish calendar. Sukkot, the autumn harvest festival, is over. Today is *Simhat Torah*, "Rejoicing in the Torah." Miriam is in synagogue in Jerusalem. Shlomo, Milton, Dr. Feinstein are all in synagogue, dancing and singing, holding the Torah in their arms. Shlomo, in honor of his great learning, has surely been named either *hattan Torah*, "bridegroom of the Torah," who chants the last portion of Deuteronomy; or *hattan B'Reshit*, "bridegroom of In the Beginning," who renews the yearly cycle of Torah by chanting the first portion of Genesis.

Elisheva does not go to synagogue or sing or dance, but in her room she silently reads the end of Deuteronomy, in which Moses dies and is buried; then, the beginning of Genesis, in which the world is created. Like Jews everywhere, she says, "*Hazak hazak v'nithazek.* Strong strong and we will strengthen ourselves." Like Jews everywhere, she turns her body to face Jerusalem, and asks for abundant winter rains in Israel.

Then she goes for a walk alone in Central Park. She thinks of Daniel, and for the first time she feels nothing but relief. She walks firmly, with a long healthy stride, enjoying the motion of

203

her body and the swish of her long raincoat against her legs. She inhales the fresh, wet autumn air. She stops to admire a large maple, its brilliant red leaves covered with water droplets. The tree is itself, nothing but itself.

She calls Daniel from a pay phone. "I just saw this tree. I have to tell you about this tree."

Daniel laughs. "Where are you? Come on over."

She takes a crosstown bus, then an uptown bus. Daniel has left his front door unlocked for her. He is lying in bed, he waves her to him, he has such a lovely smile, he looks so relaxed and expansive. How nice, at last they can relax with each other.

She throws off her raincoat and sits beside him. "Daniel, I have to tell you about this tree. It was just like you. I saw this beautiful tree, and all I wanted was for the tree to be itself, and all I want is for you to be yourself. Daniel, I think I'm finally accepting you. I think I'm finally loving you the way I want to."

With the warm smile still on his face, he pulls her down beside him on the bed. He kisses her, a long, gentle, sensuous kiss. She knows that this time they are going to make love; she is only a little bit surprised. When he begins to unbutton her blouse, she murmurs, "You've taken a shower since your last time at the trucks, haven't you?"

"Yes."

"You don't have V.D., do you?"

"No."

He doesn't seem nervous at all. She is the one who is nervous and hesitant, because she is afraid she may lose the tree feeling. But the way they make love is no threat to the tree feeling; it is no threat to anything. They grasp each other by the shoulders and shake one another a little: that is what it's like. Friendly but not at all passionate. He has no idea where to touch her—he doesn't even seem to notice that she has breasts—but he knows how to kiss and thrust, and nothing goes wrong.

Afterwards, he says, "Is that all there is to it?"

"Well, yes, sometimes that's all there is to it."

"Oh. Do you want to sleep over?"

"Sure."

She cuddles her back into his warm chest and belly, and feels his semen running down the inside of her thigh as she falls asleep.

In the morning she discovers a small bloodstain on the sheet.

"Look," she says. "Either I was a virgin again, or I just got my period."

She goes to the bathroom to check. "Thank God, it's my period. I don't have to worry about pregnancy this time."

Daniel looks horrified. "You mean what we did could have made you pregnant? It never even occurred to me that what we were doing could have made you pregnant."

"Don't worry," she says. "I may never do it again."

———

Dear Elisheva,

Thank you for trusting me enough to tell me about the changes in your religious life. You're right, this kind of questioning isn't for me. I don't think I could ever consider giving up the *mitzvot*. But I understand the difference between us. You have begun a serious and important search. I want to be in on it and to know where it leads you.

How is Daniel? Are the two of you still planning to return to Israel after your wedding? (Please say yes. I miss you very much.)

Elisheva, there's something I need to tell you. I've been seeing Milton lately. The truth is, we've fallen in love, and we're talking about marriage. I've never been so happy in my life. The only thing that's bothering me is a feeling of guilt towards you. I hope you're not angry with us and you don't feel hurt or betrayed. I know you and Milton never really hit it off, but I still feel a little bit wrong to have gotten involved with him. Is it okay with you?

Milton sends best wishes to you and Daniel.

Love from your *ḥavera*,
Miriam

———

Dear Miriam,

What wonderful news! *Mazal tov* to you and Milton. He's a very lucky man. May you have many happy years together.

Daniel and I have called off our engagement. I don't think I want to go into the details right now, but it's a good decision for both of us. Of course I was upset at first, and I'm still somewhat unsettled, but I know this is the right choice and it's another step in what you call my "search."

In a funny way, I've never felt as close to Daniel as I do now.

We're much looser with each other, now that the pressure to marry is off. We spend almost all our time together, and we talk constantly. It's turning into a very sound friendship, something like what you and I had in Israel. And it would have been a disastrous marriage—take my word for it!

Daniel and I have been talking about starting some kind of project together. A school, or maybe a community center. We do work very well as a team—that's what first brought us together, in the peace movement, and then we sort of lost track of it.

As of now, I don't picture that I'll be returning to Israel soon, but it's hard to say. I'm really loving New York. It's such a lively place, crackling with energy, everything moving so quickly. This city gives me a buzz. I'm even enjoying the noise. It's a good place for me to be right now, a good place for making changes fast.

Be well and happy. I have only good wishes for you and Milton. Promise me you won't waste any more time feeling guilty.

Love,
Elisheva

4

Elisheva sits on a folding chair and stares at the altar. Except for sightseeing, this is the first time she has entered a church since she was ten and accompanied a classmate to Confession one Saturday afternoon. She is just as uncomfortable now as she was then, just as uncertain whether to sit or stand, to talk with someone or be quiet, to look around her or straight ahead.

She doesn't want to be here, but she promised Daniel, when he found the ad in the *Village Voice*:

> OPEN MTG. OF NYC GAY COMMUNITY
> Topic: End of GLF, where to go from here, how to pull together. Sun. 8 p.m., St. Augustine's. OPEN TO ALL.

"But I'm not a member of the gay community."

"I am, and I want you to come with me. See, it says 'open to all.'"

"But I've never even heard of a GLF."

"Gay Liberation Front. Bill and I used to be members. I'll tell you all about it before the meeting. I promise. Please come. I need your support."

"But, it's in a church. Why is it in a church?"

"St. Augustine's is a good church. They give us free space for gay liberation meetings. You'll like it."

She doesn't like it. It's too big, too cold. It's a church. And she's the only woman so far, and it's already 8:30 and the meeting still hasn't started, and Daniel's over there talking with someone named John, a guy he knew in the old GLF days. John seems nice enough, the other men seem nice enough, but there are only twenty of them. Where are all the rest, the ones she sees cruising the West Village whenever she looks out her window or leaves her apartment? And why aren't there any women?

At last, two women come in together, followed immediately

by a third, younger woman. They all sit directly across the semi-circle of chairs from Elisheva and begin to talk with each other.

Oh my God, Elisheva thinks, that must be the women's side. I'm sitting on the wrong side. Then she remembers, this is a church, not a *shul*. This is a gay liberation meeting. She is here because she promised Daniel, not because she wants to meet women. Sit still, Elisheva.

She sits very still, looking at her hands. Soon Daniel comes to sit next to her, with John on his other side. Elisheva restrains herself from glancing at Daniel's knee, to make sure John isn't fondling it the way Mr. Wilbur did at the movies. *Tisht'kee*, Elisheva. Quiet yourself. *Ha-kol b'seder*. Everything is okay. The meeting will begin. Everything will be okay. *Ha-kol b'seder*.

John speaks first. He's the one who called this meeting. So, Daniel goes for leaders. That's the problem, she's not enough of a leader. Oh, God, what's the matter with her tonight? She is reverting to all the old ugly feelings, the ones she thought she was done with: jealousy, insecurity, he rejected me poor me what am I to do? Remember the tree, Elisheva, remember the tree. She imagines the splendid trunk, the red leaves falling all around her. Rake them in, burn them, rake them in, burn them. There. Better.

Listen to John. John wants to go around the circle, everybody say something. Oh God, what is she going to say? Good, he starts in the other direction. They speak, one male voice after another. "I came out in '67, I was a founding member of GLF, now I'm active in GAA." Daniel told her about GLF, but what the hell is GAA? Gay something something. Gay Alcoholics Anonymous? Gay Automobile Association?

She is shocked to hear a woman's voice, even though she saw the women enter. She looks up. Three women, one speaking—GLF, GWLF, GAA—and the other two staring at Elisheva. She blushes, but she keeps looking back at them. The woman speaking is dark and intense, doesn't smile; the other older one is blonde; both are wearing jeans and sweaters; the young one is in overalls. They look like regular women, not strange at all. But the young woman is so very young, maybe just starting college; that's too young to decide you're gay; Elisheva disapproves.

Now the blonde one is speaking; why do they keep staring, what do they see? What is Elisheva wearing, and why can't she remember anything tonight?

208

Elisheva looks down and remembers. She is still wearing the same outfit she put on this morning to teach Hebrew School: a yellow turtleneck and a plaid jumper, navy and red and yellow in big squares, the blocks of primary color proclaiming, "I'm straight! I'm straight!" Oh God, and nylons, and conservative pumps with stacked heels. Why didn't she change into her new second-hand jeans?

Suddenly she hears the voice of the man to her right, and after him will be her turn, and what on earth is she going to say? *Shmee Elisheva Rogin. Oy va voy! B'anglit! B'anglit!* In English, Elisheva, please remember, you're in New York City, they speak English here. English, remember?

"I'm Elisheva Rogin." One of the men asks her to repeat it. "El-ee-shay-vah. Um, I just returned to the U.S. after two years in Israel, and I came here tonight to accompany my friend Daniel. Also, I'm interested in learning more about the gay movement."

"I'm her friend Daniel." Laughter. "I was active in GLF for a while, and then I tried to go straight, but now I know myself better, and I know I'm gay. So I'm back."

John says, "Welcome back." There is some applause.

The meeting continues. Elisheva hardly listens. Why didn't anyone welcome *her* back? Doesn't she count for anything? After all, she said she'd been out of the country for two years.

Good Lord, what nonsense. This isn't the welcome wagon, it's the gay community. She just announced she was only accompanying her friend Daniel, and then she expects an ovation. She just said she was here to learn, and she isn't even listening.

She makes an effort to listen, but doesn't learn much. More initials, and plans for another meeting in a few weeks.

John says, "I hope more women will attend next time. If we're going to form an umbrella, we need a better balance . . . Yes? Ann?"

The young woman says, "Can anyone give me a ride home?"

Daniel volunteers. Then the meeting is over, and he leans toward Elisheva to whisper, "That woman sure is attracted to you."

"What woman?" Elisheva is blushing again. A woman, attracted to her?

"The small one with dark hair. She was looking you over the whole time. Come on, you know which one I mean."

"Are you sure? I didn't notice. I mean, I noticed all the women looking at me, but not *that* way."

"Is this modesty, or didn't you see? I'm going to have to give you another lesson in gay culture. You don't even know when someone's cruising you."

"You mean the women cruise, too? How come I don't see them in the streets? Do they cruise in some other neighborhood?"

"I don't know. I guess they must cruise somewhere, or how would they meet? Hey, we'd better go. John is ready to lock up, and he and Ann need a ride home."

When Daniel opens the car door, Ann jumps into the back, and then John and Elisheva each wait for the other to climb in back with her. Oh, well, when in Rome, Elisheva thinks, and gets in back.

Daniel and John talk softly in front. Elisheva tries to think of something to say to Ann. She's never talked to a lesbian before. What do you say to a lesbian?

But Ann breaks the silence. "Listen, can I ask you something personal?"

"Sure."

"Are you gay?"

Elisheva hesitates. "I don't know yet."

"Oh. This is my block."

Daniel stops, and then leans forward to let Ann out on his side. "Thanks for the ride," she says, and turns to Elisheva again. "Good luck, sister. I hope you figure it out soon."

"Thanks."

Daniel takes Elisheva home next. "John lives close to my neighborhood," he says.

"Nice meeting you," John says.

And then she's alone in her apartment, alone again, exchanged for John. She did what she promised, accompanied Daniel, but he traded her in. Fat chance John lives near him, fat chance. Daniel moved there especially because it's a Jewish neighborhood, not a gay one, and John's not even Jewish. Gentile man preferable to Jewish woman. Any man preferable to any woman. That's what he likes, remember? They're his people, remember?

Elisheva! The tree, Elisheva, the tree. Remember the tree. Why are you returning to the jilted lover routine? Let it go. He's your friend. You accompanied him as a gesture of friendship.

You weren't his date. Get rid of those reflexes. He's not hetero-sexual. And you?

Nope, not ready to think about, eat something and go to bed. Eat something: chocolate chip cookies, glass of milk. Like after school. Sit in front of Deborah's drawing, look at those placid water buffalo. Good.

Go to bed. Go to sleep. Good luck, sister.

———

"I entered my apartment with you. I went to a lamp and turned the switch. No light. You disappeared. I crossed the apartment and tried the second lamp. No light. Someone had disconnected the lamps and was hiding in the apartment. The phone was disconnected, too. I had locked the door from in-side, so I knew a getaway would be difficult. Someone soft was standing behind me. A woman."

"Very simple," says Daniel. "I'll have to use it in my psych paper on homosexuality. It's a classic dream. I don't 'turn you on' anymore. Now only a woman can excite you. You're wait-ing for the right woman to come along."

Elisheva pinches his cheek and puts on a Bubby Sadie accent. "Oy, will you look at this boychik of mine? Such a *keppele*! Only one month in psychology school, and already he's an analyst!"

Daniel laughs. "Does that mean I'm right on?"

"Of course it's a lesbian dream. That's just the obvious part. I've had lesbian dreams before, but never one in which the woman was a danger or a threat. This is the part I don't under-stand. I know a woman would never break into my apartment to attack me, so why would I dream that?"

"Vell . . . " He strokes a beard that isn't there. "Maybe it's your *feelings* for women that are sneaking into your apartment in a threatening way."

"Ouch. That's a little too smart. No, this time I mean it. Very smart. So, why do I perceive my feelings for women as so threatening? What do I lose if I become a lesbian? The accep-tance of society. Big deal. I never felt I had that in the first place."

"You know, Ellie, all of this is very intellectual. Maybe it's different for women, but if I were the one asking those ques-tions—"

"You'd go down to the trucks and figure it out there. Oh,

shit, I'm sorry. That was mean. You're being so helpful, too. I'm sorry."

"It's okay. I owe you one. More than one."

Elisheva looks out the window of the coffee shop. Rain, umbrellas, people with newspapers over their heads. Subway station across the street. The people disappear into the sidewalk, feet first. They emerge from the ground, head first.

His voice startles her. "Have you been attracted to any women lately?"

"No, not since I came back from Israel and got involved with you. It's like I shut off that whole side of myself, anything that would interfere with the marriage plan. Aren't we lucky you weren't able to do the same? God, what a mistake we almost made." She and Daniel shudder simultaneously, then break into matching grins. How nice it is, this easy friendship. How could she have thought they were meant to have anything else together? This is just right. She will find a mate, she knows she will. There is no hurry. "Daniel? What if it isn't any better with women?"

"You mean sex?"

"No. I mean life. I feel like I've already used up the men. What if it isn't any better with women?"

———

At the top of the stairs is a closed door with a sign:

WOMEN'S CENTER
Women Only, Please

"Uh-oh," says Daniel. "I guess I know when I'm not wanted."

Elisheva watches him descend the staircase, open the outer door, and walk out. She can just see his shoulders, a patch of tan raincoat, through the small glass pane. She waits long enough to be sure he will stay there, he will not leave her here alone, and then she enters.

It is a small office: two old desks, with a woman seated at one of them, talking on the phone. She is turned away from Elisheva, but appears quite young, about Elisheva's age probably. Her short brown hair stands out from her head like that of an elf, and she is wearing a sweatshirt and overalls. Damn, Elisheva thinks, here I am again in a skirt and heels.

"Okay," the woman says into the receiver, "meatloaf will be fine. Yeah, I'm staffing here till six. No, I'm not coming straight home. None of your business, Mom, just leave the meatloaf in the oven. Please. Okay. Yeah. Listen, Mom, I gotta go. Somebody just walked in. Yeah, I'll be careful. I promise. Bye."

She hangs up and turns toward Elisheva with a pleasant, quizzical question. Surrounding both of her eyes are enormous black-and-blue circles, horrible bruises from eyebrow to cheekbone.

She says, "Can I help you?"

Elisheva opens her mouth but can't seem to get a word out, can't stop gaping, stop gaping, don't stare at her, poor thing, father probably beat her, or someone on the street, no wonder no men are allowed here, she's even younger than I thought, maybe eighteen, don't stare.

Finally the woman says, "Oh, it's the raccoon face that's bothering you. Don't worry, I wasn't mugged. I just had a nose job. My mother talked me into it. She thinks I'll be more attractive and then I'll go straight. I told her it wouldn't work, and who wants to be straight anyway, but she finally got me to say yes. I mean, I always hated my nose—it was pretty ugly, you shoulda seen—" she makes a Pinocchio shape with her forefingers—"and she's still supporting me and everything, at least till I finish high school, so . . . "

"High school? You're still in high school? And you work here?"

"Sure. It's the Women's Center. I'm a woman. Why not? Listen, my name's Irene. Can I do anything for you, or you just want to look around?"

"I'm Elisheva. El-ee-shay-vah. I think I'd just like to look around, if that's okay."

"Sure, go ahead. There's a bulletin board in the hall, all kinds of announcements, and this little room over here is a library. You interested in joining a women's group? I can sign you up— there's one starting next week."

"Oh. Yes. That sounds very nice. Thank you."

Irene produces a clipboard from a desk drawer. "Here. Put down your name and address and phone number—you got a phone?—and somebody will call you to tell you where the first meeting is."

Elisheva signs up and then scans the bulletin board. Many women are looking for places to live. There will be a marathon reading of works by Virginia Woolf on the radio, and volunteer readers are needed. This weekend the Women's Gallery will hold

213

a grand opening and conference, with workshops and special interest groups. Elisheva writes down the address.

Then she moves on to the library: four shelves of books published by feminist presses, a woman seated in an easy chair, and a pot of coffee. The woman looks up and says hi, and Elisheva understands why Daniel had to wait outside. Elisheva came here because it is a place for women, and so did this other woman, and so did Irene. If a man had been sitting in the easy chair when Elisheva entered the library, she would have felt betrayed. It wouldn't have made any difference that he was some woman's friend or husband; she still would have felt betrayed.

On the top shelf are several copies of a book titled *Lesbians*. She takes a copy and leafs through it. Some drawings of women's faces. She likes them: strong, determined, expressive. Some photographs of women walking together, smiling, kissing each other, playing softball. She likes them: vital, sweet, ecstatic. Some poems by lesbians, about their lovers and friends and jobs and families and ideas. She likes the poems: they are full of love.

"Of course," she says to herself. "Of course. It's so simple. This book is about me. I am one of these women. I am a lesbian."

5

Men line the streets on the way to the Women's Gallery. They stand around with open bottles, making comments to each other when Elisheva walks by. She feels endangered, as she never does in her own neighborhood, even that time when the lock was broken overnight. She will have to leave the conference before dark.

A man leans close as she passes. He whispers, "Honey, I'd like to bite you to the bone."

Elisheva keeps walking, shudders and keeps walking, hears steps behind her but it's a woman, tap tap the woman passes, high-spirited, high steps in high-heeled boots; she flings her hair from side to side. Elisheva feels raw in the nipples, as though she is outgrowing her skin.

Upstairs, a roomful of women. Elisheva knows she won't recognize any of them, but then she does: Irene with the two black eyes, talking with another very young woman across the room, both of them waving their hands wildly and laughing. And many, many other women, different ages, thank God not all of them are eighteen, some are thirty, fifty, more.

Elisheva finds a list of workshops, remembers the man who wanted to bite her, chooses Self-Defense. It's in a smaller room over there, past Irene.

"Hi." Irene salutes. "This is my friend Flo, you know, like 'go with the flow.' This is—wait, let me try—El-ee-shee-vah. She's new in the movement. What workshop are you going to?"

"Self-Defense."

"Yeah? Me too. Flo's going to Feminist Child Care. Hey, it's almost time, isn't it? See you later, Flo."

When Elisheva and Irene enter, several women look at them with enormous pity, and a few get up and come running over. Oh my God, Elisheva thinks, what on earth do they know about me? What is wrong?

Then one of the women calls out, "Irene! What happened to you? Were you attacked?"

Irene, laughing, tells her nose-job story. One woman moans, "Oh, Irene! You had such a cute nose. It wasn't ugly at all." Another says, "But I thought your mother was a nice woman."

"She is," Irene says. "She just wants me to be happy. She has some weird ideas about what would make me happy, that's all. Anyway, I let her talk me into it, so it's my fault."

"Yeah, right, blame the victim. I think you need some self-defense against your mother."

Elisheva ducks out of this conversation and moves toward the circle of chairs. She thought she would see no one she knows, but she saw Irene, and now she freezes at the sight of someone . . . is it? Maybe not. Yes, definitely. Deborah. Deborah, recognizable but different somehow. She's changed, looks stronger, more sure of herself. She's changed, or perhaps Elisheva's memory-image was inexact, betrayed Deborah, made her more slight and frail than she really is. Deborah, sitting right there, more beautiful than memory, the long, pure profile, the thick hair lying like a braid of copper down her spine. Deborah, sitting like a dancer or a bareback rider, lifts one arm to smooth back an escaped tendril at the right temple, and in the generous precision of that gesture, the real Deborah and the Deborah of memory become one, familiar and strange, known and imagined. Elisheva remembers Deborah floating in clear water, swimming with sure strokes, the pebbles at the bottom, so many colors, and the poncho Deborah now wears, woven cloth and rich embroidery like the Old City.

Deborah, sitting right there, doesn't see Elisheva frozen like a game of statues, planted on the ground like a stone woman, all breast and belly, a prehistoric woman, the stone the builders rejected, frozen for centuries, then coming to life, trembling, full of desire, melting into flesh, moving. Moving, swimming through a lake of silence toward Deborah, who now sees her, leaps to her feet, speaks in the familiar husky voice of Elisheva's dreams. "You—but how?" "It's a long story I'll tell you" "Oh it's good to see you again I never thought and you're wearing the bracelet" "Yes I love it more than anything thank you and the drawing too you look wonderful" "Are you living here did you see my painting in the gallery first one ever shown I'm so excited" "No I just got here I can't wait to see it how exciting how wonderful to see you can't wait to see you when can I see you"

Then the workshop is beginning and Elisheva leans as close to Deborah as she dares, she smells fresh and healthy, and it's time to share self-defense ideas but Elisheva doesn't want to defend herself against this arousal she feels again so near to her, and now it's okay to feel it, no need to push it away as she did before, before she knew it's okay to feel it. But what if Deborah is straight, she might be, might want a man the way Daniel wants a man or some other way, might want a man, most of them do, you know. Doesn't matter, well does matter but it's okay to feel.

Now better listen, not to defend against this sweet desire but to protect it, important to protect it from that man who wants to bite you and there are others too, they will surface now that you're on your own, no big tall Daniel at your side, gentle Daniel never hit anyone in his life but they don't know that, they just saw you belonged to him and they better stay away better not bother you better not say those things. Now you're on your own, going to find out how much difference his presence made, probably a lot, makes me damn angry, say it:

"I recently broke off an engagement, and on the way over here today some men were bothering me down the street, and I realized I'm going to have to handle that kind of thing again. It started making me pretty angry, to see how dependent a woman can become on one man to protect her from all the other men."

Several women nod in agreement. Irene says, "Well, sisters, what are we going to do about it? No woman should have to hang out with some man just for protection."

Elisheva protests, "I didn't say I wanted to be with him just for protection, only that without realizing it, I was coming to depend on his presence to protect me."

One woman says, "Who's going to protect you from *him*?"

"Oh, I wouldn't have had to worry about that. He's not that kind of person. We had some other big problems, but violence wasn't one of them."

"Well, you're one of the lucky ones," the woman responds. "My husband beat me once a week for ten years until I got it together to leave him. And I never would have thought he was that kind of person before we were married, either."

Irene persists, "That's why we have to be able to defend ourselves. How many women here would come to a self-defense class if we got a teacher at the Women's Center? Hey, great, that's probably enough. Come see me after the workshop, and I'll get your name and phone number."

"Irene, you must have the biggest phone number collection

in this city," another woman teases. "Everywhere I go, there you are, asking for phone numbers." Some laughter, and Irene looks displeased. The woman quickly adds, "Look, I'm only kidding, honest. This Irene is a real dynamo. She works harder than anybody else I know. It's going to be a bad day for the women's movement here if Irene ever leaves town."

Deborah speaks up. "I like Irene's idea of offering self-defense instruction through the Women's Center. I've been taking a class at the Y, and it's made a big difference in how I feel on the street. When I'm out walking, I try to imagine a sphere around me, like a shielded area that's mine and nobody can enter it without my invitation. I feel much more powerful and secure now, and the men keep their distance most of the time. Of course, there are always the real creeps. That's why we need to know some good techniques to use in a tight spot."

Irene passes around a sheet of common-sense tips: Walk near the curb, not near the buildings. Keep your keys out. Carry a police whistle. Yell "fire," not "rape." Stay away from Nathan's in the Village, because there's a rapist who hangs around there and follows women out.

"Oh, him?" Deborah says. "That little pipsqueak? You could fight him off with one hand tied behind your back."

"Don't be so sure," another woman says. "He carries a knife."

Deborah demonstrates a judo technique to get rid of an attacker's knife—oh, she is magnificent—and then the workshop is over. Deborah is surrounded by women who want to learn the technique, so Elisheva wanders out to look for Deborah's painting. The gallery is full of paintings; why didn't Elisheva see them before? Now, try to guess which one is Deborah's. That one, the large landscape, hills like a woman's body, textures of clay—no, not Deborah. That one, a woman running, a long stride like Deborah's, but the artist is not—

"Oh, here you are. Come see my painting."

Deborah leads her to the left, to a small painting Elisheva never would have chosen, a watercolor, but wait: it's a lake, a woman swimming in the lake, another woman sunning on the shore. And there's the title: *Kinneret*.

———

Fourteenth Street. Stores full of junk, wares spread out on tables over the sidewalk, crowds of people jostling each other, everyone's in a hurry, everyone's got something to sell or buy, loud music from every doorway, merchandise neon pink bilious green plastic shoes and handbags. Chartreuse sweaters, Grandmother Lowenthal says chartreuse is the ugliest color in the world, nobody should have invented it but there it is on Fourteenth Street. Imagine it a leaf, a new leaf barely budded, nearly the same color, a new yellow-green, so fresh in nature, why is the imitation such a flop? Have to ask Deborah, not only about chartreuse but about all the colors, every single one and all their combinations. Why watercolors why not oils or something else, sculpture even, tactile and rounded, dimensions move around in space like judo or the women's dance at the church last weekend. Arms and legs in all directions, intricate rhythms and Elisheva knew women were watching her, new in town, a pretty good dancer, you'd think she'd grown up on the Supremes instead of chamber music. Never danced so well before, that's what it does to you, getting ready to come out, sure of it now, and isn't it nice, the relief of knowing and then the excitement of women's bodies all around her, moving to the music, and now it's all right to look and enjoy them, so many, all different, and I'm one too.

But why watercolors why colors you can see through and once it's there you can't change your mind it's there forever.

Of course everyone wants to be known to live openly and here I am you can look right through me once I know who I am you can't do anything to change me.

Like Lisa in Hebrew School today, sat there with her knees apart and one hand stroking the crotch of her tights while Elisheva explained verb forms. Stroked herself right between the legs and looked straight at Elisheva, daring her to say no, stop. Elisheva ignored, just kept talking, no reaction is better when a kid is testing, but maybe she wasn't only testing, maybe she was looking for acceptance of her body, her urges, herself. Or if she was testing, maybe it was her own courage she was trying to expand, her own courage and the room for her in the world.

Come on now, people can't go around masturbating in public. Lisa should have been warned about the consequences; not everyone will be as accepting as this teacher. She should have been warned but maybe not, maybe better to let her feel good about her body as long as possible, let her be strong, like little Dina strutting naked around the apartment, *"Guf ḥamud, guf ḥamud."*

It's a dilemma but at least Elisheva is teaching Hebrew, not religion. That would have been one contradiction too many, teaching religion and not attending services. She'd have to focus on ethics instead of religious practice but then the parents would complain and she'd be fired. And it's just as well she lost the job leading temple youth group, canceled after two meetings because not enough attendance. Just as well, for the kids would have asked personal questions and the parents wouldn't have liked her answers and she'd have been fired.

Now the problem is money, not enough, she'll have to get another part-time job to supplement. Grandmother Lowenthal's engagement check is running out, but next week the women's group is meeting at Elisheva's apartment; she has to get at least a rug, a chair, fabric for pillows, so the place won't be so desolate. That's why she's here on Fourteenth Street, but she doesn't see anything she likes out on the sidewalk. Maybe she can't afford good taste but she won't use Grandmother Lowenthal's money to buy a chartreuse rug.

On the corner a discount import store, stuff in the window isn't too bad, and sure enough, inside she finds a red fake Persian rug and a wicker basket chair with red cushions. Good. The fabric will be easy; Daniel promised to go with her to the Lower East Side and show her the wholesale yardage outlets. Now that he's not supposed to marry her anymore, he always does what he promises. A good friend, a terrible fiancé. That should be his epitaph.

A good friend, and maybe they will work together again. Some kind of gay center, a small comfy place for drop-in and counseling, maybe a hotline-switchboard too. John seems interested, and they'll bring up the idea at the next gay community meeting. Wonder if Ann will be there again, so I can tell her yes, I'm a lesbian, though I haven't lesbied yet.

Daniel thinks it's funny, Elisheva saying she's gay when she hasn't even gone to bed with a woman yet, but that's the way she is, had to know it for herself first. He likes to tease her, though, maybe admires her a little too.

"Do you know how much you've been talking about Deborah, ever since you ran into her? Go ahead and call her, already. You're attracted to her, aren't you?"

"Oh, will you look at the matchmaker here? As soon as he doesn't want me for himself, he has to find another taker."

"You didn't answer my question."

"Yes, I'm attracted to her. I've never been so attracted to

anyone in my life, not even you, not even the shrink's wife."

"So call."

"But why hasn't she called me? I don't think she's interested. I don't even think she's a lesbian, probably."

"Maybe she's just as chicken as you are. Call her!"

So Elisheva called, and Deborah's warm, husky voice answered: a project to finish for art school, working hard, but it's turning out well, let's get together on Saturday. That's only two days away, and Elisheva shivers with excitement and with the streetlights going on just this minute, maybe it's getting cold too, so she balances the rug on her shoulder and the chair wrapped in brown paper at her hip, down Sixth Avenue and home.

6

"Gay Switchboard," says Elisheva into the receiver. A man's voice. "Um, I'm doing research at NYU, and I wondered if you would answer a few questions for me?"

"What kind of questions?"

"I'm studying child-rearing patterns, especially with regard to discipline and punishment. Did your father ever spank you, and if so, did he pull down your panties first?"

"Go to hell." She hangs up as hard as she can, then thinks, maybe that was a mistake, maybe pain in the eardrum turns him on. Oh well, too late.

The Switchboard ad has been running in the *Village Voice* only a few days, but the call volume is already pretty high. About one in four is a crank or a heavy breather. Elisheva's usual strategy is to transfer all male callers immediately to Daniel or John; tonight they're both tied up with emergencies. Daniel is persuading someone not to take a bottle of pills, and John is consoling a man whose wife won't take him back now that she knows he's gay.

Elisheva thought Daniel was just pulling a fast one when he talked a phone company supervisor into installing the Gay Switchboard phones immediately. "Extremely urgent," he said. "Highest priority." She'd never heard him use words like that, and she thought, well, he's just trying to impress John. Finally he said, "We expect to receive many calls from suicidal people." That did the trick.

Still a lot to learn, she thinks. This is serious business, counseling strangers who want to kill themselves because they might be like her. She didn't think she'd be able to handle the really desperate calls, but then last night she did, just as Daniel is doing now. She forgot most of the instructions from the peer-counseling handbook she and Daniel and John and Ann all read before the Switchboard opened, but somehow she did a few of the right things anyhow, and she talked that woman back to life. But next time, what if she fails? What if someone dies because she says the wrong word?

It's a good thing she didn't know what she was getting into with this work, or she never would have started. And next week the drop-in center will open too, and who knows what that will mean? Don't think ahead, Elisheva. You'll only scare yourself.

Daniel is saying, "That's right. Now flush the pills down the toilet." But the other person could lie, could say, yes I flushed them, and then hang up and swallow them down with a last laugh. She is more nervous than last night when she was the one doing the counseling, and she doesn't want to send waves of fear to Daniel, doesn't want to infect him, he's doing just fine, he'll know she's nervous and then he'll fuck up and someone will die.

Elisheva leaves the switchboard and goes to the other room, plenty to do there and she'll still hear the phone ring. Two rooms, a tiny one in the back for the phones and a small one in the front for the drop-in center. The landlord gave permission to tear down the plaster and expose the brick walls, and it's going to be nice and homey. Everyone will donate a piece of furniture until they get a grant or find an anonymous benefactor, or maybe the weekly dances will bring in enough money.

She puts on a dust mask, picks up a chisel and a hammer, and chips away more of the plaster. Physical activity is good for nervousness, must remember that.

A lot to learn, but she *is* learning, and she was the one who got the Switchboard listed in the phone directory, contrary to policy. The supervisor explained, "gay" was one of the words not approved for listing.

Daniel said, "How about 'homosexual'?"

The supervisor consulted his computer printout and said, "No, I'm sorry, that's not permitted either."

John snapped, "You got 'faggots' and 'dykes' on your paper there?"

"Yes, as a matter of fact, I do. You can't use those words either. Sorry. I wish I could accommodate you. I didn't make up this list, you know."

Ann said, "Well, maybe we should talk to the person who did. What a stinky regulation!"

The supervisor wrote something on a piece of paper. "Here is the name of my boss, but he's quite a conservative man. I think

223

your best bet is to come up with a name that isn't too—"

"Obvious?" Elisheva said.

"Well, yes, of course that would defeat your purpose, if you want people to be able to reach you in times of crisis. Wait a minute, I see that 'queer' isn't against the rules. . . . no, that wouldn't do, would it?"

"Queer Switchboard." Daniel shook his head. "Strictly a last resort."

The next day Elisheva thought of a different approach. She called the business office, and when a clerk answered, she said, "I just arranged for a telephone installation yesterday, and I want to make sure the listing is correct."

"Your number?"

Elisheva gave the new number.

"Oh, it's a good thing you called. I don't see any name listed here. Your last name, please?"

"S-w-i-t-c-h-b-o-a-r-d."

"What an unusual name. How do you pronounce it?"

"Svitchbard. It's Scandinavian."

"Really? How interesting. Your first name?"

"Gay. G-a-y."

"Do you want us to list your first name or just your first initial? Most women prefer to list only the initial, to discourage obscene calls."

"No, I want to list my whole name."

"Okay, Miss Svitchbard, you're all set."

Oh boy, Elisheva thought as she hung up, wait till the gang hears about this one. Switchboard, Gay.

By now there is a large pile of old plaster at her feet, and the air is heavy with white dust. She picks up an armful of plaster chunks and dumps them into a garbage can in the middle of the floor, then goes back for a second armful.

The phone rings. Damn. She is busy. What do they want from her, anyway? She doesn't know anything yet. They should give her some time. She's tired. Maybe she needs some food. Did she eat anything today? A grilled cheese. Many cups of coffee. Is that all? She should eat something. Right after this call she'll run to the corner and get a sandwich to go. Goddamn. I'm coming. Gotta drop this plaster first. There. Better not be another obscene call. The clerk was right. I should have listed myself as Svitchbard, G.

"Hawump?" Goddamn. Forgot to take off the dust mask. Pretty funny. Forgot to say "Gay Switchboard," too. Okay. "Hello. Gay Switchboard."

"Hello, um . . . "

Good, at least it's a woman. "Can I help you?"

"Yes, I mean, I hope so. Shit."

Elisheva is moved by the woman's hesitation, and the voice, something familiar about that resonance. My God, it's Deborah. "Deborah?"

"Yes, how'd you know? Who is this? Elisheva?"

"Deborah! What are you doing calling here? Does that mean you're gay? Why didn't you tell me? We spent that whole afternoon together, and you never told me. Oh, I'm so glad. Why didn't you call? Why are you calling here? Oh, damn, I'm supposed to be helping you, and instead I'm giving you the third degree. I'm sorry. I must be tired. Deborah? Are you still there? I'm sorry. Do you want to talk to someone else, somebody you don't know, maybe you'd feel freer? I'm the only woman here tonight, but I could get Ann to call you back tomorrow. Deborah? Are you still there? Please talk to me."

"Hi." Her voice is so quiet, and then she laughs, she is wonderful, I could love her. "Elisheva? I'm still here. I'm just laughing because, well, it's funny, isn't it?"

"Yes." They both laugh now.

"Well, I called because I think I'm on the verge of coming out, and I wanted to talk to somebody. I didn't know before, that's why I didn't tell you. Shit, maybe I did know. I was scared. I'm still scared. Can you understand that?"

"Of course. It's scary. It has been for me, too."

"Really? But you sounded so sure of yourself, and then starting a gay center and everything. Shit. This is your gay center, right? Maybe I knew you'd answer, too, maybe . . . but you never said anything about a switchboard, did you? Well, maybe I knew anyway. Maybe I did. Listen, you've had a big effect on me, you know that? I've been thinking a lot about you. I mean, I guess I was calling to talk about you, so it's probably a good thing you answered." Swallow, Elisheva. Swallow first, and you will be able to talk. No good? Try again. "Elisheva? I feel kind of awkward asking you this—please don't think I'm a creep—but do you already have someone? Are you involved with this Ann, or somebody else?"

"No, no, I'm not involved with anyone. No. Oh, I'm so glad

you called."

A long silence, and they both laugh again.

"Well—" Deborah's voice, happy and playful now, "I guess we'd better get to each other before it's too late."

"Yes. Yes, let's do that. Deborah? I've been living on cheese sandwiches and coffee for weeks now, how about having dinner together tomorrow? There's a nice café right down the street. Both of the waitresses are lesbians, you might have seen their picture on the Christopher Street poster."

"No, I've never seen a Christopher Street poster. I'm new at this, remember?"

"Well, so am I. Don't worry. We'll manage. Deborah? If we feel like it, there's a women's dance tomorrow at the church. The dances there are usually a lot of fun. We can drop in if we want. Let's have dinner and see."

"Yes. Okay. Great. See you then. Thanks. I mean, bye."

Elisheva hangs up slowly. She hears applause. She must be very tired, and excited. But it's not a hallucination, it's Daniel and John, leaning against each other, grinning and clapping like a pair of imps. She could get mad but they look so cute, and she's too happy, everything is perfect.

The phone rings. Daniel answers, then says, "Elisheva, it's for you," wiggling his eyebrows.

"Hello, Elisheva?" It's Deborah again. Oh God, maybe she changed her mind. She doesn't want to see me after all, she doesn't want me, she doesn't want, the Lord is her shepherd, she shall not want—"Elisheva? I was so excited, I forgot to ask you where the restaurant is, and we didn't say what time . . . "

"Oh, right! I forgot too. Let's meet at the library, okay? We'll walk over to the restaurant together, okay? Eight o'clock?"

"Great. Elisheva? Is some kind of show going on there? I hear applause."

"No, it's just us, you and I are the show. It's Daniel and John giving me a hard time."

"Oh. Let's take a bow for them. You bowing?"

"Yes, I'm bowing, almost pulled the phone out of the wall too. Deborah? Are you there?"

———

A good dinner, no tomatoes, then the dance. They dance well together but don't stay long, so nice this arousal wants to be private. They walk, cold outside, very cold, puddles turned to ice, Elisheva's smooth soles keep sliding on the pavement the ice, slippery and nice this sensation, no need to be too careful, Deborah's there and puts an arm around her. "Just to keep you from falling," she says, and they laugh and walk, an arm through an arm, close, holding tight, the bracelet gleaming between them at streetlights. Back to Deborah's apartment on Fourteenth Street, she was there all the time and Elisheva never even knew. A small apartment above a bagel and bialy factory. When Deborah says it she slips, "bagel and bialy festival" instead. They laugh more, and Deborah does a little jig, "Oh the great bagel and bialy festival," she sings and they laugh.

Now Deborah puts on an Aretha Franklin album, and Elisheva finds an Irene joint, they smoke it and nuzzle, they stroke and lick each other, they know just what to do how on earth did they know how on earth could they not have known? They knew all the time, must have, she knew, or not, but she knows.

She licks her body her fingers such aroma such flavor she licks herself on her fingers her own body on the fingers of a woman a woman's body on her fingers. A lap of petals of desert blossoms pungent as sage and the winter succulents that bloom when nothing else will, just enough water, just enough and it is plenty it is the juice of a pomegranate of an oyster. Acacia and mustard, the smell of healthy sweat earth and root yellow blossoms as in the Holy Land, this is the holy land this tingling tip of the world. A yellow iris like a cat a corn husk doll in the World Book maize a packet of spice from the Canary Isles. Marmalade and curry, a plum for each one in the class, oh these kisses are sweeter than any. A goldfinch, a warbler, a warm yellow throat. The gold and copper of her hair, wiry and soft, a glow like a spot of sunlight collecting between trees and buildings, between toes. Egg yolk and citrus, a wet hillside, yellow, and green soon to come. The yellowish gray underside of a rain cloud, we pray for rain every fall, for water in the holy land, seeds of water condensing. As in a *mikva*, seeding the tap water with living water from a flowing stream, the seed water makes all the water living water, all of it alive and yellow with life like foxtails in cats' fur scattered on the dirt catching sunlight and water growing into grasses, and oh such excitement a new arousal on the wave of the last like ripples of grass always fresh and pure this arch of her back long and lithe as a purr. Legs shivering like stems underwater, carried by the current but rooted.

"Elisheva?"

"Mmm?"

"I'm moving to California in a month, for graduate school."

"I know. You already told me."

"Well, what are we going to do?"

"Wait and see. What else can we do? Don't be sad, Deborah, please don't be sad. Listen, we found each other from Israel to New York, we can manage from New York to California."

"Okay. Promise?"

"Promise. Deborah?"

"Mmm?"

"What do you think of chartreuse?"

"One of my favorite colors. When it's right, just the shade of a new leaf. I'll show you with watercolors in the morning. Why?"

"I don't know. But I'm glad. I'm glad you like chartreuse."

7

Deborah Blumenfeld. Deborah Field-of-Flowers. My Deborah. My sister, my bride. You are a fountain of gardens, a well of living waters, a stream flowing from the green North.

He who wrote of dust and ashes forgot the cycle of water evaporating and condensing, moisture exchanged, never lost. He forgot the vulva folding in upon themselves, the hills of chaparral in the early morning, their deep moist shadows of dew like a secret hiding from itself. He forgot the petals of the seven-year plant just after watering, how they hold each drop firm to drink at leisure. They steal nothing, nor are they robbed; all that they surrender is returned.

Even in the desert, there lives a green, green wadi where fruit trees flourish. Even in the desert, there lives a tropical plant, *Shika'on ha-Sinai*, "Drunkenness of Sinai," with its lush purple blossom and large green leaves. Even in the desert, there lives a people, the Bedouins, who know where to find water on a sun-baked plain, whose walled gardens bloom in the desert, whose strong dark coffee and sweet mint tea refresh travelers who otherwise might perish of thirst.

The man who wrote of dust and ashes forgot the miracle of immersion. He forgot the fog that hovers at the breath of the sea. He never heard the laughter of women at the Turkish bath, the scrubbing of each other's skin and the pouring of fresh water over each other's shoulders. He forgot the Song of Songs.

Nothing is lost, not even what has been ruined, not even what has been forgotten. Nothing is lost.

Even when the water is dead, dammed up, even then it can be seeded with living water—a small trickle suffices—and the drops of living water from a stream bring all the water to life.

Even when we scatter seeds on the dry ground of autumn, we can weep over the crops, and our tears suffice until the rains return.

It is written in the Song of Ascents:

Return like the streams of the Negev,
the winter rains in the desert.
Those who sow in tears
will reap in joy.

———

My Deborah. How did I choose you, how did I know? There
are other women I have loved, but you were meant to be my
lover. How did I know? How did you? And how did we put up
with each other in those first difficult years, after the euphoria
wore off, when the desire to touch became less urgent, no longer interrupted our talk, and we had finally to listen and know
we were not the same person, not even identical twins, but different in ways that jarred and chafed. Nothing had prepared us
for the attention our love required—not my years of listening to
the cello, not your years of training an artist's eye. We both resented it. But how did we know the rich fulfillment that
awaited?

———

Nothing had prepared us, and yet somehow all history con-
spired to bring us together: two Jewish women brimming with
love for one another. So sweet was our delight, it seemed to in-
fuse with meaning the centuries of suffering that had preceded
us. "Those who sow in tears will reap in joy." We were the harvest; our love was the first fruit, the springing forth of life from
the ashes of our people.

Batya, the automobile in which Deborah and I crossed the
river Jordan, was given to Deborah's Aunt Anna as compensa-
tion for her years of suffering in the camps. A sin-offering required by law. The car trivialized Aunt Anna's scars, her memories of torture. And yet the car helped Aunt Anna get around,
made her life easier in the hilly city of Haifa. Deborah and I
were powerless to erase the scars, the memories, the deaths that
Aunt Anna's survival symbolized. We had no way to justify
these things, to make them acceptable. We did what we could:
we let Batya bring us together, we let ourselves fall in love, we
let our love perform its small miracle of healing, increase our
strength to work in the world. *Hazak hazak v'nithazek.* Strong
strong and we will strengthen ourselves.

"Female power," Deborah called it. The power to work. The

power to make peace, to supply nothing to war, not even our love, to keep ourselves for each other, a peace-offering of our life together. The power to return to the source. The Law of Return. We have returned to our Biblical names, to the origins of our Jewish female power. We have raised our arms in the arc of sacred dance. We have danced to the rhythm of the timbrel. We have sung the ancient songs, and the sounds of the first language have hummed in our throats. We have wept over the crops.

The first law in the Bible is a simple one: *Pru u-r'vu u-mil'u et-ha-aretz.* Be fruitful, increase, and fill the earth. How Miriam and I once argued over this line!

"It means just what it says," Miriam insisted. "Have babies. Have lots of babies."

"Where does it mention babies?" I said. "There are many ways to be fruitful, many ways to increase, many ways to fill the earth."

We are learning, Deborah and I, the meaning of this law, which is also a promise: You will be fruitful, you will increase, you will fill the earth.

We are learning the meaning of the chant of the mothers of all tribes:

> We will pour forth peace in the midst of the earth,
> we will increase love in the midst of the fields.

The promise and the law are the same. The promise of return, the Law of Return. It is written in the Song of Ascents: "In the return, we are like those who dream."

We dream of fruitfulness. We dream of planting ourselves down into the soil to spring up again, fresh and flowing with sap. Or like the bramble, sending out tiny shoots from our base, sucklings to lap up the moisture of deep loam; or bending forward, plunging head and hands into the earth like a diver entering the water. From the old body, new vines: rockrose, dewberry, blackberry, brambleberry.

We dream of flourishing from our own grave, from the grave of our people.

———

The first year of our living together, Deborah had nightmares nearly every night. She woke up screaming and wept in my arms; sometimes we wept together, because her dreams fright-

231

ened me too and because it hurt me to see her in pain. The dreams were always the same: gangs of armed men chasing us through hallways and alleys. Sometimes the men were Nazis in uniform. Sometimes in those dreams she couldn't get me to believe the seriousness of the threat, just as her parents had been unable to convince any of her other relatives that the time had come to leave Germany.

"But you've always been Jewish," I said to her. "You've always known what happened to your relatives. Why are you having these dreams now?"

At first she couldn't answer. Then she said, "Maybe I can afford to have them now, because I feel safe with you."

But the nightmares continued. Finally she said, "The men aren't chasing me because I'm Jewish. They're chasing me because I'm a Jewish lesbian. They're chasing us both because we're Jewish lesbians. As long as I was a Jewish straight woman, I felt all right. Now I feel in danger. There is no protection against the kind of danger I fear. Judo doesn't help. Nothing helps. I don't know if I can stand this. It may be too much for me."

That was not what I wanted to hear. I wanted Deborah to feel the same way I did: happy and invincible. I wanted her to feel, as I did, at ease in lesbian identity, sure of the rightness of this new life, certain that nothing could go wrong now that I knew who I was.

In her dreams, Deborah couldn't get me to believe the seriousness of the threat to us; in waking life, she couldn't get me to believe there was any threat at all. What a frustration we were to each other! Deborah refused to share my joy, as I refused to share her terror. Her nightmares receded, and fights with me took their place. My stubborn optimism, my denial of danger, was now her enemy.

"Don't you see?" Deborah insisted. "We're homeless. Nowhere on earth are we welcome. You lived in Israel. You know we couldn't live there as lesbians. How can you be so complacent?"

"Our home is each other," I answered. "We don't need any other home. How can you deny the reality of what we have together? How can you let your fears ruin our happiness?"

We struggled for a long time to change one another, each viewing the other as a traitor to an important cause. What made us think we had to convert each other? What made us polarize

232

into warring camps? And how did we finally come to see the truth: that each of us was fighting with a side of herself. Deborah was voicing my fears as well as hers; I was expressing the secure happiness she was afraid to feel, lest it be taken away. Once we recognized the nature of our struggle, we were ready to make peace. We were ready to listen to one another. We were ready to give each other help.

———

I still see it the way I saw it then: I healed Deborah's fear of lesbianism, and she cured my fear of music. I don't know how I did it; I don't know how she did it. But one day my mother's hegemony over the world of music came to an end. There was no more hesitation for me, no more conflict. I went back to school and studied ethnomusicology, as I had told Deborah I wanted to do on the day we first met. Deborah gave me this. She gave music back to me. I don't know quite how, but she did. Perhaps it was simply her example, her devotion to art, her pleasure in doing the work she loved, even if her whole family thought she was crazy. Bless her.

———

Because I was no longer Orthodox when Deborah and I got together, and because she never had the slightest interest in Judaism as a religion, at first she didn't quite believe I had ever been one of those hopeless fanatics. By now, she believes it. Her once-vague sense of the Jewish calendar has sharpened to the extent that she always knows when a Jewish holiday is coming: when Elisheva suddenly grows irritable and restless.

If I give vent to an inexplicable fit of anger, Deborah never asks me, "Are you about to get your period?" She asks, "Isn't it almost Yom Kippur?"

In California, in Israel, in New York, in Pennsylvania, in Wisconsin—everywhere I have lived—there is always a hot spell during the Days of Awe, the ten-day period from Rosh Hashana to Yom Kippur. I remember Bubby Sadie baking dozens of honeycakes in a steamy kitchen, to bring a sweet year for the entire family. Later, I counted off the years by holidays I spent sweltering in synagogue, nylon stockings sticking to the back of my skirt, while I sweated with my father over the words of the prayers. Then the ecstatic Yom Kippur at the kibbutz, the atmosphere of effortless communal worship. I can never go back to that state, don't want to; it is not right for me anymore. But

233

what is to replace it? My years of Orthodoxy made me too much of a purist to accept a modernized hodge-podge of Christian form and Jewish content such as I find in every American synagogue: a rabbi serving the same functions as a Protestant minister, an organ playing in the background. My years of feminism have made it impossible for me to tolerate not only Orthodoxy, but the patriarchal forms of any religious institution. Even in the gay synagogue, where the English version of the prayers has been de-sexed, the Hebrew remains unmistakably what it always was: prayer to a male God. And do I really want to substitute a rabbi for a minister? And if not, what can I do to commemorate the days I still recognize as holy days? What can I do to acknowledge my kinship with Jews everywhere? Who will be my community?

I suppose I'm saying the same thing Deborah said: "We're homeless." No community in existence is completely our community.

On Rosh Hashana and Yom Kippur I cancel my classes at the university. "In honor of the Jewish holy days," I tell my students. At home with Deborah, I am at a loss. There is nothing to do, but it feels wrong to do nothing in honor of the Jewish holy days. Sometimes I bake, as Bubby Sadie did, even though it's much too hot. Sometimes I work at home. This year I wrote letters. Deborah paints, as she always does. I am touchy, difficult. It's all right for me to work if I want to, but it's not all right for her to ask what work I've done or to suggest non-Jewish activities like going to the movies or shopping for plants. I resist belonging to a community, even a community of two. I am determined to sweat out the holidays alone.

This year I wrote letters. I wrote to Miriam, to Yardena, to Zahava, to Shlomo and Ilana. I had not written to any of them in the nine years since I came out as a lesbian. During the first year, while I fought Deborah's fears with all my strength, I was afraid to write to my friends in Israel, afraid they would hate and scorn me once they knew I was a lesbian. At the end of that year came the Yom Kippur War, and then I didn't write for fear of learning one of my friends had been killed. After that year I was ashamed to write, because I hadn't written in so long.

But during the Days of Awe 5741, I wrote letters. I asked each friend to forgive my long silence. I told each friend that I had applied for a research grant, to study the folk songs of

Yemenite women in Israel, and if I got the grant, I would return to Israel in the spring, with my lover Deborah.

They forgave me. I got the grant. The rains of winter are gone, blossoms appear on the land, and the time of singing has arrived. The fig tree puts forth her green figs, and the vines in bloom send out their fragrance. *Kumi lakhi ra'iati yaffati u-l'khi-lakh.* Arise, my love, my fair one, and come away.

8

Shir ha-ma'alot: a song of ascents.
In the return to Zion,
we were like those who dream.
Then was our mouth filled with laughter,
and our tongue with song.

The photograph shows Yardena and me, leaning close to one another, grinning in unison. Before us, a coffee table spread with delicacies: a platter of small almond cookies, slices of sweet green melon, clusters of purple grapes, cups of mint tea.

Deborah took the picture. She sat across the table from Yardena and me, grinning too, the three of us mute with delight. After the flash went off, Yardena kept her arm around me. She spoke to Deborah in Hebrew, and I translated: "Elisheva was like a sister to me, *b'hayai,* upon my life she was. When I lost her, you got her instead."

Deborah said, "And now I have brought her back to you."

Like an interpreter between two diplomats, I translated for them all evening. I was astonished that they both knew exactly the right things to say; and their words, so infused with love, moved me beyond the embarrassment of being the subject of their conversation, beyond the awkwardness of speaking for them, into a realm of contentment where I needed no words of my own. As once I had floated in a calm sea of music, warmed and nourished by waves of sound, I now sat listening, lulled by the voices of two women I loved, each speaking one of the languages I loved, and my own voice swaying between the two. It was as if Deborah and Yardena represented two sides of my soul, reunited now as two figures in a dream are united for the dreamer.

On the way back to the hotel, I said to Deborah, "I am perfectly happy."

A few days later we saw Yardena again, this time in the company of Hayim and five-year-old Moshe, thanks to whose birth the government had finally helped Yardena and Ḥayim obtain a better apartment. There was nothing wrong; we were glad to be together; but now no one had much to say, and in the absence of the symbolic magic of our first encounter, in the absence of the day-to-day contact of neighbors, it was clear that Yardena and I had little in common, that we no longer knew quite how to communicate with each other, that Yardena had not understood what I meant when I called Deborah my lover, that she had translated the term into something she could understand: roommate, or good friend. If I told Yardena, "We are lesbians," she would say, "*Mah zeh?* What's that?"

Deborah and I watched the family do what families do: tease and bicker and laugh. After a while Deborah began to sketch, and Nadav's girlfriend came around to say hello, and Yardena brought out an album of snapshots of Nadav and Yonah in army uniform. Moshe trudged out in his pajamas to kiss his mother goodnight, and then Deborah and I left, promising to call soon.

It was the same when I saw Miriam, Shlomo and Ilana, Zahava. I was happy to see them, content to sit in their presence once more, moved that they still cared for me, and I for them; but we quickly ran out of words.

"It's normal," Deborah said. "There's been a ten-year gap between you and these people. You've forgotten how to talk to each other. And look how much your life has changed. We've only been here a week. Don't be too disappointed. It will get better."

"I'm not disappointed," I said. "And it won't get better. It doesn't have to get better. This is the way it is."

Deborah didn't believe that I wasn't disappointed. But I truly was not. I had expected so little and feared so much from this renewal of contact with my old friends. I knew in advance that they were no longer my community, that Israel was no longer my home. I knew that the Law of Return did not apply to Deborah and me; homosexuals were in the same legal category as criminals and mental defectives, "undesirables" who could be denied the right to immigration as Jews. I, the first Rogin to feel no fear when questioned by an immigration official, was now the only Rogin officially unwelcome in the homeland of our people.

I knew all this in advance, and anticipated a terrible sense of alienation: from my old friends, from Israel, from Jerusalem, from the self of ten years ago who had intended to stay, the new immigrant who had just taken the name Elisheva, who was just learning how to keep *shabbat*, who wanted to get married and lead a traditional Jewish life. I feared that when I saw my old friends, when I brought together my past and present, the two would destroy each other in a great explosion, like matter and anti-matter.

In the face of such extreme fears, how could I be disappointed? On the contrary: relief heightened my pleasure in each reunion, and each letdown seemed quite mild. And if I no longer had much to say to my old friends—well, that was all right. After the first month of our stay, the month Deborah and I had agreed to use for a vacation, I could occupy myself with a year of research, throwing myself into my work, making myself too busy to see anyone but Deborah and the Yemenite women whose music I would be studying; I could use my profession to distance myself from Israel: "I'm only here as a scientist." After that month, I could forget my younger self, could abandon finally her search for spiritual wholeness and community, could leave her forever standing at the gate of the Old City, waiting to enter.

––––––

Deborah and I rented a jeep and drove around the country, heading first for Yam Kinneret, the Sea of Galilee, where ten years ago we spent our first day together. The lake smelled bad, the water was murky and not so blue as we remembered, the hills not so green. The land was not uniquely beautiful or blessed. All of it could have passed for California, on a smaller scale. It was intimate, close, like the yard of a home, like the home of childhood, not so large and magical in reality as in memory.

Deborah disliked the sense of confinement, the finality of the borders. She refused to believe we couldn't drive right through into Syria or Jordan.

"Stop!" I would shout. "Turn around! We can't go any farther."

"Sure we can," she said. "Don't you see? The road continues straight ahead."

"You're crazy! There are Syrian missiles pointed at us right this minute. Stop!"

She stopped the jeep, got out with her camera, and walked to the barbed-wire fence to take some pictures of a Syrian village. While she was gone, I slid into the driver's seat and turned the jeep around. Then I ate, in frantic haste, four or five biscuits from a tin we carried with us.

Deborah returned with an innocent smile. "Let's go down there. I'd like to draw some of the houses."

Clenching every part of my body, I said, "Deborah. That village is in Syria. We can't get from here to there. Please, Deborah, take this seriously. We are putting ourselves in danger. We could be shot at." My words had a familiar ring, as though I had said or heard them before. Then I remembered, and began to laugh. "Do you see what's happening to us? We've traded places. Remember when you had those nightmares, and I wouldn't believe there was any danger?"

"That was different. I was right and you're wrong." She started laughing too, and we collapsed into a hug.

"Thank God you came with me for this year," I said, inhaling the wonderful golden scent of her neck. "I would be too cautious without you."

"You, cautious? Only when it comes to the Syrians."

"No, I mean it. You make me braver than I am. You enlarge my vision of what is possible."

"Anything is possible. I learned that from you."

The U.N. officer found us parked there like a couple of teenagers on a date. "Excuse me," he said, "but you are in a demilitarized zone. You must leave immediately. Didn't you see the sign?"

"No, we didn't," I said. And drove back into Israel.

We both loved the extremes, where there was little habitation: Sinai and the Golan. "It's because we're American," Deborah said. "We need open spaces and wild frontiers."

"Because we're American," I repeated, trying it on. "Are we? I don't feel very American."

We had argued this one before. I always said I was more Jewish than American; Deborah always said we were as much American as Jewish. But this time I meant something different.

"Here in the Sinai," I said, "nationality seems irrelevant. What difference does it make where we're from? The desert doesn't care. The Bedouins don't care. If the Bedouins don't recognize national boundaries, why should I?"

"Want to be a Bedouin?"

"I don't know. Maybe I do."

"Want your mother to have cut off your clitoris when you were five years old?"

"Deborah! You know that isn't what I mean."

"But it's part of the package, isn't it?"

"It wouldn't have to be." I felt foolish, misunderstood, desolate. I had accepted my inability to communicate with Yardena, but if Deborah didn't understand me, what hope was there? And I didn't want to think about clitoridectomy, didn't want to imagine my mother with a knife in her hand, coming at me to cripple my sexual pleasure for life. I couldn't stand to think that the women we passed in our jeep, the women who waved at us and pulled their veils up over their faces at the same time, the graceful, elegant women who served us coffee in their palm-frond huts, the women whose beauty and competence I admired when I watched them herding their flocks—I couldn't stand to think what had been done to them, what they had done to their own daughters.

No. That wasn't what I had meant at all. Deborah didn't understand me.

I pulled my sunhat forward until it shaded my eyes. We were sitting at the edge of a plateau, directly over a fault, and I peered down at the line where the earth had cracked, and at the jumbled mountains to both sides: strata vertical and diagonal, chipping away from the top in large hunks; and the place where granite once split, and magma thrust upward into the crevice, making a heavy black streak in the mountain. That was what I loved about the desert: it showed the life of the earth, the earth's history and character. It showed what was under the surface layers of vegetation and topsoil, what was older and deeper.

And the people of the desert, the Bedouins, seemed to know something older and more central too. Their flocks and gardens, their stone wells, their ability to live with scarcity. And the women, the women—they knew something I needed to know.

I suddenly remembered Michel, the Turkish fellow at the *ulpan*, who called me his little Bedouin. He was a jerk, and he understood. How could Deborah not understand?

By now Deborah had pulled out her sketch pad and was drawing a twisted, striped mountain. With a sure hand she captured the landscape's harsh beauty. I understood why she loved the Sinai: in a few days she had compiled enough sketches to keep her painting all year. She had drawn canyons of sandstone filigreed by the elements, and date palm oases, and hills nearly buried in sand, and wadis speckled with thorny acacia, and camels grazing among rocks. For her, the Sinai was a parade of long vistas and dramatic shapes. For me, it was something else. But what? How could I expect her to understand, when I didn't even understand?

———

That night, like the Children of Israel, we made camp at the foot of Jebbel Mussa, the mountain known as Mount Sinai. We lay on our backs in our sleeping bags, and stared up at the dark sky and the darker silhouette of the mountain. We didn't talk; there was no sound but the whistle of wind.

At three in the morning we started the climb. We hiked in silence, in darkness, passing the water bottle back and forth. "This is the walk Moses took," I said to myself in time with my stride. "Moses climbed this mountain to receive the Law."

When the light began to break, I saw the safe, generous path ahead, and the massive steps of rock. We passed under an arch of stone, and on the other side, we paused to watch the sun rise over the saddle of the mountain. The rocks around us shone red, and purple, and white. The air shimmered with light.

I tell you it was a holy trek, a holy mountain, a holy desert. I wanted to stay there forty days and then forty more, like Moses, until the mountain had taught me all its secrets, until the word of the Law was mine. I could have become a hermit in that desert, surrounding myself with sandstone and granite, curling into myself, turning toward the interior, leading my flocks down the wadi to the source of water, squatting on the ground, pulling rock and sand up around me like a blanket.

There were no Bedouins at the top of Jebbel Mussa, but it was there that I understood my wish to become a Bedouin. My wish had nothing to do with Bedouin society, nothing to do with the real lives of Bedouin women. It was not the wish to be part of a tribe. It was the opposite of all this, a desire to live solitary in the desert. It was a temptation of sorts: the temptation to renounce the search for community, to give up all human ties, to abandon the effort to communicate with others. It was the temptation of silence.

———

When we returned to Jerusalem, I called no one. We took a room in a hotel in the Arab sector, close to the Old City. I withdrew into myself. I still conversed easily with Deborah, in the comfortable familiarity of years spent side-by-side. I was willing to talk with her about anything except myself. When she asked, "How are you doing?" or "Are you okay?"—and she asked more and more frequently—I shut myself tight. To answer seemed futile, maybe even dangerous.

As we walked the streets of the city, everything I saw confirmed my sense of hopelessness in human society and my desire to retreat into solitude. In Miriam's old neighborhood, where the Hassidim's harmless, quaint disapproval had once amused me, the walls were now covered with violent, threatening graffiti: "*Mavet l'meholelei shabbat.* Death to those who defile the sabbath." And while the Jewish side of the city prepared for a boisterous Independence Day celebration, the Arab neighborhood around our hotel was taut with bitterness.

"Things have gotten worse," I said to Deborah. "I used to feel optimistic, as though peace was a possibility. Not now. The Arabs are too angry, the Israelis are too tired."

"The Israelis seem tired to you? Look at Yardena and Ḥayim. Look at these soldiers." She pointed at two young men, each with a machine gun slung over the shoulder, each walking with an arm around his girlfriend, laughing and shouting, ignoring the PLO graffiti on the wall, ignoring too the Arab merchants who drew back slightly into the doors of their shops when the Israelis passed. One merchant spat on the sidewalk, and as if that were a signal for action, a young Arab ran out into the street and yelled at the soldiers' backs: "*Achtung! Achtung!*"

He yelled it with full knowledge of the word's significance for Jews. He meant: "You are like Nazis to me."

I froze, and felt Deborah freeze beside me. The soldiers paid no attention, just kept walking.

"That was horrible," Deborah said. "Everything about it was horrible. Maybe you're right. Maybe there can never be peace."

"Please don't agree," I said. "I don't want to be right this time."

We both perceived the manner of the two soldiers as an affront to the Arabs, a show of modern sexual ease. "Here we are, invading your culture," they seemed to be saying. "Your children will be like us if you are lucky."

But all this was subtle undertone. The four Israelis didn't aim

242

their actions at the Arabs, behaved more as if the Arabs didn't exist. That always has been the worst affront.

"Even so, he had no right to yell such a thing," Deborah said. "How can he compare the Israelis to Nazis? What armed Nazi would have ignored an insult shouted at him in the ghetto? The man who shouted would be dead now, in any other military occupation."

I thought for a minute. "What you say is true, but it doesn't help."

Only at night did I feel any hope. Each night we spent in that hotel, we were awakened by the cry of a *mu'ezzin* from the minaret of the mosque next door. I would lie in the darkness, enjoying the long call of the nasal, thin voice, the ornamented cantillation so similar to that of the Yemenite music I was studying. For a crazy moment, I would think, "We are so much alike, we Semites. What divides us in the modern world seems petty and superficial in comparison with the things we have in common, the thousands of years we have lived in this part of the world, the way this land shaped us, our voices, our music. Why don't we make fools of those who wish us to be enemies? Why don't we talk to each other? Why don't we make peace?"

———

Miriam had told me there was a women's center somewhere in downtown West Jerusalem, and the day after the *achtung* incident, Deborah and I set out to find it. We went to Zion Square, and asked the women waiting there; we asked shoppers in a department store, in a bakery, in a pharmacy; we asked policewomen and women soldiers. Finally a bookstore clerk said she thought she knew which street; she had seen a flyer advertising a Saturday-night coffee house for women at a place called *Kol Ha-Isha*, "The Woman's Voice."

Someone could have taken the women's center I first entered in New York—the day I left Daniel behind and walked in alone —and transported it to Jerusalem and called it *Kol Ha-Isha*. There was the same narrow flight of stairs, small office, combination bookshop-library, meeting room. I half-expected to see Irene's raccoon face at the desk, to hear her talking with her mother on the phone. But there was no one at the desk, no one in the library, no one in the meeting room. Down a long corridor, some women were arguing loudly in Hebrew.

"The Woman's Voice," I said to Deborah. I listened for a

moment: "But we met at my apartment *last* week." "*Eyn lee zman*, I have no time for more meetings." "Who took the account book?" "What's the difference? There's no money."

At the end of the corridor, we found three women crammed into a tiny kitchen.

"*Shalom*," I said, and then with more volume, "*Shalom!*"

"Ah, we have visitors. *Shalom*." The woman smiled broadly, extended her hand, and switched to English. "My name is Shula. What kind of coffee do you want, *ness* or *botz*?"

"I'm Elisheva. This is Deborah. *Botz* for me, please." I turned to Deborah. "What do you prefer? *Ness* is instant, *botz* means mud—it's a kind of weak Turkish coffee with sediment at the bottom."

"Yum, yum," Deborah said.

Shula laughed. "You should try *botz*. Then you will understand the Israeli character." She began to pour and stir, adding more sugar at each step of the process. "This is Esther, this is Yokheved."

Esther said, "You are new immigrants?"

"No," said Deborah. "Tourists."

"Even you?" Yokheved looked at me. "You have lived in Israel. You knew what is *botz*."

"I lived in Jerusalem ten years ago."

"*Nu?*" Shula gave me a cup. "So this time are you here to stay?"

Deborah and I looked at each other and laughed. We had yet to meet an Israeli who did not ask this question within five minutes.

Shula laughed too, at herself. "You did not expect us to be different at *Kol Ha-Isha*, did you? We are the Jewish Agency for feminists."

I stopped laughing. "The real Jewish Agency does not want us," I said. "We are lesbians."

"So am I. So are they." Shula pointed to Yokheved and Esther. "Do not pay too much attention to this law. It is a bad law, *b'vadai*. Maybe some day we will succeed in getting it changed. But for now, everyone ignores it. You could become citizens tomorrow if you wanted. No one in the Ministry of the Interior would check on your private life. *Nu*, so this time are you here to stay?"

"Leave them alone, Shula," Esther said. "They just arrived."

"*B'seder, b'seder*," Shula said. "All right, okay. But at least I

244

will get them to come to my Independence Day party. No lesbian can resist Israel after one of my parties." She turned to us. "You will come, yes? Good, good."

Yokheved said, "You need a place to stay? We have a couch in our apartment."

"I see what you mean about the Israeli character," Deborah said. "Drinking mud coffee must be what makes Israelis so hospitable."

Shula said, "You want another cup?"

———

I spent the night of the Independence Day party sitting in a corner, berating myself. Everyone else seemed to be having fun; Deborah was dancing up a storm; why couldn't I be like her, and give myself over to the communal merriment?

Until the previous day, I had assumed there were no lesbians in all of Israel; and now here I was, in the same room with thirty lesbian feminists from all parts of the country. Ten years ago, if there had been such a thing as *Kol Ha-Isha*, if there had been a community of lesbians, even just a few, I would have felt ecstatic. Nothing could have pried me away from Jerusalem then. What had happened to me, that I now sat sullen, dissatisfied? I couldn't seem to converse with these women. Everything they said rubbed me the wrong way. I found them more Israeli than lesbian: all shout and brag, all argument, singing and dancing with that overwhelming Israeli energy, sociable without cease, unable to drink even a little wine without becoming either sleepy or obnoxious, unable to leave me alone when I clearly didn't want to talk to anyone.

Even Deborah's enjoyment rubbed me the wrong way. Why was everything so easy for her? She danced with grace and abandon; she looked beautiful in the embroidered vest we'd bought for her in the Old City; she had no difficulty making conversation with these women, even though I knew their language and she didn't.

And how could she, how could any of them devote themselves wholeheartedly to celebrating the birth of a country that did not welcome or accept lesbians, a country that branded us "undesirables"? How could they greet Independence Day with such unabashed revelry, when all of us knew things were getting worse and there would never be peace? Had Deborah forgotten that the people who lived around our hotel thought of us as

245

Nazis? Even the *mu'ezzin* whose nightly call to prayer delighted me, even he probably thought of us as Nazis. There was no hope.

For the first time in years, I missed Dr. Feinstein. I had entered analysis with him when I discovered I couldn't get along with men. Maybe he would understand now why I couldn't seem to get along with women either, why I was unable to talk with anyone, why I lacked interest in a community that would have thrilled me in the past, why I felt unfit for human company, male or female.

I pictured him, and shook my head. He would not understand. He would think the whole problem was that I had left analysis, left Israel, given up seeking a husband. Yes, that was how he would view my lesbianism: as a failure of persistence in looking for a man to marry.

If anyone would understand, it was Deborah. She knew me better than anyone, and she wanted to help. From across the room, I heard her hearty laugh. "I love her," I said to myself. "I still love that woman."

I still loved her, and yet I didn't know how to talk to her anymore, didn't know how to get back to a state in which I would want to try to talk to her again. With each day of silence, I moved farther from that state. With each day of silence, I edged toward isolation; perhaps, without heeding the signs, I had already crossed the border and entered that particular danger zone.

———

"Come. We will show you the Old City." Esther and Yokheved stood in the doorway of our hotel room. Yellow morning sunlight fanned out around their heads, as in a medieval painting of a visitation.

"No, thank you, I don't think I want to come. How about you, Deborah? Why don't you go without me? My research begins next week; I need to do some preparatory work. And I already know the Old City."

"*Shtuyiot*," said Yokheved. "Nonsense. Nobody knows the Old City. Today we will show you *our* Old City. Another time, you can show us *your* Old City."

"Have you ever tasted *knafeh?*" Esther said.

"I've never heard of it," I said.

"Then you must come."

Esther led the way to a tiny pastry shop in the Moslem Quarter. We shared a table with a veiled woman and her two little boys. Honey dripping from our fingers, we ate the marvelous concoction: a layer of melted goat cheese, a layer of roasted semolina, and warm honey poured over the top.

"You like it?" Esther asked. "Good. It is a very old recipe in this part of the world—maybe thousands of years, maybe only hundreds. I don't know."

Across the table, honey was drizzling down the chins of the two boys. Their mother found a handkerchief in a pocket of her long black dress and tried to wipe the children's faces, but she succeeded only in smearing the dark honey until it formed the shape of a large mouth around each boy's small mouth. Yokheved said something in Arabic, and the woman replied, lowering her veil until we could see that she was smiling.

"What did you say to her?" Deborah asked when we left.

"I said *knafeh* is good for the skin. And she said soapy water is better."

The Arab woman could have been Yardena; her sons could have been Nadav and Yonah. But now Nadav and Yonah were soldiers, like the two we had seen walking with their girlfriends; and the little boys' older brother might be the young man who yelled after the soldiers, calling them Nazis. Some day these boys too would wash the honey from their faces and enter the battle.

"You think too much." Yokheved poked me in the ribs. "Why do you think so much?"

"I like to think."

"Ah, I know where we should take you next. The Christian Quarter. *Nakhon*, Esther? Right?"

"Wait a minute," I protested. "I'm not Christian. I just like to think."

"This has nothing to do with Christian. If you like to think, you will like where we are going."

The narrow alleys were more crowded than before, the din louder, and we progressed slowly through the throng of shoppers, mules, men with pushcarts, busloads of European pilgrims, soldiers, women carrying infants.

"Here." We climbed a small set of stairs and entered a doorway, into a burst of silence. It was a monastery of some sort, built on the white roof of a larger building. There were a few

247

white plaster huts, shaded by very old grape vines that grew there as if by a miracle, their trunks thick as trees. One monk was sitting on a bench, reading.

Deborah, Yokheved, and Esther moved on to the chapel. I stood motionless, transfixed, in the white light of silence. I would gladly have become a monk, or one of the plaster huts, or a weathered vine, in order to stay in that magical silence. I would never leave, never speak again, never touch anyone. I would hear nothing but the throb of that silent world.

What I had felt in the Sinai was the pull of silence; what I felt now, in the Coptic Monastery, was silence itself. I became a cell of whitewashed brick, static and unyielding; a recluse with no tongue and no ears, forever and willingly confined to that cell; a book from which all writing had been erased; a scorched stone, varnished and sealed by the silent light of the sun. I became an absence, like the final silence after the final war.

I don't know how long I stood there, vanished and stilled. Then I felt my voice well up in me, and Deborah was looking into my face, her hair like a crown of copper, and I was weeping.

"I'm back," I said.

"Good," she said. "I've missed you." As Andrée had once done in a dark bus, Deborah reached for my hand, and I twined my fingers through hers.

In the beginning was sound. In the end will be silence. We live in the middle, the region of speech.

It is not yet time for silence. As long as we are alive, we will struggle to understand one another, to make ourselves known, to say what we mean, to listen with our whole bodies. As long as we are alive, we will struggle toward community. We are nowhere at home, but in talking with each other we will build a home of language, a nest of words.

Tonight Deborah will ask how I am, and I will try to tell her. As long as we have breath, we will raise our imperfect voices and join the clamor of humanity.

When Zahava's mourning was over, she stepped down from her *mirpesset*, crossed the street, and tried to speak to a neighbor. When the Children of Israel stood poised at the shore of the Red Sea, they took a deep breath, and then, in a powerful gesture of trust, in the faith that someone who loved them would not let them drown, they stepped forward, toward the water. Then Moses sang, and Miriam sang and took a timbrel in her hand, and all the women went out after her with timbrels and with dances.

The time of singing has arrived. In a moment Deborah and I will join Esther and Yokheved. We will pass through the doorway, descend the stairs, and return to the noisy, crowded streets of the Old City.

About the Author

Alice Bloch is the author of *Lifetime Guarantee: A Journey Through Loss and Survival* (Persephone Press, 1981). She was born in Youngstown, Ohio, in 1947, and since 1972 she has lived in the Los Angeles area. In the intervening years she studied literature and languages at the University of Michigan, Cornell University, and the Hebrew University of Jerusalem. Some day she will live in Jerusalem again.

Other ALYSON books you'll enjoy

Don't miss our free book offer on the last page

THE MEN WITH THE PINK TRIANGLE
by Heinz Heger; $4.95

Here is the true story of a chapter in gay history that has long been hidden from view. In 1939, the author was a young medical student, in love with the son of a Nazi officer. In March of that year the Gestapo abruptly arrested him for homosexuality, and he spent the next six years in concentration camps. Like thousands of other homosexuals, he was forced to wear a pink triangle on his shirt so he could be readily identified for special abuses.

Richard Hall, book columnist for *The Advocate*, praised this as "One of the ten best books of the year" and *Gay Community News* warns that "You may find yourself riveted to your seat" by Heger's narrative.

REFLECTIONS OF A ROCK LOBSTER
A story about growing up gay
by Aaron Fricke; $4.95

No one in Cumberland, Rhode Island was surprised when Aaron Fricke showed up at his high school prom with a male date; he had sued his school for the right to do so, and the papers had been full of the news ever since. Yet until his senior year, there would have been nothing to distinguish Aaron Fricke from anyone else his age. You'd never have guessed he was gay — and Aaron did his best to keep it that way. He created a shell around himself as protection against a world that he knew would reject him if it knew the truth. But finally his anger became too great, and he decided to make a stand.

Now, in *Reflections of a Rock Lobster*, you can read Fricke's moving story about growing up gay — about coming to terms with being different, and a lesson in what gay pride can really mean in a small New England town.

BEYOND THE FRAGMENTS:
Feminism and the making of socialism
by Sheila Rowbotham, Lynne Segal and Hilary Wainwright;
$6.95

The last decade has seen the women's movement gain strength dramatically among all classes of society. At the same time, the left has too often floundered, as fragmented groups of party liberals and leftists struggle helplessly against a growing right-wing trend.

There's an important reason for all of this, say the authors of *Beyond the Fragments.* It lies in the very different structure of the women's movement as compared to that of most socialist organizations. This new book shows what the left must learn from feminism if it is to become an effective force for grassroots change.

ROCKING THE CRADLE
Lesbian mothers: A challenge in family living
by Gillian E. Hanscombe and Jackie Forster; $5.95

Lesbian mothers are often in the news these days, but usually they get just superficial treatment, triggered by child custody cases. Here is the first book to thoroughly look at topics such as the social and personal aspects of lesbian motherhood; the implications of artificial insemination by donor; and how children feel about growing up with lesbian mothers.

Both authors have long been active in the lesbian movement, but their book assumes no special knowledge or experience on the part of the reader. *Rocking the Cradle* discusses questions ranging from the most basic to the most specific, from "What is a lesbian?" to "How can women administer artificial insemination on their own?"; all in a style that is clear and thought-provoking.

ONE TEENAGER IN TEN
edited by Ann Heron; $3.95

One teenager in ten is gay. Here, 26 young people tell about how they came to discover their homosexuality; about how and whether they told their parents and friends; and what the consequences were.

THE NON-JEWISH JEW
by Isaac Deutscher; $5.95

Isaac Deutscher — whose biographies of Trotsky and Stalin have won him world-wide respect — writes here of his vision of Jewish life, contemporary and traditional. The essays in this book discuss the "remnants of a race" after Hitler; the Jews under Stalin; the Zionist ideal; the establishment of the state of Israel; the Israeli-Arab war of 1967; and the perils ahead — all with great insight, and with a style that appeals to both scholar and layperson.

BETWEEN FRIENDS
by Gillian E. Hanscombe; $5.95

Lillian Faderman, author of *Surpassing the Love of Men,* writes that *"Between Friends* is an achievement. [The author explores] many of the vital lesbian and feminist issues of our day — monogamy, communal living, living with men, sexual relations with men, racism, lesbian motherhood, boy children in the lesbian community, the place of love in a radical movement. She succeeds both in involving the readers in the emotional lives of her characters and demanding of the readers a serious re-examination of their beliefs about the sorts of lives lesbians and feminists ought to be living."

NO BOSSES HERE!
A manual on working collectively and cooperatively
by Karen Brandow, Jim McDonnell and
Vocations for Social Change; $4.95

The collective work situation can be one of the most human and fulfilling experiences around. It can also be the most frustrating and de-energizing. Here's a practical guide for people working in collective situations, or trying to create a collective or cooperative work structure. The authors, from long experience, look at the many problems that may arise in such groups, and ways of solving them.

Get this book free!

When were you last outraged by prejudiced media coverage of gay and lesbian issues? Chances are it hasn't been long. *Talk Back!* tells how you, in surprisingly little time, can do something about it.

If you order at least three other books from us, you may request a FREE copy of this important book. (See order form on next page.)

To get these books:

Ask at your favorite bookstore for the books listed here. You may also order by mail. Just fill out the coupon below, or use your own paper if you prefer not to cut up this book.

GET A FREE BOOK! When you order any three books listed here at the regular price, you may request a **free** copy of *Talk Back!*

BOOKSTORES: Standard trade terms apply. Details and catalog available on request.

Send orders to: **Alyson Publications, Inc.**
PO Box 2783, Dept. B-48
Boston, MA 02208

— — — — — — — — — — — — — — — — — — —

Enclosed is $_____ for the following books. (Add $1.00 postage when ordering just one book; if you order two or more, we'll pay the postage.)

☐ Between Friends ($5.95)
☐ Beyond the Fragments ($5.95)
☐ The Law of Return ($7.95)
☐ The Men With the Pink Triangle ($4.95)
☐ No Bosses Here! ($4.95)
☐ The Non-Jewish Jew ($5.95)
☐ One Teenager in Ten ($3.95)
☐ Reflections of a Rock Lobster ($4.95)
☐ Rocking the Cradle ($5.95)
☐ Talk Back! ($3.95)
☐ Send a free copy of *Talk Back!* as offered above. I have ordered at least three other books.

name: _____

address: _____

city:_____ state:_____zip:_____

ALYSON PUBLICATIONS
PO Box 2783, Dept. B-48, Boston, Mass. 02208